LAST RESORT

Abhinav Ramnarayan

***

PROLOGUE

She stood, panting, in absolute darkness.

Something was brushing against her leg and she didn't know – or even *want* to know – what it was.

She wondered for a wild moment if this was hell – if she had just died without realising – and if this is what it was, complete darkness, complete loneliness, and demons approaching.

She collected herself and tried to calm her breathing and listen for any incongruous noises. For a few panicked seconds, she held her breath and listened.

Just the steady *drip drip drip* of rain on leaves. Her breathing became a bit more normal, but still sounded ragged and loud in her ears.

In theory, the presence of the forest around her should have been reassuring in the cover it provided. Better here than in the open meadow. But why was it not a reassuring thought? Why was every ounce of her body hoping she would come out into the open again?

She was on the verge of a nervous breakdown. Who knew what beasts had already caught her scent and were heading in her direction? And even if they stayed away for whatever reason, would she ever, ever find her way out? Or would she finally collapse and die from exhaustion and her body steadily decompose somewhere in the depths of these woods?

Unbidden came the image of a rotting trunk she had seen fallen on the forest floor a few days back. It was crawling with insects, and birds in turn came to find the insects. It was a veritable hothouse of life.

Back to the earth, back to the elements. The circle of life. Bizarrely, the thought gave her some courage, and she pulled herself from the very edge of terror and tried to take stock of the situation.

Right. So, you don't know where you are and you can't see anything. What now?

She ran her fingers over her hand torch and found the button. Could she risk it? Or would the demons see and be attracted like moths to a flame?

She had to risk it, she realised. It was no good blundering in the dark. She cautiously flicked on the switch, partially shielding the torch head so the light only fell in a forward direction.

Blessed light poured out onto the dark trunks up ahead, and she could have sobbed with relief just to be able to see again.

But the relief was short-lived - her heart sank again when she realised that all she could see was thickset trees all around and no sign of a footpath or a break in the forest. She slowly moved the torch in a circle and suddenly the light jerked as she caught sight of the tail of a snake as it slithered into the undergrowth.

She screamed involuntarily and then clapped her free hand to her mouth. *What have you done, you idiot?*

She closed her eyes to keep the tears from leaking out, and, with a tremendous effort of willpower, she turned off the torch.

Her heart was thumping again. She whimpered slightly and tried to listen.

At first, there was just dripping. And then – the hackles rose on the back of her neck – she could hear faint cries. Mostly unintelligible, but she could make out a few words, speaking a strange language.

She tried to tell herself she was imagining it, they couldn't possibly have heard her, it wasn't that loud a scream. But – her heartbeat quickened – there was no mistaking it: the voices were getting louder.

Her already pounding heart was now drumming against her chest, threatening to burst out. She stifled a sob and stumbled in the direction away from where she had seen the snake, stretching her hands out to prevent herself from running into trees. She kicked her feet out as she ran so that she could feel any roots that may trip her up.

Her training now kicking in, she shifted smoothly from a slow jog to a full run.

"Ah!"

A blinding pain shot through her skull and she tried to stay on her feet, her head swimming, the bile rising in her stomach. What had she done? She must have run into a low hanging branch or something, she thought dazedly.

She steadied herself and continued blindly, feeling something hot and sticky running down her forehead. She hoped she hadn't fractured her skull.

She was dizzy and weak now and only willpower was keeping her on her feet, keeping her moving. She experimentally started running again and felt the pain shoot through her forehead and transmit itself to the rest of her body.

She was done. She couldn't do it. She stopped, hand on knees, breathing in deep rasps.

It was too much, she thought; she needed a rest.

She thought with relief of just collapsing and lying there and letting whatever beast or demon come and take her.

"There! I heard her!' "Where? Where?" "That way!"

A shock went through her body and she jerked out of her stupor. A horrible image ran through her head. Her, lying on the floor, and three horrible hulking figures ripping her clothes off, grabbing her body, dirty fingernails scraping against her skin, stained teeth biting her lips...

Survival instinct kicked in and a much-needed shot of adrenaline coursed through her veins. She automatically straightened up and began moving her legs.

Throwing caution to the wind, she turned on the torch and sprinted through the trees. She would beat them. She would. She had to.

There was a cry behind her – was it a bit fainter now, or was she imagining it? Under normal circumstances she knew she could outrun them, but who knows what that blow had done to her head?

The dripping became a hammering as the rain came gushing down now, drowning out all sound. Her adrenaline rush was fading, and her body started to flag again. She forced herself to keep moving her legs, back and forth, and she tried to breathe deeply rather than in rasps.

Several feet above her, the roof of the forest grew thick and soggy under the beating torrent and visibility went down to almost zero. Darkness spread across the mountain.

* * *

1. ARRIVAL

The large man next to him, not content with taking up most of the double seat they were squeezed into, was now sleeping on his shoulder.

For the umpteenth time, Harsha cursed himself for not booking the train earlier and getting a proper seat of his own. He had been so impressed that Indian Railways now had a website. He had blissfully bought a ticket back in London and had felt very pleased with himself for avoiding a potentially long queue at the train station.

It was only when he reached the Chennai train station that morning that he realised that the act of buying the ticket online had merely put him on the waiting list, and he had listened aghast to the station master who said that he hadn't been assigned a seat.

But in another weird quirk of the Indian railway system, those on the waiting list could get into the "unreserved" compartment. The seats were first-come, first-served, though, so Harsha had stood by the toilet for the most part of the journey, leaning dangerously out of the doorway occasionally to get some fresh air or smoke an illicit cigarette.

He had finally got a seat when they left the town of Gudiyattam. He wouldn't have thought of Gudiyattam as anywhere special but clearly he was in a minority — a host of his fellow passengers had stampeded for the exit, nearly running him over in the process.

And now, here he was, sinking lower and lower in his seat so that his neighbour would wake up and leave his shoulder alone, wondering whether he should go back to standing by the doorway. He had forgotten what a brilliant, if slightly terrifying, experience that was. Harsha remembered sitting on the steps of the doorway with his schoolmates on a class trip, competing with each other to try and grab a few leaves from passing bushes. He shuddered at the recollection. It was incredibly stupid; any one of them could have died...

The man next to him snuggled up, his oil-slicked hair brushing against Harsha's cheek. *If he begins to drool...* Harsha thought viciously to himself.

He tried to focus on the positives. Looking over the man's head, he could still watch the scenery from the open window.

India's rural landscape really is criminally undersold, he thought to himself. He watched the rolling hills, the farmlands, the occasional houses and the kids running up to wave at the passing train.

The landscape, the gentle movement of the train from side to side, the steady clacking of the rails, the wind rushing in through the windows, the afternoon sunshine — it was all very soothing, and despite the shoulder rogue he felt his eyes close slowly.

"Coffee! Coffee, coffee, coffee, coffeeeee!" Harsha jerked awake and looked blearily at the uniformed member of train staff. "Coffee?" the man asked him inquiringly, in case he hadn't got the message.

Harsha shook his head. Generally, Indian train food was really delicious, but the coffee was execrable. He hoped someone would come by with the tea sometime. It was usually so sweet that your blood vessels instantly went into panic mode, but at least it tasted good.

He considered reading, but the only book he had brought — in a weird fit of wanting to improve his knowledge — was a work of non-fiction on the causes of the 2008 financial crisis. He wished he had thought to bring the Pulitzer Prize-winning book he had been recommended or — if he was completely honest — something like Harry Potter instead.

The train slowed steadily and eventually came to a halt at a station. Harsha looked out curiously. It was a tiny little rural station with just two platforms, trees leaning over almost all the way to the railway track on one side, and plants growing in the gaps between the flagstones that made up the platform.

On the other platform sat a group of children — Harsha did a double take — not children! Monkeys! Sitting there and staring out onto the tracks, looking for all the world like they were waiting for a train. He laughed quietly to himself, and despite himself, his spirits began to lift.

He really was in rural country now, and he hadn't been to the Indian countryside for well over ten years, maybe closer to twenty.

Only a couple of passengers got on at the stop, one of them lugging in two sacks of rice, presumably to sell in a bigger town.

One of them nodded at Harsha as he went past him in search of a seat.

As the train started up and moved out of the monkey station, Harsha saw a tiny station master's office bearing the legend "Peranumbut". He realised, with a start, that he was nearly at the end of the journey. He was scheduled to arrive at his destination — the town of Ramananpettai — in about twenty minutes.

He got up, leaving his sleeping companion without any regrets, and starting getting his suitcases out from the shelf above the seats. May as well go wait by the doorway now — Azhar had warned him that the train only stopped for a minute at his station.

"Coffee coffeecoffee!" The coffee vendor had obviously gone to all the carriages and was making his way back. He said something to Harsha, who said: "No Telugu, sorry."

"Oh, do you want any help, sir?" the man asked in Tamil instead. They were officially in Andhra Pradesh now, but close to the borders of Tamil Nadu and Karnataka, and many of the staff spoke the languages of all three states and possibly Hindi and some English as well, putting Harsha — who only knew English and a smattering of Tamil and Bengali — to shame.

"Thank you, I am fine," Harsha said, smiling at the man, who nodded and resumed his rounds, leaving Harsha feeling even more cheerful. There had been a genuine warmth about the offer of help, and Harsha was feeling good to be in India after a long time.

The man with rice was standing by the open doorway and the two of them nodded awkwardly at each other. Presently, the train slowed again, and the man started pulling at the sacks.

Apparently, he was also getting out at the station, and Harsha started to stress about how they would get everything out. As the train came to a halt, Harsha saw the "Ramananpettai" sign as they moved past and readied himself to embark, his heart beating slightly faster.

To his annoyance, the man with the rice squeezed past him with one of the sacks and jumped out as the train came to a halt, but the annoyance melted away when the man turned and gestured to Harsha to pass out his suitcases.

Between them, they bundled all the luggage out, but even so the train was moving when Harsha finally jumped out with his heavy knapsack. Utilising the experience of his university days, he ran forward a little to keep from falling.

Panting and red-faced, he took stock of the station of Ramananpettai.

His first impression was that it was more like a toy station than a real one, and the old colonial-style station-master's office reminded him forcibly of the station in Cromwell, Derbyshire, where he had once gone for a wedding.

It was empty apart from his fellow passenger. Trees fringed the platform and leaned their branches over a few benches, sheltering them from the streaming sunlight.

All he could hear was the chugging of the train, which was getting softer, the sound of birds and the chatter of the odd monkey.

The man with the rice sacks waved him a cheerful goodbye, and, displaying strength that belied his slight frame, hauled a sack over either shoulder and marched off towards a footpath that led out from the middle of the platform.

Harsha followed him with his eyes and saw what looked like a town just past the trees, and beyond that, a small mountain, patched with different shades of green. Harsha was able to distinguish, even from this distance, farmland from forest on its broad slopes.

"That must be it," he muttered to himself. He shouldered his knapsack, picked his suitcases up in either hand and walked in that general direction.

The feeling of goodwill was fast being replaced by minor panic. Where the hell was Azhar? And how was he supposed to get there in his absence? Harsha was not even sure he remembered the name of the resort. Would people be able to direct him? Would he be able to get a bus?

All the details were on email — he hadn't bothered to write anything down. "Idiot," Harsha said to himself.

Luckily, just then, a man came out of the office and, spotting him, headed in his direction. He was short and portly, with a luxuriant moustache and uniform buttons creaking over a massive paunch. He was the very caricature of a station-master.

"Where you want to going?" the station-master asked.

Damn, he couldn't even remember the name of the resort!

"Er... I am going to the... er... mountain resort?" Harsha said, and luckily the man nodded.

"Mr Azhar's hotel, yes? There is bus for you," the man said, and Harsha was impressed. Clearly, old Azhar was a bit of a personality here. Or maybe that was just how small towns worked, he thought, as he followed the man — who had taken one of his suitcases — out on to the footpath. He wouldn't know, having only ever lived in Chennai and London.

"It is very beautiful and peaceful here," Harsha said to the station-master in Tamil.

"Soon will become busy," the man said, persisting with English. "Chennai to Bangalore train stopping at this station soon. Next year coming. Very, very busy soon," he added gloomily.

They came out past the trees and headed towards a little car park, empty save for a minivan that Harsha eyed nervously. Vans and mountains did not combine well, as far as he — or to be more specific, his stomach — was concerned.

A man was sitting by its shade and reading a magazine, but he jumped to attention when the pair of them approached him. "Hello Vembu sir! Ah, Mr Harish?" Harsha nodded, not bothering to correct him.

The man ran up to help him with his suitcase. "Mr Azhar sir waiting for you! Very happy, very happy to see old friend," the man said, also in English.

"*Rombananri*," Harsha said in Tamil.

"Ah, *neenga* Tamil *thana*!" the man said delightedly, lapsing gratefully into the language. "*Naanum*! From Palladam, near Coimbatore. Selvam," he ended, pointing towards himself.

Selvam was a short, trim man wearing a faded checked shirt and khaki trousers. His clean-shaven face was well defined, and he had bright, humorous eyes. Harsha liked the look of him immediately.

He turned to the station-master, thanked him, and stood a bit uncertainly, wondering whether the man would be offended if he offered to tip him.

The man fortunately made the decision for him, rapping out a smart "Goodnight!" before turning to walk back up the footpath to the station in the afternoon sunshine.

Selvam chattered away as he opened the back of the minivan,

clearly delighted to be speaking in what he called "shudha" Tamil, or pure Tamil. "Over here, sir, they speak Tamil but they have terrible accents!" he confided as he stowed one suitcase away.

Harsha was glad that his mother insisted on speaking to him in Tamil on the phone, as it had helped him keep touch with the language — just about.

"I also speak with an accent," he said self-consciously.

"Yes, sir, you are coming from England, so you speak like that. It's ok, no problem," the man said forgivingly, taking the second suitcase from him.

"Er ... can we keep the windows open? I have motion-sickness, you see," Harsha said as he went round to get into the passenger seat.

"Sir? It will be a little cold up in the mountain, but no problem, sir. And don't worry, I will drive carefully," Selvam said, getting in and patting the dashboard.

"Right," he said, turning and smiling at Harsha. "Are you ready to go to Pipal Resort?"

"That's what it was called! Yes, I'm ready, Selvam," Harsha said, buckling his seatbelt (much to the driver's amusement).

Selvam turned the ignition on and they eased out of the car park. Harsha took a deep breath, looking at the mountain ahead of him.

2. MOUNTAIN

Despite the promise, Harsha began to feel queasy the minute they hit the mountain road.

They had skirted the edge of Ramananpettai — a colourful little town divided by a river that flowed down from the mountain ahead of them — and on its very edge had picked up some passengers ("Just giving them a lift!" Selvam explained) who were chattering loudly at the back of the minivan. Harsha's head was beginning to hurt.

As he had not brought any medication, he purchased a lime at a juice shop on the edge of town, which he now held up to his nose. It was an old trick his mother had taught him when he was a child and they had had to take a long car ride to visit relatives. It seemed appropriate that he was going 'old school' on a visit back to India.

Fighting a silly urge to bite into the fruit when the van suddenly lurched downwards for a short stretch, Harsha asked: "How much longer?"

"Oh very little sir, very little, just one hour! We will make a small stop in the village to drop these people off and you can go to the toilet there," the man said cheerfully.

"One hour!" Harsha said faintly and buried his nose in the lime. He tried to distract himself by looking out of the window — and admittedly, the view was stunning, and growing more beautiful as they went further uphill.

About halfway up the mountain, a light mist crept over the acres of farmland that stretched out in strange, sloping patches in myriad shades of green. Looking downhill, he saw that the farmland abruptly ended in a thin line of forest near the foot of the mountain — they must have come around the curve of the mountain, because he had seen no forest near the station.

The further the car went forward, the more the forest intruded into the mountain and the farmland receded, and Harsha felt, after a while, as though the forest was creeping up the slopes to meet him. And then, as the car curved, he saw up ahead that the line of the forest rose dramatically and the farmland ended. The car plunged into the midst of the jungle. It happened so suddenly that it caught Harsha by surprise.

Now all around the car were great trees in twisted shapes, with creepers snaking around their thick trunks, and moss and lichen lapping at their feet.

Harsha's mind went back to hikes in English and Welsh woods. Those walks had had their own slightly otherworldly quality, the whole *Lord of the Rings* thing, particularly under grey English skies and with rain and wind passing through the leaves. But this: this was wild, tropical forest, thick with a darker shade of green and a sense of danger lurking in the air. The chatter behind them had faded to a slight murmur of quiet conversation.

"Are there any wild animals here?" he asked, and his voice came out in a whisper.

"Lots, sir! Elephants, monkeys, snakes — and there is even a black panther, sir," Selvam said casually.

A black panther! Harsha looked around hurriedly. What a great story that would be to take back to London, if only he could see it! But no sign of the great cat — or indeed any other form of wildlife — appeared to disturb the wall of vegetation on either side.

"But also leeches, sir. Lots of leeches!" Selvam said, somewhat less romantically. "One word of advice, sir: if you have leeches, just let them finish drinking your blood and go on their own. If you pull them off, it will bleed a lot."

"Perhaps I won't get any, if I'm careful."

"You will," Selvam said with conviction.

Presently, they came out of the forest and Harsha blinked in the light. They appeared to have come all the way around the mountain again, because he could see the town where his train had arrived, much further below than the last time it was visible. It was evening now and lights were already coming on in some of the houses. The river winked and shone in the overcast, half light. Harsha was both charmed and spooked by the surreal beauty of the scene.

Soon, they plunged into the forest again and his mind began to drift. Inevitably, his thoughts turned to what lay in store at the top of the mountain.

As a journalist, he was used to putting himself into new and sometimes unnerving situations, so he was reasonably adept at handling the unfamiliar. He sometimes even enjoyed the experience.

But this was different. Azhar, the chief troublemaker back in college, was now managing a resort in the hills, and had invited the old gang to come and stay for a week.

Harsha was not at all sure why he had agreed to come — he hadn't met them for nearly a decade, and the last meeting had not been a pleasant occasion. In fact, it had been so fractious that it had ended their days together and they had all gone their separate ways.

That was nine years ago, just after university had ended, he remembered. Harsha had landed a job at a well-known newspaper. In his day job, he was meeting politicians and businessmen, and in the evenings going to cocktail parties full of beautiful people. He had lost a lot of weight after being obese through his teens, and the subsequent attention he'd been receiving had gone to his head.

He cringed when he remembered how condescending and patronising he had been to his old university friends, the ones who had stuck by him when he had been fat and lonely, and had made him feel — for the first time in his life — accepted for who he was, without judgement. They had even made him feel good about himself with their clumsy affection and admiration for his talent with words.

I was a real idiot, he thought to himself. But the reality is, once they had left college and got jobs in different sectors, they had grown apart.

But now, for some reason or other, he was going to spend a week with them. These people, who were both familiar and strange — old friends he had drunk, smoked and read poetry with, and at the same time people whose lives he did not relate to now. Some were even married.

So why had he accepted the invitation? There had been many reasons; Azhar's insistence was one of them, nostalgia for a past life was another — but, if he was honest with himself, the defining factor had been Maya. Once Azhar had told him she was coming, he had agreed on impulse to join, and could not think of a way of taking back those fateful words.

You foolish, foolish man, he said to himself.

"Are you from Chennai, sir?" the driver asked, breaking into his thoughts.

Harsha pulled himself out of his reverie with difficulty and said:

"Oh? Ah, I grew up in Chennai, but my father is from Bengal and my mother is from near Chennai."

"Ah! Bengali!" Selvam said, nodding as though Harsha had conveyed some great secret to him.

"And you are from errr ... where was it again? Palladam. Right. Do you go back there?" Harsha asked politely.

It was always strange to come back to India where everyone talked to you all the time. At times it was more pleasant than the chilling silence of the London Underground — but there were times when you did want your space, to sit in silence and think.

"Once or twice a year, sir. My wife and children are there."

"Really? How come you don't ask them to move here?"

The man shrugged his shoulders. "Wife does not want to leave her family. But it's hard to get a driver's job there, sir, it's a very small town, and everyone wants to be a driver."

"How did you decide to come here of all places?"

"I used to work for Abid sir — that's Azhar sir's father - in Chennai. I really did not like Chennai, though, sir, especially the weather! I used to wake up dripping in sweat. Terrible," the man gave a little shudder. "So I asked Abid sir if I could work somewhere else and he sent me here. Much, much better than Chennai."

The man gave a little sideways look to see if he had caused offence, but when Harsha chuckled, he grinned and continued: "The job is very good, sir. Not so much driving, I do a lot of other work, but I really like the resort. It is beautiful."

Harsha was intrigued by the thought of his college friend as an employer. "Is Azhar a good boss?" he asked.

The driver nodded. "Very good, sir, he is a very friendly person with everyone, I think everyone in the resort likes him a lot." The man frowned and continued: "Some people take advantage of his good nature. I wish they had worked for his father. Then they would know!"

They went too fast over a slight bump in the road and were jolted slightly out of their seats, and the driver apologised.

"Don't worry. Actually that's the first real bump — this road is very good," Harsha said.

The driver caught the tone of surprise in Harsha's voice and grinned, saying: "The head of the local Arasur panchayat lives here, so he makes sure the roads are good," he said.

"Arasur?"

Selvam looked at him in surprise. "Arasur, that's the name of this mountain, and the village as well."

Harsha went red. "I am sorry - I just forgot," he lied. The truth was, he hadn't bothered to find out.

"It's ok, sir," Selvam said, the cheerful smile returning. "It is a small place. But Rajaratnam is the head of the panchayat. He ruled for the maximum ten years, then he stepped down and his wife became the head of the panchayat, then after that he became the head again. You know how it is," the man said.

Harsha laughed. "Politics!" he said.

The driver shook his head. "This country will never change, sir. But at least the road is good. I'll show you his house soon, when we come to the village."

"Are we near yet? It seems a strange place for people to live," Harsha said, looking around at the wild terrain.

"It is a farming village, sir. The mountain weather is good for planting coffee, so that's what they do. The resort is just after the village."

Almost on cue, they came out of the forest and Harsha saw houses scattered on either side. The architecture was old-fashioned, built low and with wide porches and large, heavy doors, though most of them were open.

It was extremely picturesque, but Harsha couldn't help feeling an odd sense of displacement. This was his country, but he felt far removed from his surroundings, and felt a momentary pang for the Victorian buildings in the City of London and the red-roofed cottages in the city's suburbs.

The bus stopped in front of a little roadside shop under a massive tree covered in light, heart-shaped leaves. The tree was so tall and wide that it seemed to create a sort of village square or meeting point with its canopy, with a number of people sitting on benches that had been put out in its shade. Others stood chatting by the shop.

All the passengers filed out, greeting some of those people before heading in different directions. One or two of them looked curiously at

Harsha and he looked away self-consciously, trying to ignore another quiver of his stomach.

Selvam squirmed uncomfortably in his seat and then said to Harsha: "Sorry, Harish sir, I will just go ... er..."

"Call of nature?" Harsha asked, sympathetically and nodded. Selvam grinned in relief, slipped out of the van and disappeared behind a clump of trees.

Harsha's eyes followed the man a little forlornly. He felt oddly lonely in this unfamiliar village, with an uncertain few days ahead of him. He looked around the patch of village curiously and noticed a side road leading out on up the hill a few hundred yards until it reached a massive iron gate and brick-red compound wall, and a massive house beyond — at least four times bigger than any of the others, the only one with more than one floor.

The house was painted in a ghastly pink and constructed — he thought, with his middle-class sensibilities — with all the tastelessness of new money. It towered over the village.

With a sudden decision, Harsha clicked open his seatbelt, slid open his car door and jumped lightly down onto the dusty pavement of the village square.

The cold mountain air ran its icy fingers over Harsha's neck and face, but he drank in great gulps of air gratefully, scanning the beautiful, wild slopes as he turned towards the shop. He hesitated, feeling shy to join this group of villagers who seemed to be having such a jovial time, but reminded himself he was a journalist (and therefore not afraid of anything) and marched up towards the outlet in question.

As he got closer, he realised with a sort of shock that the roadside shop was made entirely of clay — *could this be any more rural?* — with a little cubbyhole for the shopkeeper to lean out and sell his wares. Shampoo sachets hung from the roof and sacks of rice and lentils stood in front of the shop, and the branches of the tree hung protectively over it.

Five men were laughing, chatting and exchanging remarks with a group of three middle-aged women seated on a nearby bench, resplendent in their colourful saris and wearing wide grins to match. Harsha self-consciously sidled up to this group and they turned to look at him in surprise but made way for him to reach the counter. They continued their conversation in some combination of Tamil and Telegu that Harsha couldn't quite follow.

"What will you have, sir? Some hot tea? And some hot bajjis, freshly made?" said the shopkeeper, a cheerful-looking man with bushy eyebrows and an impressive paunch. He spoke in Tamil. Harsha saw a stone frying pan lying in one corner of this versatile little shop, sizzling with bits of batter and chilli. His stomach gave another lurch.

"Er... do you have anything to drink?"

"Whatever you want!" the shopkeeper declared and turned and opened the door of a little fridge with the air of a conjurer pulling a rabbit out of a hat.

"Er... oh wow, you have Red Bull here!"

"Only the best!" he declared, grinning and showing a set of *paan*-stained teeth.

"Er... I will have... oh, just a bottle of Limca, please!" Harsha said, spotting the fizzy, sugary lemon drink that he had guzzled down in bucketloads in his childhood. If that wouldn't settle his stomach, nothing would!

The shopkeeper took out the drink, opened the cap with another flourish and handed it to Harsha, who pushed a 10 rupee note over to him and smiled his thanks. The shopkeeper took the note with a benign nod of the head, but then his expression changed shockingly fast as he looked beyond Harsha at something.

Harsha noticed that the noise around him had stopped and all the villagers had fallen silent. He felt a chill go down his spine.

"Please take your drink and go," the shopkeeper muttered urgently, his friendly manner disappearing.

"What?" Harsha asked, bemusedly.

"At least stand to one side," the man pleaded.

Harsha turned around stupidly and saw a slim little man in a pure white shirt and trousers — almost like a uniform — walking towards the shop. Behind him stood a bulkier and more commanding man, looking — it seemed to Harsha — in a malevolent manner towards the people by the shop. A frisson went through the group.

The white-clad man walked daintily up to Harsha and said:

"Please to move from here, Mr Rajaratnam has business here now."

"Mr ... who?"

The man looked at him as if he was mad. Harsha turned and saw the look of panic on the shopkeeper's face, took pity on him and moved out of the way, clutching his drink.

The uniformed man stood to one side and the bulky man began walking. Ponderously, and in his own time, he made his way towards the shop and the villagers quailed as though he had threatened to beat them. The bulky man did not glance at any of them, instead focusing a pair of tiny red eyes on the shopkeeper. He stood for a moment in front of the shop, and from his side perspective Harsha saw the corner of the man's lips rise in a sneer.

"Subhash, you seem to be doing very well here." The man spoke in a hoarse, deep voice and also spoke Tamil in a cultured accent.

"Ye-es, yes sir," the shop-keeper said, nodding furiously. "It is going well."

The bulky man nodded and sighed. "It is a simple life you lead, Subhash, but a good one. The goods arrive at your shop. You sell them at a profit." At this, he looked up sharply at the shopkeeper, who quailed and nodded his head furiously again. "The state has given you so much... stability. And you — you pay your dues to the state, of course. That is how the system works. Then your children are educated by the state." At the mention of his children, the shopkeeper jumped.

Rajaratnam patted the side of the mud hut a little vigorously, so that a tiny crack appeared in it. "How easily this beautiful, stable democracy crumbles. We have to make sure it is always strong. Isn't that right, Subhash."

"Yes, sir," the shopkeeper said again, hanging his head.

There was a moment's silence and then the bulky man turned and walked away. The other villagers appeared to be trying to shrink into the earth.

The uniformed man marched smartly towards a nearby jeep and opened the door for the bulky one to sedately clamber into, before running towards the driver's seat. The jeep revved up and raced off down the road, and as Harsha had expected, it made its way to the road that led up to the garish house that stood at the top of the village.

There was a general sense of the day ending, with the villagers all beginning to disperse, the chatter and laughter no longer as apparent.

"Your change, sir," the shopkeeper said, in a subdued tone.

"Never mind, keep it," Harsha said, and the man just nodded without smiling. Harsha made his way towards the van thoughtfully. "Who was that man?" he asked Selvam, balancing his Limca bottle between his legs as he put on his seatbelt.

"That is the panchayat head I was telling you about, sir," Selvam said, as he turned the ignition and eased the van into gear. "He is the one who made sure this road is so good!"

Harsha watched the jeep take a turn and disappear towards the giant gates he had seen earlier and couldn't help wondering if what he had just witnessed was just a natural diffidence towards the local honcho or something more sinister.

As they drove past the main village, the road ended and the minivan bumped and shook over a dirt track. Little clay huts sprang up like moles on the skin of the earth. There were one or two people doing day-to-day things such as hanging up their clothes or drawing a kolam on the porch of their house. They paid no attention to the van as it went past.

And then it was empty farmland again: rows and rows of freshly dug earth and a few cows and goats grazing in weedy fields beyond.

As they turned slightly, following the curve of the mountain, Harsha looked to his right and gasped.

Just above them sat a long rectangular building with large glass French windows. It was ringed by six cottages, some higher up the slope and some lower, but neatly arranged around this central structure.

The cottages had dark blue roof tiles and cream walls, and they were, in turn, surrounded by and interspersed with trees of different types. In the middle was one large tree very similar to the one in the village square, recognisable by its lush canopy of light-green, heart-shaped leaves. A sort of concrete platform or dais had been built around the trunk of this great tree, and one or two people were sitting on it and drinking something.

Above the building, the mountain stretched away into mist.

It was worth coming just to see this, Harsha thought to himself, as Selvam drove between two of the cottages and parked in front of the rectangular building.

"Welcome to Pipal Resorts," Selvam said, grinning at Harsha's open-mouthed admiration.

3. AZHAR

As the van arrived, a man hurriedly came out of the building and stood, hands on hips, with a big grin on his face. Harsha stepped out of the van, staring at him.

"Azhar! Bloody hell... it's... wow, you look exactly the same!" Harsha said, grasping the man's hand. Azhar, however, pulled him into a big bear hug. "Man, I never thought you would actually come!" he said, nearly lifting Harsha off his feet.

"Easy, tiger!" Harsha gasped, embarrassed but secretly ple v ased at this warm reception. He stepped back and looked his friend up and down.

"Seriously man, you look fantastic!" he said, and he couldn't quite keep the envy out of his voice.

If anything, Azhar looked even better than before. Dressed in a short white kurta and jeans, he was trim and muscled. His hair was longer, neck length — nothing like the close shave Harsha remembered — and clustered in curls under a small cap.

Upon closer inspection, there were a few lines on his forehead and around his eyes, but this suited him, giving him a more rugged and mature look.

What was Bollywood thinking, rejecting this vision of human perfection, Harsha thought to himself, remembering Azhar's brief, abortive attempt at a career in cinema.

Keeping these thoughts to himself, he instead pointed to the cap and asked: "What's this stuff, man? Turned religious in the end?"

"What, and give up my fine wine?" Azhar laughed. "This is just for appearances. Dad likes me to greet all guests like this. Namaste, welcome to Pipal Resorts," he said, putting his hands together and bowing with mock obsequiousness. "Where we are all about the *people*," he added, playing on the word. "Good eh? I added that last bit!"

"Very witty indeed," Harsha said solemnly, before breaking into a laugh. "It's great to see you again, man!"

20

Azhar turned to the driver, who was standing there and smiling indulgently at the two of them, the suitcases and knapsack neatly set down by the side of the building, causing Harsha to feel a pang of guilt.

"Thank you Selvam, you can leave those there," Azhar said, casually. "Why don't you go get some tea?"

Selvam nodded and winked at Harsha as he headed to the back of the rectangular building.

"This is the main dining hall ... meeting place ... kitchen, whatever you want to call it," Azhar said, gesturing at the building. "Come on, I'll show you inside."

"It's perfect. In fact, this resort is beautiful — how many people can you house here?" Harsha asked as he followed his long-lost friend through the main entrance.

"Each cottage has four rooms with separate entrances, so we have 24 rooms here. Right now, just four are taken apart from you lot, since it is winter. But this summer they were all full, and I'm trying to convince my dad to put in some money to build more," Azhar said.

Harsha looked around the dining hall, which was a lot bigger than it had seemed from the outside. It was the size of a good-sized restaurant with several tables, big and small, scattered around. It was mostly empty, except for a couple in the corner who took no notice of them.

There was a little area on one side which was clearly meant as a sort of sitting area, furnished with two sofas, a coffee table and a large-screen television. A man was ensconced in one of the couches, his face buried in *The Hindu* newspaper.

At their entrance, he put the paper down and stood up, smiling.

"Hey Harry," he said, getting up laboriously and walking up to them.

Harsha looked at him and then said in surprise: "Shane! Shanny! Bloody hell!" and strode up to him.

Shane — also known to his friends as Shanny, or Shannon — had always been a presence in Harsha's life during university days. Shane had had a whole host of fellow Anglo Indians to choose from for making friends with at the Catholic university they'd all gone to; but instead for some reason he had chosen to hang out with Harsha, Azhar and the rest of the rag-tag, eclectic bunch that had made up their gang of friends.

Shane had never been in the limelight, but more on the periphery, chuckling at the antics of free spirits such as Azhar, and priding himself on contributing clichéd little statements and aphorisms at odd, and often inappropriate, moments. But Harsha also remembered him as a steadying presence, one who had always been there to lend a hand or bail his friends out when any of them had got into trouble.

Grabbing him by the hand, he pulled Shane into a half hug, and said: "You look great, man!" He hoped the words sounded genuine.

The truth was that Shane looked different. A more-than-slight paunch bulged out, belying Harsha's memory of a tall and slim teenager. The cheeks were a touch bloated and his hair, still curly, had a stringy, unkempt look.

Marriage and parenthood really do age a person, Harsha thought to himself. He hoped he himself didn't look that much older, especially if Maya was going to be here.

He shook himself and tried to focus on Shane, who was saying something.

"Sorry man, say that again?"

"Just saying it's strange seeing you without this," Shane said, miming an enormous pot belly in front of Harsha's now-flat stomach. A slightly malicious edge to his voice reminded Harsha of the less-than-cordial terms on which they had parted last time they met.

Azhar stepped up at this: "Yeah, all of his weight has transferred on to you, bugger," he said, rudely slapping Shane on the stomach.

"A case of the pot calling the kettle black," Shane said, twinkling. They all laughed, and the couple looked up at them from their coffee.

"Sorry, sorry to disturb you," Azhar said to them, his overly solicitous tone almost making a mockery of the apology. Harsha noticed their eyes flicking nervously to his cap.

"Enough of this," Azhar said under his breath. "Let's just go to my office and get a drink or something. Unless you're hungry, Harsha?"

"A drink sounds perfect," said Harsha.

"Ok good, we'll eat later. I have some alcohol in my office, and there are some biscuits and chips and stuff in case you get hungry," Azhar said, heading for the exit.

"Azhar *bhai* has a creative definition of the phrase 'office supplies', as you can see," Shane said, as they followed him, giving his trademark chuckle that Harsha remembered so well.

Azhar had gone a little way down the footpath, but at this he turned around and said: "You need to stimulate your brains before you work, man!"

"I remember that used to be your policy in college as well — and I can't remember it ever worked very well," Harsha said, smiling.

"Stop raking up old tragedies!" Azhar said, his voice slightly muted by the sharp breeze that flowed against them.

They were walking up the hill now, past the higher row of cottages — which were a lot bigger than they had seemed from a distance — and Harsha saw a seventh cottage a little further up the hill, hidden from the road by a line of trees. He stared at it, open-mouthed, charmed by this secret hideaway.

It was identical to the others, except that it had black tiles rather than blue. The mountainside was a bit steeper there — the others had been built on a relatively level stretch of land — and Harsha thought that it must command a spectacular view of the valley. It was by far the best location of the lot.

"That's your office?" Harsha asked, running up to catch up with Azhar.

"Yes — but it also has two rooms at the back, just for my family to stay when they come — a bit bigger than the others. One of them is for you — you will like it." Before Harsha could thank him, Azhar bellowed: "Murugayya! Murugayya!"

From the cottage in front of them emerged a short, skinny man clad in a white shirt that was a touch too big for him, and black trousers. Harsha immediately had the impression that he was uncomfortable in this formal garb and would be more at home in a *dhoti*. He came running down the hill slightly sideways in a crab-like manner.

"Yes sir, coming sir!" he yelled in obsequious tones. Harsha, used to the pride-bordering-on-arrogance of the English working class, couldn't help feeling a stab of disdain.

As he came up to them, Azhar stepped forward and clapped him on the shoulder, and the man squirmed at his touch.

"This is my right-hand man, Murugayya, a genius at organising things. Murugayya," he continued, in mock sternness. "I told you to stop calling me 'sir'!"

The man moved his head from side to side, signalling assent in that peculiarly Indian way.

"Yes... Mr Azhar," he said uncomfortably.

"Murugayya, this is Harsha, my old friend. Yes, another one. Can you please go and organise to get his luggage up here please?"

Murugayya launched into action and loped off downhill.

Azhar yelled at his retreating figure: "And don't carry it yourself! You're supposed to be the one in charge!"

He caught Harsha's eye and shook his head despairingly: "The poor bugger just does everything, refuses to delegate. Even the cleaners order him around."

Harsha laughed. "Who is he? And what does he do?"

"Well, he is technically the manager of the resort, but he does absolutely everything — he organises the provisions, he takes the guests on tours, he would even do the cleaning if I didn't stop him. I don't know what I would do without him," Azhar said fervently, walking up to the open door of the cottage. "Worth putting up with all that caste stuff. Why are you standing there gaping like fools, come on in!"

"What caste stuff?" Harsha asked, following him in. "Oh my god, Azhar, this is ... this is beyond description! What a place to work from!" he exclaimed, thinking of his own slightly soulless cubicle back in London.

"Not bad, eh?" Azhar said modestly, turning around and standing in the middle of his office. It had seemed gloomy and overcast outside, but the light was streaming in through long windows on one side of the office, lighting up a corner where two computer tables stood adjacent to each other, flanked by bookcases on either side.

In the centre of the room on a dark blue carpet was a sofa and two large, comfortable chairs that faced each other, a coffee table between them laden with books and a vase filled with fragrant, white flowers. On the other side, by more long windows was a tall table with a kettle and two mugs, and behind it a drinks cabinet. In the far corner of the room was an ornate writing table with a little cubby hole filled with notepads and pens.

The windows on this side of the room were open and the fronds of some tall plant outside occasionally swayed inside in the breeze. All the furniture was teak, so that you had an impression of warmth despite the slight chill of the breeze.

Harsha was lost in a daydream in which he was doing his writing on that beautiful writing table in the corner, when he realised that Shane was talking to him.

"Say that again, man?" he asked, placing a hand on Shane's shoulder.

Shane smiled. "Same old Harry, daydreaming away. I was just saying that he is a *dalit*."

"Who is a *dalit*?"

"Murugayya, you nut!"

Harsha shook his head.

"Murugayya! The guy you met two minutes ago!" Shane shook his head in disbelief. "Come on, you must be pretending! You can't have forgotten already! The resort manager!"

"Oh him! Yes of course, Murugayya. Murugayya."

Shane laughed loudly. "The leopard never changes his spots, eh, Harry?"

"You're one to talk! Still talking in little clichés, huh?" Harsha asked in mock outrage.

"Let him be, Shanny — what he needs is some alcohol, to stimulate the brains, man!" Azhar walked towards the drinks cabinet and opened the little glass door. "What will it be, Harry? Scotch? Rum? Bourbon? I've even got some..." he picked up a bottle and inspected it. "Cointreau," he said, uncertainly.

Harsha wrinkled his nose.

"Or do you want some beer?" Azhar asked, opening a mini fridge at the bottom of the cabinet.

"Now you're talking!"

They settled themselves on the sofa, Azhar popping open the beers with a Swiss army knife. "Look at the three of us! We should be in a movie or something."

"A modern-day Amar Akbar Anthony," Shane said, drawing a laugh from the other two.

"So Murugayya ... he's a *dalit*, eh?" Harsha said, taking a mouthful of his beer, savouring the taste of barley swilling around his mouth and feeling better for the first time since the van ride.

Azhar didn't say anything, but Shane said: "Yes, he's an untouchable."

"Does that matter?" Harsha asked, leaning back and crossing his legs.

"Not in my hotel," Azhar growled, a slight tone of pride in his voice. Harsha looked at him in surprise.

"So what's the problem then?"

"Damn villagers," Azhar barked.

"Easy, easy. None of them are here," Harsha said, remembering briefly how alcohol always had the effect of bringing out Azhar's rage.

Azhar did not answer straight away. He took a sip of his beer and stared out of the open door. Harsha followed his gaze and could see the central resort building away in the distance, and far, far beyond, he could just about make out the town at the foothills, not quite hidden by the mist that lay between.

"The guy was employed by my father as a cleaner," Azhar said suddenly. "He was a hell of a worker, and suddenly one day we found that he was talking to the foreign guests, chatting away easily. He had picked up English in something like one year. My mother liked that, because her Tamil and Telugu are worse than mine. Soon he was doing tours of the mountain for the North Indian and foreign guests and when I took charge I found he was basically running the place. So I just decided to make him the manager." He paused to drink his beer, finishing it in one gulp.

"Was your father ok with it?"

Azhar jumped up easily off his chair. "I'm getting another beer. You're still a hell of a slow drinker," he said, indicating Harsha's half-full bottle, before turning away. "The guy was too good to waste," he said over his shoulder, as he opened the mini fridge. "He works like a demon, so I just pulled weight with my dad, told him he must respect my decisions. Not that he gives a damn about your castes and shit, he just didn't want trouble from the village."

"They're not *my* castes, I don't care about them!" Harsha said as Azhar collapsed onto the sofa beside him. "And you know what — I've never come across anyone who does! Literally no one in Chennai cares about it." From the corner of his eye, he caught Shane's smile and he turned to him.

"What is it, Shanny?"

Shane said: "Well... you are from the highest caste."

"I most definitely am not!" Harsha said, hotly. "I mean — so what if I was? But I am not!"

"Come on! Of course you are!"

Harsha sat up in annoyance. "Shanny, are you seriously telling me which caste I am from? My father is one of the *naths*, from Bengal — the community of weavers — it's a backward community by definition!"

"And your mother?"

"Fine, she is a Brahmin — but I am a mixed caste — and this is pointless anyway 'cause I don't give a damn what caste I am! I never have."

Azhar unexpectedly came to his aid. "Shane, why the hell are you interrogating him? How does it matter what caste he is from?"

Shane smiled a little bitterly and said: "It does not matter to you, and it does not matter to me — but it does matter to society, and you can't deny it. Harry may not be a full Brahmin or whatever, but he looks like one, and..."

"Hang on," Azhar cut in. "He looks like one? I don't agree at all. The thing I've always felt about Harry is that he could be from anywhere in India. Not dark, not fair, not too tall. Slim, but not skinny. He literally just needs to adopt an accent and he could pass off for Tamil or Punjabi or Bengali or anything. He is like the stereotypical Indian. And a good looking bugger as well."

Shane and Azhar turned to look at Harsha critically and Shane nodded slowly.

"Why would it matter what caste I am if I don't care about it, or take advantage of it in any way?" Harsha persisted, ignoring this exchange.

"It's cool and breezy at the top of the mountain," Shane said.

"Oh, fuck off," Harsha said exasperatedly, but then he chuckled slightly. "Dammit, Shanny, you always had a way of riling me up."

Shane leaned forward and clinked his bottle against Harsha's and smiled at him apologetically. "Sorry bud. I didn't mean to insult you. Maybe I've got my own baggage here that I need to deal with."

"Of course, man," Harsha said, forcing himself to smile as he took another sip of his beer.

"Anyway," Azhar said hurriedly. "The Murugayya appointment was trouble, right from the start."

"From the village?" Harsha asked, turning to him.

"Oh yeah."

"What sort of trouble?"

Harsha had an unrestricted view of the mountain through the open door in front of him, and he thought he could see Murugayya's slight figure tugging at his suitcase. He felt a pang of guilt at having judged the man's obsequiousness.

"They started stealing from the resort. Mobile phones, laptops and once even the damn water pump. That's why we have to keep this stuff locked up now," Azhar said, gesturing at the high-end desktop computer in the corner. Harsha looked at it for a second and then his gaze shifted to the books and ledgers stacked neatly on the other desk.

"Murugayya prefers paper," Azhar said, following Harsha's gaze. "God knows where he learnt to read and write in this damned mountain. Sent him to Chennai for a computer literacy course. Total waste of money."

Azhar took a long pull of his beer and smacked his lips. "Harry, I'll tell you this. You can keep all your English ales, give me good old Kingfisher any day."

Harsha took another sip himself. After that agonising bus ride and in this unfamiliar environment — albeit a beautiful, mist-laden one — the familiar-tasting beer felt like a prop. He felt like he had never tasted anything more delicious.

There was a moment's pause as the three men applied themselves to the serious business of slaking their thirst.

Then Harsha said casually: "Where are the others?"

"Juni is coming only for the weekend, worse luck, so we still have four days. Some family wedding. The twins ditched, totally useless things. No point relying on women once they've had babies," Azhar said.

"All of them?" Harsha asked, trying to keep the bitter disappointment out of his voice.

"Well, Maria and Jackie ditched. But don't worry, your babe is already here, but just asleep."

Harsha felt his heart lift, but this was accompanied by another jolt of nerves.

"She is? And why are you calling her my babe? You're the one who dated her in college," he said.

"Yeah well. She should have dated you. I was an idiot back then, sleeping around and shit," Azhar said comfortably, with no visible signs of regret. "I can't help myself man, it's in my nature. It's just that..."

"'I love women and I love sex'," Shane and Harsha chanted together and they both laughed.

"Idiots," Azhar said, but without rancour.

"How come there are no women in your life now, Azhar *bhai*?" Shane asked.

"Just taking a break, man! Bombay was a bit much for me."

It was a comfortable afternoon, and Harsha leaned back on his sofa. It would have been too much to say he was completely used to these new surroundings, but listening to Shane and Azhar talking softly, reminiscing about professors and classmates from the past, with a beer in hand, was extremely comfortable. He felt his eyes close involuntarily as their familiar voices washed over him.

4. MAYA

The fire alarm was going off again. Just the routine fire alarm test they do every Tuesday, Maya thought to herself, continuing to type away in the chat window. But it was a weird one, screeching intermittently rather than at a stretch. And it refused to go away.

She looked up in puzzlement at the colleague who sat next to her in her office. For some reason, her face was a blur and refusing to come into focus. What was going on?

Maya woke up with a start.

"Wassgoingon?" She turned in her bed, blew away a strand of hair and looked around at the unfamiliar room. It wasn't massive, but it was comfortable. A desk rested in one corner and a lamp sat on a bedside table. A large window was directly opposite her, wooden blinds drawn, and a baroque painting depicting a rural scene — replete with sheep and milkmaids — dominated the opposite wall.

She turned and blinked at the old teak dresser on the other side, where her jewellery and makeup were neatly arranged, and tried to shake away the sleep from her head. She finally reached out and switched off her screeching phone alarm and sat up in bed, still dazed, trying to separate her dream from reality.

I'm not in that stupid office in the United States of bloody America. I'm in India! She felt a jolt of fierce joy, terror and fear, all in equal measure. She scrambled out of bed with excitement and terror coursing through her veins, waking her up more effectively than the alarm had, and made her way to the bathroom.

She blinked in the bright light of the bathroom and glanced out of the window at the waving trees outside and shivered slightly. There was something ethereal and eerie about being here on this isolated mountain, on the edge of a tropical forest, especially compared to the glass towers and the buzz and lights of Seattle.

This is much better, she told herself firmly, forcing herself to remember the loneliness of the semi-detached suburban home that she shared with her husband.

That she *had* shared.

Would he still welcome her back?

She splashed her face with water to complete her transition to the waking world and then looked up at her own reflection in the mirror. She still had her large, lustrous eyes, the full lips that she forced into a grimace to check her bright, even teeth before she checked for lines all over her face — there were just the beginnings of crow's feet about her eyes. She sighed. There was no doubt that she was exhibiting the first signs of age as she approached her 30th birthday.

As she brushed her teeth, she looked at her reflection again, quizzically, and said out loud: "What the hell have you done?"

She had abandoned her husband. Her family. Her life. She had just stood up and walked away, using up a good chunk of her savings in the process. A text message and an email is all that she had left Naveen with, explaining where she had gone. Her mother had not even received that.

And why?

It had been either that or jump in front of a train. It was that simple. When Azhar had called her and babbled something about a college reunion back in India, she knew she had to go — or give up on everything. It was a last resort. A final effort before giving up on life. "I'm coming," she had said, barely pausing to take down details of the place.

Maya ran the shower and jumped in before she could think too much, feeling the cold water washing away the vestiges of her sleep, and thought to herself about stories. Her story was that she was a good woman, a good housewife. Her husband's story was that he was a hardworking family man. What simple descriptions with which to condemn two people to a lifetime of boredom and depression! Poor Naveen. He was as much a victim as she was, in his own way, even if he got to fulfill some sort of ambition at the IT firm where he worked. But he lacked that rebellious streak that Maya had held deep inside her for years and just wouldn't be denied any more.

She stepped out of the shower and toweled down her slender frame. Walking into the bedroom, she chose a top and a pair of jeans at random. She wasn't here to impress anyone. She was here to escape another life.

She heard some creaking noises through the wall, and she thought vaguely that it must be Harsha, who had been allocated the adjoining room in this resort block. How did she feel about Harsha? With Azhar and Shane, she had felt a certain level of comfort, a familiarity and lack of judgement that provided a sanctuary from her humdrum existence. Even the endless reminiscences about college didn't bother her.

With Harsha, it was different. Of all the group of friends from university, he was the one who was the real success. He had been a well-known journalist in India, and if that wasn't enough, he had gone to England and had become a successful journalist there.

When Maya compared this with her own life, she almost felt choked up with jealousy. Couldn't that have been her, in a parallel universe where women had the same choices that men did?

She shook her head to try and rid herself of these toxic feelings and took a deep breath, trying to remind herself of what a sweet boy Harsha had been. How hopelessly in love with her he had been, even when she was dating Azhar back in the day.

BANG BANG BANG. A sudden loud hammering on the door rudely interrupted her chain of thought, and Maya's heart leapt into her mouth, beating hard against her chest. She gulped and asked: "Who... who is it?"

"It is Murugayya, madam!" The resort manager's voice was distinctive, and she calmed immediately. No one could be threatened by poor old Murugayya. But what the hell did the man mean by knocking the door down with that racket?

She walked up to the front door and flung it open .

"Yes, Murugayya?" she barked in annoyance. And then looked down — she hadn't quite gotten used to how short he was. Murugayya backed away in alarm.

"Sorry," she mumbled, feeling a little sorry for her bad temper. "Er... what is it?"

"Mr Azhar sir has asked you to come down to the dining room, madam."

"Oh... er... Thanks Murugayya. What's the time?"

"Six thirty, madam."

The man looked up at her, and the light from the open doorway lit up his face. A long, drooping moustache gave him a permanent air of melancholy, and despite a young-looking face, the lines on his strong cheekbones and forehead gave him an air of wisdom. Most of all, his fine, grey eyes shone brightly, and when he smiled, as he did now, the edges of his eyes crinkled in full-blooded enjoyment. Maya felt some tug of emotion as she looked at the man's expressive, strangely beautiful face.

"Azhar sir wants you to join him for dinner. Sir is really happy with all his friends here with him," he confided. "I have not seen him like this for years!"

And then, as though slightly taken aback by his own familiarity, he stepped back and bent over slightly again.

Maya stepped forward and placed a hand on his shoulder: "That's good to hear, thanks again Murugayya," she said.

The corners of those liquid eyes crinkled again as the man grinned, his moustache forming a partial curtain over his pearly-white teeth, before he turned to go.

"What about Harsha... the other man?" Maya asked, quickly. "Is he coming down as well?"

"I just woke him too, madam. He said he will come in half an hour."

Maya briefly considered waiting for Harsha, or even going up to knock on the door herself. But a rumble in her stomach settled the issue and she said. "Give me one minute, Murugayya, and I will come down with you."

Soon after Murugayya had woken him up with his thunderous knocking, Harsha sat on his bed and blinked blearily for a few minutes, trying to centre himself and get used to the idea that he was in some remote part of India rather than in his tiny flatshare in London.

It took him maybe 15 minutes before he finally got himself up to smoke a quick cigarette in the bathroom, wash his face and then pull on a random T-shirt from his open suitcase. Then he remembered that Maya would be there and he tried on a few others, looking at himself critically in the wardrobe mirror, before finally settling on a dark grey H&M number that hugged his slim frame and somehow mysteriously seemed to accentuate his shoulders while also hiding his slight paunch.

As he pulled on his jeans (which had been lying on the carpet by the bed in the exact shape in which he had stepped out of them) his thoughts drifted to Murugayya, and he chastised himself for judging the man too early.

Was Shane right? Had he just been wilfully blind to all the caste problems in this country?

Some people have hard lives, he thought to himself, as he buckled on the leather belt. And then he remembered that Azhar had promoted Murugayya and felt a gush of affection for his old friend.

He stepped out of the door and stopped short. He could see the lights of the resort further down the hill, but his immediate surroundings were shrouded in a darkness that, as a city boy, he was completely unused to. He reflected briefly that there were very few places in the city where there was no street lamp or light of some sort.

"Sir?"

Harsha jumped and said: "Good god, Murugayya, you scared me!" A torch-light flicked on to briefly show the resort manager's smiling face, and Harsha looked at him in wonder. In that remote place, there was something almost ethereal about the man. Murugayya gestured and turned, and Harsha followed the man as he went downhill with that weird crab-like gait.

"Who else is at dinner, Murugayya?"

"Azhar sir, Shane sir and Maya madam," the man called out as he loped downhill.

Harsha quickened his pace.

When they reached the entrance to the large dining hall, Harsha hesitated. He looked around for Murugayya, of all people, for some moral support, but the man had disappeared after depositing him by the large French windows.

He took one step forward, looking at the trio around the main table, and particularly at the girl sitting facing in his direction. To Harsha's relief she showed none of the signs of going to seed that Shane had. She was still tall, slim and bright-eyed with a lovely, wide smile and even teeth. The only difference was that she had short hair now — it suited her, Harsha thought.

But despite the slightly boyish appearance this gave her, she looked older, more mature. Looking at it objectively, he could instantly see why his teenage self had fallen hopelessly in love with this lovely woman, though if anything she was even more beautiful now.

He shook himself and took another step forward. At that moment, she threw her head back and laughed, and Harsha stopped and smiled to himself as he remembered her strange, gurgling laughter from a decade ago, like the sound of water falling on rocks.

Azhar, who was next to her, looked up and saw Harsha. He stood up quickly.

"Dude! What are you doing standing there like some damn bodyguard! Come on in," he bellowed, gesturing urgently with both hands.

Harsha twisted the French window open and stepped in carefully.

"Sorry dude, I... err... I just had a smoke so I was waiting for the smell to go away," Harsha felt the lameness of this statement even before the table burst into laughter.

"Still the same old Harry," Shane said, whatever that meant. Harsha walked up to the table, avoiding Maya's eyes for some reason he couldn't fathom.

"How are you guys doing?" he asked the table in general. "How come you're all alone here, are there no other guests?"

"It's off season so we have very few guests. They're mostly ordering food in their rooms," Azhar said. "Tomorrow you will probably see..."

"Harsha," Maya cut in, and he forced himself to look down at her. She was wearing eyeliner and lipstick, he noticed. That was different.

"You are totally ignoring me," she finished, pouting slightly, a nasal twang to her accent betraying her last few years living in the United States.

"Err...." Why did he have to go back to his awkward teens now? Surely he had come a long way since then?

"Harry is just a bit dazed and confused," Shane said, clapping Harsha on the back.

Harsha decided to go for honesty: "I just felt a bit shy. I'd forgotten how beautiful you are," he said, smiling slightly.

"Wah wah! *Shabhash!*" The other two cheered, and Maya shook her head, smiling.

Shane looked amused: "Is this the guy who couldn't talk to girls at all back in the day?"

"Dude, you don't know this guy, man, he is a dangerous fellow! I hung out with him a bit after college. Lock up your daughters!" Azhar said, pulling a few airtight containers towards him and opening them. "We kept the food hot for you. Here, have some chapatis, there's korma and butter chicken. And some wine that I kept for this occasion which ... er... well, there's a little bit left. I'll go get another bottle."

As if in response, Harsha's stomach rumbled loudly and he pulled up a chair and sat down, as Azhar scrambled up from his seat and went back into the kitchen, emerging a minute later with another bottle of white wine.

"It's not quite as good as the other one... but it's decent. A Sauvignon Blanc from Marlborough. That's in New Zealand," he said as he walked up to the table and picked up the corkscrew.

Harsha was less interested in the wine and more interested in the huge piles of food in front of him.

"This smells amazing, man," he said, spooning massive helpings of chicken on to his plate. "God, it's good to have some home-cooked food!"

For a while, he concentrated on his food, letting his friends' chatter wash over him, and it was only when he had almost cleaned out his plate (which didn't take long), that he looked up to see Maya regarding his enthusiasm with some amusement.

"How is married life treating you?" he asked, mopping up the remnants of the gravy on his plate with a piece of chapati.

Her face hardened slightly. "Oh you know... It's alright. Naveen is a good guy."

"Is he ok with you being here? With dangerous men like Azhar and Harry?" Shane asked.

She shrugged her shoulders, clearly irritated at the question.

Harsha quickly cut in: "And how's... er... San Francisco?"

She smiled: "Nice try. We are in Seattle. It's a beautiful city, though it rains a lot."

"Look at all you people, in Seattle and London and shit. Even Juni's in New York or New England or somewhere," Azhar cut in.

"New Jersey," said Shane.

"Whatever. Only Shannon and I are in Hamara Bharat. *Meri desh ki darti*!" he sang out suddenly.

"How many drinks down are you, man?" Harsha asked, laughing.

"I stopped counting hours ago, dude! This is supposed to be a reunion anyway, we're not in church. Harry, some more wine?"

Mouth full of food, Harsha just nodded.

Azhar poured the Sauvignon Blanc somewhat unromantically into a coffee mug before handing it over.

Taking a sip, Harsha sighed comfortably and said: "When's Juni coming?"

"Only on Friday. And I told you, those girls ditched. And god knows if Ricky is even alive."

Harsha felt a pang thinking of Richard, the brilliant singer whose voice had been ruined by extensive drug abuse. For one sickening moment he wondered if Azhar's casual question might be a legitimate one — was Richard alive?

He looked sideways at Shane, who had been Richard's closest friend after university. His face was impassive, but a brooding silence had fallen over the group.

Harsha tried to think of a change of subject, but nothing came to mind.

"Do you remember Richard's singing?" Maya asked. Harsha looked at her. Her eyes were looking away at the distance, lost no doubt in a memory of Richard singing — there had been plenty of occasion for that. Their old classmate had played in a band that had been well received at the local pubs and wildly successful in inter-college cultural events.

Shane smiled, and so did Harsha, but Azhar was looking uncharacteristically low. Alcohol fuelled, Harsha realised, as Azhar poured out a generous glass of wine and tossed it down.

Maya asked: "Is it true he had lost his voice towards the end?"

Harsha knew she meant toward the end of college, but it took on a sinister meaning in his mind. Also, he couldn't help feeling he had noticed a slight edge in Maya's voice when she asked. Had he imagined that?

Shane answered: "Pretty much. He could hardly speak. His throat was completely messed up from all the weed and whatnot."

"Can't be weed," Azhar slurred. "Weed's goo' for you. Medi... medi... medicinal and shit."

"That's enough drinking for you," Shane said calmly, pulling the bottle away from him.

"Fuckin' shpoi ... Shipo... Shpolshport," Azhar said, leaning forward menacingly.

"A smoke?" Harsha cut in hurriedly, remembering Azhar's habit of enjoying a cigarette with his drink.

Azhar switched his slightly unfocused gaze to him, and his forehead crinkled in thought. "Yeah!" he bellowed suddenly and pulled himself out of the chair and stumbled towards the French windows, Harsha hurrying after him.

They stood outside and smoked quietly, Azhar swaying slightly. The night air had turned almost uncomfortably chilly, and some of the clouds had cleared, revealing a myriad stars, more than Harsha had even known existed.

"Gorgeous, yeah," Azhar said.

"Really stunning. You barely see any stars in London."

"Stars? Who's talkin' about bloody stars? I meant Maya," he gestured with a thumb back into the dining hall. Harsha turned and watched Maya chuckle at something Shane had said.

"You still fancy her?" Harsha asked and almost laughed at the expression of panic on Azhar's face.

"God no! I ruined her life enough back in college. I would never go back there, even if she wasn't married," Azhar said virtuously. "She's changed," he added thoughtfully. His speech became less slurry as he spoke, as the cold night air cleared his head. "Don't get me wrong, still a nice girl, but not so sweet and innocent anymore. Something's wrong. She's changed for sure."

Harry remembered that feeling he had had when they had talked about Richard — the hint of excitement in Maya's voice. Most journalists were malicious gossips, and Harsha had recognised that tone: it was an edge to the voice he heard when some of his colleagues were discussing office indiscretions or someone's fall from grace.

Everyone has changed, Harsha thought, and for the first time the thought saddened him. Life had gently battered them over the last dozen or so years — Shane had become visibly older, Maya had become malicious, and Harsha himself — yes, he had become more cynical.

"Still has an amazing body though," Azhar said, making a ridiculous gesture with his hand.

"Dude!" Harsha said, pulling Azhar's hand down and glancing back toward the hall.

They both burst into laughter.

"Man, you at least have NOT changed one bit," Harsha declared.

5. MEETINGS

Maya's eyes fluttered open the next morning and she felt a wave of jetlag, wine headache and confusion all come crashing down on her at the same time.

She stared up at the clean white ceiling of her room, trying to pick apart and calm the maelstrom of thoughts and emotions that were rushing through her head. One of them stood out as most imperative: Harsha.

She had been dreading, almost hating, the idea of meeting him again. But instead of the jealousy and resentment she had expected to feel, she had only felt nostalgia, regret — and a most unexpected and unwelcome wave of attraction.

She sat up in her bed and pushed her hair back, blinking, and briefly glanced at the wall that separated her from Harsha. Her mind drifted to that moment when he had walked into the dining hall the night before.

He had always been a good looking man, particularly after he had worked off his teenage obesity, but she had forgotten how slim he had become. Since she had last seen him, he had also acquired a broadness about his shoulders. Meanwhile, he still had those melting, dark brown eyes, and that unwittingly fashionable tousled hair that fell over his forehead and accentuated his high cheekbones.

But it wasn't even that. It was that air of world weariness that he had acquired that was most attractive. He had shed the arrogance that had put her off so much in the years after university had ended and had regained some of that the shy innocence that had first made her warm to him all those years back. The effect of all of this put together had been quite devastating, and Maya still felt quite dazed by it.

"I have a husband!" she scolded herself, and fell back onto the bed and closed her eyes again, trying to ignore the tightness about her temples. What would poor Naveen be doing now? He would know she was safe. But she had better call him and update him, at least to keep him from any further worry. The thought of reality intruding into this little haven of peace made her forehead throb even more.

BANG! BANG! BANG! A pounding on the door added to the pounding inside her head and she groaned even louder, before eventually pulling herself out of the bed, untangling herself from the bedsheets and shuffling over towards the entrance to her room.

"YES?" she bellowed, throwing the door open. Murugayya, looking odd in shirt and trousers, took a step back, startled by her response. He glanced at her tousled hair and her pajamas, and licked his lips nervously.

"Sorry, madam," Murugayya said, looking away from her. "Azhar sir said to come for breakfast."

"To hell with Azhar," Maya mumbled.

"Madam?"

"Nothing, nothing," Maya said crossly. "Clearly Azhar has never heard of jetlag."

"Ah, jetlag," Murugayya said wisely, to Maya's surprise. "Best is to follow the normal routine and in two days you will be alright, madam," he said.

Maya smiled unwillingly and said: "You are right, Murugayya. Tell Azhar I'll be down in half an hour."

Murugayya nodded and was about to leave when Maya spotted another face peering around from behind the man's legs. It was a tiny face dominated by a pair of large black eyes. Maya managed to muster up a smile.

"And who is this?"

"My son, Jagannathan," Murugayya said proudly. "Jaggu, say hello!"

The boy continued to peer in silent wonderment at the strange woman, arms tightly clasped around one of his father's legs. He must have been all of five years' old.

Maya's heart melted.

"Hello, Jaggu, how are you?" she asked in English. The boy mouthed "hello" and buried his face in the back of his father's knee.

"Say it properly!" His father said sternly. "He speaks very good English, madam, he learns it very quickly!" he said, speaking in Tamil himself.

"I am sure. If he wants some practice, I will be happy to help."

Murugayya's face radiated delight, and Maya felt guilty for her bad temper.

"Er... I'll see you in half an hour then, ok?" Maya withdrew hurriedly, the image of Murugayya's bobbing head imprinted in her mind as she shut the door on father and son.

As promised, she walked into the dining room half an hour later and was told by one of the cleaners — Leela, she thought her name was — that Azhar was in the "meeting area".

Momentarily baffled by these vague directions, she wandered around until she found the others sitting on the stone platform built under the large, umbrella-shaped tree she had seen when she first arrived at the resort.

Shane and Harsha were sitting under the shade of the tree's thick, heart-shaped leaves, while Azhar was standing nearby, immaculately dressed in a dark blue shirt and jeans.

Shane noticed her first: "Morning, sleepy head," he said, smiling affectionately up at her. Shane had always been a dependable friend.

"Ah, there you are, bloody hell, it's almost eleven!" Azhar said, sounding considerably less patient.

Maya murmured something incomprehensible and said: "Where's breakfast?"

"Lunch is ready in an hour. Here's some coffee." Shane poured out some steaming coffee into a mug from a flask and Maya grasped it like it was the elixir of life.

"By the way, where in this wilderness can I get some mobile phone reception?" she asked Azhar.

"You have to go down to Ramananpettai."

"Seriously? No signal anywhere on your resort?" Harsha asked, moving to make some room for Maya. She blushed slightly, remembering her feelings from the night before, but sat next to him without comment.

Azhar sighed. "It's a long story, dude. I have been trying to get the local authorities to set up a linking station by the village — which would be better for everyone — but there's this panchayat head, who is blocking it for some crazy reason. He is one difficult dude."

"Why, what's his problem?" Maya asked lazily, taking a sip of her drink. "This coffee is heavenly, I must say."

"Made from local beans," Azhar said, absentmindedly. "He wants me to pay for the damn thing, as though I own the infrastructure — or can even afford it. Anyway, there's a landline you can use in the dining room and in my office."

Maya focused on her coffee but Harsha nodded, as he patted his pockets. Probably looking for his cigarette lighter, Maya thought. "Might be good for me to lose touch with civilisation for a bit anyway," Harsh said, finding his quarry and fishing out a battered lighter and a crushed packet of cigarettes. "And what are we doing today?"

"I was originally going to take you guys up the mountain trail today, but I've got some tasks to do unfortunately, and besides, his highness decided not to bring any sports shoes with him, so I will have to go down to the town and find him a pair," Azhar said, grinning at Harsha.

"I didn't know there was hiking involved, idiot — 'your highness' is a bit harsh," Harsha mumbled, lighting his cigarette.

"Prince Harry," Shane said slyly, and the three of them burst into laughter. Harsha hurriedly took the cigarette out of his mouth.

"Ok, you guys are NOT calling me that!" he said sharply.

Maya thought he looked genuinely hurt so she leaned forward and put a hand on his shoulder. "It was just a joke, Harsha — relax! We all know you're nothing like that."

"Just... well... I'm not... life in England isn't that... work really hard..." Harsha muttered, scowling at the floor.

His sulky expression amused Maya all the more, and she couldn't help laughing again, setting Azhar and Shane off as well.

"Hahaha, Prince Harry!" Azhar said again, as though hearing it for the first time.

Finally Harsha looked up and smiled weakly at the three of them and shook his head.

"Be careful or I'll have you all executed," he said, finally, earning a friendly punch on the shoulder from Shane.

It was so relaxing out there under that beautiful tree that Maya felt her heartbeat slowing, and all the issues and worries of that morning seemed to recede. It was so peaceful to sit under the tree and chat quietly, with the sounds of birds and the distant clang of vessels from the kitchen as background.

"What is this tree, Azhar?" Maya asked. "It's very beautiful."

"Dude. This is a *pipal* tree. It's where the resort gets its name!" Azhar said, jumping lightly up onto the platform and placing one hand affectionately on its slender trunk. "These trees are all over the mountain! That's why the village is also named after it. Arasur," he said.

Light dawned on Maya. "Of course!" she said. "Arasamaram! Arasur — it all makes sense now."

Harsha looked up with keen interest. Maya knew that this sort of wordplay would appeal to him. "Arasur and Pipal Resorts. I like it! Very clever. Was that your idea?"

"What do you think?"

"Well, whoever came up with it, it is a beautiful idea," Harsha said, approvingly.

Azhar nodded soberly as he sat down beside Shane. "I think so too, but some of the villagers... well, they thought we were insulting them by calling it by the Urdu name or something. I don't know, who knows how these people's minds work!"

"Seriously?" Harsha asked, grinding out his cigarette.

That seemed utterly ridiculous to Maya. But she supposed that people who actively wanted to be offended could find anything to get offended by.

Azhar shrugged his shoulders. "Anyway, as I was saying, I can't take you up the mountain trail today as I do have to get hold of some help for the hotel — one of our cleaners hasn't turned up for three days, and we have to get hold of some temporary staff."

Maya leaned back and squinted as a ray of sunshine made its way through the *pipal* tree's leaves and fell on her face. "One of your cleaners has gone missing?" she asked, sounding mildly interested.

"Oh you know how it is! None of them like taking holidays, they just disappear anyway and suddenly turn up and say they went for their grandmother's funeral in Tirupati or wherever," Azhar said, moodily kicking a bit of dirt as he spoke. "I wouldn't have expected it from Lakshmi, but still... I suppose I better fix the situation or Murugayya will stay up all night doing her work."

Maya looked curiously over at Azhar and tried to reassess her happy-go-lucky university boyfriend in this new role of responsibility. It was incredibly incongruous, like watching a dog playing a piano, she thought to herself.

"Anyway, you don't have to worry about us, we can entertain ourselves," Shane said soothingly.

Azhar nodded his thanks and said: "Here's what I had planned for the week, anyway, and you can choose."

Ticking them off his fingers, he continued: "There is an elephant trek with a local tour guide who comes here when we need him. You could visit the school nearby — the owner is a friend of mine and I could get Murugayya to take you. There is a temple in the village of Arasur that is very ancient and historic — crumbling but charming. Or, finally, we could go to the pool."

Maya put up her hand.

"This is not a classroom, Maya, what is it?"

"Why do you want us to go to a school?"

"Oh, it's a bit more than that. This mad, rich French guy came and bought huge acres of forest land and set up a school. The classrooms are all in different places so you have to trek through the forest to get to them. It's really quite kickass, wish I had gone to a school like that. The guy is a bit mad, but he's a decent enough fellow, and maybe Prince Harry will like talking to him about England or France or whatever. Shane has met him."

Shane made a slight expression of distaste and said: "The school is very beautiful, as Azhar said. Definitely worth seeing. As for Laurent — let's just say he's not my type."

"Ah there's no harm in Loco!" Azhar said, flicking some dust off his shirt cuffs. "He's had a strange life. Made loads of money as a banker but his wife left him."

Shane looked at him in surprise. "How do you know that?"

"He told me after a bottle or two of wine! Even showed me his wedding ring! Poor bugger still wears it."

Shane shook his head. "Wonders never cease. I never thought you and he would be drinking buddies."

"He's the only one around here who drinks wine. Good wine anyway," Azhar explained.

Harsha yawned and said: "Not sure I really want to socialise today. Tell me about this temple?"

"I knew you would be interested in that, with your history and culture and all that. It's a very ancient temple, built when this used to be part of some old kingdom. *Pallavas* or *Hoysalas* or something. The temple priest is quite a personality around here — I'm a bit scared of him, to be honest," Azhar said.

"And the pool?"

"Oh, that's the best part!" Azhar said, enthusiastically. "It's a natural pool nearby, created by a series of waterfalls that go all the way down the mountain — perfectly clear, and on a day like this, the water is not too cold. It's pretty amazing, actually," he ended, modestly.

"Sounds good to me, but maybe for tomorrow," Maya said. Her head felt like it had stones in them. Jetlag was becoming worse as she grew older. "Though if I feel up to it I might do this mountain trail later this afternoon though. Is it very hard?"

"It won't kill anyone," Azhar said.

A smiling, saree-clad woman came out from the back of the hall and said: "Lunch is ready, sir!"

"Thank you, Kuppi," Azhar said, and there was a general move to the dining rooms.

"You guys go ahead, I have some stuff to finish up," Azhar told them, and Maya thought he looked a bit hassled, but she let it go and walked to the hall behind Harsha and Shane. She heard Azhar bellowing: "Murugayya! Murugayya!" behind her as they went into the hall.

6. DISCOVERY

Since there were very few guests at this time of year, the kitchen staff had laid just one long table in the centre of the room. A couple sat next to each on one side of the table. Another man sat sipping a coffee by the sofa in the corner, in defiance of the implied edict to sit at the central table. He was reading a Telugu paper and did not look up.

The couple eyed them nervously and then introduced themselves as Bhaskar and Mala, a couple from a village further south. The man looked distinctly nervous when Maya went round to his side, even though she sat one chair away from him.

Shane and Harsha chattered away — they appeared to be quite comfortable in each others' company already, as men often were — so Maya sat mostly in silence, occasionally volunteering a remark. Finally, she turned to engage the couple in conversation.

Bhaskar, it turned out, had actually spent five years in the United States, studying technology and working in a tech firm in San Francisco for awhile.

It was such a bizarre collision of worlds that Maya could barely get her head around it. So she asked the question that was closest to her heart: "Did you find it difficult to move back to India?"

The man swung around to look at her a little nervously, and then shook his head vigorously. "No no. I love it here, though I would like to live in a big city like Coimbatore."

Maya had to hide a smile at Coimbatore being referred to as a big city. She tried to think of an American equivalent — New Jersey, perhaps — being referred to as a sprawling metropolis.

"Of course, some things you miss. Like the freedom over there," Bhaskar said thoughtfully. "Nobody knows or cares what your background is, or your gender or caste... That was nice."

"I completely agree," Harsha said, warmly, joining their conversation.

"You should not say that," Mala, the wife, said sharply, to everyone's discomfort. "Whatever it is, this is your country!" she declared, training her fine eyes indignantly on her husband and then on Harsha, as though it was somehow his fault. Maya had to hide a smile as she watched Bhaskar squirm and Harsha's taken aback expression.

"Yeah Harry, you are starting to sound like a proper NRI, bitching about India all the time," she put in, referring to his status as a Non-Resident Indian.

Harsha was stung by this grievous insult. "Hello, you live in the US!" he declared.

"Yeah but I never said I liked it," she said and then stopped and looked down at the table. She hadn't expected to feel so hurt by this gentle banter.

A second awkward pause fell over the table, relieved by Kuppi bearing a massive tray full of dishes.

"Dammit!" said Harsha, looking at the platter of curries and steaming chapatis. "I wouldn't have had so much of that soup if I knew this was coming!"

After lunch, any semblance of a plan was stymied by Azhar, who came down and told them he would be busy for the rest of the day.

"So sorry, guys," he said, looking hassled, but hurrying away almost immediately.

"What's he so busy with?" Maya asked Shane, who replied quietly: "I think he's having some trouble from the village. From the panchayat. Or maybe it's this cleaner? Who knows."

He did not elaborate, and Maya did not ask.

In the absence of any other ideas, Maya suggested they brave the mountain trek. Shane said he had work to finish, which everyone understood to mean a nap in his room.

So, it was just Harsha and Maya. She felt her stomach flip over slightly at the thought.

"Should we ask Bhaskar and Mala if they want to come?" Harsha asked her as they walked back to their rooms.

"Are you embarrassed to go with me alone?" Maya asked, smiling slightly. She often found that level of directness was quite good for hiding her own nervousness.

"Er... no no! Let's not ask them," Harsha said hurriedly as they came up to their respective rooms. "Shall we get some rest first, meet outside here at three o' clock?"

She said goodbye at her door and went into the room. She lay on the bed and picked up her phone and stared at the last text she received from her husband and read the words for the hundredth time, while trying to block out sounds of Harsha's presence in the next room.

Maya stepped out of her room at three o' clock, armed in her hiking boots and tiny backpack, enjoying the novel sensation of feeling slightly chilly on an Indian afternoon. She walked a little both ways, taking in the mountainous scrub, the long lines of the leaves and the woods that covered part of the mountain above her. She was determined to enjoy the natural beauty around this resort. Questions about her own life could wait for another day. As for Harsha — she was his old university friend, and she would treat him as such, and enjoy it for what it was.

She heard the clicking of a door opening and turned to see Harsha walk out of his room, a cigarette dangling from his mouth, and smiled briefly at him. He was wearing a black T-shirt that hugged his shoulders over khaki trousers and a pair of Reebok shoes. A thin gold chain dangled over his t-shirt, ending in a simple ring pendant.

"The best that Ramananpettai had to offer," he said, grinning and holding up his right foot so she could inspect his shoes. "Azhar dropped it off an hour back."

"Very nice," she said. She tried not to notice that he was looking at her in open admiration — she knew her boots suited her — and nodded to him instead.

He just said: "Nice Pearl Jam T-shirt. Juni would approve."

She smiled. "I have grown to appreciate them since moving to Seattle."

"Shall we?" he asked, his eyes shining with warmth in the old way that she remembered so well from university days. She nodded in response.

He cleared his throat. "So, as far as I can remember, this is the path that we must take," he said, pointing to a footpath that fringed one side of the woods. "Azhar said it goes all the way to the top of the hill, but we shouldn't be fooled by how nearby the summit looks from..."

He broke off as she leaned in towards him to better look at the path, her shoulder brushing against his chest, her hair barely an inch from his face. He smelled of cologne.

She briefly grasped his arm and said: "Alright then, let's go."

"So, I think it will take two hours to get all the way to the top, where there is a lookout point where we can see waterfalls and..."

"Stop talking and save your breath for later, fat boy," she said impishly, sticking her thumbs in the straps of her rucksack.

"What the... I'm not... Not anymore..." he spluttered, looking down at his trim figure.

"Sorry, force of habit," she said, smiling at him again, and he grinned in response. She didn't normally hold with fat shaming, but this was *Harsha*.

They set off at a smart pace, and in about 20 minutes the track wound to the left and the woods — which turned out to be a small stretch of forest — obscured the view to the resort.

Ahead of them the path was fairly level grassland, interspersed with a few clumps of trees and a thicker and darker stretch of forest lay to the right, contrasting sharply with the brightness of the open landscape up ahead.

Initially Harsha had led the way but soon he began to flag and she pressed ahead.

In a little while, as they passed a fold in the mountain and a vast panorama of farmland and forestland stretched out before them, she realised could no longer hear Harsha's footsteps behind her. She turned to see him gasping as he tried to keep up, and smiled.

"Come on, hurry up!" she said, mercilessly.

"Hang on, I'm going to take a picture!" Harsha called out, though instead of taking out his phone, he just bent over, resting his hands on his knees, and took some deep breaths.

"Come on, Harry, the view will be even better at the top," she said, running back to him. "Just a little longer, fatso!"

"Not... fat... smoker!" Harsha managed, wheezing slightly.

"That is *much* worse!" she laughed.

She walked towards him and Harsha, focused on the ground in front of him, nearly walked into her. She held up two hands to his chest to avoid the collision. For a second, she left them there and they looked at each other, her eyes tilting slightly inquiringly, the half-smile back on her face.

She broke her gaze eyesight first and patted his chest, saying: "Your heart is beating really hard."

"Yeah, I think I know why," Harsha said in a rush. "I mean, because of the trek I mean," he added hurriedly, laughing quickly. "We... yeah, so I never asked — what's your husband's name?"

Oh, why did he have to bring that up now?

"Naveen," she said, shortly.

"Oh... And how is it going with him?"

They reached a ring of trees surrounding a soft patch of grass, a natural sitting point. He flopped down and took deep gulps of air.

"Oh, alright, you know," she said, unslinging her backpack and pulling out a big bottle of water and passing it to him.

He drank in great gulps until she pulled it away from him. "Don't finish it."

"How did you meet him?"

"My mother arranged it all. How beautiful the view is!" she said.

Fortunately, he took the hint and dropped the subject.

It *was* very beautiful. There were large stretches of tall grass on either side of the road, leading out on to a dark line of forest on one side, and in the silence they could hear the call of birds and the distant sound of running water. Down below them, the slopes of the hill stretched out until it knelt at the feet of the village Arasur.

As they sat in the silence, the breeze picked up and made an almost imperceptible rushing sound as it swept through the grass. The sound should have been a soothing one, but it was starting to bother Maya slightly — like a dripping tap when you are trying to sleep, she thought to herself.

It seemed that this sense of disquiet had come over Harsha as well, because he kept looking around as though searching for something.

Maya followed his gaze and looked to their right at the vast expense of hillside greenery and then to the left, where a dark line of trees signified the start of the forest, unforgiving and mysterious. An irrational flicker of dread came to her just for a second, as though anything might creep out from the darkness between the trees.

"Look at that skeleton tree!" Harsha said suddenly, pointing behind her towards the peak of the mountain.

She turned and saw a bare tree in the middle of a meadow, a little way away from the forest wall. It was dry and twisted, like an old woman with distorted limbs bending under the weight of the years.

The hackles rose on the back of her neck, and she shook herself to try to rid herself of that feeling of spookiness, accentuated by the low moaning of the wind rushing around the thick grass.

Harsha stood up abruptly and walked past her, his eyes fixed on the tree.

"Is something wrong?" she asked, her voice sounding loud and unnatural in the silence.

"No, no, nothing..." Harsha said, and she thought he was trying to sound reassuring. "I think I saw something up there. Just give me a minute, just wait here for me."

She felt slightly panicky as he picked his way through the tall grass, walking uphill.

"Where are you going, Harry?" she asked.

"Don't worry, Maya! I've just seen something... Wait here! Don't come up."

Well, she couldn't possibly listen to him if he was going to act this protective. She hesitated for a moment and then scrambled up and ran lightly after him, leaving her backpack behind. He was halfway towards the gnarled old tree when she looked past him and saw a flash of red, startling against the various shades of green and brown.

"I think there's something there," Harsha called out, and there was a terrified edge to his voice that made the hairs on the back of Maya's neck stand up.

"Something? What do you mean, something?" she asked querulously.

As she moved closer to him, the stench hit her. Sharp, pungent and utterly awful.

She realised with shock that the flash of red she had seen was a strip of cloth, bordered with gold lines.

A sari.

And the sari was still wrapped around a person.

The smell of decomposition was unmistakable when Harsha shouted urgently: "Maya! Don't come here!" He turned and saw that she was just ten yards behind and said sharply: "Don't look! Just go back!"

She ignored this and continued to walk towards him until she reached him. Together, they looked at the decaying remains of a woman, facing the sky and the end of her sari flapping in the blowing air. Maya gripped Harsha's arm tightly, breathing hard.

After the initial shock, she could see that there were cut marks all over the dead woman's face and the exposed arms and legs. They were looking not just at a dead body, but one that had been mutilated and ravaged. Harsha leaned over to the side and vomited violently, and her own legs felt like jelly. She felt like collapsing right there — and she felt like running away from this horrible place.

"It's ok, it's ok," she said to Harsha, soothingly and meaninglessly, putting an arm on his his back.

"I'll be fine," he said thickly, hands on his knees. She squeezed his shoulder and they both stood there in the shadow of the lonely tree, while the light faded around them.

7. MURDER

Within hours, the hill was swarming with people, a handful in an official capacity, and the rest of them mourners or curious onlookers, peering through the grass in the fading light. The air was thick with wailing.

Harsha was already sick of the pot-bellied police officer who was questioning him, pausing every few minutes to look lasciviously at Maya, even though she had pulled on a hoodie to cover her T-shirt, giving her a relatively unremarkable appearance.

"We have told you everything, can we go now?"

"Just one or two more questions, please," the man leered, and Harsha bridled. The man was on some sort of weird power trip, perhaps fuelled by some class anger. Understanding this didn't help Harsha feel any better about it.

"How did you know she was here? It is nowhere near the path."

"I did not know she was here. I just saw her sari," Harsha said wearily.

"All the way from the path? Through all this grass?" the man asked incredulously.

"Yes, dammit!" Harsha said in English.

"Oho, come to speak Peter English is it? I will ask you once to not use that kind of language. This is a serious business," the man said with relish, as though he had won an argument.

"Well, what are you suggesting?"

"Just that your story doesn't make sense."

Harsha closed his eyes briefly, trying to contain his irritation. He opened his mouth to say something cutting but was interrupted — perhaps fortunately — by Azhar, who came striding up and said heavily: "It is Lakshmi. My cleaner. Body has been there for three days. Nobody noticed it. Absolute nightmare."

Feeling the tension in the air, Azhar looked from Harsha to the policeman and asked: "What's going on? Everything alright here?"

The man said greasily: "Oh nothing sir, just a few routine

questions."

Harsha said nothing, but Azhar looked at him and then Maya and said: "These people know nothing, they just arrived here yesterday. Why don't you let them go get some rest? They have had a hard time."

The policeman ignored this and instead demanded: "How do you know the body was three days old?"

"How the hell should I know? That's what your inspector told me," Azhar said, pointing to a trim, uniformed man who was facing away from them and talking to some of his staff, who were nodding repeatedly. "Go ask him if you want."

A mingled look of respect and dread came into the man's beady eyes, and his head bobbed back and forth. "Yes, sir," he said, presumably cowed by the mention of his superior.

"You may go," he told Harsha and Maya, who were already making their way down the slope.

Maya placed one cool hand on Harsha's arm.

"Take it easy, Harry," she said.

"The dickhead!" Harsha said. "He was totally enjoying that!"

"I know, but relax."

"And the way he was looking at you! It made my blood boil!"

Maya sighed: "Do you think I'm not used to men looking at me, Harry? Just let it go, ok?"

He had no idea why some fat policeman on a power trip was making him so angry, but he continued to fume all the way down the hill.

When they reached the residence, he was about to go to his room — he was exhausted from the day's events — but Maya said: "Harry, can you come stay in my room for a bit?"

He froze and then slowly turned to her and said: "Er... what?"

"It's nothing like that!" she said hurriedly, blushing. "I just... I... I don't want to be alone right now."

"Of course!" Harsha said, feeling foolish. "So sorry, Maya, I didn't even think ... er... of course."

He followed her up to her door — the entrance to Maya's room was adjacent to his — and looked back up the hill as she fumbled with the key. He imagined a crowd around the dead woman's body and thought of a swarm of ants around a dead cockroach. He shivered.

She finally got the door open and they went in. It was the same as his room but neater and smelling of the perfume he was beginning to associate with her now. He awkwardly sat on the chair by the desk, pulling his trousers over the neck of his shoes so his feet wouldn't smell up the room. She sat on the bed opposite.

"You asked me about my marriage," she said abruptly. He assumed she was trying to talk about more normal things, though her marital life wouldn't have been his first choice.

"Yes, but if you don't want to talk about it..."

She sighed and said: "You know my father died... What is it, six years ago?"

He nodded. "I did hear about it, I am so sorry."

"Oh, I'm over it... Well, as much as you can be. But you know, after he died, just days after he died, they started looking for a husband for me."

Harsha said nothing.

She continued: "I didn't want to do it, but it was relentless. The whole family was on my case: cousins, aunts, uncles, people I couldn't remember and others I didn't even know existed, they all went on and on and on. It was as though the whole happiness of the household was dependent on my marriage. Even at my father's funeral they were at it.

"I finally caved and agreed to meet a few men, though nothing more. I liked one of them quite a lot and chose him, and we were married a few months later."

"You were ok with that? Getting married to him?" he asked incredulously, unable to be silent any longer.

She hesitated. "Well, it's hard to know whether it was because I liked him or if I just wanted to get my family to shut the fuck up. But that's not even the point. I was supposed to be mourning my father and all I was left doing was preparing for the wedding and the move to the US, quitting my job and everything." She shook her head and fell silent, staring out of the window.

He hoped she wouldn't cry. He would have no idea what to do if she did. Should he be holding her hand or something? He made a move forward, then lost his nerve and tugged at his shoelaces unnecessarily instead. He cleared his throat and then said: "Is he ok to you?"

She dragged her eyes from the window and laughed softly. "Oh, he is fine, fine... he is a very gentle man, very much in love with me I think, and maybe even a bit scared of me. I take out all my frustration on him which I know is unfair.

"It's not his fault, but life in the US is so lonely. I spent almost two years just minding the house, and then... Well, my job is just mindless. Typing up notes for lawyers. I had a real job here!"

Harsha was sympathetic, but only to an extent. What hope was there for the rural women of India if the women in the city, supposedly educated and empowered, caved in to societal pressures? But he did not want to articulate this, so he wisely said nothing.

"Do you think she was raped?" Maya asked suddenly. The blunt question broke Harsha instantly out of his reverie.

"Eh? Er..." The honest answer was yes, but he didn't want to say that. "I have no idea," he said instead.

"Must have been raped. You have no idea what it's like being a woman in India, Harry," she said, staring out of the window again.

This was too much. "Well, obviously I don't, but surely you are not comparing your problems with being raped or... or... or killed?"

"Of course not, but it's part of the same problem - it's the role we are expected to play, be available for sex whenever the men want it," she said.

"You just said your husband is quite gentle."

She shook her head impatiently. "I mean *in general*. I had to give up everything and go to the US, and now I am stuck there, while he gets to live the life that he wants."

Harsha was unnaturally irritated by the tragic tones in her voice.

"Then don't do it anymore," he said shortly. "Come back to India and pursue your career."

She looked up at him, stung. "Because it's that easy, is it?"

"Why is it not?"

She shook her head. "You are a man, you won't understand."

He shrugged. "Maybe not. But I don't see it as an insurmountable problem."

"Well, I have to ask him to give up his job in Seattle and come back with me, and what will he do when he comes here?"

"He can't get an IT job in India?" he asked, the sarcasm in his voice barely hidden.

She shook her head: "No Harry. It's too late for me. My youth is gone, the best years of my life."

"Man, stop this Emily Dickinson thing! Go look in the mirror and tell me again your youth is gone! You're still barely past 30, for crying out loud!"

She sprang up and looked down at him, breathing hard.

"God, Shane was right, you *are* still a patronising asshole!" she barked.

The blood rose to his face and he opened his mouth to say something when there was a knock on the door. Neither of them moved or said anything, and presently, the door opened slightly.

"Can I come in? I have coffee!" Shane said cheerfully from the doorway.

Maya still stood there without saying anything, so Harsha finally said: "Come on in, Shanny."

He came in, smiling faintly, flask in one hand and three cups dangling from the other.

"Not interrupting anything, am I?"

Maya turned away and muttered incoherently: "I... er... bathroom." She marched away to the toilet and slammed the door shut.

Shane poured out the coffees and then sat on the bed Maya had just vacated.

"How are you doing, buddy?" he asked, leaning concernedly forward towards Harsha.

"Maya was just telling me how right you were when you called me a — what was it? — a patronising asshole," Harsha said resentfully.

Shane threw his head back and laughed loudly, catching Harsha off guard.

"I was asking about the dead body you found earlier on the hill. But clearly, this is more important," he said. "The truth always hurts, Harry boy, but it's best that you know this about yourself. What's that thing you once quoted to me from Hamlet?"

"Er... from Hamlet? I can't think what it might be."

"The thing about being true to yourself?"

"Ah, the Polonius speech," Harsha said, and then chanted automatically: "This above all: to thine own self be true; And it must follow, as the night the day; Thou canst not then be false to any man..."

"There you go, Shakespeare said it."

Harsha smiled reluctantly: "How are things out there anyway?"

Shane became serious. "Pretty bad. Do you remember us talking about Lakshmi, the cleaner, who had gone missing? That was her. She was a bit of an oddball — lived on her own, which is very unusual for this area, but apparently people were used to her eccentric behaviour."

"No family, then?"

"I don't think so, but have to ask Azhar for more details. I think her parents died when she was young, she somehow managed not to get married off, so maybe that's why she is seen as unusual. Struggled to get a job anywhere except here, so she was fiercely loyal to Azhar. Azhar is quite upset."

"Any idea who did it?" Harsha asked again.

"They have absolutely no clue, but it was a pretty horrible murder. Whoever did it hacked her with an *aruval* — you know, that sickle type of thing that farmers use to slice the crops?"

"I know what an *aruval* is, idiot. Any idea why she was killed?"

Shane shrugged. "The rest of the staff are terrified, talking of leaving their jobs immediately. Azhar is under a lot of pressure."

"Poor guy. Is he ok?"

"Upset, but dealing with it. You wouldn't believe it is the same Azhar, the way he is taking charge of this and calming everyone down. Murugayya is being an absolute champion as well."

Harsha had a feeling Shane was doing his share of calming people down too. Shane had always been good in an emergency — like when Richard had had that horrible drug-induced seizure in class.

Maya came out of the bathroom, ignored Harsha and said to Shane: "I would like to be alone for a while please. I can't handle people lecturing me and giving me more problems right now."

Shane said calmly: "This is not the time to be a drama queen, Maya. Both you and Harry have just had a very bad experience and are not in a normal state of mind. You need each other — we all need each other to be calm and supportive right now."

There was an awkward silence.

And then Maya said: "It's bloody annoying how you are always right, Shane. Yes, I admit, I do need you guys right now."

Harsha said: "I should apologise, I..."

"No, no I should have..."

"Why don't you both apologise to each other?" Shane suggested, with a tone of authority.

"Sorry," Harsha and Maya said together, and looked at each other in surprise.

Harsha turned to Shane, who was grinning from ear to ear.

"Don't enjoy this so much, you fool," he said, but he couldn't help smiling as well.

He turned to Maya and sobered down instantly at her expression, as they sat there in silence for a moment, thinking of a dead woman none of them had known.

8. POLICE

A scene of complete mayhem met Harsha's eyes when he came down to breakfast the next day.

The cleaning and cooking staff were milling about, guests stood aimlessly outside the dining hall and a large pile of provisions had been dumped unceremoniously on the ground outside and both the van and the police jeep stood empty at random positions on the driveway.

"What the hell is going on?" Harsha said to the air.

No one seemed to be paying any attention to him, but years of working as a journalist had taught him not to put up with that. He grabbed the arm of the woman he recognised as the cook as she hurried past.

"Hi, sorry *akka*, but what's going on?" he asked.

She wrung her hands in frustration and said: "I don't even know! The police took Selvam, the driver, for questioning last night and he hasn't come to work today! And two of the cleaners and Millie, the other cook, are too scared to come to work," she said and snorted. "Or maybe they are too lazy! So just the two of us trying to do everything. You will have to wait for food, sir, I am having to do everything and I've only just managed coffee and biscuits!"

"Never mind the food," said Harsha, ignoring a loud rumble from his stomach. "Where is Azhar?"

"No driver, so Azhar sir has gone in his car to bring the provisions from the town, all of this HAD to happen on the day when we have run out of rice and lentils! Nothing left in the kitchen!"

"No provisions? Then what is that?" he asked, pointing at the pile of provisions. "It looks like it could feed an army!"

She looked at him pityingly. "That's only for today, sir. He has to shop for the whole week! His friend," here she mimed a pot belly and puffed out her cheeks. "Has gone with him to help."

"Shane, you mean?"

"Yes sir. Shane. Sorry, sir, but I'm really busy!" She hurried away to the pile of provisions in question and began picking at the bags.

So, he was all alone. For a brief moment Harsha felt a bit lost and aimless, but this was not about to last.

"Sir! Sir!" a voice bellowed and he turned to see Murugayya sprinting up to him, this time clad in a traditional *lungi* and shirt, his Hawaii slippers flapping as he ran. Behind him the rotund policeman from the previous evening was following, panting at the unaccustomed exercise.

"Sir!" Murugayya said once more, in a pleading voice, as he reached Harsha, before stopping to take a couple of deep, heaving breaths.

"What is it, Murugayya, please calm down and tell me slowly," Harsha said firmly. He did not like the panicked edge to the man's voice.

"Sir," Murugayya said again. "The police took Selvam for questioning yesterday, and he is now in the hospital."

"What? What the f... what happened?"

Murugayya held up an imaginary stick and brought it down violently on an imaginary person two or three times.

"They beat him, sir! He has six broken bones and 12 stitches!" he gestured to a spot above his eyebrow.

"What? They beat him? What the hell, what for?"

"Sir, I don't know! But they are doing it to everyone, sir, and now they want to take me for questioning, sir! I can't do it, sir, how will I work, what if I die, I have a son, sir!"

The rotund policeman caught up with his quarry finally and immediately starting yelling, in-between gasps. "How dare you run away from me! I told you not to move!" he bawled into Murugayya's face. His round frame and Murugayya's rake thin one made an odd contrast, particularly with the resort manager cowering from the other's bullying stance.

Murugayya stepped away and shrank towards Harsha, who put a reassuring hand on his shoulder.

"What do you want, constable?"

The main raised his lathi and pointed at Muruguyya (who cringed even more) and said: "This man is to accompany me to the police station. Inspector's orders."

"Are you taking him for questioning?"

"Yes... sir!" You could tell the constable immediately regretted the involuntary honorific.

Harsha regarded the man calmly. "Then can you please have the courtesy to wait until the owner of this resort is back?"

The policeman's eyes bulged and Harsha watched in fascination as a vein throbbed in his forehead.

The constable took a deep breath and then bellowed: "How dare you tell me what to do! You cannot defy the law! My orders are to take this man immediately! You can take it up with the inspector if you have any objection!"

"Sir, please sir," Murugayya whispered to him, and Harsha saw real fear in the man's eyes. He looked a completely pathetic object, and yet who was Harsha to judge him? This was a man who was used to being beaten down and expected nothing more from life. Pride was a luxury for people who had some sort of basic human rights and expectation of justice, should they be wronged.

"What's going on here?" The three of them turned to see Maya standing there, and despite everything, Harsha was momentarily distracted by her simple but gorgeous *salwar kameez* with leaf patterns around the sleeves. It made her look instantly slimmer and younger, and he noticed she had put on just a touch of eyeliner.

She looked at him, giving him a slightly cheeky grin, and he blushed, remembering the events of the previous evening. He had slept on the floor of her room at her request, but she had kicked him out hours later, saying her nightmares were preferable to the sound of his snoring.

"Madam, you stay out of this! This is none of your business!" the policeman barked, waggling his finger at her (after looking her up and down).

She lifted her eyebrows in an expression of magnificent disdain. "Excuse me?"

The constable subsided and muttered something about not meaning to offend anyone.

"Ok everyone, just calm down for a second, please," Harsha said in as commanding a voice as he could muster. Miraculously, everyone went quiet. He paused for a second and then made a decision.

"You, sir," he said, pointing at the policeman. "If you absolutely refuse to wait until Azhar comes back before taking this man for questioning..."

"My orders are very clear — to bring him back immediately," the constable said sulkily.

"... then I am coming with you as well."

A hand plucked at his sleeve urgently. "Sir, sir, they will beat me, I might die, sir, I have a son!" Murugayya said in desperate tones.

"One second," Harsha said to the policeman, and without waiting for a response he pulled his smaller companion a little away from the group and said to him: "Murugayya, I cannot stop the policeman from taking you. But I promise I will come and I will make sure they don't beat you."

"Sir, what can you do? You don't know what they are like..."

"Murugayya, I have given you a promise!" Harsha said sternly, and that quietened the man down.

They moved back to the group where Maya was, nose in the air, pointedly ignoring the policeman's scrutiny.

"You cannot come," the constable said as soon as Harsha and Murugayya returned to the group. "The inspector told me to bring only him."

"Either I am coming or no one is coming."

Maya took a step forward and said: "I want to come too."

"Maya, no! Someone has to tell Azhar what happened and get him to sort this shit out."

"We can tell Kuppi. The cook," she added, seeing his bemused expression.

"It looks to me like she has enough on her plate," he said.

She was about to argue but he forestalled her, saying: "Maya, listen to me, I am not being protective or anything, we genuinely need someone to stay here. And I think I should be the one to go with Murugayya."

She hesitated and then said: "For some reason he seems to trust you. Fine. But what do you want me to do?"

By this time, the other guests had recognised a voice of authority and came crowding up to Harsha and one of them said: "What is going on? Where is our breakfast? Why are the police everywhere? Do we get a discount?"

Harsha put an arm on Maya's shoulder and he couldn't quite hide a grin as he said: "This lady here will be delighted to help you."

He steered Murugayya to the police car, the constable still muttering as he followed them.

He glanced back and gave Maya a cheeky wave and saw her glaring at him, her face like thunder.

He chuckled to himself and got in the passenger seat of the car, earning another frown from the policeman.

The ride down the mountain was dreadful. Despite the excellence of the road, the jeep was a rickety old thing, making the van ride to the resort from earlier in the week seem like a pleasure ride, and Harsha was forcibly reminded that going downhill was even worse for his stomach than going uphill.

He found that the view, spectacular as it was, made him feel even sicker when he looked at it, so he kept his eyes studiously on the road in front of him.

Every now and then, the jeep appeared to swoop down like a plane taking a dive, making his bile rise. The policeman drove in hostile silence, and the only noise from within the jeep was Murugayya's words of prayer at the back, eyes closed and hands pressed tightly against each other.

"*Om namonarayana... om namonarayana...*" the man repeated again and again. It was putting Harsha nerves on edge to hear the same words repeated over and over in a voice laced with terror, particularly with his stomach giving a swoop every now and then. His head started to throb.

"Quiet back there!" the policeman snapped suddenly. Murugayya ignored him and continued praying. Harsha focused on the road, wondering if this awful, awful drive was ever going to end.

They finally reached Ramananpettai after what felt like a lifetime and drove through its streets. It had a certain charm about it, but it was not quite as romantic as it seemed from the top of the mountain.

They negotiated the narrow, dusty streets, and every here and there a little tea shop emerged, with jars of sweets in front and lines of shampoo sachets hanging from the roof. There were a few men and women outside some of them, enjoying a mid-morning cup of tea.

There was a large crowd around one shop. The shop sign said: "Golten Wines". Harsha frowned at it, thinking there was nothing even remotely golden about the cramped little shop front — assuming that "golten" was a misspelling and not some bizarre Telugu name.

Finally, they stopped in front of a red brick building that, across India, meant "police station". Harsha was surprised to see that it was a colonial building and he wondered just how old this town was.

They slammed the doors shut as they got out of the old jeep and walked up to the entrance — surprisingly clean in Harsha's (admittedly small) experience of police stations — and into the building. It was at this point that his mood took a complete 180-degree turn.

Taking charge of the situation had secretly given him a bit of a thrill at the top of the mountain. But when he walked into that police station, his heart fell with a thud, and he wished he had never come anywhere near Azhar's damned resort. He wished he was back among the red roofs in England with its (comparatively) neat pavements and well organised public services, and above all, a predictable life. This kind of crazy situation simply did not happen there, not unless you were really living on the margins or had some direct connection to London's dark underbelly. If you didn't, you could live your whole life without any direct experience of it.

"Sit here," their policeman said, pointing to a bench in what Harsha assumed was a waiting room of some sort. His nerves gave an additional jangle.

Despite the heat outside, the room was dimly lit and cool. It had two uncomfortable wooden benches on either side, and a policewoman with a bored expression was taking down notes as three different people gabbled away at her. There was a general feeling of fear and anger in the air, and the smell of sweat drifted across the room.

Harsha watched as the three people got more and more worked up until the policewoman — who, he noticed to his surprise, was quite attractive — raised her lathi and threatened to beat them all indiscriminately if they didn't speak in turn. While possibly not out of the police manual, this approach certainly seemed to work, and things quietened down.

A man with a broken nose made room for Harsha and Murugayya and they squeezed on to one of the benches. On the far end of the bench, an emaciated woman was breastfeeding her baby. Harsha tried not to look at this uncomfortable sight. Without ceremony, Murugayya resumed his prayers next to Harsha.

Their own policeman went away briefly through a door at the far end, but was back in front of them in five minutes. "I hope you enjoyed the drive," he said maliciously to Harsha. "The inspector won't allow you to come in when questioning this fellow."

Murugayya rocked back and forth in the middle of his prayer.

"He is not going in without me."

The policeman laughed nastily in response. Being back in his environment seemed to have given his arrogance a boost.

They waited for what felt like hours, though it was probably about 30 minutes. Murugayya continued praying right through this period, while Harsha took out his phone to find that he had been flooded by messages, now that he was back within range of a mobile phone tower.

He scrolled through them briefly — one was from a London colleague asking him if he fancied a pint, another from his phone company offering a new deal, a third from the Labour Councillor from his neighbourhood in London informing him a council meeting was postponed and the rest were from his mother asking him, in passive aggressive tones, if he was enjoying his time in India. He knew she hated that he was in the country but not in his parents' home. He texted her back briefly and then put away his phone in irritation and went back to staring at the opposite wall, looking resolutely away from the breastfeeding woman.

Finally, the fat policeman returned and said curtly: "The inspector wants to see you now."

Harsha sprang up and said: "I am going with him."

"No," the man said, and Harsha noticed suddenly that the expression of triumph on the man's face had been replaced by baffled fury. "He wants to see just you," he bit out, pointing at Harsha.

Harsha's mouth fell open, but he collected himself, patted Murugayya on the shoulder, and followed the policeman into an inner room.

The miasma of body odour was a lot less prominent here. In fact, despite the smallness of the room, it was clean. And one window on the far side let the sunshine flood in, lighting up the childrens' paintings on one side and a list of commendations on the other. The inspector was sitting at a table, writing in a notebook with a cheap ball-point pen. "Sit down," he said, without looking up.

Feeling horribly like an errant student in front of the college dean, Harsha sat on a metal, foldable chair and looked at the man in front of him. A label on the table informed him that he was in the presence of Inspector A. Palanivel.

"Thank you, Mr Ezhumalai," Inspector Palanivel said sharply in English, still not looking up, and the constable left the room immediately, shutting the door behind him.

Finally, the inspector looked up, and Harsha could not help feeling impressed and intimidated in equal parts. Here was no fat, unfit policeman. Palanivel was trim, neatly dressed and though he wasn't obviously muscled, there wasn't an ounce of fat on his sinewy arms. He had a small, neat moustache and his eyes were sharp and calculating. Harsha made a gesture as though to shake his hand but put his hand down when nothing was forthcoming from the other side.

"Mr Devnath," Palanivel said, without preamble, "I will not have you interfering in our investigation." Harsha did not know how the man had found out his surname.

Harsha tried to stay calm. "Sir, I do not want to interfere in your investigation. All I told your colleague is that I don't want to stand by while you beat Muru... I mean, the resort manager. He has done nothing wrong."

"That is not for you to say."

"Be that as it may, I don't want any harm to come to this man. It may not be obvious, but he is a very senior person in the resort and his well-being is very important to the owner of the resort, who happens to be my friend and associate. However, I can guarantee that he will answer all your questions truthfully."

The inspector leaned forward and looked at Harsha sharply. "*You* will guarantee? And who are *you*, if you don't mind me asking?"

This is where it all falls apart, Harsha thought to himself, but nevertheless he launched into the speech he had mentally rehearsed in the jeep.

"Who I am is not important at the moment, but you can take it that I am speaking on behalf of Mr Azhar, the resort owner. He and his family have been an important part of the local community here for almost three decades."

The inspector looked steadily at Harsha, who did his best to return the gaze without flinching or looking away.

Finally, the inspector said: "Mr Devnath, do you know how many cases I am dealing with right now?"

Harsha shook his head, confused by this change of topic.

"I have fifty cases pending, and more come into my in-tray every week. Don't look so surprised. Last year, when I came to this post, I had one hundred pending. I have brought that down. Yes, I had to use strong methods to do it; otherwise, this region would have descended into chaos. They have had no real law and order for decades. It's a forgotten place that people don't want to think about.

"Now you tell me, Mr Devnath, what would you do if you were in my position? How would you get through all these cases? How would you solve..." he glanced down at a sheet on his desk, and then said: "Eight murders, 22 burglaries, 7 cases of assault, 3 allegations of rape..."

Harsha's head reeled as the inspector read out the entire list to him. Finally, the inspector looked up at him expectantly, and Harsha realised he was waiting for a response.

Harsha cleared his throat and said: "Er... I guess I would question all the people with knowledge of the matter, inspect the scene of the crime, send out for information to..."

The inspector cut in: "Yes, I can see that you have been watching a lot of American crime dramas. I have seen them too. But using those methods, cases don't get solved in one hour, in time for dinner. They would take about a month or two. Let's assume a month. I get two or three new cases every week, sometimes more. How far behind do you think I would be if I treated every crime as you suggest?"

Harsha did not say anything.

The inspector gestured around the station. "These are not well paid men and women. They are not well trained. You think of us as villains. But where do most policemen and women live? In the slums. I have the chief inspector on my back about these cases, and ultimately the head of police for the state. She does not want to know how I deal with cases. She only wants to know how many are solved and how many are pending.

"Once again I ask you Mr Devnath, if you were me — *what would you do?*"

Harsha opened and shut his mouth, and finally said, truthfully: "I don't know."

The man relaxed and nodded. Finally, he yelled out: "Mr Ezhumalai! Bring Mr Murugayya in."

A few minutes later Murugayya came in and, without preamble, fell on the floor and prostrated himself in front of the inspector's desk.

"Inspector sir, please sir, don't hurt me sir, I have a son, sir."

"Be quiet," the inspector said briefly. Murugayya subsided but stayed on the floor.

Inspector Palanivel stood up, twirling his pen in his fingers.

"This man," he said, pointing at Harsha with his pen, "has vouched for your character. So, I will ask you a few simple questions and let you go."

The inspector looked up at Harsha and added: "In private."

"If you..."

"I will not lay a finger on him," the inspector said calmly.

Harsha looked into the other man's eyes and believed him.

"I will wait outside," he said and moved towards the door.

The inspector resumed his seat and started writing again. "Oh, Mr Devnath," he said, just as Harsha was leaving.

"Yes?"

"I would like you to come for questioning tomorrow. At 11am, please. Constable Gautami will show you the paperwork on the way out. Thank you."

9. COLLABORATION

By the time he was done with breakfast the next morning, Harsha had a full-blown strategy planned out.

He poured himself some more coffee, watching the steam rise from his mug.

Azhar sat opposite him and said, nervously: "It will be fine. It will be fine. Don't worry. Just keep calm."

"I'm not worried, Azhar."

"Yeah, yeah, no reason to be," Azhar said, chomping at his fingernails.

"So, what will you do once you drop me at the station?" Harsha asked. Selvam was yet to recover from his police inflicted injuries, so Azhar was doing the driving duties.

"I have some work in town," Azhar said vaguely.

Maya came up with a bowl of cereal and sat beside Azhar, looking at Harsha with concern.

"Don't worry, Harry, I bet he just has some routine follow-up questions. Let's face it, that fat policeman was not very bright."

Harsha sighed and said: "I'm not worried, Maya."

And the truth was, he wasn't. Despite the ominous summons from the inspector the previous day, he was reasonably sure that his education and middle class background protected him from the sort of treatment meted out to so-called lower members of Indian society.

And much as he abhorred this in theory, he couldn't help feeling grateful for the protection it conferred upon him at that moment. Remembering how Murugayya had grovelled in the inspector's room, he shivered. *There but for the grace of God, go I*, he thought to himself.

There was also something else, something that Harsha was not even sure if he should acknowledge, even to himself. The fact was, this whole episode had made him feel alive in a way that he hadn't in all his years as a journalist in England, where he had felt more corporate drone than intrepid reporter. Of course, he wasn't working at the moment, and a woman had died, so it wasn't right to be excited or to be enjoying it. But a part of him *was* enjoying it. It felt like he was actually doing something rather than sitting on his backside in an office, and it just felt right! Was that wrong?

He was in the middle of this complex train of thought when Shane came up, passed him a glass of water and said: "Don't worry, Harsha, it will all be fine."

"Guys, I am not worried!" Harsha said impatiently. "I know it will be fine!"

A silence fell as they all sipped their coffee (which tasted as heavenly as it had the previous day) and then Azhar took a deep breath and said: "I've arranged for a van to come this evening. There is a late train to Chennai and I think all of you should be on it. I can arrange..."

"I'm not going anywhere," Harsha said flatly.

Maya looked at Harsha and then said quietly: "Me neither."

Shane said: "What happened to all that stuff about going into business with me, Azhar *bhai*? Bailing already?"

Maya smiled at the two of them. "Are you guys going into business together?" she asked.

"Look, we will talk about all that later," Azhar said, sounding tense. "Right now this is a crisis and I don't even know if this resort is going to exist in a month. That panchayat dude is putting pressure on us to sell it to him. He has been wanting it ever since he saw how successful it has become over the last couple of years."

"But you don't have to sell, surely?"

Azhar moodily stirred some sugar into his coffee. "I don't know man, Dad asked me to seriously consider it. It's ultimately up to me, but I can't rule it out. We have many hotels and this one has been nothing but problems. I thought I had turned things around, but poor Lakshmi... People are starting to say this place is cursed."

Harsha looked at him in surprise.

Seeing this, Shane said by way of explanation: "It's the Muslim thing. Apparently some people are saying that this is what happens when you work for a Muslim or some such thing."

"It's not even just that," Azhar said wearily. "It's also because I hire all these dalits. It wasn't like a planned thing — they just happened to all end up here, and they work really hard and do it with a big smile. They are definitely one reason for the success of this place, and ... I don't know."

"You should be proud, Azhar," Maya said, quietly. "We all really admire the way you have hired so many people from disadvantaged backgrounds in this place, and promoted them as well."

Azhar looked up and smiled for a second, but his face fell almost immediately after and he looked furtively down as he placed his hands on the table.

"I ... I ... don't deserve any credit for that," he said heavily. "I had no clue what I was doing, I just hired whoever turned up and then kept the people who worked hard."

"That's how it should be though, mate, a meritocracy!" Harsha said earnestly, leaning forward. "You can't help it if these backward idiots can't handle that!"

Azhar shrugged and said: "Whatever it is, backward or not, I have to ask the question — is it worth it? I mean, poor Lakshmi, I can't even..." He trailed off, looking uncharacteristically woebegone, and Maya put one sympathetic hand on his shoulder.

"Did you know her well?" she asked.

"Know her well? I mean, she was an employee, so not that well — but she was a good one — very loyal, would work all kinds of stupid hours to get the job done," Azhar said, soberly. "I'm not sure she had much of a life going on outside or anything, but still — she was great," he ended, lamely.

There was a silence and then Maya said: "Whatever you decide, for now we are not leaving."

"Maya, at least you should think about..."

She flared up at this. "Why 'at least' me? Because I am a woman?"

"No, no!" Azhar waved his hands in self-defence. "I only meant because you have a husband and..."

"So what? Shane has a wife! Anyway, that's none of your damn business."

"We... I'm just saying... ok..." Azhar took another deep breath and then said: "Ok you know what, never mind. Can I just say how much I really appreciate this, I mean..."

"Oh, shut up," Maya said, but this time with a small smile.

"You promised us a holiday, and we are not leaving till you give us one," Shane said jovially.

Azhar nodded, glanced at his watch and stood up.

"Harry, time to go, buddy."

Harsha felt a jolt of nerves — maybe he wasn't as calm as he thought? — but he forced a smile and said casually: "See you guys in a bit."

He apparently wasn't fooling anyone because Shane clapped him reassuringly on the shoulder and Maya came round and placed a hand on his arm, asking: "Should I come with you?"

"I'll be fine," he said again and walked quickly out with Azhar.

Azhar's car was parked out front, and Harsha momentarily forgot his troubles.

"Wow! An Audi Sport! Nice car!"

Azhar grinned. "Present from Dad for turning the resort around to profit."

"Man, I had no idea it was THAT profitable!"

As they walked up to the car, Azhar asked casually: "Wanna drive?"

Harsha's mouth fell open. "Are you kidding me?"

He was so used to taking the underground in London that driving itself was a rare pleasure. Driving an Audi sportscar on a beautiful, empty mountain road — now that was something else.

As he eased the car out onto the main road and accelerated, feeling its powerful engine respond, he felt like he was going to explode with pleasure. This was one of those occasions when he seriously wondered if he had made the right choice in opting to be a penniless journalist.

They sped down the road in silence.

As the excitement wore off a little, Harsha cleared his throat and asked politely: "So... You are enjoying running a business, then? You seem to be doing really well."

A tiny snore came by way of response. Harsha glanced at his friend, smiled to himself and drove on in silence, enjoying the view and the drive.

Inspector Palanivel was standing and looking out of the tiny window of his office, hands clasped behind his back, when Harsha was shown into his room.

Harsha had just a second to admire the trim profile before the man turned around and said: "Please sit down, Mr Devnath."

Harsha sat down uncomfortably, placing his mobile phone and notepad in front of him.

The man frowned at the notepad. "What is that for?"

"I was going to take down some points of interest if possible."

"I would prefer you don't do that," the inspector said politely.

Harsha opened his mouth — he had meant to insist, to establish his credentials as a journalist straightaway and control the conversation if possible — but the inspector sat down as though the matter was closed, and Harsha left the notebook untouched. The inspector had his own notebook and pen, of course, and he opened it now and began to take notes, much to Harsha's annoyance.

"So, Mr Devnath, on the evening of October 14..."

"The afternoon."

"Oh, I'm so sorry!" the inspector said with mock solicitousness. "In the afternoon, you and Mrs Pandey came across the body. Can I ask what you were doing there?"

"We just went for a walk."

"For a walk?" His tone was politely sceptical.

"Just for a walk. Up the mountain. To get some exercise."

"I see. And then?"

Harsha gave him a short account of how they had found the body, though he avoided any mention of the premonition of evil he had had, which had led him to explore the hill more closely in the first place. He didn't want to sound like a nutcase.

Finally, he said: "And then by the evening you came to inspect the body. Though I should add, we conveyed all this and more to your colleague. Mr Ezhumalai I think the name is?"

The inspector's eyes flickered, and Harsha smiled to himself. It appeared that both of them shared the same opinion of Constable Ezhumalai.

"A few additional questions, Mr Devnath. First of all, what did you notice about the body when you came across it?"

"It was badly hacked. And the sari was... all over the place."

"Anything else?"

Harsha wracked his brains. "I guess it was arranged neatly, as though someone had put it there. So maybe... it... the murder... was done somewhere else."

The man nodded. "Anything else?"

Harsha searched his memory again, but what did the man expect? "Frankly, no. I'm sure you can understand it was quite a horrible sight for us. We were not thinking rationally."

"What did you do next?"

"Well, I said I would wait there and Maya should go down and alert Azhar and tell someone to call the police."

"Why did you feel the need to wait by the body?"

Harsha was beginning to sweat now.

"I don't know, it just didn't seem right to leave it there."

"Didn't you feel scared?"

"Scared? Why scared?" Harsha asked, but he remembered how terrified he had been standing alone with the dead body in the darkening mountainside, hoping desperately for someone to come quickly.

"Scared that the killers would come back?" the inspector asked, as though it were an obvious point.

Harsha decided to go on the offensive. "So, it was more than one person?"

Another flicker of the eyes. But the inspector ignored his question and instead asked: "Did you do anything else while waiting?"

Harsha could only remember hugging himself, trying to stop the uncontrollable shivering.

"No."

"Didn't look around, look at the body?"

"I'm not sure what you mean, look at the body."

The inspector asked: "Did you do anything else while you were waiting for the others to come?"

"No, absolutely nothing."

"Then who came?"

"I don't know, a bunch of women, I remember because they were all crying loudly, people were shouting, torches everywhere. It was pretty mad, it's hard to remember."

"So, it was dark by then? Can you remember who exactly?"

Harsha thought for a minute.

"I guess it was the cook, Kuppi, I think her name is... Two cleaners, Millie and Leela I think... And Azhar and Shane, and then... Murugayya. And his son, for some reason, was tagging along behind him."

"Did anybody else do any searching, any detective work?" the last two words were infused with a slight sarcasm.

"Not as far as I know."

The man looked at Harsha impassively and then said.

"Alright, thank you. You may go."

"Are you missing something, inspector? Something that was supposed to be on the body, but isn't?"

"I said you may go, Mr Devnath," the inspector said, returning to his writing.

"Listen, Inspector Palanivel, I am only trying to help."

The man looked up, sighed and put down his pen. "You have read too many detective stories, Mr Devnath. Members of the public don't suddenly turn up and solve crimes in real life. And believe it or not, I actually know how to do my job."

Harsha went red. "I know that! I'm not saying I can solve this crime or do any detective work as you call it. But..."

He took a deep breath and decided to plunge right ahead with his plan. He said: "I still think I can help."

The inspector's eyebrows climbed up towards his hairline. "How exactly?"

"Er... so... I am a journalist..."

"Whom with?"

"The Times," Harsha said casually, hoping the inspector would not probe further.

But the man was too sharp. "The Times of India?" he asked.

"Of London," Harsha conceded reluctantly.

The man leaned back, losing interest.

Harsha pressed on: "But it doesn't matter. You were saying yesterday that you don't have time to gather background and information on every single crime. As a journalist I can go around and ask some questions for you, people will be more willing to talk to me."

The man shook his head, a sceptical look on his face.

"Look," Harsha said patiently. "I'm not saying I will ask who had a grudge against Lakshmi, or where people were on the evening of October 11th or anything like that. I'm just talking about getting some background information on the area, the politics and the culture of it. It may not be useful at all, but it can't hurt can it?"

The man paused at this and looked at him. "I can't stop you from asking questions," he said. "But why on earth would an English paper be interested in this?"

Harsha smiled a little. "Oh, the English love reading about India. And they absolutely love reading negative stories especially, I think so that they can feel superior. Also, I can always sell the story to an Indian paper, I am not a permanent employee, only a freelancer. And in India, people want to read stories... of this nature."

"Of this nature?"

"Well... of violence against women. It's, well, you could call it flavour of the month."

"Flavour of the month?" the inspector asked, flatly.

Harsha shrugged. "I could phrase it differently, but what I mean is newspapers are willing to publish such stories, as violence against women is becoming a serious subject. But look, the point is, I don't have to do a story at all. Azhar has already asked me to write a travel journalism piece on this resort. I can just go ahead and do that, and as I speak to people I can try and get an idea of village politics and who the important people are, who knew Lakshmi, and so on, all of which may be of interest to you. The one thing I have learned in my profession is that people love to talk. There may be some things they tell me voluntarily that they may be scared to tell the police."

The inspector leaned forward: "Look, Mr Devnath, I cannot prevent you from doing your story. But if you interfere in this investigation..."

"No no! I'm not going to..."

"If you interfere," the inspector continued implacably, "I will have you arrested. And once you are in here, I will not promise any special treatment for you."

Harsha exhaled in frustration. "Are you saying that you don't want my help?"

"Your help? No. If you have any information that you think might be relevant, of course it is your civic duty to inform the authorities."

Harsha thought he felt a chink of light penetrate the blinds.

"I see. And how am I to... er... inform the authorities?"

The man paused in thought, flicking that ball-point pen over his fingers again.

Finally, he said: "I will be inspecting the crime scene again in..." He glanced at a calendar by his desk. "... Today is Wednesday, on Friday evening I will inspect the crime scene again. Around 6 o'clock."

Harsha smiled: "Do I need a password as well? Or a special codeword?"

"Mr Devnath, I am not allowed to officially interact with the press except through the appropriate channels. That was no problem as long as this town had no press. Now it has one — you."

Harsha nodded. "I understand," he said.

"And Mr Devnath. No questions to people about the murder please."

Harsha said: "Sir, I don't mean to be rude, but freedom of the press is..."

"Mr Devnath, I am asking as a personal favour. If you wish to help us, please do not get directly involved. Otherwise I will have to... how to say... wash my hands of you, as you say in England." Palanivel pushed himself back slightly from the desk.

Harsha nodded again and said: "Thank you. I will see you on Friday."

"Good," the man said and, leaning forward, returned to his writing as though he had forgotten about Harsha's existence.

Harsha left the station, smiled at the policewoman — Constable Gautami was it? — at the door and walked out to find Azhar reading a copy of the *Deccan Chronicle* newspaper and leaning against the bonnet of his outrageous sports car.

"What took you so long?" he asked, the newspaper rustling as he folded it shut.

Harsha shook his head. "Long story, dude, I'll tell you on the way back. Can I drive again?"

Azhar threw him the keys and walked round to the passenger seat, newspaper tucked under his arm.

"Oh, by the way," Harsha said casually, as he climbed into the beautiful vehicle. "You asked me to do a travel journalism piece for you, and I'm going to work on it over the next few days."

"I asked you what?" Azhar asked, bewildered. "Are you stoned or something, Harry?"

"Never mind, we'll discuss it later."

In five minutes, Harsha forgot all about Inspector Palanivel and lost himself in the pleasure of driving.

10. WINDMILLS

"You're doing WHAT??"

Maya winced, Shane smiled quietly to himself and Harsha looked calmly across at his friend, who had stood up from his chair and was now standing over him. Half of Azhar's well-sculpted face was in shadow, the rest lit brilliantly by the late afternoon light coming in through the windows of his office.

"Just helping out the police a little. Not investigating or anything, just getting some background info. Plus, I'll write your travel piece for you."

"Just... just helping... police... WHAT?!!" Azhar bellowed. "What the fuck is the matter with you! Who do you think you are, Tintin the detective or something? With that dog, what's the dog's name, Sonny or something?"

There was an absurd pause as all present tried to remember the name of Tintin's dog.

"Snowy?"

"Whatever! You've read too many books! You've become like that Spanish madman, what's his name?"

"What Spanish madman?" Harsha asked blankly.

"You know that fellow who reads all those books and goes mad? Don Corleone or something! Shanny help me out here!"

"Don Quixote?" Shane suggested.

"Yes! Him! Harry, you've gone mad, reading too many books! Like Don whatsit."

"Look, Azhar, I am not going to do anything crazy, I'm just doing that travel journalism piece! If I come across anything of interest, I will tell the police, and that's it. I'm not trying to solve any crimes or anything."

Azhar pulled his swivel chair in front of the sofa where Harsha sat and leaned forward, just two feet away from him. "Look, Harry, I'm under a bit of pressure here. First, all the guests are leaving, I have to compensate them. Some of them are furious at being questioned by the police. They all blame me. The villagers are after my life — many of them think I am somehow responsible. My accountant is on the way to negotiate repayments. That panchayat dude is putting pressure on me to sell the land to him and my dad wants me to do a deal."

Harsha opened his mouth to say something but Azhar ploughed on.

"It's too much man, and if you guys won't go to Chennai as I suggested, at least behave yourselves, dickheads!"

Harsha exchanged glances with Maya and then said: "Tell me more about this 'panchayat dude' anyway?"

"Who? Oh yeah. His name is Rajaratnam. He is a big landowner here, owns much of the coffee plantations, and he is also the head of the panchayat of Arasur. He lives in the village. He sold us the land for this resort to start with, but now he wants it back, especially after seeing how successful we have been with it."

Harsha nodded. "The guy who lives in that big pink house, right?" he asked, his mind going back to his incident in front of the tea stall on his first day at the mountain. The man had come across as some sort of sinister mafia lord, though Harsha wasn't sure if he was overplaying it in his head.

"Yeah, the house that looks like a bloody cake," Azhar said.

Harsha went to the fridge, took out some beers and passed them around. Azhar had fished automatically for his Swiss army knife.

"Azhar, listen to me for a sec. People like Rajaratnam are the kind that we should try and talk to. We can't rule out that he may have had something to do with..."

"There you go with this Tintin shit again!" Azhar said, standing up in exasperation.

"Dude, just relax ok? I'm not saying that guy did it. I'm just saying that these are the kind of people I need to speak to. I need to get the lay of the land and I will have something to give the inspector."

"We," said Maya quietly.

"What?"

"We have a few people to speak to, you mean. Or are you forgetting our existence?"

Azhar looked around at Shane and Maya and said: "What the... So now you're The Three Investigators, are you? Or is it The Three

Stooges?"

"Hey, stop comparing us to books and movies! This is nothing like that! We know the difference between fiction and reality!"

Azhar stood up and addressed the group: "Guys, please, can I just make a polite request that you all stop this?"

When there was no reply, he lost his temper.

"Bloody hell, Harsha, this was a damn murder, it's not a game!"

"I know that!" Harsha said, standing up as well. "This is not a game to me, Azhar, it's my job! I am a reporter, I've had training in reporting under adverse circumstances. That's training for war reporting, if you must know. This is not an ego trip, ok?"

"Well, why don't you do all that adverse reporting when you go back to England?"

Harsha flopped back on to the sofa. "I don't get to do any of that stuff in London. Most of the reporting there is online. I am at my desk all day, reading wires and making phone calls. And a bit of ripping off other newspapers. Only the star reporters get to do field work."

Harsha stared down at his hands, shook his head and continued: "I don't know man, ever since this murder happened, I felt like there's a story here to be told, and I want to tell it. I want it to be my contribution or something. This... This is why I got into journalism in the first place."

Azhar looked at him for a minute, his expression softening slightly.

"The prodigal son returns..." Shane muttered.

Azhar sighed and said: "Alright Harry, if you are going to do a story I won't stop you. Just please be aware and try not to make things worse for me or make me lose my business."

"The aim is to help you *keep* your business."

Azhar nodded. But he turned to the others and said: "You too need to be more careful. Maybe it's best you let Harry do this on his own. Shane, you're supposed to be helping me with my business anyway. Are you still serious about that or what? And Maya..."

"Don't even try," she said sharply.

Azhar threw his hands up in despair. He turned to Harsha: "I'm trusting you to make sure she doesn't do anything mad."

"I'll take good care of her," Harsha said, his grin widening at the look of consternation on Maya's face.

"So," Azhar said, sitting on a table next to Maya and putting an arm around her shoulder. "What's next, Tintin?"

"Well," Harsha said, taken aback by this sudden change of tack from Azhar. He racked his brains for something that sounded important.

Finally, he took out his notebook and said: "I've made a list of key people that I think I should find a way of talking to. I'm hoping you can help add to this."

"Shoot."

"So there's your hotel staff. The cooks. Kuppi and... er..."

"Kuppi and Millie," Maya said. "And the cleaners are called Leela and Ammani." Harsha wondered briefly how Maya had got to know them in barely two days.

Azhar shook his head at this, leaning forward to pick up his beer. "Millie has left and Leela's father doesn't want her to come back. Selvam is in the hospital. Right now, only Ammani and Kuppi are here. And Murugayya, of course. It's probably a good thing most of the guests are leaving or we would have no one to take care of them." He took a long pull of his beer, looking uncharacteristically sober.

"Right," Harsha said, thrown by this. "I'll speak to whoever is left. Outside of this, I thought that French schoolmaster — what was his name again?"

"Laurent," Shane said, with an admirable stab at the French pronunciation. "I can take you there whenever you like, Harry. Now if you want."

Azhar nodded. "The guy is always happy to receive guests. Loves entertaining people."

"Ok, great," Harsha said. "And then there's Rajaratnam. And I still want a word with that guy in the village who owns that kiosk. Subhash, I think his name was. Anyone else, Azhar?"

Azhar thought for a second and then said: "The local temple priest. He knew Lakshmi very well. There was some controversy a few years back because she started going to the temple, even though she is... was... a dalit."

Seeing Harsha frown in puzzlement, Maya said: "Dalits are sometimes not allowed to enter temples. Seriously, Harry, how can you be so clueless?"

"Oy! I wasn't wondering about that. I was wondering why the priest knew Lakshmi well."

"Because he somehow managed to convince the village to allow the whole dalit community in. I don't know the details. This is just stuff I heard from my dad. I wasn't involved in this place then," Azhar said.

Harsha nodded. "Definitely worth asking about. At the very least, this is useful background. Anyone else?"

Azhar leaned back, his forehead creased in thought, when Shane shifted in his seat on the sofa and said: "Azhar, why not just give these two a little history of this region? Just so they understand what this place is all about?"

Harsha felt a minor stab of irritation and then nodded, grudgingly. That was an entirely sensible suggestion and one he should have thought of in the first place.

They all sat in that sunlit office and listened as Azhar, hesitantly at first, and then with growing confidence, talked about Arasur, the name of both the village and the mountain on which it was situated. The village apparently dated back to the British Raj, when farms were first established on its verdant slopes. It being a profitable business, particularly when growing substances such as poppy for opium prodcution, the area was then taken over by the *zamindars*, wealthy landowners who ran a sort of feudal system.

Azhar's father first bought land there soon after a panchayat, or local district, was established, as part of an expansion of his hotel and resorts business across hill stations in Tamil Nadu. But it wasn't until fairly recently that he had built the resort itself, after the panchayat had laid some good roads running from Ramananpettai to Arasur, making the property far more accessible.

For a while, everything had run smoothly with the village, as long as only a handful of tourists trickled through. But when Azhar took over, he had invested in marketing, and the resort had boomed. It was then that trouble with the village had begun — particularly with the head of the panchayat.

"Somehow, all the politics of Muslim and Hindu and caste and whatnot hadn't mattered when we weren't making any money," Azhar said, ruefully. He hesitated and then said: "We could probably sell it for an absolute bomb now. But... I mean... it is my baby — you know?"

Harsha stirred, and looked around at Maya and Shane. Maya, like him, was also drinking in this fascinating story of a little patch of Indian countryside and how it had developed over the years. Shane was watching Azhar keenly, a proud smile on his face. Harsha realised he must be thinking of how much Azhar had changed and matured over the years. He looked at his happy-go-lucky friend of old and marvelled at the change as well. At that moment, Azhar looked up and met his eyes and grinned in that old way that Harsha, rolling back the years.

"Alright, reporter sir? Anything else I can help you with? What do you want to do first?" he asked.

Harsha put his beer bottle down on the coffee table and then looked at the floor, thinking deeply. He had two-and-a-half days before he was supposed to meet the inspector. Despite his bluster and his confident air, he didn't have any clue where to even begin with the investigation. Is this how all journalists felt at the start of a big story? He briefly wished he knew of some experienced reporter who could give him advice. At *The Times*? He dismissed that thought quickly. A colleague from an old job in India? He felt oddly reluctant to share this story with anyone. He wanted to be the one to stumble through it himself.

"Ok, let's just start with talking to some of the people you mentioned," he said finally.

"I'm warning you, it may not be easy to get hold of Rajaratnam. And he may not be that friendly."

Harsha shrugged his shoulders. "Being unwelcome is part of the job. I would get nowhere if I stopped doing my work because people are not polite," he said.

"Oho, big shot reporter. Who else do you want to speak to?" Azhar asked, standing up with a sigh.

"Maybe I'll speak to your staff tomorrow. Could you let them know? And Shane — why don't you take me to meet this French dude now?" Harsha asked, and his heart gave a little flutter. Despite everything, even though he had fought to be in this position, it was still scary to move so far outside of his comfort zone.

Shane nodded in that reassuring way of his and stood up as well.

"I'd like to come as well," Maya said, quietly, and Harsha nodded, smiling at her.

"The Three Stooges," Azhar said, shaking his head. "If you don't mind, I'm not going to join this circus show. You go ahead. And please don't upset him!"

"Don't worry, Azhar *bhai*, we will watch our Ps and Qs," Shane said, grinning.

Azhar turned to Harsha: "And what if he doesn't give you what you want?"

Harsha smiled faintly. "I will just have to find some other windmills to charge," he said.

11. SCHOOL

It wasn't a run of the mill school entrance.

After trekking through the forest for about half an hour, the sound of water growing louder and louder, they reached the river. It was a magnificent sight, rushing at breakneck speed down the mountain slope. Even though the bank rose up several feet from the water, they were regularly showered by spray from the raging torrent below.

Harsha could see the raw stumps of branches of trees that had grown too close to the river in more peaceful seasons — hacked off neatly by the water, as though chopped by an axe.

There was no way they could hear each other over the din of rushing water, so Shane gesticulated downhill.

They walked down a small footpath, treacherously close to the edge of the bank, and Harsha felt a rush of adrenaline course through his veins.

They reached a bridge, a string of wooden planks stretched about six feet above the water, and tied to trees on either side by means of a rope. The knots looked solid, snaking several times around two tough trunks, but Harsha looked at the swaying trees doubtfully. Shane confidently led the way, and Harsha brought up the rear. A few steps on the creaking bridge though, and he quickly hurried back to dry land.

Maya looked back and then tapped Shane on the shoulder. They both looked back at him quizzically and he gestured for them to go on.

To his annoyance Maya came running back and asked him a question, but he couldn't hear a word above the roaring water. He shook his head.

She put a hand on his shoulder, tiptoed up to his ear and yelled: "Are you not coming?"

In turn he yelled into her ear: "Let's do it one by one. One... by... one!"

She nodded and ran across the bridge and he watched her light frame enviously. What it must be to be at the peak of your fitness and so fearless!

Once Shane and Maya were safely on the other side, he stepped cautiously onto the bridge. It creaked under him and he glanced down, regretting it instantly. One small slip...

He focused instead on Maya, who was smiling encouragingly, and quickly made his way to the other side.

The noise of the river receded behind them as they walked deeper into the forest. There were no visible signs of thinning, but they came upon a slim path leading uphill that was laid with stone steps.

They did their best to avoid getting scratched by the wall of shrubbery on either side and suddenly came out onto a small stretch of meadow. In the very centre of this clearing was a squat, wooden building, with smoke puffing out of one chimney.

"Arasur School," Shane announced.

Harsha took a good hard look at the man standing by the doorway, arms folded. He was tall and thin, a light stubble of white hair on a rather pink face.

He was wearing a red polo t-shirt, khaki trousers and a white hat with a black band around it, forcibly reminding Harsha of middle-aged members of Lord's Cricket Ground.

He smiled at the three of them, his eyes twinkling. "You city people enjoying your time in the countryside?" he asked, with a pleasing French accent. His eyes moved from Shane, who was breathing heavily, to Maya, who had twigs and leaves in her hair, to Harsha, who had his hands on his knees. His smile broadened.

"Laurent Coroller," he said, shaking hands with the men and kissing Maya on either cheek. She looked embarrassed but not displeased. "You can call me Loco if that's easier. Everyone does."

"Hi Laurent," Harsha said, pronouncing it as well as he could.

Laurent's eyes narrowed as he looked at Harsha again, nodding approvingly. "Not too many people can pronounce my name around here. Come on in," he said, opening the door wide with a flourish.

Harsha caught hold of Maya's elbow and said: "Just give us one second, Laurent."

The man nodded and politely turned away as Harsha began to whisper urgently into Maya's ear.

A few minutes later, Maya and Harsha walked in to find Shane sitting comfortably on a colourful divan and talking politely with Laurent. The inside of the house was not — as one may have assumed — split into many rooms like a normal house. Instead it appeared to be one large, long room, almost like a studio, with a kitchen and toilet attached.

The walls were lined on one side with thousands of books, and on the other, with rows and rows of DVDs, only relieved by a 42-inch television screen. On the far side, a large French window led out onto a perfectly manicured garden with a stone fountain at its centre.

"Nice set-up!" Harsha said, looking around appreciatively.

"Thank you," Laurent smiled. "Can I get you some coffee or tea?"

"Coffee would be lovely," Maya said, and the others nodded.

"Mala!" Laurent called out. "Some coffee please, and biscuits."

He sat down on an easy chair and sighed. "Not getting any younger, I'm afraid. So, which one is the journalist?"

"That would be me," Harsha said, smiling as his sat on the divan opposite Laurent and looked at the Frenchman. Close up, he thought the man looked a bit exhausted, with bags under his eyes and a slightly haunted look. But his eyes were alert and a piercing blue. Maya sat on another chair next to Laurent.

Laurent reminisced for a while about journalists he had known at The Times during his time in London, none of whom Harsha was familiar with, punctuating his talk with dramatic hand gestures, and then Harsha took out his notepad and pen and gently steered the conversation to the matter at hand.

"Well, I spent several years working as a banker in Paris and then in London, making my, how to say, my fortune," Laurent said, before adding wryly: "This I did successfully, but, you know, I lost two marriages in the process. Then I decided I wanted a complete break," Laurent said, making a slicing motion with his hand. "Is that shorthand you are writing in? Very impressive!"

Harsha smiled his thanks and waited.

"Anyway, to resume, my grandfather was stationed in Pondicherry — and the stories he used to tell! Tigers in the backyard, cobras and mongooses fighting on the side of the street... Probably all lies, but still. Elephants! I really loved the stories about elephants, gentle creatures with tremendous, violent power when provoked. A bit like me," he said, turning to Maya and winking. She smiled weakly.

Laurent stood up and walked to the window and said: "We had elephants here once, almost all the way to the house — they were escaping some, what to call, some poachers, and broke through my electric fencing. Cost me a fortune! But it was worth it! A whole herd!" He turned around, his eyes sparkling.

"You have electric fencing? Is that necessary?"

"Black panthers!" Laurent declared gleefully, by way of explanation, raising both hands to convey just how incredible this was.

Harsha thought he understood why the man had started a school — there was something child-like about him.

He asked the question anyway.

"Why not start a school?" Laurent answered, flopping down on the easy chair again. "I had to do something! I couldn't just sit around in the middle of a jungle like some crazy hermit, you know," he added, laughing.

A smiling lady brought in four coffees and some goodies. There were macarons that looked authentic. This eccentric Frenchman must have them shipped in somehow, Harsha thought to himself.

"Thank you, my dear," Laurent said to Mala, who nodded affectionately at him. "I like the kids as well. Very sharp, no opportunities here in this crazy country — no offence, you know, but it's true — and they are always smiling. That lifts my spirits, to see the poor little fellows so cheerful despite everything...

"For a while it was only poor kids who came, but I must have been doing something right, soon everyone wanted to come here. We have 100 students now, god knows where they all come from! I've hire six, sorry, seven, teachers including the sports master. And we started with just the two of us!

"I only got board approval three years ago. I must say, your Education Ministry... it is a ... how to call it... a snake pit! But I did get something out of all those miserable days working in an investment bank. I do know how to... make things happen," he said, winking at Harsha, though his expression changed comically as he hurriedly added: "That's off the record, of course!"

Harsha laughed. "Don't worry, I'll just say you did it through sheer perseverance."

"Ah, I like the sound of that!" Laurent said, snapping his fingers in approval.

Harsha asked: "And do you interact with the village much?"

"Not if I can help it. Days, sometimes months, go by without me having to go there. I have a jeep hidden away nearby, so I can go all the way to Ramananpettai or even Kuppam if necessary." He pronounced it 'coo-palm'.

Shane interjected, to Harsha's slight annoyance, asking: "You may not go to the village, but if the kids come here, surely the parents also come here to complain and so on?"

The man eyed Shane and said: "Spoken like a true parent! Am I right? Ha, I knew it. Yes, they do, they are constantly complaining. But the good thing about *pro bono* work is — I don't need to do it. If they don't like it, they can send their kids to the corporation school."

Now that Shane had intervened, the floodgates were open. This time, Maya asked: "But what about the kids? Surely they shouldn't be punished just because their parents are rude to you?"

The man frowned at the accusatory tone in her voice. "My dear, if you were not so lovely I would refuse to answer that question. The truth is, children leave here all the time for reasons I don't like. The middle-class children because I don't focus enough on the exams. Some other children because I let in someone from such and such caste. And worst of all, because the children need to work, or the girls need to get married. If I fought every single battle, I would have no energy left.

"So, I let them come and go as they please. They don't have to attend any classes, though if they do, I expect complete discipline and hard work. The truth is, none of them misses a class unless something really earth shattering happens. They are so thirsty to learn, it's remarkable. Incredible little bastards."

Maya looked annoyed at the man's language, while Shane looked amused. As far as Harsha was concerned, the man was giving the children a free and — by the sound of it — good education, so it wasn't his place to judge.

Harsha folded his pad and said: "Thank you so much for your time." His companions looked up at him in surprise, but the man just nodded.

Shane was trying to catch Harsha's eye, but he ignored it and said instead: "It's so good of you to give us your time. The school is very beautiful. Would you show us around sometime?"

"Anytime at all! Right now, if you like. I can show you the main classroom where you can meet some of the kids. They have some sort of performance planned tomorrow as well, if you're interested, as part of their class. You're welcome to come watch if you like, they love an audience!"

"Sounds great," Harsha said, and they all stood up.

"It is a good walk up the hill, you know. Do you feel... umm... energised after your coffee?"

Harsha heard Shane sigh beside him.

"After you," Laurent said, theatrically opening the door for Maya with a little half bow. He stepped out himself. Harsha was about to follow when Shane pulled him back in.

"What are you doing, man? I was trying to get his view on the village, and you let him ramble on about something else! And then you just ended the conversation!"

Harsha walked towards the door. "Trust me, Shanny," he said and walked out.

Laurent was chatting away with Maya, though he stopped briefly to say: "This way!" to the boys before picking out a path that went, as promised, steeply uphill.

Harsha caught up with the two of them and listened in on the conversation, walking slightly behind, trying not to make this obvious.

After a bit of general chat, Maya said: "You must be such an important person here. I'm sure all the parents come to you for advice."

Laurent shrugged modestly. "I do feel a bit like a, how you say it, a pastor at the confessional, you know. And I do try to keep it all to myself! Never was the gossiping type."

Maya laughed and said: "Wow, you must know pretty much everything that goes on around here!"

Harsha held his breath. It seemed a bit obvious to him and Laurent had been a sharp banker trained in the rat race of the City of London. But it turned out, he was not impervious to flattery.

"Oh well... I do get a few insights into this region, you know. I can tell you one thing. I thought French politics was complex. But what goes on in your country — it is incredible, no? There's Hindus and Muslims, castes, languages, regions, races. God, how do people keep from murdering each other as they walk past each other on the street!" he asked, throwing his hands up in the air.

"So much hatred, so much hatred," he said after a pause, heavily and dramatically. There was definitely something of the actor about Laurent. He took a few breaths as they traversed a particularly steep part of the mountain, though he was doing much better than all his younger companions, who were all gasping for air now, even Maya.

"I think we should pause for a bit," Laurent said, listening to their breathing in amusement. Shane gratefully put his hands on his knees and took deep rasping breaths.

Panting himself, Harsha went up to Shane and put a hand on his shoulder and asked him if he was alright. Shane was too out of breath to reply, which was just as well because Harsha was listening to the conversation between Maya and Laurent.

"We just had an example of that violence at the resort," Maya said quietly.

There was a pause, and then Laurent spoke without his usual flourish. "Yes, that is a very good example." Harsha was surprised to hear genuine anguish in the man's voice. "Lakshmi was a very, very good woman."

"Did you know her?" Maya asked, seemingly casually.

Shane's eyes widened as he looked at Harsha. Harsha put his finger to his lips and the two of them continued to stand a little way away from Maya and Laurent, though within earshot.

"A little bit," Laurent said. "But... it was only a matter of time before something like this happened."

"Why do you say that?"

"For one reason or another! Whether it's caste or religion, take your pick. Muslim owner hiring untouchables on his resort! Going into rooms, changing the sheets. Muslims own the place, making a load of money. Accident waiting to happen."

"You seem to have understood Indian society very well! And why do you think it happened?"

Laurent stuck his hands in his pockets and smiled a little bitterly. "Lady, look at any war in the world and tell me what they have in common."

"Er... religion?"

"Ah, no no, you're not looking deep enough."

"I don't know..."

"It happens for a resource of some sort, most often land. The crusades? Land. World War 1? Land. Israel and Palestine? Land. Iraq? The oil *in* the land."

"What has this got to do with..."

"The question you have to ask is — who benefits most if your friend leaves the resort? That's where your answer lies," the man said, with that bitter smile still etched on his face. And then, just like in the house, his expression changed rapidly and he turned to Harsha (who quickly looked away) and said: "Hey, Mr Journalist. Were you listening to all that?"

Harsha turned to face Laurent. "Listening to what?" he asked, in as innocent a tone as he could muster.

The man looked at him, his eyes shrewd and calculating, without the sparkle that had lit them up previously.

Brusquely, he said: "This way. Hurry up." The schoolmaster plunged without warning into a thin path that led up the hill. The others followed, trying to keep up.

"How did I do?" Maya asked quietly.

"Perfect!" Harsha said. "So he thinks someone is doing this to get hold of the resort! Who would it be?"

Shane's heavy panting cut into the conversation as he walked up to them and asked Harsha: "What did you do, magician?"

Harsha grinned. "Nothing special. An old journalist trick. People will tell you the most juicy stuff when you close the notebook and stop taking notes. Getting Maya to ask the important question — that was just a bit of improvisation after I saw the way Laurent manhandled Maya as he kissed her on the cheeks. Though I have to admit I never thought it would work so well. OW!"

"What? What happened?"

"Damn... branch... full of thorns... hit my tongue. For god'th thake Maya, be careful! Don't pull the branches back like that and let it go! It thwung back and hit me in the damn thongue!"

"Maybe it's a sign that you shouldn't talk too much, Harry,"

Shane said, his voice brimming with amusement, while Maya laughed out loud openly.

"Thcrew you. Thcrew you both," Harsha said, spitting, as they both collapsed with laughter.

12. STORIES

"I remember we watched Gajini together. She, my husband and me. We took a bus, hanging from the footboards, all the way to Salem! Four hours! And then the ticket master refused to let us into the movie I wanted to see! Luckily, my brother's friend was a cleaner there and..."

Harsha tuned out the rest of Ammani's words. He had a long day ahead of him, and he needed to make sure he wasn't taking in irrelevant information, nice as this anecdote was. He moved on his uncomfortable stool, adjusted his pad on his knee and waited.

Ammani continued to talk in a solemn monotone as she crouched on the floor and ground the heavy pestle in her hand into the rice, sweat forming in little beads on her forehead. Harsha admired the strength in her muscled arms, and the effortless nature with which she was able to talk while engaged in back-breaking labour.

At the first break in her story, Harsha jumped in and said: "I'm sorry, Ammani, but can I ask you to start from the beginning?"

"Oh? Yes, of course, sir, we first decided to go to the cinema when..."

"No, no, no," Harsha said, hurriedly. "I meant - from the beginning. How did you get to know Lakshmi?"

The pestle paused, and Ammani turned her black eyes up at him in surprise, using the back of her wrist to wipe away a wisp of hair from one of them.

"How did I know her? Sir, we are from the same community. We all know each other."

Even though the hotel staff now called Maya and Shane by name, they still called him "sir", which rankled slightly. But Harsha shook himself and tried to bring his focus back to what was relevant.

"Ok, so you grew up together? Went to school together?"

"Only for a short time, sir," Ammani said, resuming the grinding. "Soon, after her parents died, she stopped school and got a job."

"And where did she live?"

"In her house, sir," Ammani said, as though he was being stupid. Harsha remembered those tiny clay houses of the dalit community of Arasur, and realised that there was no reason why Lakshmi couldn't have gone on living in that house even without her parents. No one was going to come and claim it.

"I think she got a job cleaning someone's house," Ammani said, thoughtfully. "Soon we all left school and got jobs — I was working in the town. Then when we found out Azhar sir was hiring we all applied here. And he hired us all."

Ammani spoke of Azhar with a mixture of indulgence and awe that for some reason made Harsha feel slightly emotional. Whether it was pride, or affection, or both, he couldn't quite figure out.

"I'm sorry, Ammani, but can you go back a little? To your school days? What was she like?"

The picture of Lakshmi forming in his head was starting to take shape, and he felt a mingled excitement and sadness as the dead woman's life story unfolded in front of his eyes. Everyone he had spoken to so far had had a different opinion and reaction when asked about Lakshmi, but the one common thread was how much she seemed to have affected people's lives.

Laurent had been full of quiet sadness. Murugayya had openly wept, while Selvam had quietly said that Lakshmi was a "special one". Ammani seemed to view her with something approaching idol-worship and awe.

Everyone also said she was "unusual". Already Maya seemed to have embraced Lakshmi into the sisterhood, and was taking her death personally, as though she had been a close friend.

"And then, sir, she stood on the footboards herself, saying to that man that if he can do it, she could as well — and she caught hold of an orange from a tree by the road and nearly fell out! It was crazy! Risking her life to prove a point! But that was Lakshmi," Ammani said proudly, as the story about the day of the cinema made a return.

It was a pity Harsha had only so much time. Peeling back the layers of someone's life like this was fascinating, though he wouldn't have admitted as much to the others, in case he sounded callous.

As it was, though, he had to cut this interview short, as he wanted to get some coffee before going down to the village. He wanted to talk to Subhash the shopkeeper, the local temple priest and to the head of the panchayat, Rajaratnam. They were apparently the three most prominent personalities in Arasur.

"Ammani," he said gently. " Can I ask you again — what do you think happened? And why?" He had told the inspector he would not ask these questions but Azhar had sworn his staff to secrecy.

Her face darkened: "There are enough cheap men in the village. I've seen the way they looked at Lakshmi. I know what went through their minds."

"But this kind of crime? Are they capable of it?" He didn't want to mention the manner in which Lakshmi had been slashed repeatedly with knives.

She grudgingly said: "Maybe not. They wouldn't have the guts, and plus Lakshmi would have been able to handle them. But still, it's more likely it is them than what they are saying in the village."

The minute she said those last words, she clapped her hands over her mouth in horror, making Harsha twice as suspicious in the process.

"Ammani, what are they saying in the village?"

"Pah! I don't listen to that," she said, returning to the pestle and twisting it around the mortar ever faster.

Harsha watched the heavy stone smash the rice and lentils into pulp and shuddered slightly. In the right hands, that pestle was a deadly weapon.

"What do they say?" he asked insistently.

She tossed her head. "Some nonsense about how this resort is cursed because it is owned by a Muslim. But I don't say that sir!" She added quickly. "After all that Abid sir and Azhar have done for us..."

"Us?"

"You know... lower castes," she said cautiously. "All we could do before was clean the village. Clean the toilets. I mean, they say caste is abolished and all that, but we don't get any other jobs!"

"And with Azhar?"

"Well I guess we do some cleaning here as well, but it's different," she said with conviction.

Dignity, Harsha thought. We all want to live with dignity.

"Well thank you, Ammani, I will leave you now," he said, and stood up.

Despite the early start and the hurried breakfast, he felt fresh and alert for the first time in years.

Was it because he was finally doing his job? Was it an adrenaline rush?

Before he left the room, he said: "One final question, Ammani."

She looked up at him inquiringly.

"What are you grinding that for?"

She displayed a pearly-white set of teeth. "Masala dosai tomorrow," she said, and his mouth watered. He would have to do a lot more trekking or this holiday would be ruinous for his waistline.

He went into the hall where the others were sitting around a table sipping coffee.

To his surprise, Bhaskar and Mala were still there, possibly the only guests left in the resort apart from themselves.

"Not too scared to stay?" he asked them as he passed by them.

Bhaskar grinned: "It is like just after 9/11, no? Safest time to fly."

Shaking his head and smiling, Harsha joined his group.

"Any luck?" Azhar asked, and the three leaned forward conspiratorially.

Harsha poured out his coffee and said: "I've learnt a lot about Lakshmi, and that in itself is interesting, but not much in terms of what could have happened or who might have done it. Except that the village folk have got it into their heads that your resort is a cursed place run by Muslims and dalits."

He leaned back, savouring the smell and taste of the freshly brewed coffee. "Also, driver Selvam has some crackpot theory about how this has to do with the dispute between Tamil Nadu and Karnataka over the Cauveri."

"The Cauveri river doesn't flow anywhere near here," Shane pointed out.

Harsha shrugged: "The man is convinced that 'those kannadigas' are capable of anything."

"To be fair, that's a good point."

Azhar shook his head. "Only you South Indians can waste time and energy fighting over such a filthy river."

"Hello, you were born and brought up in Chennai, you can't just become a North Indian whenever you like," Shane objected.

"Yeah, yeah that's why that professor, what's his name, called me Osama Bin Laden's nephew, right?"

Shane threw his head back and laughed! "T.K! I'd forgotten about that!"

"Yeah dude, hilarious, saying that a terrorist is my uncle."

"It was kind of funny," Shane insisted.

"Anything else, Harry?" Maya asked loudly and pointedly. She placed her hand on Harsha's arm. The joint discovery of Lakshmi's body appeared to have broken a wall between them, at least as far as physical contact was concerned.

Harsha cleared his throat, forcing himself not to look down at the delicate fingers now clasped firmly around his arm. "Well, something that may or may not have any relevance: apparently some college students were camping nearby. Apparently, some of them made some lewd remarks to Lakshmi when she went past. That's according to Kuppi."

Azhar chimed in: "The inspector already interviewed and cleared them. I went down to the police station while you were doing your Tintin thing over here."

"Oh," Harsha said, deflated. "In that case nothing much. But at least we have ticked all of Azhar's staff off the list. The only cleaner who is left — Ammani. The cook, Kuppi. Murugayya, and driver Selvam. Anyone else?"

"That's it, at the moment. You might be able to speak to Leela in the village," Azhar said.

"Fair enough. I will probably need to talk to Murugayya again, when he is not so shaken," Harsha said.

"He is busy today — but you can talk to him tomorrow any time."

Maya let go of Harry's arm, leaned forward and pulled the coffee jug to her and poured a little into her mug. "Did the inspector tell you anything else? Who ate all the biscuits!"

They all looked around at Shane, who did not even have the grace to look guilty, but merely rubbed his belly in mock relish.

"We don't need Tintin here to figure that out," Azhar said sardonically.

"Come on, stop calling me Tintin!"

"I could do your hair for you," Maya said, turning to him,

grabbing hold of his fringe and holding it up in a tuft.

"Get off!" he said, pushing her hands away. They both broke off and turned to see Shane and Azhar exchanging glances.

"Anyway," Harsha said. "I'm going to go down to the village in a bit. When is lunch ready?"

"How should I know? I don't have food in my pocket," Azhar said.

"And you just had breakfast an hour ago!" Maya objected.

"Two hours! And all this detective work is very exhausting, I need to keep my strength up."

"Fatso," she said, poking the side of his stomach.

He caught hold of her hand and held it for a second before letting go and asked the other two — who were watching them with identically neutral expressions on their faces — if they were going to join him in the village.

Neither of them were. Shane, in the absence of his young children, was taking every opportunity to catch up on six years of lost sleep, and Azhar had paperwork to finish.

"Really sorry, guys," he said seriously, "I didn't mean to be so busy while you were here. And there's only a couple of days left before you leave!"

They looked at each other.

"Er... Azhar, we thought we would stay here a bit longer if you don't..." Harsha snorted with laughter at the delighted look on Azhar's face.

"Just one thing," Maya said. "We want to pay for it. You are losing enough money from all the guests who left."

Azhar stood up. "The day I take money from my friends is the day I stop working in this business!" he declared.

"I'm not sure that's in the business manuals," Harsha said jovially. "Anyway, since we are your guests, how about organising some lunch for us?"

"Idiot, I'll make you work in the kitchens next!"

Fortunately, this was rendered unnecessary as Kuppi came in and announced lunch. She gave Harsha a coy smile as she left.

Maya slapped him on the shoulder. "I think she likes you!" she said.

"Good god, Maya, you are in such a violent mood!" Harsha

complained, rubbing his shoulder. "Please don't do this sort of thing when we're in the village!"

"Don't worry, Tintin, I'll be on my best behaviour," Maya said playfully.

Harsha did not deign to respond to this.

Fed and watered, they left the resort around 2pm. They walked through the meadows just below Pipal Resorts until they reached a vast stretch of farmland, covered in acres and acres of coffee plants; short, bush-like plants with glossy leaves that glinted in the afternoon light.

Ignoring the road, as Azhar had told them to, the pair of them walked across the footpath that cut through the coffee plantations.

Soon, they crossed over to paddy fields, which were waterlogged after the torrential downpour from earlier in the morning, with the long stems waving in the slight breeze, lush with water droplets.

It was an almost empty landscape — in the distance they could see a farmer leading a bullock through the fields.

They marvelled quietly at the tranquillity of the scene, and how it contrasted so sharply with the violence of recent events. It really did feel like nothing bad could ever happen in that idyllic landscape.

Soon, they reached the clay huts that Harsha had seen on his bus ride into the resort. It felt like an age ago.

He tried to stop himself from peering in, but even when temptation got the better of him, the entrances were shrouded in darkness.

They walked in silence until they reached the main square where Harsha had first stopped and bought a drink and had encountered the panchayat chief. As ever, there was a clutch of people around the clay structure, jostling the sacks of rice and lentils that flanked the entrance, and this time Harsha was able to smile indulgently as Maya went into transports over this quaint sight.

"Ah! Welcome!" the shopkeeper Subhash said as he spotted Harsha. It appeared the man remembered him, and Maya's addition to his company only improved matters. "Red Bull eh? No — sorry, Limca!"

Harsha grinned at being remembered in this manner and said as they approached the shop: "Limca would be lovely. Maya?"

"Fanta for me, please," she said cheerfully to the shopkeeper, who gave her a shifty grin.

The villagers who stood nearby nodded amicably at the two of them, though one or two couldn't resist eyeing up Maya, and she shifted uncomfortably beneath their scrutiny. She had swapped her T-shirt for another *salwar kameez* but Harsha guessed even this was unusual around here, where most women wore saris.

Harsha took a swig of his Limca and turned to the nearest man, a young chap who had a light cloth turban tied around his head, hanging over a clean shaven face and an honest expression.

"How are you?" Harsha asked, and got the familiar head bob and a smile in return, though the man remained silent. The others looked on curiously.

Harsha felt a bead of sweat drip down the side of his forehead. Getting these folks to chat was proving impossible. "Can any of you point me to Rajaratnam's house?" he asked in a desperate bid to get a response, perfectly aware of the pink monstrosity at the far end of the village.

The silence grew thicker and one or two of the men exchanged glances. The clean-shaven chap pointed out the house to Harsha, who pretended to be interested and nodded as the man gave him brief, terse directions to get to the panchayat chief's house.

"Thank you," Harsha said, taking another sip of his Limca and smacking his lips. He turned to the group and asked: "Is he a good man? We are supposed to meet him for a chat. I want to get an idea of what kind of a person he is."

There was a pause and then, unexpectedly, they broke out into a chorus of responses.

"Very good man!"

"He takes care of the village."

"Look at the road!"

"He is very good to us."

And then the comments subsided and the villagers all looked away, unsmiling. It was such a bizarre performance that Harsha shook his head slightly in disbelief and glanced up at the shopkeeper, who had a slightly troubled look in his eyes, but still managed a smile and said: "You have a meeting with him, sir?"

There was a look of respect in his eyes, and... maybe a bit of fear? His manner had certainly changed from the jovial greeting he had started with.

Harsha said: "Not yet, but I am hoping to speak to him for a travel journalism piece. Do you know him well?"

"Oh yes," the man said, an unfathomable expression on his face. "Around here, we call him The Eagle."

"Why an eagle?" Harsha asked curiously.

Subhash hesitated and then said: "Because he is single-minded and gets what he wants. Please, I don't know any more."

Harsha and Maya looked at each other and then he turned to the shopkeeper again.

"We also want to meet the temple priest. Is the temple far away?"

"The Murugan temple? Not at all! Just 10 minutes that way," the shopkeeper declared, some of his gusto returning as the topic moved away from Rajaratnam. "It is a very beautiful place. Very ancient temple. You must see it!" he declared.

The group around the shop had edged away as though Harsha and Maya were carrying something contagious, and Maya looked at them in some bewilderment.

"Did we say something wrong?" she asked the shopkeeper.

"Oh, no, not at all, madam," the man said. He hesitated and then leaned forward conspiratorially and whispered: "They just... want to be peaceful. Don't want any trouble."

"What trouble could they get into?" Maya glanced at Harsha to see if he was taking notes, but the last thing Harsha wanted to do was to make an already nervous man even more scared. So he leaned against the side of the shop in as casual a manner as he could muster.

"Please sir, the shop is a bit fragile, if you don't mind not leaning like that on it," the shopkeeper barked at him sharply.

Harsha hurriedly straightened up and cleared his throat, trying to look nonchalant.

Maya hid a smile and then asked again: "Is there a problem, Mr..."

"Subhash, madam."

"Mr Subhash, why is everyone acting like they are scared of us? Is it just because we are not from here?"

The man smiled a little from under his bushy moustache, his expression melting in the face of Maya's simple candour.

"No, madam, we are normally very happy to have tourists coming here. It is good for business, they are usually polite and clean. Usually." Subhash hesitated and then leaned forward and said in a lower tone: "It is the business with... Lakshmi. It has everybody a bit worried."

Maya nodded sympathetically. "Was she very popular?"

"Very pop..." Subhash looked at Maya in surprise, and then a thoughtful expression came over his face. "I suppose you have to say... yes, in her own way..." He shook his head as though to clear his thoughts and then said: "I don't know about such matters, madam! I am just a simple shopkeeper!"

"Surely you know everyone who comes and goes here? I would have thought you were a very important man!" Maya declared. "I'm sure you know everything that happens around here?"

Harsha was lost in admiration. Maya was a natural. He wished he could convince her to become a journalist — she would make a fantastic one.

Subhash shook his head, but his chest swelled with pride. "I will say this, madam. If you are looking for answers on what happened with Lakshmi... our priest will know. Nobody better than him. That's all I can say! As for who knew her best - have you visited our local school? Ah you have! Well, that is a very good starting point! And as for Rajaratnam..." His eyes took on a shifty hue again and he leaned forward conspiratorially. "Be careful. He is a very dangerous man. A very dangerous man. Like all politicians in this beautiful country!"

He laughed uproariously as Maya thanked him for the information. Harsha pulled out his wallet to pay for their drinks but Subhash waved it away theatrically.

"Oh no no!" the man said. "On the house!"

Harsha and Maya thanked him repeatedly and then walked away from the group, Harsha nodding pleasantly to the villagers and getting a few respectful nods in return.

"Was that uncomfortable or what," Harsha muttered to Maya as they turned towards the path that led up to the pink house.

"This is not such a happy place," Maya replied, troubled.

"Let's hope this famous priest is a little bit more forthcoming."

She didn't say anything in response, and they walked through the winding mud roads of the village, looking at the pretty little houses with their brightly-painted doors and windows. A few women sat outside some of the houses, though they mostly ignored Harsha and Maya, looking away or rocking babies on their laps. In England and parts of Northern Europe, Harsha would not have been surprised by the less than warm welcome. Here in India, the lack of warmth was conspicuous, and he felt a little chill go down his spine.

13. TEMPLE

They walked to the edge of the village and looked down on the other side of the mountain in awe. Where Pipal Resorts was surrounded by forest land, this side of the mountain was covered in farmland, with long lines of thick, dark-green coffee bushes lining the mountainside in tiered rows, interrupted by little rivulets of water where farmers had carved out small irrigation canals.

The soil here had a dark-brown, rich and fertile look to it compared with the grey-brown mossy forest floor on the other half of the mountain. The whole scene was a bit like getting a massage for the eyes.

"I'd love to explore this side of Arasur some time," Harsha said, with enthusiasm.

"If we have time," Maya said sternly, and his expression became serious again.

Filled though they were with the landscape's lovely contours and the natural beauty of the coffee plantations, they were still not prepared for the temple.

They turned the cleft of the hillside just past the first coffee plantation, as instructed, walked up a furrowed path past a line of neem trees and then gasped.

It was an ancient, crumbling edifice, with the stone wall of the perimeter on one side entirely collapsed inwards to a 45-degree angle. On the other side, the wall was simply missing in parts, leading directly out to the fields. The whole picture was incredibly romantic, like being transported back several hundred years.

The Murugan temple itself was in reasonable shape. Many of the carvings had faded with time, but the main deity that adorned the entrance was lovingly taken care of.

As they walked past a little lamp room in front of the temple itself, Harsha caught hold of Maya's arm and pointed under the crumbling outer wall. A pair of eyes regarded them warily.

"Look!" Harsha said, pointing. It was a stray dog, regarding them with the sad expression that dogs all over the world seemed to specialise in. Beneath the dog, a litter of scrawny puppies tumbled over each other to try and get to the mother's teats.

Maya started forward but Harsha held his grip on her arm firmly. "We don't know anything about this place, Maya. The dog could have any old disease," he said.

Maya nodded reluctantly and they made their way to the main entrance of the charmingly-rundown temple.

The main tower was taller than it looked from a distance, and they craned their necks to see the top as they passed under the arch of the entrance. As their eyes adjusted to the light, they looked around in wonder at the carved animals at every nook and cranny — here a monkey, there a tiger — and wondered at the amount of effort that had been poured into building this tiny countryside temple.

Harsha started as a man emerged from the inner depths of the building and headed towards them with a metal plate. On the plate was a little lamp and a container with holy ash and red kumkum powder on it. Could he have expected them?

As they had been taught, they both cupped their hands over the flame briefly and touched their eyes, Maya with alacrity and Harsha awkwardly. Maya applied a bit of the kumkum powder to her forehead, and they stood awkwardly, waiting for the priest to finish his prayer to the main Murugan deity that was right before them, the focus of the temple.

Unlike many representations of Murugan, this particular statue had a benign, Buddha-like quality to it. It was entirely black; Harsha knew that Murugan was seen as a Tamil god, and was rare in Indian mythology for being represented with dark skin. Many South Indians, who were dark-skinned themselves, identified with this younger and less-favoured son of Siva and Parvati.

Finally, the priest put down his plate and came to them, smiling.

"Let's talk outside. This way," he said, leading them further into the temple and out towards a back entrance. "Do you know much about Murugan?" he asked as they walked. "He is often laughed at. The less intelligent of the two boys — Ganesha, or Vinayakar, was seen as the intelligent one. Do you know the story of the contest between the two brothers?"

Oddly, Harsha did know the story. Ganesha, the elephant god, and Murugan, the younger brother, decided to compete on who could go around the universe quicker. Murugan, on his peacock mount, raced to be first, crossing many hurdles and enjoying a most uncomfortable journey. In the meantime, Ganesha lay at his ease, popping a laddoo or two into his mouth. But at the most crucial moment, he stood up and went once around his parents, Siva and Parvati, and then supplicated in front of them, thus winning the contest.

"And what do you think of that?" the priest asked, sitting on a porch cross-legged and looking at Harsha and Maya with piercing eyes. He was a lot younger than Harsha had expected; around Harsha's own age, not far above 30. He was short, with thick, wavy hair and piercing eyes beneath beetling brows. Harsha had a momentary sense of deep intelligence behind those eyes before the lids closed on them, and he wasn't sure if he had imagined it or not. Behind the priest, the mountain rose up dramatically and farmland melded into forest before the treeline disappeared into the clouds.

"Er ... I don't know," Harsha admitted.

"Murugan is a South Indian god. Mostly worshipped here in Tamil Nadu," the priest said, calmly. "I don't know where this story came from, but they are laughing at us, calling us fools."

Harsha felt massively aware of his non-Tamil roots and tried not to meet the priest's gimlet eyes. But the man just nodded, satisfied at this reaction.

"How can I help you today?" he asked, finally.

Harsha waited. They had agreed that Maya should take the lead on this conversation as the resident Tamil and practising Hindu.

"Can you tell us about Lakshmi?" Maya asked finally.

Harsha's eyes flickered. This wasn't how they had agreed to approach this talk. He would have preferred for them to reach this subject in a roundabout way. But Maya had taken matters into her own hands.

The priest's impressive brows contracted and a brooding look came over his face.

"Everything is God's will," he muttered, looking unhappy. "Lakshmi was a good, God-fearing woman. She had very little... support in her life. But Lord Murugan supported her — or so I thought."

He paused and Harsha heard Maya's intake of breath as she prepared to ask her next question and he quickly gripped her hand to make her stop. Sometimes it was good to just let someone talk.

The priest looked out across the fields. "Without any parents to protect her, she could have gone anywhere. She was helpless. But... she was also a fighter," he said, smiling to himself as though lost in a sweet memory. "She would come here every Monday, even though I said she couldn't come in..."

"Because of her caste?" Maya asked, and Harsha could tell she was trying not to sound accusatory.

The priest recoiled as though she had slapped him, but he recovered and looked at Maya steadily enough.

"Yes," he said, finally. "But she would just come and sit outside, where she could see the god, and she would pray.

"Eventually, after a few months of this, I couldn't bear it any more and I just told her to come in." The priest looked slightly shocked at his own effrontery.

"A brave decision," Harsha said gravely, and the priest sat up a little straighter. "Did it cause any problems?"

"Any problems! Ha! The whole village stopped coming to my temple! Especially after all the dalits started coming on Mondays! For almost a year I was only doing *puja* for these dalits!" The man shook his head in disbelief.

"And then?" Maya asked, interested despite herself. The priest shifted his piercing eyes to her.

"And then they started coming back," he said, pointing his finger at her dramatically. "The ones who could no longer walk all the way to Ramananpettai at first, then all the ones for whom Murugan was a special god. There is only a Vinayakar temple in town," the priest said.

A special god. It was funny how so many Indians adopted one of their many gods as the one just for themselves. Sometimes it was Ganesha, the accessible elephant god with the rotund belly, at other times Saraswathi, the goddess of knowledge; and often Lakshmi, the goddess of wealth. For others, it was Murugan, the underdog.

Maya glared at Harsha as though wondering whether he understood any of this, and he smiled to himself. *I'm not as Anglicised as all that, Maya*, he thought.

"Finally," the priest continued, "We reached this arrangement where the dalits came here on Mondays and the rest of them visited on other days of the week. An imperfect solution, but a solution."

This time, neither Harsha nor Maya were inclined to break the silence. There was a grim look about the priest's face, but a tone of wonder came into his voice. "Yesterday," he said, "Everyone came to pray. Dalits. Non-dalits. Brahmins. Everyone. I have never seen anything like it." This last sentence came in an awed whisper. Maya and Harsha were now sitting at the edge of the porch, leaning forward and drinking this in.

The priest just shook his head and said: "She changed the village. And... and she changed me. Yes, she changed me."

To their immense astonishment (and embarrassment, in Harsha's case), tears rolled down the priest's face and splashed silently onto the stone floor of the temple porch.

They sat like that in the afternoon silence for a few minutes, with only the sounds of the priest's sniffles, bird calls and a gentle breeze blowing through the coffee plantation as accompaniment.

Finally, Maya and Harsha exchanged glances before she leaned forward and said: "I am so sorry about what happened."

He looked up at her and bit his lip to control his emotion, unable to say anything more.

"Why do you think it happened?" she asked, gently.

His expression hardened and he gathered himself and said: "She was a young, vulnerable woman. This world is not a safe place for such people."

"Do you think anyone in this village is capable of anything like this?"

He laughed bitterly at this. "Who better to know what demons a man carries inside him than the priest?" he said, sardonically. "But honestly? This is a very downtrodden place. Very few people around here are capable of something like this." Maya sighed in disappointment, and the priest looked at her, pursing his lips. "But very few people doesn't mean that no one is capable," he said, and the two of them sat up straight.

When he looked at them again, his expression had switched from grief to calculation. He looked at both of them, one after the other, as though considering exactly what he was going to say. Finally, he said:

"This mountain is a gold mine. You understand me? A gold mine. And where there is gold — there are people who compete for it."

Both Maya and Harsha tensed. This sounded important.

"Who do you mean?" Maya asked in a coaxing manner.

The priest smiled bitterly at her and said: "Who do you think is most powerful here? Who are the landowners? The leaders?"

Maya didn't say anything, but Harsha stirred and said: "Rajaratnam, the panchayat head. He also owns much of the land."

The priest kept his expression carefully neutral. "Anyone else?" he asked.

"Laurent — the schoolteacher."

The priest nodded thoughtfully. "I hear he knew Lakshmi... quite well," he said, and Harsha's breath caught for a second. Was the man saying what he thought he was saying?

After a second's silence, the priest asked: "Anyone else you can think of?"

There was an even longer silence after this, and then Maya said reluctantly: "I suppose, Azhar."

Harsha felt the blood rise to his face. "Just because he is a..." he began, hotly, but this time it was Maya who placed a restraining hand on his, and he went quiet. They were here for information, not to start a fight.

He took a deep breath and said: "Why would any of these people hurt Lakshmi?"

The priest shrugged his shoulders. "She was young and vulnerable. She may have just been caught in a turf war. Or she may have upset someone powerful. These are just ideas. I don't know. I don't have any insight. But you asked me what I know — and I told you what I know."

Maya glanced at Harsha and then nodded and said: "Thank you for your time and for talking on such a difficult subject."

The priest nodded curtly and stood up.

Harsha couldn't contain himself. "Was there anything between Laurent and Lakshmi?" he asked in a rush.

The priest looked at him knowingly and said: "Look, there were three men in Lakshmi's life. Azhar, who was her employer. He gave her a job when she was struggling and she would have done anything for him. Then there was that schoolteacher man, who was following her everywhere — but she was not interested in him." He hesitated and then said: "Then there is Rajaratnam. It was an open secret he was... interested... in Lakshmi. And he is also really interested in that resort. I can't say more than that."

Harsha did his best not to look at Maya. This was beyond anything they had hoped for. The priest had been an absolute fount of information.

They walked back through the temple to the front porch. The dog with the puppies looked mournfully up at them as they walked past towards the path that led back to Arasur.

"Is there any bad feeling in the village towards Azhar?" Maya asked, sounding worried and voicing Harsha's own concern.

The priest scratched the back of his neck, considering his words. This was not a man who gave an answer without thinking twice.

"I think some people think he is responsible somehow for Lakshmi's death. Most do not, but... there is some resentment anyway."

"Because he is a Muslim?" Harsha asked, quietly.

Another pause as the man thought. "I don't know if it is that. I think some people see him as a foreigner. A North Indian. The name of his resort — that wasn't a great idea."

Maya shook her head, crestfallen. "He thought it was a nice gesture, called it Pipal Resorts. It was a tribute to Arasur."

The priest looked at her, nodding slowly. "I can see how it could have been like that. But people think he is bringing all these strange urdu names to the region. It is how people think. Not me — I think he is a good man," he finished, scowling at his feet.

"Thank you for your time," Harsha said. "You've been very helpful."

The priest nodded and then, strangely enough, took out two business cards from the fold of his dhoti and handed one to each of them. Harsha read the name 'Maheshwaran Shastrigal' and saw a mobile phone number on the business card before he put it away. Another incongruity about this odd priest.

"Thank you very much for coming," the man said. "It was a pleasure talking to people who care about Lakshmi. Come back for puja any time."

Maya nodded. "It is such a peaceful spot. I will definitely come," she said.

"Come on Monday if you can. I have a feeling it will be special," Maheshwaran said. He looked out onto the mountain slopes and said: "She has changed this place forever."

Harsha was so quiet on the way back that Maya started to worry about him. When she couldn't bear it anymore, she prodded him with her elbow and asked: "Everything ok? You seem very down."

"Oh? Down? No, no. Not down. But… just thinking."

"About what?" Maya asked, waving to Subhash the shopkeeper as they walked past the town square.

"Just thinking that I have no right to judge India. Yes there's caste, yes there's religion. But it is full of surprises. That temple, in the middle of nowhere — who would have thought it would be the centre of some kind of cultural revolution? Incredible."

Maya smiled and looked sideways at Harsha, and thought to herself that India wasn't the only thing full of surprises.

14. STUDENTS

The husband walked up to his wife, caught her by the shoulders and said harshly: "Are you going to give me the money or not?"

"No, you fool, leave me alone. This is your fault, so you get us out of it!"

"But I can't, you wretched woman. That debt collector is going to beat the hell out of me and then what will you do? Who will gather the harvest?"

"I do all the donkey work anyway! All you do is drink and cry about how much money you owe! If you worked as hard as you drink, we may never have had these problems!"

The man strode up to her and slapped her across the face. "Give me the money!"

"No! My grandmother left it to me! And we already gave you enough as dowry!"

He slapped her again and she fell to the floor.

She crawled to the tiny kitchen area in the corner of the room and picked up a stick.

"If you touch me again..."

The man strode to the kitchen and picked up another stick and they faced each other.

At this point, the pair of them stopped and turned to face the audience. The 'wife' said with a shy smile: "We want you to pretend that we are holding stone pestles. And also, this sauce is a bit brown, but it is supposed to be blood."

And without another word the two of them fell to beating each other furiously with the sticks, jumping up and down and running around the plastic chairs as they tried to reach each other, discreetly emptying brown sauce over each other to represent their bleeding wounds.

The most chilling thing, Harsha thought, as he watched the tiny thespians on stage, was that this was supposed to be comedy. And indeed, the thirty or so children who comprised the audience were rolling on the floor, some of them in tears of laughter.

At one point the 'husband' stopped running and let out a yell of frustration. "What did I do in my previous life to deserve this curse of a woman? I must have been a murderer! Or I must have beaten my children! I must have been a murderer of children!"

Each fresh declaration was accompanied by a big cheer from the audience.

Laurent turned to his shocked companions and said, with a wry smile: "Tragic, isn't it?"

Finally, the play ended with husband and wife holding each other and the money lender (who sported a massive fake moustache) brandishing a whip.

The audience cheered and cheered, and Laurent stood up to applaud. The four guests followed his example, clapping, as the little actors bowed to all corners of the room.

"Dinner is served!" Laurent declared, drawing the biggest cheer of the evening, and a massive sigh of relief from the four guests.

The kids rapidly split into two and went to either side of the room and sat cross legged on the floor, as Mala came in with a huge pile of banana leaves. She proceeded to lay them on the floor in front of each child while other teachers and one or two of the older children came in with rice and sambar and vegetable curry and served small portions of each onto the leaf plates. Within minutes, all the plates were full and everyone was tucking in.

"Not bad, not bad at all," Azhar said, stuffing his mouth. "Much better than that sh... The stuff they served us in my school."

Shane didn't bother with talking, but just applied himself to the serious business of eating. On Harsha's other side Laurent tried to talk to Maya but she was engaging in conversation with a bashful teenage boy on her other side, while his friends giggled and whispered to each other.

One of the girls sitting on the opposite side called out to Maya, saying: "Ma'am can I tell you one thing?"

"Of course, my darling, what is it?" she asked, warmly.

The girl seemed to lose her nerve but at the prompting of her friends, she said haltingly: "You are so beautiful, like a movie star ma'am! You should be in Kollywood! Or even Bollywood!"

Maya reddened with pleasure and smiled her thanks.

Harsha turned to Laurent, who looked incongruous sitting cross-legged on the floor with a banana leaf, but also extremely comfortable. Harsha said: "So innocent in some ways, but in other ways..."

Laurent replied: "I told you, India is a country of contradictions. But... I love being around these kids. I couldn't ask for anything more."

Harsha looked at the face of a man completely at peace with himself and felt a stab of jealousy. How is it that this Frenchman had found peace in India and he, Harsha, was struggling so much for it in England?

As Laurent looked away to talk urbanely to one of the children, Harsha watched him. Could he be a killer? Was the priest Maheshwaran right to suspect him? The problem was, Harsha had absolutely no idea how to even go about investigating a crime of this nature. What on earth could he possibly know about criminals? He had absolutely no experience.

At this point, Laurent turned and caught his eye and Harsha laughed weakly. He had intended to ask Laurent about Lakshmi — but how the hell was he supposed to begin that conversation? His nerve failed him and he started a conversation about London instead.

They talked for a while about England and, around them, the students began to leave. With the noisy chatter receding, Harsha could hear the rain pattering down on the roof. After the last one had gone, Laurent turned to his guests and said: "How about a nightcap?"

They migrated from the floor to the sofa and chairs and had a few drinks while Mala and two of the older girls from the school cleared up, having rejected the few half-hearted offers of help from the others.

Laurent seemed to have forgotten the journalist trick Harsha had played on him earlier, and was all charm, and Harsha couldn't remember the last time he had enjoyed an evening so much.

But after a few drinks, conversation became harder and harder as the sound of the rain on the roof got louder. Finally, Laurent stood up and looked out of the window.

"I am afraid you may have to stay the night here," he said.

"What? Why?" Harsha, Maya and Shane looked at each other in panic.

"Kind of you, Laurent, but I think we would prefer to go back!"

Shane said, politely.

"There are four of us! There's not enough space here!" Maya added quickly.

Laurent shook his head.

"I can't let you cross the river in this rain. Azhar, you know."

They turned to Azhar, who had a resigned expression on his face. He nodded at their looks of inquiry and said: "Flash floods. They could happen at any time and it's not safe to cross the river when it's raining like this. People have died in the past, washed away in seconds. It's my fault for not paying attention to the weather."

"This is the jungle, city boys and girl," Laurent said. "I have some spare duvets and pillows. But in this building, there's only my bedroom. It will have to be the mat for you kids, I'm afraid."

Nobody was particularly happy with the situation but they resigned themselves to it and followed Laurent to a cupboard in one corner of the room. While there were a number of pillows, it turned out there were only two duvets.

"Er... Is everyone feeling cold? If so, I'm afraid you're going to have to share..."

The group all shuffled their feet awkwardly as they realised that Maya was going to have to share a duvet with one of the boys.

Maya glanced at Shane, who looked back at her with such an expression of panic that Harsha couldn't help chuckling. Maya looked down at the floor, rather that at one of the others, but Azhar settled the matter by saying: "I don't think anyone but myself can put up with Shane's snoring. Come on, we will take this one. You two lovebirds will have to take the other."

Maya looked so downcast that Harsha said, softly: "Maddy, it's a big duvet. And you can obviously trust me to be a gentleman."

She looked up at him and smiled. "I never doubted that. I was just... feeling sad about... something else."

Harsha did not pursue the matter, but instead pulled one of the duvets to one corner of the room.

"Lights out?" Laurent yelled over the hammering of the rain, once they were sorted.

They nodded and gestured assent. Laurent flicked the switch off and headed to his own bedroom.

There was a momentary silence and then Shane said: "Harry? What do you think? Laurent of all people?"

Harsha shook his head. "I have no idea, man. No idea at all."

"Your Maheshwaran priest is off his rocker," Azhar said sleepily. "Laurent, a killer — impossible!"

"Guys, maybe we shouldn't discuss this here?" Maya asked urgently.

But she needn't have feared. Harsha could barely hear himself speak over the sound of the pounding rain. Tired as he was, he simply couldn't sleep over the hammering on the roof.

The others did not seem to be having the same problem — before too long, he could hear assorted snoring coming from the boys' sleeping spot.

"Harry!" A voice said by his ear and he started and scrambled around.

"It's just me you idiot, Maya," she said. He was aware that she was very close to him. He could feel the heat from her body.

Well, this was unexpected. He turned around to face her, half expecting (and half hoping) she would do something.

"I feel... really lonely," she said.

He could feel his heart thumping against his chest and gave silent thanks for the sound of the rain, which drowned it out.

"I don't know what I'm doing. I've left my family to come here..."

"They know you are here, right?" he asked, frowning.

"Of course! Well maybe not that I am here with three guys, they think it is a big reunion and all the girls are coming. I won't be showing them too many pictures. I didn't lie, but... To my husband..."

He knew nothing was going to happen now. He couldn't make a move even if she could. "Listen, Maya, it's not a big deal. Everyone lies, and in your case, it is more an omission of facts to spare his feelings. As long as your conscience is clean..."

Now that he had grown accustomed to the dark, he could make out the shape of her eyes from the porch light, the gleam in them. She was even closer than he thought, he could lean forward very slightly and kiss her.

Instead he added: "Don't worry, you have nothing to feel guilty about."

"It's not just guilt, I... just don't want to go back. I want to be here. My way of life... It just cannot go on. It hit me like... like... like a religious conversion the other day."

Harsha did not say anything. Her eyes were gleaming now either through excitement or from unshed tears.

She said: "It's really scary, as though the floor has disappeared from under my feet. The future I had in my head, however boring or crap or whatever else — it has disappeared. I feel scared and... lonely."

He took a deep breath and then laughed quietly. "I don't know what to say, Maya."

She was quiet for a minute and said: "Don't say anything. Just be there for me."

And her hand found his.

15. HONCHO

Maya woke up burning with embarrassment. It wasn't just that she had spent the night holding hands with another man (*Holding hands! Was she in kindergarten?*) but it was also the fact that she had let her personal issues overwhelm her.

She turned and looked at Harsha's body, facing away from her towards the French window, and cringed. Naveen's compact little body, with his somewhat-feminine shoulders and pointy ears, rose in her mind and she felt a catch in her throat.

Every day since she had left their Seattle home, she had been wracked with doubt. Why was it that in real life you never knew if you had made the right decision? Had she taken a much-needed break or had she just run away from her life and responsibilities like a child? She thought of her mother, and her mind hardened. How on earth would they salvage their relationship? Would they, ever? She felt nothing but anger when she thought of her mother, no matter how much she tried to look at life from the other person's point of view.

She got up quietly, edging her way out of the duvet, walked up to the French windows and looked out at the sodden lawn. Laurent's garden had that washed, post-rain look about it, and she could almost smell the wet grass and the soaked earth. The little fountain bubbled away.

Maya took a deep breath. What was done was done. Her own life would have to wait to sort itself out. Right now, she needed to focus on Lakshmi. She desperately wanted to focus on Lakshmi. She had never met the woman but felt a strong sense of kinship with her.

Bringing her killer to justice had quietly become a minor obsession with her. There was nothing else going on in her life — nothing that she wanted to return to. This was everything, at the moment.

She didn't know how long she stood there, looking out into that beautiful garden, but eventually, she heard some movement as Azhar woke the other boys up and she turned to smile at them. Whatever other mistakes she had made, she had done one thing right — that was to come to Azhar. No one could have been more understanding or less intrusive in that moment. No one could have been more supportive than Shane. As for Harsha — she hurriedly shelved that thought as she watched Harsha get up from the floor and fold the duvet inexpertly.

The door behind her creaked open, and Laurent emerged, resplendent in a purple dressing gown.

"Would you kids like some coffee?" he yawned and headed over towards the kitchen area. "Toilet's over there," he said, pointing vaguely in the direction of his bedroom door.

Five minutes later, Laurent approached the sofa with a tray holding a steaming French coffee press and a plateful of biscuits, a benevolent smile on his face. Maya jumped up and gave him a hand with the tray, thanking him profusely and breathing in the soothing scent of freshly-brewed coffee.

As he handed her a cup, she glanced at his pockmarked and sorrowful face, and couldn't help but admire his strong cheekbones and the vitality in his blue eyes.

Could he be a killer? She liked Laurent, but if he was Lakshmi's killer — she wanted to bring him down.

Laurent placed the tray on the coffee table and then pushed down the plunger slowly and expertly before serving each of his guests. The boys murmured their thanks and they all sat in silence in that beautiful studio-like room and sipped their coffee.

Eventually, Azhar said: "Thanks so much for hosting us last night, Loco. Appreciate it. Come and stay at the resort some time if you would like."

"Oh I will take you up on that!" Laurent said cheerfully, settling into his easy chair and looking piercingly at Azhar from over his cup.

Maya forced herself to look at Harsha, as though looking at him might help her get over the embarrassment of the night before. She found that he, in turn, was looking steadily at Laurent, as though trying to read the Frenchman's mind.

With a flash of insight, Maya realised Harsha was wondering the same thing that she was; whether Laurent was capable of such a gruesome crime.

"Would you like to stay for breakfast?" Laurent asked, urbanely. Maya's eyes narrowed. How did the man hold it together so easily?

It was Harsha who answered: "Thank you, Laurent, but we cannot. Maya and I have an appointment with Mr Rajaratnam, the panchayat head."

Laurent stirred his coffee absentmindedly. "For the travel piece?" he asked, with studied casualness.

Harsha hid a smile. "Yes," he said, finally. "For the travel piece."

As soon as they said their goodbyes and left to walk back to Pipal Resorts, Maya caught up with Harsha quickly, pushed aside a low hanging branch and said quietly: "What did you make of Laurent?"

Harsha didn't say anything for a second, and then he said: "Sir Arthur Conan fucking Doyle."

"What? Have you finally lost it?" she asked impatiently. "I was talking about Laurent."

"Yes, yes," Harsha said, equally impatiently. "I was just thinking about Sherlock Holmes. And how easy it is for Arthur Conan Doyle to write a character who can just look at someone and just tell immediately by the ink on their fingers that they were up at 8 pm on Thursday night in the conservatory, or whatever. Or that this person was killed by his aunt with a letter opener because of the way in which the cloth on his shirt tore."

"Stop babbling and focus," Maya said sternly. Harsha grunted in response.

The path back towards Pipal Resorts was surprisingly unchanged given the violence of the rain the night before. The trees above them held raindrops that splattered down on them, and the footpath was muddier than usual, but apart from that the forest of Arasur was as tranquil as Maya remembered it.

Harsha sighed deeply as he slid down a particularly muddy part of the pathway down and said: "I learnt nothing at all from that evening. I have no idea whatsoever about Laurent."

Maya nodded thoughtfully. "I didn't notice much either. Other than the fact that he is grieving desperately, and hiding it."

There was no warning as Harsha stopped and caught hold of her hand, staring at her. Maya yelped as they both slid down the path, catching hold of each other to keep from falling.

"Oy! Watch out there! I have no intention of carrying you back to the resort!" Azhar called out from behind as Shane and he caught up with them.

"Keep your eyes on the path, Prince Harry," Shane said, dimpling.

Harsha ignored them both. "What do you mean, grieving?" he asked, staring at Maya.

Maya wrenched her hand free and directed her most ferocious glare at Harsha as she massaged her wrist. Manhandling her like that!

"Wasn't it obvious? He has clearly been crying recently! You just have to look at how swollen his eyes are — and the bags under his eyes as well!" she said, crossly. She crossed her arms and looked up at Azhar and then at Shane, and frowned when they shook their heads to signify they hadn't noticed either. "Men," she muttered.

Shane and Azhar chuckled at this, but Harsha continued to stare at her. A patch of sunlight penetrated the canopy above them and fell on his face, highlighting his serious expression.

"He hid it extremely well," Harsha said, finally. Maya nodded. Laurent had been absolutely charming the whole evening and that morning. "Azhar — are you sure that Laurent was close to Lakshmi?" Harsha asked, turning to him.

Azhar shrugged his shoulders. "I only heard the same gossip that you heard, that he was crazy about her. But Ammani told me confidently that Lakshmi did not have a relationship with him or encourage him in any way."

Harsha stared out into the distance.

"Does it all mean anything? That Laurent hid how upset he was?" Shane asked, finally, when Harsha showed no signs of either saying anything more or resuming their journey towards the resort.

Harsha was quiet for another moment and then he just said: "Let's keep going. We have a long day ahead of us."

Harsha was being mysterious, and Maya did not like it. He was quiet over breakfast and he was quiet all the way to the village (they had been driven down by Azhar this time) and Harsha was sitting under the village pipal tree in silence, looking towards the road that led up to Rajaratnam's house.

Maya shook her head and walked towards the shop, smiling at the villagers who were congregated around it as usual. Did they ever actually do any work? It felt like they were getting used to her presence, because none of them stopped in their chatter, and one or two even greeted her.

Subhash the shopkeeper welcomed her as a long-lost friend, of course, and asked her dramatically how cold she would like her Fanta.

"Very cold, please!" she smiled. Subhash popped the bottle open with his usual flourish and handed the fizzy drink over to her. She took a sip and then smiled at one of the men who came up and asked for tea. He grinned at her, his pearly white teeth gleaming in the sharp afternoon light, and said in English: "Myself Ragu. 10th standard pass," he said, and the men around him collapsed into giggles. He turned to frown at them. "What did I say wrong?" he asked in mock outrage.

Maya smiled weakly, happy that some of the formality had melted away, but also annoyed that she seemed to be the target of some sort of joke.

"How are you, Ragu?" she asked in English, smiling.

"Very well, madam."

She took another sip of her drink, eyeing Ragu. How could she take advantage of this new friendliness and wipe that smile from the man's face? She decided to go for the simple and direct approach.

"What do you think happened with Lakshmi, Ragu?" she asked. Ragu's expression froze, and the giggles around him ceased instantly.

Ragu licked his lips and looked to either side nervously. Maya glanced at Subhash, and the shopkeeper was staring at her in surprise.

"Madam — I do not ask such questions," Ragu said, reverting to Tamil. "It is too big for me. I just do my work and leave that to the police."

Maya nodded, already regretting the impulse that had led her to ask this question in the first place. Thankfully, Harsha came up at that point and said shortly: "Shall we go?"

As they wound their way up to the pink mansion, carefully avoiding the jeep tracks that had splattered mud to both sides of the road, they realised it was even bigger than they had first thought.

Closer up, the house loomed over the entire village, its immense bulk casting a wide shadow over the nearest dwellings. Maya was forcibly reminded of the churches in small American towns, built to such a large size that wherever you were in the town, you could them and navigate your way to the centre.

As they approached the broad compound wall that snaked around the main edifice, she started to feel drowsy and had to stifle a few yawns. She recognised the sensation from writing exams back in the day — the body forced you to relax when you were tense. She could see that Harsha felt it as well. He was no longer walking confidently ahead, instead staying by her side as though they had strength in numbers.

"On this occasion, let me do the talking, Maya," he muttered. "But please observe it all very closely. You see things that I don't."

She nodded. She was both flattered and relieved at this role he had assigned her. Perhaps it was lame on her part, but she was terrified at the idea of talking to this Rajaratnam, and was more than willing to let Harsha take the lead.

They walked up to the black iron gate, which was carved in ornate style ending in the shape of some sort of bird — an eagle, Maya realised, spotting how the metal twisted to represent a sharp beak. Through the bars of the gate, they could see a large man sitting in the shadow of the porch, his face shrouded in darkness.

Harsha pushed at the gate, but it refused to budge. Maya pointed silently to a buzzer on the gate post and Harsha pressed it briefly. To their irritation, the man on the porch had not moved through this whole exhibition.

Instead, the front door opened and a smaller, slimmer man dressed in a white uniform came out of the house and hurried forward to press a button on one pillar of the porch. Maya wondered if this was the assistant that Harsha had described from the incident in the village shop. With a clicking sound, the gate opened smoothly and Harsha and Maya slowly proceeded onto a paved pathway up to the porch.

There was some indeterminate — but delicately arranged — shrubbery on either side of the pathway and an actual lawn beyond that. But Harsha and Maya only had eyes for the odd pair ahead of them.

When they reached the porch, the assistant gave an odd little bow and stood back to allow them to climb a couple of stairs and walk through the pillars on to the porch. The roof of the pink house protruded out to cover them in shade, and some beautiful cane chairs were arranged on this raised porch around a glass coffee table.

Maya stood there, feeling remarkably out of place among the three men. Why wasn't Harsha saying something?

As if on cue, Harsha stepped forward with a somewhat ghastly smile on his face and spoke to the bulky man in the chair. "Good afternoon Mr Rajaratnam, a pleasure to meet you, sir," he said, and Maya admired the measured tones of his voice. He was certainly dealing with the uncomfortable situation better than she was.

"And you," said the man, not attempting to rise, but holding out his hand to give Harsha a brief handshake.

Rajaratnam was not obese, exactly, but there was a certain bulk about him that was more than a little intimidating. His face was thick set and jowly — not ugly, but not remarkable either. He had one large mole on his left cheek, and Maya thought absurdly of Marilyn Monroe and hid a smile.

The man indicated the cane chair across the coffee table from him and Harsha glanced back at Maya before sitting down.

Did it sting that Rajaratnam was ignoring her completely? Yes it did. But she was used to being ignored in favour of a man, so she sat silently on another chair that was slightly set back from the two of them.

"So, Mr... Devnath is it? How can I help you?" Rajaratnam asked, speaking slowly and carefully.

The chair was very inconvenient for interviewing from — it was built for leaning back. Maya put her fingers together and looked at Rajaratnam carefully, determined to observe every tic, every expression on his face.

Harsha was struggling between leaning back and perching on the edge of the uncomfortable chair, and Rajaratnam and Maya both watched silently as he took a notepad and pen out of his knapsack and tried to balance it comfortably on his knee while sitting on the edge of the chair. It would have been funny if Maya hadn't been so much on edge.

"Sir, I am writing a travel journalism piece about Arasur," Harsha said. Maya had heard him rehearse this part of the speech in the car on the way there. "I was hoping you could tell me a bit about the history of the village and the surrounding area. I am told that you have been responsible for a lot of the village's prosperity, and that you are the head of the local panchayat. I was hoping I could get your views on this region."

The man's eyebrows rose. "All this for a travel piece?"

"Well, depending on how much more I get, I could write a wider piece on the region and its place in Tamil Nadu and in India," Harsha said, stumbling slightly over his words.

"And what has this mountain got to do with India?"

A bead of sweat appeared on Harsha's forehead.

"It could be a story about India as a growing nation, of how local entrepreneurs are driving the Indian economy forward. Depending on how much information I get."

"And you think that your English newspaper would be interested in me?"

Maya re-evaluated Rajaratnam. Yes, he was still a scary man. But he was also clearly an intelligent one. She looked at his expressionless face and felt a pang of worry for Harsha. Was he sharp enough to handle this canny operator? She was not sure she was, and hoped Harsha was different.

"It depends on how I sell it, sir, and on our conversation," Harsha said, smiling slightly and shrugging his shoulders as though such matters were above his pay grade. It was very nicely done, Maya thought with a gush of pride.

Rajaratnam looked searchingly at Harsha for a minute and then said: "Alright. Ask your questions and we will see."

Harsha glanced at Maya, as though to draw strength from her. She sent him good vibes and luck through her thoughts. Harsha turned to Rajaratnam again and took a deep breath.

16. RAJARATNAM

For all that this was a small town, Harsha could tell that Rajaratnam was a good politician. He did not answer any of the questions directly, and had a knack for bringing the question back to the subject he wanted to discuss. Initially, this was the standard of the roads in the area. The man seemed obsessed with this.

"You tell me, Mr Devnath, have you seen such beautiful roads anywhere else in Tamil Nadu? Or even India? Of course, some of the highways are ok, but when it comes to rural road networks, they just lay superficial gravel roads, which are destroyed when one or two trucks go past..."

This went on for a while and perhaps it would have been quite interesting if Harsha's mind wasn't elsewhere.

"Did you grow up here, sir?" he asked at the first gap in the conversation.

"Oh yes! This is my home," he said, spreading out his hands. "When I was a boy, this was a run-down place, grinding poverty, hardly any food to eat even though there were paddy fields all around us!" he laughed. "No education, no schools nearby, so the only options were to work here as a farmer, and take on more and more debt from those moneylenders at ridiculous interest, or go to the cities to work as a construction labourer. By the time I was 19, 20, all I saw around me was empty houses and debt."

He shifted forward, the chair creaking under him, and he pointed a finger at Harsha. "What would you have done in that situation Mr Devnath? If you had not had the fine education that you clearly had, speaking your beautiful English?"

Harsha had enough experience as a journalist to resist the temptation to get into a debate. Instead he said: "I can honestly say I don't know what I would have done. What did *you* do?"

The man leaned back. "That was the time of M S Swaminathan's green revolution. Genetically modified crops and chemical fertilisers. We were already steeped in debt when my father fell sick, poor man.

As the eldest son I inherited his wealth. Or rather, his debt!" he laughed bitterly.

"I recognised that I had to gamble to try and get some of that back. I bought into the government scheme for high-yielding crops and changed our fortunes bit by bit. Moneylenders were hounding us, threatening my wife. I was young, but even in those days, I knew how to deal with that," he said, stretching his arms out and Harsha noticed that as large as the man was, there was a healthy layer of muscle on his body.

"I am guessing with your Western education, you are against GM crops," Rajaratnam said, eyeing his interviewer beadily. Harsha could honestly say that he had never even thought about genetically modified crops in his life, so he cleared his throat non-committally.

"Nowadays these damned environmentalists parade around saying that GM crops are ruining the land," the man's voice, so placid up to now, rose in anger. "What the hell do they know of the situation before the green revolution? Bloody academics and students, pretending they understand the situation that farmers were in back then."

He leaned terrifyingly close to Harsha and tapped his notebook. "That was off the record, you understand?"

Harsha nodded.

The man spread his arms around, encompassing the entire village, and even the entire mountainside before them. "I changed the fortunes of not just my farm but the entire village. I bought all the failing farms and made them use high-yielding crops. Within ten years — just ten years, Mr Devnath! — this was a prosperous village. Soon, we shifted to coffee, and profits doubled again! There was only one thing left to deal with."

"And that was?"

The man hesitated and then knocked on the front door. The man in white uniform came out. "Do you and your companion want anything? Coffee? Or tea?"

"Coffee would be lovely, thank you," Harsha said. Maya shook her head.

After the servant had withdrawn, Rajaratnam asked: "How are things at the resort? The owner is a friend of yours, isn't he?"

Harsha recognised the change of subject and reflected that he would have to navigate this conversation carefully.

"The death of poor Lakshmi has shocked people," Harsha said, observing his quarry carefully. Was there a little flicker of the eyelids? "But Azhar is trying to settle things down again. He is confident that things will be normal again soon, once the initial shock wears off."

The man's expression was neutral now. "I see," he said finally. "So, do you have any more questions for me?"

Harsha said gently: "You were mentioning the troubles you had to deal with in the village, sir?"

The man sat silent for a few minutes, and then looked pointedly at Harsha's notebook. Harsha shut it and put down his pen.

Rajaratnam smiled and said: "You come from Kolkata, Mr Devnath?" Harsha did not bother to correct him. "You don't understand the situation here in the old days," Rajaratnam continued. "We were basically back in the days of the *zamindars*, even if that name was not being used any more. Do you know, if a lower caste woman wanted to speak to the high-caste landowner, she was not allowed to wear anything above the waist?" The man glanced at Maya for the first time and smiled at the flash in her eyes.

"Different times. Tamil Nadu, for all its problems, is a better place now. The landowner squeezed every last drop out of the farmers, forced them to grow crops that made money for him, not crops that put food on their tables. The English made them grow opium, and after they left, the Indian landowners made them grow spices that they had never heard of or knew how to use. What was the difference for them? Nothing." He spat out onto the side of the porch.

Trying not to look at the blob of saliva that could be seen in the grass, Harsha asked: "Was this when you grew up?"

"Ha! No! I am talking about my father's time. By the time I grew up those landowners had left for the bright lights of the city and the farmers were left to fend for themselves. Now they had no money to invest in the land, and that's when the moneylenders came in. What sort of interest do you think they charged?"

Harsha went for a high number. "Forty percent? Fifty percent? Sixty percent!" he amended, seeing his interviewee shake his head.

"Sometimes they charged up to 200 percent!" the man declared.

"200 percent, but how..."

"Exactly," Rajaratnam said, leaning back with a sigh. A silence fell between them, and Harsha was remembering the little play enacted by the children of Laurent's school. Had things really changed since the days Rajaratnam was referring to?

"So there you have it," Rajaratnam continued, ticking points off his massive fingers. "The English, the *zamindars* and then the moneylenders ran the place. I saw it as my duty to break this cycle."

"And how did you do that? Moneylenders have their *goondas*, don't they?"

"The moneylenders themselves are *goondas*, Mr Devnath."

"So how did you defeat them?"

The man smiled a little nastily and looked speculatively at Harsha, adjusting his position on his chair. He pursed his lips, his eyes boring holes into Harsha, who instinctively just waited for the response.

"Did you see carving on the gate on the way in, Mr Devnath?"

Harsha's eyebrows rose, and he had to resist the urge to exchange glances with Maya. What on earth was this all about?

"Some sort of bird, wasn't it?" Harsha asked finally.

Rajaratnam's brow knitted together and he frowned at Harsha. "Not just any bird — that's a *pambu kazhugu*. A serpent eagle. It specialises in killing snakes. And this mountain — it was full of snakes. Oh yes, it was full of them."

Harsha felt a shiver go down his spine. This time he did glance at Maya, and she looked similarly shaken. Was Rajaratnam saying what they thought he was saying?

"Do you mean to say that..." Harsha began, but Rajaratnam raised his hand to stop him. Harsha was so unnerved that he actually stopped talking immediately.

Rajaratnam's lip curled and he said: "Even if you throw your notebook away, Mr Devnath, I will not tell you any more. Let us just say Gandhi would not have approved, but sometimes when you turn the other cheek, the world just keeps slapping you. There are times when you have to slap back."

"Gandhi did get us freedom."

The man waved this away. "He was dealing with a different opponent. The British were still recovering from the Second World War, and they had convinced the world they had the moral high ground, which Gandhi destroyed brilliantly. But what I... what we were dealing with was a tough set of moneylenders with a complete stranglehold on this region. They did not care about morals. The only way was to fight fire with fire."

"And you did that?"

Rajaratnam waved his hand towards Arasur below them. "Let's just say that down in the village, they call me The Eagle. I go one step further and consider myself the *pambu kazhagu*. The Serpent Eagle."

"I heard," Harsha said, neutrally. "And now you represent this village in the local panchayat?"

"Someone has to represent the interests of this region," the man said, virtuously. "Clearly the people of this village believe I am the right man."

The false tone of self-sacrifice irritated Harsha, so he decided to ramp up the questions.

"Also, you are now the biggest landowner in this region, are you not?"

"Yes, that is true. But I charge a sustainable rate of rent, so that my tenants can earn good money."

"Why not sell them their land back, so they can be completely free?"

He laughed. "Mr Devnath, they are people dealing with several generations of debt. Do you know the land prices these days? They may like the idea of buying land, but they cannot deal with that level of debt. Until such time they are back on their feet, I cannot in good conscience allow them to burden themselves in that way."

"But..."

"Mr Devnath, is this all for your travel piece?" the man's eyes had narrowed, and Harsha backtracked.

"No sir, I was just interested — you see, I have not taken out my notebook."

The man stood up painfully, his voice taking on a slightly menacing tone. "It's interesting isn't it. A big city journalist comes along, asks these questions, trying to understand problems beyond his understanding."

Harsha looked at Rajaratnam, his mouth opening and closing in surprise.

Rajaratnam towered over him now and Harsha fell back into the easy chair with a flop. "If you want, you can go speak to the villagers and ask them how much I have done for this place," the man said, waving his hand wildly to indicate the village that lay below the house.

"I... sir... I didn't mean..." Harsha stammered, alarmed at the turn the interview had taken.

"I have work to do," the man said. "Finish your coffee and leave."

And with that, he went into the house, slamming the door shut behind him.

"Dammit!" Harsha said, picking up his notebook, which had fallen to the floor.

He turned to Maya, who had stood up silently. He sighed. "I cocked that up. I didn't even get a chance to ask him about Lakshmi. But his superior tone was really annoying me," he said in self-justification, half expecting her to remonstrate with him.

But she just smiled at him, a strange look in her eyes.

"What?" he asked, slightly embarrassed by her steady scrutiny.

"Nothing. Shall we go?"

They made their way back towards the gate and maintained their silence until they had safely left the panchayat leader's house and were making their way through the winding village streets. Finally, Harsha said: "I shouldn't have pissed him off. It was a stupid mistake, a rookie mistake, imposing my views in an interview."

"Relax, Harry, he was being incredibly sensitive. And you got some good information from him."

"In stories, people are always able to talk to suspects about murders and gauge their reaction. They don't write stories where people just refuse to talk to you or cut you short — or where you make a mistake and cock it up," Harsha said, bitterly.

He was silent until they crossed the concrete houses and reached the clay huts that indicated the poorer, low-caste section of the village.

"You are being too hard on yourself, Harry. You did a good job. You got him to tell you a lot of stuff."

Instead of being consoled, he felt irritated by what he felt was her condescension.

"Maya, I have worked as a journalist for ten years. I should have known better."

"Why are you attacking me? I am just trying to help!"

"Well, just, I don't know..." he mumbled. Harsha took a deep breath and then said: "What did you think of him?"

Maya pursed her lips. "Do I think he is capable of murder? Yes, absolutely. He more or less hinted that he had done it before, when dealing with moneylenders."

"Did he?" Harsha asked, smiling. "I think he was very careful not to do that."

Maya opened her mouth, but before she could respond, a voice rang out from behind them.

"Maya madam! Madam!"

"What now?" Harsha muttered.

They turned to see a young woman of about twenty standing there, a stack of twigs and firewood in her hands. Harsha recognised her as one of the cleaners.

"Oh hello, Leela!" Maya said warmly, stepping back towards her. "I haven't seen you for a few days! How are you?"

Leela came right up to them, smiling and greeting Maya like a long-lost friend. Harsha stood there awkwardly, noticing little details like how Maya's bun had come untied, and the single dimple on Leela's right cheek as she talked.

He was just about to suggest that they move on, when Leela said, hesitantly, "Madam — will you come and eat with us?" She looked like she regretted her question as soon as it came out and she looked down at her feet.

"Of course, Leela!" Maya said at once, and the woman looked up and smiled beautifully, Harsha thought.

Maya looked back at Harsha, who said: "Go ahead, I'll see you later."

Leela said: "But sir, you must come as well! My father has wanted to meet you!"

"Wanted to meet me?" Harsha asked in surprise.

She stepped forward and lowered her voice. "We all know that Azhar sir has asked you to find out who killed Lakshmi!"

Maya and Harsha looked at each other in blank shock, and then

Maya burst out laughing.

"Leela, that's not true! Is that what everyone is saying? The whole village?" Harsha asked sharply, panicking at the thought of the inspector's reaction to this rumour if it reached him.

"No, sir! Only the people who work in the resort! They are saying you are a detective from England!"

"Good god! This is terrible! It's not true, Leela, not true at all! I need to speak to Azhar about this, God knows what he's been telling everyone! Leela, I am just a journalist, and I am not investigating anything!" Harsha said, his voice sounding panicky and whiny in his own ears.

"He is just being modest, Leela," Maya said, her voice bubbling over. "He is a detective — in London he is known as 'Tintin'."

"Dammit, Maya..."

Leela looked at the pair of them one after the other, confusion on her face.

"Sir, will you come or not? I don't have anything special to eat, but still it would be wonderful..."

Harsha glanced at his watch. It was 3 pm, and he was meeting the inspector at 6 pm (assuming the tenuous appointment was still on).

"Of course, Leela," he said finally. "At least to make it clear to your father that I am not a detective."

Leela smiled and led them to one of the clay huts. It was dark apart from a small lamp in the corner, but after Leela had set the twigs alight in the tiny clay oven on the side, they could see around clearly.

Small as the place was, it was decorated with various inexpensive ornaments and one lovely Persian rug, which Harsha guessed must have been a present. He felt oddly moved by the clear effort that had been put into making the tiny hut a home.

Shortly, a wizened old man came out from what must have been the only other room in the house and put his hands together in greeting. He could not have been above forty-five, but farm work had both strengthened his limbs and aged him at the same time, giving him an impressive set of wrinkles around his eyes and mouth.

"Myself Dasa," he said, twisting his slender body into a sort of bow, before carefully sitting down and arranging his limbs into a cross-legged seated position.

"I am Harsha, pleasure to meet you, sir."

The man turned his face enquiringly to Maya, who hadn't said anything, but Harsha cut in.

"This is my companion, Maya. But you can call her Snowy. Ow!" he rubbed his arm where Maya had pinched him. "That hurt, you..."

"You...?"

"Snowy. Female dog. You know, a bi... Ow! Stop pinching me!"

Harsha turned to daughter and father, who were looking at them indulgently. *They think we are husband and wife*, Harsha thought embarrassedly.

They chatted awkwardly for a bit, as Leela went away to prepare some food, and then Dasa looked at Harsha and said: "You are trying to find out who did it?"

"Who did what?" Harsha asked, though he knew the answer.

The man pointed to his daughter, who was now heating something over the stove, the spicy smell of sambar filling the little hut as she stirred.

"It could have been her, you know," Dasa said heavily. "The previous day she was walking up that mountain path. Sir, we have our hopes on you."

"Please, Mr Dasa, don't have your hopes on me! Whatever people say, I am not a detective. And I am not investigating this crime, I was just asking some questions to get some background. If you want answers, you need to go to the police!"

The old man shook his head. "The police, they are no good. They don't stand for us. They just beat us. When they took my daughter for questioning, do you know what I was doing?"

Harsha shook his head.

"Praying. I just lay in the temple and prayed that they would not harm her."

"Appa, I was perfectly safe," Leela said in embarrassment. "Gautami madam is very good to us."

The man shook his head. "She knows nothing about the world," he confided in Harsha, cocking his head towards his daughter, much to her irritation. "We are nothing to the police. Not even human. Only you treat us as human, both of you. And Azhar sir, god bless him, even if he is a Muslim, he is still a good man."

Harsha wisely let that last remark pass. "The inspector is an intelligent man," he said, instead. "If anyone can find the killer it is him. We are just ordinary people."

The old man leaned forward: "Sir, with respect, you are not. You are *educated* people. Educated people have changed the world. Look at Gandhi, he was an educated man. Educated people have a voice, they can make a difference — they have the platform. That is why we are asking you and not doing it ourselves. The inspector, he may be intelligent, but he is part of the police. The police are not for us."

Leela put out banana leaves in front of Maya and Harsha. "There is no vegetable to go with the *sambar sadam*," she said apologetically. "But I do have some *appalam*." She opened a tin box and soon the air was loud with the crackling of frying *appalams*.

Though he had had lunch, Harsha enjoyed his meal thoroughly.

"Absolutely delicious," he said, with perfect honesty, as he dug his fingers into the steaming food in front of him. Leela and Dasa beamed at his obvious enjoyment of the simple meal.

"Leela, are you coming back to work for Azhar?" Maya asked.

She did not answer but looked at her father. He shook his head firmly.

She smiled sadly and said: "My father won't change his mind."

"What will you do for money?"

"Right now, Azhar sir is continuing to pay my salary. He is not accepting my resignation, he wants me to think about it before I quit completely."

"He is a very good man," the father said, only a little grudgingly.

Harsha and Maya glowed in the reflected glory of their friend.

They left the hut in an hour, their earlier argument forgotten, and both of them lit up with the warmth of the house they had just left.

Finally, Maya said: "Just when you despair for this country, you meet some people who make you feel like there's no better place in the world."

The sun had come out, and they walked in silence, enjoying the view of the mountainside and the farmland ahead of them.

"What do you make of all this detective stuff?" he asked, trying to sound casual.

She shrugged. "I think it gives them some hope. Just try not to think about it."

"Oh yeah," he said. "Good plan."

He thought about expressing some of the anxiety that had risen up in him. The conversation with Leela had transformed the whole thing from an exciting game, a way of redeeming a floundering career, into something far more serious and burdensome. The hopes of other people were now resting on his shoulders, and with a feeling of horror, he realised that their faith was utterly misplaced.

What was he, after all? A glorified clerk, putting together other people's work and publishing it as though it was his. Not a true journalist, though even that may not have been enough to justify this level of expectation on him.

"Penny for your thoughts," Maya said, linking her arm with his, and driving all his anxieties away.

"Oh... Never mind. What a beautiful evening!"

They walked slowly back, drinking in the serene beauty of the mountainside.

17. INSPECTOR

After a refreshing shower, Harsha swapped his formal clothes for jeans and a T-shirt and walked on his own up the mountain path. He had insisted to his friends that he do it on his own, so Maya and Shane had decided to watch a movie and wait for his news when he returned.

All the trekking must have been doing him good, because he panted a lot less this time round, and he reached the point of the path closest to the scene of the crime relatively sweat free.

He looked around and shivered. This was the first time he had come back here since they had found the body, and the scene was as spooky as he remembered it. The grass waved in the evening breeze, while the crooked skeleton tree stood guard over the meadow. Harsha turned away from the forest, unable to stop imagining creatures crawling out of the dark between the trees.

He pulled out his cigarettes to give himself some sign of normality and was about to light one when a voice behind him said: "That's not good for health, you know."

Harsha jumped, burning his finger in the lighter flame in the process.

"Inspector! I half expected you not to come," he said, turning to face Inspector Palanivel.

The policeman was dressed in his uniform, but with a thick jacket over it, his calculating eyes regarding Harsha steadily from over his neat moustache. Noticing Harsha looking at his jacket, the severity of his face eased into a small smile and he said: "I am used to the heat. This cold weather does not suit me."

Looking at Harsha's T-shirt in turn, he pointed to the cannon insignia over the breast pocket and said: "Arsenal?"

"Yes!" Harsha said, looking at the man in surprise.

"My son," Palanivel said by way of explanation, breaking into a genuine smile. "He supports Manchester United."

Shaking his head in disbelief at this proof of the English Premier

League's remarkable popularity in India, Harsha said: "And how are you, inspector?"

"Fine," the man said, reverting to his curt manner.

They stood in awkward silence for a minute, not knowing how to proceed. The evening had turned truly chilly and Harsha rubbed his shoulders for a minute in a vain attempt to keep himself warm, envying the other man's thick jacket. The inspector stood there wordlessly, standing against the dark line of the forest.

Finally, the policeman said: "So, Mr Devnath. Why don't you tell me what you have been doing over the last few days?"

The sentence seemed to break some reserve between them, and Harsha took a deep breath.

"Well, I have been speaking to a few people in this area," he said.

He briefly brought the inspector up to date on his conversations with the various resort employees and villagers, finishing with the recently concluded meeting with Rajaratnam.

To his surprise (and gratification), the policeman took notes as Harsha spoke, squinting at the pages and occasionally biting the back of his Reynolds pen. It was strange to be on the other side of the notebook, so to speak.

When Harsha finished, Palanivel said, surprisingly: "Why don't we walk a little bit into the forest."

"Into the... sure," Harsha said, feeling slightly nervous.

They waded through the grass, past the crooked tree — Harsha noticed that the grass had been chopped down in a wide circle around the tree, about a 10-foot diameter around it — and towards the forest.

The inspector led him slightly uphill to a gap in the trees, beyond which was a small clearing. The light was immediately dimmer and had a greenish quality to it. The policeman sat on a fallen trunk, placed his open notebook on one knee, and motioned for Harsha to sit beside him. Once they sat there, there was a clear view through the trees to the path.

"This would be a perfect spot for..." Harsha stopped.

"For what, Mr Devnath?"

For lying in wait for someone who would go along the path, Harsha thought, but he didn't say it out loud.

The inspector nodded as though he had heard the unspoken

words. "Exactly," he said.

"Do you have any idea who did it?"

"Yes."

Harsha turned to look at the man. "You do? You know who did it?"

"I didn't say that. You asked if I have any ideas. Yes, I do have some ideas. But right now I don't know how likely they all are. Do you have any ideas?" Palanivel asked, looking down at the path in front of them.

Harsha hesitated. Clearly, one of them would have to take the leap of faith, and he suspected it would have to be him. "Is this between us?" he asked.

"Strictly between us."

"Having spoken to a lot of people in the village, it seems there are two people who have a motive. I don't know how strong the motive is, but they do have a motive."

He paused, but Palanivel continued to stare down at the pathway without saying anything. So Harsha continued: "Firstly, there's Rajaratnam. It seems he wants to buy Pipal Resorts, and that he was interested in Lakshmi. It could be a bid for power in the region — a way to teach her a lesson and to destroy Azhar's reputation and get what he wants."

Harsha looked sideways at Palanivel and thought he saw him nod slightly. But he wasn't going to continue without hearing something from the inspector. After a brief silence, the inspector said: "He is definitely a person of interest. As you say, he has motive and ability. He could have ordered someone to do it as well as do it himself. Good. Anyone else?"

Harsha took a deep breath and said: "Then there's Laurent. I'm not sure about this one, but it seems he was in love with Lakshmi, but she wanted nothing to do with him. He also seems to be lying about how upset he is, which I find suspicious."

This argument seemed a bit thin to Harsha as he said the words out loud, but to his surprise, the inspector looked impressed and even took out his notebook again to write it down. "The oldest motive — unrequited love," he said. "That's good work, Mr Devnath. I hadn't known about this love interest. It is something we should keep an eye on."

Harsha nodded, feeling oddly proud at this rare bit of praise. All his work hadn't been in vain after all.

"Anything I should know, inspector?" he asked, feeling it was about time he got some information in return.

Palanivel scraped the floor with one heavy boot and then sighed before saying: "You told me about your conversation with the priest. Did you consider him as a possible culprit as well?"

Harsha's head snapped towards his companion's in surprise. "Maheshwaran Shastri? Wow. Seriously? I hadn't even thought of him. He seemed to be very emotionally attached to Lakshmi."

"But that's exactly it. Where there is a violent emotion, you have to keep an eye on it. Also, I do believe Lakshmi was responsible for all the dalits entering the temple? That was a humiliation for the priest, wasn't it?"

"Was it?" Harsha felt like an idiot for not scrutinising this better.

Once again, Palanivel seemed to show that knack for reading his mind, saying: "Don't just believe what people tell you, Mr Devnath. I am told this priest was livid with anger because of the dalit situation. He has lost all his engagements — no one hires him for weddings or funerals anymore. Lakshmi more or less robbed him of his livelihood. That's intelligence from one of my constables, Gautami. And she is very thorough."

"I am a journalist — I know that you're not just supposed to believe what people tell you," Harsha said with asperity, though inwardly he burned with embarrassment. How could he have missed this completely?

"Don't take offence. You have no experience of murder investigations. You learn by making mistakes," Palanivel said, sounding almost human.

As though to make up for this, the man then said: "I believe you are leaving out one other person of interest, Mr Devnath. One person you have been careful not to mention."

The blood rose to Harsha's face. He could only be talking about one person.

"If you are talking about Azhar," Harsha began, hotly. "Yes — I don't consider him a suspect. What possible motive could he have? This whole situation has brought him nothing but grief!"

Palanivel stood up from the tree trunk and brushed off the seat of his trousers. "Too many people have mentioned his name for us to ignore it."

"Just because he is a Muslim. He has no motive," Harsha muttered and watched the inspector shrug his shoulders.

"No motive that we know of," he said. And then in a kinder tone, he added: "Walk with me. Let's look at the scene of the crime again."

They walked between the two large trees again and waded across the tall grass. The light had fallen significantly since their conversation began, and Harsha now had to strain to see in the silvery evening light.

"The other thing that you couldn't know, is that there have been some strange men in this region, doing some illegal sand quarrying by a nearby lake," Palanivel said as he walked, hands clasped behind his back.

Harsha wondered how sand could have any value, but felt there were more important matters at hand, so he didn't say anything.

The inspector continued as he stomped on a particularly stubborn bit of grass: "Some of the men were spotted coming this way that evening. And there, in that spot where we just were sitting, I found many footprints and an empty bottle of rum half hidden in the sand, and a few other signs of people having been there."

"What will you do?" Harsha asked, trying to hide his disappointment at this completely unexpected development.

The inspector shrugged. "We will have to wait until they come again to try and catch and question them. It will not be easy — there will be many of them and not enough of us."

"What about fingerprints on the bottle, DNA samples?"

"Oh yes, you saw our crime lab when you came to the station didn't you?" the man said with heavy sarcasm. He sighed and added: "If this were Chennai we could run some DNA samples and try and match them with the crime database. But I had to send what we had to Chennai. It could take several months for it to return."

"Several *months?*"

"Yes Mr Devnath!" he said, sharply. "This is not America or England. Things move slowly and there is a huge backlog of those types of requests."

He sighed again. "But in any case, there *is* no database. So even if we get the samples, what will we match it against? No, we have to do this the old-fashioned way."

Harsha looked at him quizzically.

"By questioning them," Palanivel explained.

"Ah, I see!" Harsha tried not to think about how this questioning would proceed.

A wind picked up, flowing over the top of the hill and moaning through the tall grass. The skeleton tree looked more foreboding than ever. Harsha wrapped his arms around himself and thought of every warm jacket he had left behind in his room and back in England.

After a few minutes, he said through chattering teeth: "This is very interesting, but why are you here today if you believe it could be these... sand robbers? All that I have told you could be irrelevant!"

The inspector started tracing random shapes on the ground with his boot again.

"Because," he said finally, "It still doesn't make sense."

Against his better judgement, Harsha felt his hopes rise again. Naturally, he wanted the case to close, Lakshmi to get justice and for Azhar to get his resort back to normal. But something in him wanted the case to be more complex, and, if he was honest with himself, he wanted to be involved in cracking it open.

"In what way?" he asked.

Speaking slowly, the inspector said: "*Why*? Why would they do it?"

"Inspector, you hear of many rape cases in India, a few drunk men, a woman on her own... It happens."

"Yes, but why come all the way here? And find this," the inspector gestured around the clearing, "Find this spot? How did they even know it exists? Everything about this murder says to me it was premeditated. Not just a chance encounter. And if it was premeditated — the killer was someone she knew well."

Harsha opened his mouth and then closed it again. He thought of the little spot they had just sat in, pictured a killer waiting there for Lakshmi, and his shivering increased.

"Don't worry," the inspector said, smiling. "I don't expect you to know the answer. I'm just thinking aloud."

"Inspector," Harsha said hesitantly. "I still don't understand why you are telling me all this."

This time the pause was even longer, and the boot made several more shapes on the ground. "Mr Devnath, all my colleagues believe the case is as good as closed. Once we catch the men in the quarry, they think we will get the answer we need."

"But you think there is more?"

"Yes."

"And you want me to help?"

Another pause, and then: "Yes."

"But how? Sir, I know that I am the one who approached you in the first place. But now everyone seems to think I am a detective, and I am not! I don't even know where to begin, what more I can do?"

The man stood up, put his notebook into one of his capacious pockets, and said: "You are right, Mr Devnath. It is very stupid of me, I can't expect you to help in this case. Once we have the killers, this case is likely to be closed. Just forget I said anything. Let's go."

He pulled a torch out of the jacket pocket and a stream of light fell onto the path in front of them, and the inspector slowly walked down the path without waiting to see if Harsha followed.

Slightly taken aback at the premature end to the meeting, Harsha pulled out his own tiny torch from the back of his trousers and flicked it on, the two streams of light waving crazily over the meadow as he hurried to join his companion.

As they walked back towards the path, the inspector asked casually: "Do you come walking here often?"

"This is the first time I have come here since the night of the... the incident."

Palanivel nodded as they reached the path. "I think we have investigated this scene quite thoroughly and found everything there is to find. But I don't suppose there was anything else that someone found?" the man asked, still in the casual tone.

With a thrill of insight, Harsha recognised a version of his own strategy of asking the most crucial question after the notebook was closed.

Except, he had no clue why this question was so important.

He racked his brains as to why something may have been missing.

"What sort of thing?" he asked, mimicking the inspector's casual tone, as they rounded the hill and caught sight of Arasur village below them.

"Oh... anything at all. A lighter, a card, an item of jewellery."

Harsha frowned. "Do you think someone stole Lakshmi's jewellery after she died?"

"Oh no! She did not own anything of real value. And it was all on her. These people usually keep their expensive jewellery locked away in a bank or something even if they have any."

"So we are talking about jewellery?"

"Oh no no no... nothing in particular. Jewellery was just an example," the inspector said quickly.

Harsha was tired of this game. He stopped in his tracks, gritting his teeth. The inspector walked on a few steps before realising his companion was no longer by his side. He turned around, and Harsha just looked at him. Having turned a corner in the road, he could see the resort beyond the inspector. Beyond that he could see vast stretches of farmland and Ramananpettai at the bottom of the valley, the lights coming on in houses.

"Inspector, if you want my help, you need to tell me everything. Why is this piece of jewellery or whatever so important?" Another thought clicked into place, and he added: "Clearly you thought it was important, because you cleared the grass around the body to look for it."

The inspector walked back uphill, covering the few steps between them, and stood right in front of Harsha, perhaps one foot away, and looked full into his face. *What if he kisses me*, Harsha thought wildly.

"Mr Devnath, I do not want this to go beyond the two of us."

Harsha nodded.

The inspector sighed and said: "I have seen many dead bodies. I may not be a scientist or a forensics expert but I have enough experience to read the signs."

"I never doubted your..."

The inspector cut in: "This victim was killed violently and possibly raped as well. I have seen that before, more times than I wish to count. There was only one thing unusual. The fingers on her left hand were broken."

Harsha looked at him, puzzled. "You said it was a violent crime?"

"The fingers were broken after she died."

A silence fell as light continued to fade. It was scary how quickly it became dark on the mountain.

"Are you sure?"

"Absolutely. Like I said, this is not the first dead body I have seen. The fingers were broken like twigs, and there was no blood, just congealed flesh. It must have been quite easy to do it, the body becomes very brittle after death."

Harsha had a horrible image of eating grilled prawns, snapping them into two to get at the flesh. He decided on the spot to go vegetarian for a while.

"And that's not all. There were flakes of gold in her hand," the inspector said heavily.

"Flakes of... and what does that mean?"

"It means that whatever was in her hand was gold. Or gold-plated."

The inspector walked a few further yards uphill, looking up the path as though he could still see the dead body. "She grabbed something from one of her attackers," he said, mimicking the movement with his hand. "Probably something valuable or recognisable. Maybe they didn't even notice at the time. But later on, probably in the three days the woman was lying here, someone came and took it from her hand. Maybe even the night you found the body."

"I swear, it wasn't me. I didn't even touch the body, it looked so horrible!"

Palanivel turned and looked at Harsha. "I believe you," he said heavily. "But this is why I called you in for questioning. I wanted to know if anyone else had touched the body. You told me no one did."

Harsha scanned his memory once more. He said, slowly: "I am certain no one did. At least as far as I was there, but it was very chaotic with all the women crying. I can't speak for sure, because there were people there when I left."

"Who was?"

Harsha thought for a moment and said: "Just Azhar, I think, and maybe the driver Selvam and Murugayya. A couple of men... the women had left at that point, yes, I am sure of it. Yes, I remember

Maya was sick, so I took her down to the resort. Sorry inspector, I can't remember any better than that."

They started walking back towards the resort, and they both held their torches steady so that they could see the path. Every time something gleamed on the path, Harsha's heart rate rose, expecting it to be the missing bit of jewellery. But it was always just dew on grass or a plastic wrapper or something equally disappointing.

They reached the resort, the light of the central dining room building shining brightly in the darkening evening.

"A coffee, inspector? Or dinner?"

The man shook his head and instead said: "That conversation was between us?"

"Absolutely."

"You will not tell your friends? Not even Mr Azhar?"

Harsha hesitated. "I will tell him you are close to finding the killers. But perhaps nothing about the jewellery."

The inspector nodded, hesitated and then said: "I have a feeling, Mr Devnath, that if we find that piece of jewellery — it will lead us to the killer. All the background information you gave me was important — even crucial. But I have a strong instinct that finding this item is the most important thing now. Can I give you one piece of advice, Mr Devnath?"

"Of course."

The man came up to him, his eyes gleaming in the light of the dining room.

"Don't trust anyone," he said.

Harsha bristled in indignation, but before he could say anything, Palanivel was gone, swallowed up in the darkness, with only the bobbing light of the torch indicating his presence.

18. NIGHTMARES

Harsha didn't say anything to anyone that evening, instead pleading a headache and going to lie in his room. The hurt in Azhar's eyes was palpable — he had planned a 'party' for them, with alcohol and music. Normally Harsha would have forced himself to go, but today he physically could not handle it. Instead, he had another hot shower — his third for the day — turned off the lights and lay in bed, staring at the ceiling. The noise of crickets was a welcoming sound, a lullaby almost.

But it could not stop the image playing in his head in a loop — a disfigured rotting figure lying in the grass, flies crawling through the nostrils, insects sitting on the open eyes, a mysterious figure looming over it, its shadow falling across the slashed body, and then bending to gently lift the closed hand, and then pulling the fingers back, back, back, until... Snap!

He shifted in his bed. Think of something else!

Think of your happiest memory, he said to himself. Walking down the corridor of City University London's main hall, getting that phone call, finding out he had that job at *The Times* after several rounds of interviews and writing exercises, that burst of exhilaration and joy and relief...

A wave of homesickness hit him — homesickness for London! How strange, he thought, remembering the repeated waves of homesickness that had overcome him in his first two years in England. Was he going to ever be able to move back to India, having gotten used to life in England? That fear seemed ridiculous in the light of recent events, with Lakshmi's body rotting somewhere, waiting to be cremated.

He turned the other way in bed, punching the pillow.

No wonder Maya had had nightmares, he thought to himself. He had been indulgent but not understanding of her fear and unwillingness to sleep alone.

Right now, he felt immensely lonely and afraid — afraid of the darkness outside. He avoided looking at the window — another throwback to his childhood, when after his mother read out some fairytale or the other, he would be consumed by the fear that a ghost's face would appear any minute at the window.

He turned determinedly away from the window and sighed.

"Harsha, are you alright? You look terrible!"

Harsha paused on his way down towards the main dining hall and looked at the woman in mingled exasperation and amusement.

"Thank you, Leela!" he said with heavy irony. "Hang on... When did you come back?"

"Came back to work today! Couldn't leave the other girls to do all the work," she said, smiling at him, a few palm trees dancing in the morning breeze behind her.

Her frank conversation was refreshing after the bashfulness displayed by other members of staff when talking to Harsha. He also noted with relief that she had dropped the "sir" when talking to him.

"And your father?"

She tossed her head. "He will just have to put up with it. He finally agreed when I said that you would take care of me."

"Me? Why me?" he asked in horror.

"Don't worry! I don't expect you to keep me safe!"

"Thank god for that."

"Maya will," she said, and winked at him and picked up a container that was by his feet and walked away, looking roguishly at him from over her shoulder.

Shaking his head but smiling for what felt like the first time in days, Harsha walked towards breakfast.

The despondency came over him again as he reached the door.

"Er, Leela!" he shouted, looking into the empty dining room.

She peeped out from around the corner of the building.

"Yes?"

"Sorry, Leela, but where is everyone?"

"Oh! Sorry, they are sitting under the tree," she said and disappeared.

Tree? What tree? Oh — the pipal tree that gave the resort its name. Could he be bothered to join them? Why couldn't he just have his breakfast in peace?

He stood on the balls of his feet, indecisive. He finally sighed and walked back towards his room, considering skipping breakfast altogether, but from the corner of his eye he caught movement and he turned to see his friends sitting and chatting happily under the beautiful old tree.

Maybe just a little bite, he thought to himself and made his way there. It was actually the ideal place on a dry, sunny day, and clearly the group had decided to have their breakfast there, the cement structure built for that very purpose under the canopy. Dishes of *sambar* and coconut chutney sat in the centre of the floor, and his friends sat around it along with a woman he did not know, facing away from him. A lone guest, perhaps?

With a tremendous rumble of his stomach, he remembered that he had skipped dinner and also that Ammani was going to make *dosai*. He quickened his step and reached the tree in a few strides, his depression temporarily forgotten.

Maya looked up and smiled at him. "Hallo, sleepy head," she said.

The others turned to him, and Harsha waved to them all. He glanced casually at the fourth person, who had done a double take on seeing him and was now staring at him as though seeing a ghost, mouth open.

"Juni!" Harsha exclaimed.

"Bloody hell!" the woman said, scrambling up and dusting the seat of her jeans.

"Surprise," Azhar called out, grinning.

Juni — or Junaina, as was her actual name — came up and embraced Harsha and then stood back to look at him.

"Looking good, Harry!"

"Thank you! Leela said I look terrible. You look amazing, by the way!"

Junaina waved this compliment aside impatiently and asked, instead: "Leela? Who's this new chick? And how the hell are you, anyway? We haven't heard from you in ages!"

"Doing well, Juni, and you?" Harsha looked Junaina up and down and marvelled at the change in his old friend.

Juni had always had a tomboyish quality about her, going to rock gigs with all the boys, wearing her hair quite short and usually decked in Iron Maiden and Metallica T-shirts and a range of assorted rings and jewellery. This had been replaced by a light grey, stringy top over a pair of well-fitted jeans, and the heavy gold chains were replaced by a single slim silver chain with an "Om" symbol rather than a skull or a fang, as had been the case when they were in university together.

The whole ensemble accentuated her slimness in a way those baggy band T-shirts never had, and she looked far younger and far more feminine than he remembered her, if anything.

"You're looking so different, Juni! Maybe because you're not holding a joint between your fingers," he said.

"You're looking even better man! Lost a hell of a lot of weight. No longer a fat slob," she said, clapping him on the shoulder. The appearance may be different, but the manner and vocabulary was still the same, Harsha reflected wryly.

"Right, I hate to interrupt this loving scene, but I better go to the town and organise the coaches and the trains," Azhar said, getting up and taking his cap out of his pocket and adorning it carefully around his long curls.

"What the hell is this?" Juni said, pulling the cap from his head.

"Oy!" Azhar yelled, grabbing it back. "Show some respect!" He readjusted the cap on his head.

Juni went off into a peal of laughter. "Biggest drunkard in South India now acting like a proper religious boy and all."

"Shut up, idiot, coming to my resort and insulting my religion."

"Insulting your..." Juni turned wide eyes to the other three in turn. "Did I insult his religion? Come on, tell me? What's wrong in just pointing out that..."

"Shut up!"

As Shane and Maya collapsed into giggles from behind the pair, Harsha scanned Azhar's face, currently screwed up in mock outrage, his hands held up in protest.

What had the inspector meant when he said: 'Don't trust anyone'? Surely he couldn't seriously suspect Azhar? Harsha tried to imagine his old friend as a murderer, or even as an accessory to a crime like that. The mind boggled — it just wasn't possible. He realised that he knew Azhar better than almost anyone else in the world — he knew the simplicity of his mind, his flawed sense of morals and his sanguine, but deeply compassionate view of the world. Azhar, a murderer? Ridiculous!

But then, didn't everyone have a dark side? One thing about making literature your main area of study was that you knew what human beings were capable of.

"Oy, why are you looking like a tragic hero?" Junaina said, butting rudely into his thoughts and clapping his shoulder violently in addition.

"No reason. Cigarette, anyone?" Harsha asked, switching off his thoughts and smiling around. He held out his pack, and Azhar took one. Harsha showed the pack to Junaina, who did not take one.

"I've quit. Been six years," she said virtuously.

A stunned silence fell over the group.

"How the ... what the... How on earth did *Ganja Juni* quit smoking?"

"With the help of meditation and God," Juni said, kissing her pendant and touching either eyelid.

To her obvious annoyance, the whole group burst out laughing again.

"Juni's gone religious!"

"Meditation! Wow!"

Azhar, who was hands on knees laughing, said weakly: "Too good man, just too good... But you," he said, straightening up and glaring at Junaina. "Are you a hypocrite or what? Mocking me for observing my faith, while you are..."

"Shut up guys, come on, this is serious!" Junaina pleaded.

Harsha clapped her on the shoulder and said: "Of course it is Junes, proud of you, for quitting smoking anyway. Now you and Maya can go to the local temple together. The priest is a friend of ours."

"Well I'll give it a miss this time, seeing as we're all leaving on Sunday. Such a pity I could only come here for the weekend!" Junaina said, shaking her head. "That wedding, it's not even as if I like that guy and his wife is a bloody pain in the ass."

Harsha sat down next to Maya and ripped a piece of *dosai* out of her plate and put it in his mouth unceremoniously.

"Dude, what are you doing? I'll ask Ammani to get you another plate."

"Too hungry," Harsha said, taking another large piece, dipping it in Maya's cup of sambar and putting it in his mouth.

Junaina looked at Harsha stuffing his face with a mild look of disgust and said: "I thought this chap went to England? How come he has come back even more of a barbarian than before?"

Massaging Harsha's shoulder affectionately, Maya said: "Leave him! Poor guy didn't have dinner yesterday, he is really tired. And by the way, we are not leaving on Sunday! We are staying until Tuesday at least. Maybe longer."

"What! Really? All of you?" Juni said, looking at Shane and Harsha.

"Yes of course, all of..." Maya paused when she caught sight of Harsha's face. "Harsha? You are staying, right?"

He swallowed his mouthful, banished the memory of his nightmares of the previous night, and said indignantly: "Of course I'm staying!"

"Good man!"

"Man, you had scared me there for a second," Azhar said, grinning from ear to ear. "What made you ask that question, Maddy? Of course he's staying! We're all staying and gonna have some good times!"

But Harsha only had eyes for Maya, who was looking at him in a way that was making his heart stop.

"Awesome!" Juni said, cutting into the moment. "Party time, boys and girls! I am only flying back to New York next weekend so I can stay as well! That is, if Azhar can change my train ticket?"

Azhar grinned and said: "Only if you go to the mosque with me."

"Eh? What on earth kind of logic is that?"

Harsha dragged his eyes away from Maya's face and said: "Come on Azhar, we'll all go with you! I've always wanted to go to a mosque!"

Azhar licked his lips and then said: "There's no mosque anywhere near here!" He looked triumphantly around as though he had scored a point.

"Don't you have to be somewhere?" Shane asked.

Azhar started and said: "Oh yes. And you're coming with me!"

Shane and Azhar left, chattering away about something in low voices.

"Get me some cigarettes!" Harsha called out after them. Azhar acknowledged this with a wave of his hand.

Maya looked at their retreating figures. "Do you get the feeling..."

"... that they are up to something? Yes," Harsha said.

"Never mind them dude!" Junaina said, sitting down opposite Harsha and looking at him with keen interest. "How are you man? What are you up to? How's work? Got a girlfriend?"

"One question at a time!" Harsha said, holding his hands up and laughing. "Ok, hold that thought — all questions will have to wait," he said, his eyes on Ammani, who was approaching with a wide plate piled with *dosais*.

19. AN ENDING

A tentative plan to trek through the forest that afternoon fell apart quickly, mostly thanks to the drowsiness of the beautiful sunny day. They chatted through the morning and into the afternoon, when Ammani came up, smiling, and asked if they would like to have their lunch in their spot under the pipal tree as well.

So, they ate there, having more or less sat around under the tree for half a day, and then Junaina went away to shower and change.

Maya looked at Harsha and smiled. She felt immensely satisfied and happy to be there with him, all vestiges of awkwardness between them gone.

"You look really tired, Harsha, your eyes are bloodshot. Maybe you should go back and have a nap. I'll wake you up when the others come," she said.

"What, get up and walk all the way back? No way!" Harsha said, yawning. "Even the thought of getting up is so tiring!"

He stretched out on the concrete, trying to get himself into a comfortable position. He stretched this way and that like a cat. Laughing at his discomfort, Maya moved into a cross legged position and then said: "Come, sleep on my lap."

"You'll be bored, just sitting here," he said, his voice already slurring with sleep.

"Don't worry, I have some thinking to do," she said.

He made no objection, instead putting his head on her lap and, presently, he started snoring gently. She smiled down on him. His mouth was slightly open, but he looked peaceful, she thought. She looked around — there was no one nearby, so she gently stroked his hair, pushing it out of his eyes.

What was going on with her? She had asked herself this question several times over the last few days.

Being apart from Naveen made her realise that in an odd way, she had grown to love her husband. She loved his forbearance of her many moods and his constant desire to please her — he was the rock that held the marriage together, doing everything he could to make her happy.

But... Harsha. God, there was so much history between them. A history of what-might-have-been, admittedly, unlike with Azhar, whom she had actually dated for a couple of years. But she looked at Harsha now, and she felt far more attracted to him than she had ever had with Azhar.

Men always thought women wanted a strong, macho man with a chiselled body, but that was not quite right. A man who knew his mind, yes that was attractive. The warmth and passion, that feeling of being safe with someone dependable, even if he had a slight paunch, she thought, looking at Harsha's midriff. Yes, she knew she could depend on Harsha in the same way she could depend on her husband — but there was also an unpredictability about Harsha missing in Naveen — a sudden anger that came into his eyes from time to time at something in the world that didn't fit his idea of right and wrong.

And sometimes that anger was directed at her. She responded to that, even if she raged back and insulted him at times.

Give me anything but the docile acceptance of every irrational thing I say or do, she thought, thinking of her husband, and then she felt a horrible guilt roiling inside her for comparing the poor IT software coder working away in the US with this other man who was lying in her lap.

What was she doing? She asked herself that again even as her fingers automatically went to Harsha's cheek and stroked it lightly.

She started when his eyes opened slightly. He smiled, caught hold of her hand, and mumbled: "I feel safe with you, Maya. No nightmares, no nightmares at all." And his eyes closed again. She held his hand tightly and sat and thought.

Azhar and Shane came back around 2 pm, and stopped in their tracks, looking at the scene in front of them: Harsha lying in Maya's lap and clasping her hand tightly.

"What the hell is this, dude," Azhar said quietly to Shane.

"None of our business, anyway."

"I just don't want some angry parents coming after me and saying that their daughter's marriage was ruined in my resort," Azhar mumbled.

"Then you don't know Maya," Shane said calmly. "She won't leave her husband just like that."

"Why not? Lots of people are getting divorced nowadays, even in India."

"Azhar *bhai*, trust me, you have nothing to worry about."

At this point, Maya saw them and hurriedly let go of Harsha's hand.

"Azhar! Shane! Er... He was just tired!" Maya said, her face reddening.

Harsha woke up with a start. "Wassamatter," he said blearily. "Oh - hey guys."

He raised his head and brushed against Maya's shoulder and broke away quickly, both of them red in the face now.

"We... Was just tired," he said by way of explanation.

"Bugger, I'm not your father," Azhar said. He threw a packet of cigarettes on Harsha's stomach, as though providing proof of this statement.

Harsha clasped it gratefully and began to break the seal.

"We... Any coffee going?"

Azhar bellowed without warning: "Ammani! Ammani."

"Yes, sir?" came a voice from the depths of the kitchen.

"Some coffee please!"

They listened as Ammani in turn yelled the same instructions to someone else, evidently at an even further distance away.

"God, what lungs," Harsha said, thickly.

Azhar started making suggestive gestures in front of his chest but seeing Maya, he quickly dropped his hands.

She giggled and said: "Don't be so embarrassed Azhar, I dated you remember? I'm used to your cheap ways."

"Hello, at least I only talk, unlike Prince Harry here who was happily snuggling up to you."

"Azhar! For god's sake dude!" Harsha snapped.

Shane and Azhar roared with laughter at his discomfiture, and even Maya was grinning.

"What's all this? You guys are scaring off all the birds," came a penetrating voice from the houses and Harsha turned to see Junaina walking up towards them, changed and looking refreshed. "What are you all laughing about?"

"Er, I better go brush my teeth," Harsha said, standing up and looking everywhere except at Maya.

"Hang on, Tintin, we have some news for you," Shane said, sitting on the edge of the concrete.

Harsha looked enquiringly at him, but it was Azhar who answered.

"It's all done."

"What is?" Harsha asked, shaking his head to try and dispel some of the grogginess.

"The case. All solved."

Maya's eyes opened wide and she felt Harsha go alert beside her.

"What? How?" she asked.

"Last night, the police caught some people who were doing illegal quarrying or something, and they confessed to the crime this morning. Just heard 'off the record' from the inspector," Azhar said. He clapped Harsha on the shoulder and added: "He said to thank you for your help, and that he owes you an interview if you still want to write an article about this case."

"Oh... Good," Harsha said. Maya thought he looked devastated. As far as she was concerned, she just wanted Lakshmi's murderer to be brought to justice. Her heart was pounding as she listened to Azhar speak.

"The hell are you guys talking about?" Junaina asked. "What case?"

They all ignored her.

"Man, aren't you happy?" Azhar said, looking at Harsha. "It's all over! We can just enjoy the holiday now! And pretty soon I will start getting guests again! I don't have to sell to that panchayat dude and it will be profitable again!"

And indeed, Maya noticed now that Azhar looked a lot more bubbly and carefree, as though the weight of the world had been lifted from his shoulders.

Ammani came up to them at that point with a pot of coffee and several cups, which she placed carefully on the stone dais.

"Ammani! Dance with me!" Azhar said, and grabbed her hands and began to waltz on the grass.

"Sir! Sir!" she said, laughing and panting at the effort. The others went into paroxysms of laughter while Shane started clapping in time to the dance, a big grin on his face.

Maya looked at her old boyfriend in wonder - this was the Azhar she remembered from university, spontaneous and completely mad. She hadn't realised that boy was still inside him, waiting to resurface.

Finally, Ammani pushed him away and said: "Sir, I'm warning you my husband has an *aruval*!"

"What *aruval* and all? See this?" Azhar said, pulling up his t-shirt to reveal the six-pack beneath. "No blade can cut through these rock-like abs, Ammani!"

Much as she didn't necessarily want a chiselled man, Maya couldn't help enjoying looking at Azhar's body and she saw Junaina look around in interest as well.

But Ammani just said indulgently: "Shameless boy," and to everyone's utter delight, proceeded to pinch both of her boss's cheeks before walking away.

"What the hell, dude," Azhar said as Ammani withdrew. "This is how my employees talk to me. But who cares! The case is finally closed!"

"What case, you fools?" Junaina asked in exasperation, but again to no avail.

"Azhar, the inspector told me he thought there was more to the story than just these sand quarry thieves," Harsha said, seriously, taking a cup of coffee that Maya had poured for him. "Are you telling me it's all done?"

"Yes, he told me about the cock and bull conspiracy theory he gave you. Now he thinks that's just what happened; these bastards were probably having a cup of tea at the tea shop when they saw Lakshmi walking up the mountain. They followed her all the way up the hill until they reached a lonely spot, and then..."

The unspoken next part was enough to sober them down and bring the mood of the group down a few notches. Maya hunched over her coffee, taking in the aroma of the drink and trying not to tear up.

They sat silently for a bit and then Shane said in his practical way: "Well now that the case is closed, and we know who did it, the police should release her body, so that we can all go to the funeral and pay our respects."

Last Resort

His measured voice had a calming effect on the group, and they all looked up and nodded.

"Azhar, do you really think the guests will start coming back?" Maya asked anxiously. "Surely there will be some concerns about the death..."

Azhar bounced on the balls of his feet. "Will you tell them or shall I?" he asked Shane gleefully.

Smiling, Shane waved him on.

"So, Shanny here had a brainwave. Corporate retreats! He is in charge of team building at his company in Chennai, so he is getting a couple of teams to come here next month! A winter retreat!"

"Wow!" Maya said, putting down her cup.

"Nice idea!" Junaina said approvingly.

"Well done, guys!" Harsha said, smiling affectionately at the pair of them.

" And that's not all!" Azhar bellowed above the hubbub of voices. "After that he is gonna quit and work for me, and organise all the corporate retreats, using his contacts!"

They all stood up and shook hands with the soon-to-be colleagues, clapping them on their shoulders.

Finally Azhar waggled his finger at Shane: "Now I'm gonna be your boss! No more funny stuff, yeah? Better work hard!"

"The minute you start slow dancing with me, Azhar *bhai*, that's the day I quit," Shane said, grinning.

"Man, there's gonna be dancing and partying non-stop!"

Harsha cut in: "Well we should start now! How are we going to celebrate? At least with a glass of bubbly?"

Azhar clapped his hand to his head. "Almost forgot! Have a surprise for you, Harry boy. Old Laurent has agreed to let us watch the Arsenal match on his big screen television. Can't remember who they are playing but it's at 8.30 tonight." He grinned at the look of delight on Harsha's face.

"But... but... You guys don't all want to watch football, do you?"

"We can put up with it for you," Maya said softly, looking at him.

He turned to Azhar. "Man, please don't feel obligated..."

"Dude, just shut up. After everything you have done for me over the last few days? All of you! You have stood by me right through one of the most difficult times in my life," Azhar said fervently, looking around with an almost pathetic expression of gratitude on his face.

Maya couldn't help it. She went across and gave Azhar a hug, trying to put all her own gratitude for his presence into it. Shane came over and put his pudgy arms around the both of them and then Harsha joined as well, making it a massive group hug. Maya felt the emotion almost overwhelm her in that moment, so close did she feel to this group of old friends. How had she managed to live without them for all these years after university?

"Goddamn it all!" They broke out of their hug and turned in surprise to Junaina, who was sitting on her own by the coffee pot and clutching at her forehead in frustration. "Is one of you fuckers going to explain to me what the hell is going on or not? What case are you blabbering about, dickheads?"

Laughing, Shane walked over to her and grasped her by the arm, pulling her gently upwards. "We are going up to Azhar's office now to have a drink. Let me fill you in on the way," he said, gently.

This was the cue for them all to get up and slowly make their way uphill towards Azhar's office, abandoning their coffees by the beautiful pipal tree.

Harsha hung back for a second and turned to look downhill at the mountainside stretching all the way down to Arasur and to Ramananpettai beyond. It was the clearest view yet, stretching out for several gorgeous miles.

"You coming, Harry?" Maya called out.

"In a sec! Go ahead!" he said and took a deep breath.

It was over. Initially he had been disappointed — he had been on the scent, feeling like he was finally doing the work that had made him become a journalist. It still hurt that all that work had been completely incidental to the case, but it hadn't been a complete waste. It had made him realise many things, above all else just how much he wanted to be back in India and writing about his country, telling real stories. Maybe he would take up the inspector's invitation to do a full-blown interview.

Now some of Azhar's relief flowed into him, and the whole burden of being the saviour of people like Leela and Dasa was lifted off his shoulders.

He took a deep breath and said out loud: "That's that, then."

He turned and followed his friends. All that was left to do was to enjoy the rest of this holiday.

20. A BEGINNING

Maya went out to get some fresh air. The testosterone in the room was getting a bit too much to handle, and for the hundredth time, her thoughts drifted to her mother.

Maybe it was the champagne she had chugged recklessly earlier that evening, but a euphoric love for her friends had faded, and a gentle melancholy had settled on her instead. Particularly, her last conversation with her mother was still ringing in her ears.

"You've already done enough to ruin my life, so now at least let me finish the job my own way!"

Those had been her words, in a fit of high drama and rage. She could still see her mother standing in front of her, blinking through her spectacles, her mouth turned down in disapproval and sadness.

Sometimes, she thought of that line with tremendous pleasure - it had been poetic, dramatic, and, above all, it had been true. At other times, she thought of the hurt look on her mother's face and her stomach clenched...

On an impulse, she had confessed her suicidal thoughts to Jenny, a colleague in the US. Jenny had jumped up and suggested they go for a walk. She had led Maya to Les Gove Park near their Seattle office and they had sat on the footsteps of the library before Jenny said the words Maya would never forget: "Maya, you must remember that if you end your life, your family will have a lifetime of regret, of wondering 'what if'. What they had done wrong. They would always, always feel guilty for the rest of their lives."

Bad argument! That is exactly what she wanted - she wanted her family to hurt for what they had done to her.

The problem was actually doing it. She remembered standing on the edge of the Aurora bridge, trying to steel herself... It was impossible, terrifying, and she realised that no matter how she felt about her life, she feared death more. Harsha would have quoted Hamlet's "To be or not to be" speech at her if she had confessed this to him, she thought, with a wry twist to her mouth.

She may not have had the guts to go through with the suicide, but that rebellious streak was still coursing through her veins. That's what had made her come here, to Pipal Resorts, in defiance of her family.

For a blessed few days, she had felt normal, like a student again. But now, as the holiday drew to a close, she felt the old resentments resurface and the old rebelliousness boil within her, desperate to find a way out.

She needed to do something crazy, something so off the charts that there was no coming back.

The door creaked open and Harsha came out, cigarette pack in hand.

"Hey."

"Hey."

"I'm so sorry, this must be so boring for you. The football I mean."

She pulled her thoughts back down to earth with an effort and forced a smile: "Not at all, I just needed a break. Seeing you go red in the face and yell at the television screen was priceless."

He shifted his feet sheepishly. "You know, I don't usually get that angry, only when watching football."

"It was very funny, Harry."

He nodded, not looking at her.

She laughed, and he looked up with an answering grin.

She looked at his face carefully. *He has a weird, pointed nose*, she told herself severely. And a weak chin. He wasn't that tall. He was not by any means conventionally attractive.

But it wasn't about that at all, was it? As though she could not sleep with an attractive man if she wanted to. She wasn't vain, but she knew that she was considered beautiful.

"Maya... Are you alright? You look... Strange."

There it was. The concern in his eyes, that feeling that the only thing he ever wanted was her happiness. She knew that's why he had become so angry when she had poured her heart out to him - he was angry that she was unhappy.

It came to her husband sometimes as well, but the poor fool had no idea what made her tick. He thought he could buy her an apartment and an expensive language course, and that would solve all problems. Her mouth twisted.

"Maya, you're scaring me a bit, the way you're looking at me!"

"Come here, I want to check something," she said.

He looked at her, baffled, but he dutifully came closer. She was feeling more and more crazy now so she went right up to him, reached and caught the hair on the back of his head and pulled his face closer to hers, her forearms resting lightly on his shoulders. He was inches away when she stopped him. She took a deep breath, taking in the mingled smell of his aftershave and the nicotine from the cigarettes. Normally she hated the smell of smoking but on this crazy night, it felt forbidden. And therefore — attractive.

She took another deep breath, this time inching closer so that her body was pressed against his and she could feel his heart thumping. She pulled his head down a little so she could look into his eyes, without bothering to be gentle.

"Maya — stop," he breathed.

"Stop what," she said, looking into his eyes. His lashes were unusually long, almost feminine.

"Don't stand... so close to me... I can't keep from ... from kissing you."

"What's stopping you?"

He paused and she saw all the answers flickering in his eyes. You're married, you live in a different country, you dated my best friend, we haven't met for years.

The lashes came down on those expressive eyes once or twice and he opened his mouth to say something, and then he closed them and kissed her. She released his hair and wrapped her hands around his shoulders and kissed him back.

Now his hands were on her hips and then he moved them to the small of her back and pulled her to him, crushing her and knocking the breath out of her body; but she didn't care. She just lost herself in kissing him for what felt like hours.

When she was finally out of breath she broke away and stood there panting.

He looked at her, grinning sheepishly, looking slightly dazed at the turn of events.

"Harry... Harsha..."

"Yes, Maya," he caught hold of her hand and their fingers interlocked.

She wanted to be very clear about this, so she looked him right in the eyes.

"Harry — take me to my room now."

"Er.. ok... why?"

She used her free hand to smack him on the side of the head.

"Why do you think, idiot?"

He grinned a bit more confidently, and said: "Maya, are you sure?"

"At this moment, yes. Tomorrow, I don't know."

He looked at her for a minute and then smiled a little sadly and with his free hand he caught hold of a strand of her hair and ran it between his fingers.

He didn't say anything for a few minutes, and she started to feel a horrible sense of humiliation come over her. What the hell had she done? She, a married woman, had propositioned this man and he was going to reject her, and show a sense of moral awareness that she should have had. It was too much to bear.

"Well?" she asked abruptly, tapping her foot on the floor.

The hand moved to the back of her head and with a slight sense of shock she felt him pull her towards him and kiss her again.

"God, yes!" he said.

Completely mad with the moment, the two of them laughed, and still hand in hand, they walked away from Laurent's porch.

"Wait!"

"What now?" she asked, exasperated.

"Torches. We need them. It's completely dark, not a star to be seen."

She watched in amusement as he slowly, painstakingly, opened the front door and felt for the jackets hung up in the hook behind.

Having fished them out, he turned and ran lightly up towards her and handed her one.

"Let's do it! I mean... er... let's go, I meant."

She laughed at this further evidence of his strange sense of prudery. It had annoyed her in the past, but at the moment everything about him seemed so attractive, even his odd nose.

They began the strange walk back, the light of their torches bobbing up and down, waving side by side, as they hurried towards the resort. It should have been the most romantic thing in the world, but such was their haste it was wasted on them.

Harsha's heart was pounding as he watched the crazy progress of the torchlight in front of him on the forest path. A slight drizzle had started, and they could hear the pattering of the rain on the canopy above them, as a chill rose from the earth.

Earlier in the day, he would have been wracked by moral uncertainty over their decision to sleep together. All such thoughts had fled in the madness of that kiss on the porch of Laurent's beautiful home in the middle of the jungle.

Now he just thought about how much he had hoped for this to happen, from the minute he had Azhar's invitation to come visit this resort. Maya was the unfinished chapter of his youth that always haunted him — and, of late, it had become intricately entwined with the "road not taken" — the life in India he could have led if he had chosen to stay. He blinked, trying to quell the stab of pain this thought gave him.

Never mind that, he said to himself. It's not too late. *You're with Maya now.*

And then a more immediate and more mundane problem rose in his head, and his heartbeat intensified. Sex. It was all very well for it to be a distant, unattainable fantasy, but once faced with the actual prospect, it became so real, that he suddenly felt gripped by a nasty, familiar fear — what if he couldn't perform? He took deep breaths and tried to calm himself. This was not something he needed to fear — while he was hardly a massive player or anything, he had no history of having trouble with physical intimacy.

But this is Maya, a panicky voice inside him reminded his more rational side. A fantasy that had lasted for over a decade and had, until now, gone unfulfilled. He passed his hand over his mouth, wiping off a fleck of rain, and clenched his fist, trying to will the panicked voice to go away.

The rushing of the river grew louder in their ears, overwhelming the sound of rain, as they approached the bridge. Maya ran across it lightly, earning a few warning yells from him as he ponderously and carefully went across. She waited impatiently for him at the other side.

The noise receded as they navigated the footpath. As they proceeded further and further away from the river, his panic receded, and his excitement rose. He clutched Maya's hand next to him and felt the answering pressure.

He saw a gleam of light in front of him and realised they had come to the end of the forest, and now had only to navigate a short stretch of open land before coming back to their room at the high end of the resort. They were about to break cover when he suddenly stopped and clutched Maya's arm, forcing her torch to point to the floor, and flicking his own torch off as quickly as he could.

"What now Harry! This is really getting..."

She felt him clap a hand over her mouth, and the tension in his body transmitted itself to her. She looked up at his face, just about visible in the light of the torch, and then followed his eyes, which were looking straight ahead.

They were on the very edge of the forest, and through the leaves, could spot several torchlight beams drifting across the grass, and shadows crawling around the meadow. Big shadows.

They looked at each other, and they both knew something was very, very wrong.

21. CHASE

Maya brought her lips right up to Harsha's ear, his breathing ragged and loud in her ears.

"Who do you think they are?" she whispered.

He shook his head but what he said, in a hoarse whisper, was: "I would bet my life they are Lakshmi's killers. Or connected with the killing in some way."

"We don't know that," she muttered back. "It could be... I don't know... just some random group of men."

It sounded lame, even in her ears.

Instead of answering her question, Harsha silently pointed to the nearest man. Maya followed his finger and saw what he was indicating.

The man was holding a long sickle, an *aruval*, its blade glinting in the torchlight. A quick scan of the meadow showed that all the men were holding those wicked-looking blades.

This was no midnight jaunt. These were men of violence. And she would bet — Lakshmi's killers. What were they doing here?

Maya recognised that some primitive part of her was going into fight or flight mode. The hackles at the back of her neck were rising and her heart was pounding against her chest. Awful scenarios, each more dreadful than the next, were running through her mind.

They watched as the torchlights moved methodically back and forth across the open space, just beyond the treeline. Two of them were further away, slightly downhill, and another away to the right. One man was much closer.

One of the men idly lopped off a bit of grass with his aruval, and she winced at how the grass fell apart on contact — the blade was strikingly sharp. *Who the hell were these people?*

Suddenly, Maya felt Harsha's body tense again, and he pulled his arms away from her and wrapped them around his face, turning away from the strange scene in front of them.

She realised with a thrill of horror that he was about to cough or sneeze. *Don't do it Harry!* She thought desperately, trying to will him to hold it in.

But to no avail. A rasping noise came from behind his arms and echoed out on to the plain in front of them, clearly audible over the sound of the spitting rain.

The nearest beam of torchlight froze, and without warning, without giving Maya even a second to react, it rose up and caught her full in the face. She couldn't see the man, but he recoiled a step or two at the unexpected sight and then yelled out to the others in a language she didn't know. The torchlight moved from her to Harsha and the man gave another yell.

Harsha was blinking in the light, so she took charge, grabbing his arm, and pulling him back along the footpath. They ran back the way they came, but even with the blood pounding in her head, she could hear men yelling behind her, and then the rustling of plants as they ran through the narrow forest path.

Dammit! Damn you and your bloody *cigarettes, Harry!* she thought as she pelted down the path. Despite her panic, she forced herself to take deep breaths in time with her footfalls, as her marathon training kicked in.

She went against every instinct and slowed down every now and then to let Harsha catch up - he was flagging badly, his breaths coming in painfully rasping intervals.

She mentally cursed every cigarette manufacturer in the world, and went slightly ahead, trying to steady her torch hand so she could keep an eye out for any roots or tree stumps that may trip them up.

Harsha was really struggling to keep up now but after perhaps five minutes of pure, terrified running they reached the fork in the path. Away to the right they could hear the gushing of the river, faintly. The path to the left led into the dark recesses of the forest. She looked away, spooked by the long stretch into darkness and took the path to the river. But a minute or so in, she noticed the complete absence of any echo behind her. She turned to see that, unbelievably, Harsha had stopped completely and was just standing there, hands on knees.

She ran back up to him.

"What the hell are you doing?" she asked, trying to keep her voice down.

"I... can't... anymore... you .... go... Laurent... house," he managed in between gasps.

"What?? Are you mad? You're coming with me! Come on, one minute of rest and then we go on!" The rustling started up again and she could hear the men's voices, faintly. They were still some distance away.

Taking a deep breath he said. "Look... I got us.... into this mess... you go ahead.... I will get us out of it."

Of all the pigheaded idiots...

"Shut up, you moron, and just come."

He shook his head. "We can't lead them to Laurent's house. What if they are Lakshmi's killers? What if they turn violent? It would be a bloody massacre!"

"But we don't know if they ..."

He grabbed hold of her and said: "Why would they chase us if they are just some random villagers? We can't take that chance, Maya!"

A miniscule pause and then he spoke again, and she marvelled at how calm his voice was. "You just go and I will sort this out," he said firmly.

The thrashing was growing louder.

He glanced down at her body and grinned. "You look hot, all sweaty and breathing deeply."

She felt a gush of affection and pinched him on the arm.

He pulled her to him and kissed her roughly on the forehead and then said: "Just go."

The thrashing grew ever louder, she had to decide. She nodded and said: "Don't do anything heroic like fight them. Just run, and - this is important - take deep breaths, not shallow ones."

He nodded, and she turned and started to jog up the path towards the river.

Just as she was turning a corner, she turned to catch a last glimpse of him. He was looking down the forest path from which the men were coming, torch in hand. She couldn't see his face.

He had read somewhere that the best plans, the ones that worked, were the simple ones. He hoped like hell this was true because this plan was as simple as it got.

Wait for the men to approach, shine the torch in their faces and then run down the other path yelling and screaming so they would follow him and not Maya. It wasn't just heroism. He just thought the chances of the men doing anything violent to him were a bit less than what they would do if they caught Maya. He tried not to think too much about that.

He could hear the men's shouting now — what were they, twenty seconds away? Ten?

He thought about running down the dark path and an irrational fear of the dark gripped his heart.

A wild memory came into his head. Sitting in the college library and reading Eugene O' Neill's *Emperor Jones*. He remembered the thrill he had felt at the sheer poetry of the images, a man running through the forest, while the war drums of his hunters thumped in time to the beating of his heart.

Well, you can experience the sensation for real now, he thought bitterly to himself.

Mechanically he put his hand to his chest. Yes — there it was, that two-step beat, sounding so loud in his ears.

He waited.

Panic rose in him. *What the hell are you doing?* Had he just spelled his own death sentence? He thought of death, the afterlife, no longer being alive, with a sense of horror. What was it like? Where was poor Lakshmi now?

He closed his eyes and opened them again, trying to calm himself. On the other hand, maybe the men were peaceable, and there was some normal explanation for their presence on the mountainside at midnight, and for their pursuit. But this thought sounded ridiculous to the rest of his brain.

He knew that they would do some harm to him if they caught him. *But at least they won't harm Maya*, he thought, and that thought gave him courage, and his heart filled with emotion when he thought of her.

There they were! Or at least torch light had appeared just in front of a bend in the path, and his heart gave another sickening leap in his chest.

"Action time," he said to himself, his voice trembling between chattering teeth. "Now or never!"

As the first dark shape came up towards the fork in the road, he stepped out and shone the torch right in the man's eyes, yelling. He had one brief second to take in a strong, angular face with a bristling beard before the man yelled in unison with him and slipped on the muddy floor of the path and fell. The others behind him tripped over him and fell in a pile — it would have been comical under different circumstances.

Still yelling and screaming, Harsha ran down the left fork, making sure he waved his torch all around so they couldn't miss the light.

Behind him, he heard them curse and one man angrily shout in Tamil: "Finish him off!"

The phrase and the gleaming *aruvals* the men held were enough to turn Harsha's legs to jelly.

"What have I done!" he yelled out, on the edge of hysteria now.

He sprinted down the dark path pumping his arms as he had seen Maya do, and taking deep breaths. The latter action became increasingly hard as they went on — but it was definitely working, he could hear them behind him, yelling curses after him. The path was downhill, which, given his bigger frame, was probably to his advantage.

He kept going, but his heart was burning now and he looked ahead at the path, which snaked into further darkness. Was there no end to this damned forest?

His breath just came in ragged gasps once again, and his knees were throbbing. He realised with sinking dismay he could not go much longer. And the men were almost on him.

A churning noise started up in his ears, adding to his already mounting panic. Was he bursting an artery or about to have a nervous breakdown?

He was sobbing now with the effort of running, his nose and eyes leaking, and the churning was growing louder and louder. He did not dare look back, but he was sure they must be very close now.

The churning reached its height and, without warning, he was out in open air again. He recoiled at the sudden burst of cold air and realised it was raining properly now. All this realisation came to him in a fraction of a second and then he stepped out on thin air and fell with a crash into the raging river.

His first feeling was of relief — so, this is what the noise was! He wasn't having a nervous breakdown. It was just the river, taking a turn into some other part of the forest. His feet touched the ground — it was barely eight feet deep! He kicked and swam to the surface and looked wildly around him.

There they were! Standing on the bank, but already several feet behind him, shining their torches. The current must be strong if they were already that far behind.

He exhaled with relief and then focused on controlling the movement of his body and tried to strike out for the shore.

And then a horrible thought occurred to him and he lost his stroke and flailed in the water — he had only seen two men on the bank, and there had been at least five men when they had initially started running away from them.

Where had the other three gone?

Maya! He thought desperately, as the river carried him away into darkness.

22. FOREST

He did not think of Maya for long — he couldn't afford to — he was fighting for survival now. Trying to resist the current was proving close to impossible. The river inexorably drove him on, and he could feel the rain bucketing down on him.

This was easily the most terrifying experience of his life, being driven on by the water in complete darkness. At least the men's torches had lit up the scene briefly, now it felt like he was on the wings of an invisible dragon at night.

How had this happened? He had a fleeting memory of his dull, but well ordered, life in London. He had craved adventure. But adventure, when it actually came, was beyond anything he had ever expected. His heart was bursting out of his chest. The water was freezing his limbs. His clothes felt soggy and heavy. And, good swimmer though he was, he had no idea whether he was swimming or if the river was just carrying him along. The water roared all around him, a crescendo of noise that seemed to create some sort of wall of sound on either side.

Could it get any worse?

The answer was yes, of course. But what Harsha hadn't realised was that something elemental within him had awoken. There was adrenaline pumping through his veins, his heart rate had increased to an incredible high and his breathing was deep and heavy as his body prepared him for this extraordinary, life-threatening experience. If he survived, he would remember it forever as a high that he could not replicate artificially.

But in that moment, he thrashed about and pulled himself off the edge of panic and blinked water off his eyelids, squinting to try and see through the dark.

As his vision adjusted, he had seconds to see dark shapes up ahead of him before he slammed into something hard and slippery, and felt a splintering pain in his chest. He let out a groan that was entirely overwhelmed by the sound of the water and held on to the dark shape — a rock of some sort, maybe — desperately. He kicked his legs out and met something else equally hard with his feet. More rock. He leveraged himself between the two rocks and reached out with his hand and met with what felt like the most welcome, most beautiful thing in the world. It was land. It was, against all reason, in the middle of the river, but it still felt blessedly solid.

Carefully, he lifted one sodden foot and placed it on one of the rocks, and with a gargantuan effort, lifted his body over and pushed himself onto this piece of land. He felt his aching torso strike the muddy floor, and sobbed with relief, the tears running hot down his cheeks.

He lay there, cursing himself bitterly for his so-called desire for adventure, and wondered why he had ever come to this damned countryside retreat. He thought of Azhar and tried to feel angry with his friend for having invited him to this god-forsaken place, but he couldn't bring himself to feel anything but love and longing to be with his old friend at that moment, preferably surrounded by light and warmth.

He thought of Maya, and, as though an electric current went through his body, he remembered that she was in worse peril than he would ever be. His heart started pumping again, and he thought with terror of what would have become of her if the men caught up with her. It didn't bear thinking of. Another image came to his exhausted brain — that of Lakshmi's body — only, this time, it had Maya's face. He roughly wiped his face, as though to remove the thought from his brain, and sat up.

Maya. He had to do something. He felt in his pockets — his jeans were sticking to his body, but he managed to extricate his phone and his torch. There was no signal on his phone in this wild corner of the world, but he still felt like he would feel safer if he could get it to work. He felt along its edge to the button that would turn it on, and pressed it repeatedly, held it down for ages it felt like, but nothing. Just darkness.

With a sigh, he put the phone back in his pocket and turned his attention to the torch. It was supposed to be waterproof, but that had been a hell of a ride through the river. Would it still work?

He pushed the button forward for the light and heard a squelching noise as it slid into place. No light.

"Work, dammit!" he yelled, banging the side of the torch and then

— wonder of wonders — it emitted a dim light and he nearly cried with relief. It was directed at the ground below him, which was a muddy, mossy sort of colour, and as he shone the light around he saw two tiny saplings on either side of him, their long, slim branches trailing in the water that flowed on either side, and a mighty rock ahead of him making up a tiny little island. It was almost like a watery throne, set in the middle of the river. He shone the torch beyond the island and gasped, covering his mouth with his hand.

The river was flowing over a yawning gap just in front of him — he was close to the very edge of a waterfall! He had been saved by this little island he was on. And how was he to leave it?

Calm down, Harry boy, he said to himself. He could always wait until the morning, and then, in the daylight, reassess. At this thought, a huge weariness hit him, and he was ready to fall on the muddy floor beneath him and fall asleep right away.

Another electric current went through him as he suddenly remembered Azhar's words, from what seemed a century ago.

"Flash floods. They could come at any time when it rains."

He would have to get away from the river, or risk death. He felt like breaking down at the thought of more effort, but he shone the torch wearily on either side of the island and saw the closer bank on the right side, and a convenient set of rocks he could use to navigate his way there. He carefully put the torch away in one of the pockets of his waterproof jacket and looked out despairingly into the darkness. To his relief, he found he was able to see a little — whether it was starlight or moonlight that showed a few shapes he recognised, he did not know, but he was immensely grateful for it.

With a great effort of will, he pulled himself up and walked to the edge of the little island, pushing the branches of the sapling aside, and, closing his eyes involuntarily, he waded into the water again.

The pressure of the water hit him like a truck and he swayed, expecting any second to be swept over the edge, but instead, his shoes found the floor and a new determination went through him, and he kicked off, pushing himself off rocks as he swam powerfully towards the shore.

For a few desperate seconds, he felt completely out of control, but he kept striking the water again and again, repeatedly, as though his life depended upon it — it probably did — and slowly, the pressure relented and he could feel himself making headway.

It wasn't long before he felt the bed of the pool rise up and soon he was wading onto the land. He fell to his knees and coughed once or twice, clutching the mud with his fingers. The rain was still coming down hard, but nothing could take away the feeling of being on solid ground again.

Finally, he pulled himself together and stood up with an effort. Painstakingly working the zip of the pocket of his waterproof jacket, he pulled out his torch.

With shivering fingers, he fumbled with the button and turned it on. He blinked in what felt like the blinding light and looked around.

Covering the torch with one hand from the rain, he looked blearily around him. He was in front of trees — hateful trees — but fortunately there weren't that many of them. He must be out of the forest and somewhere near the resort.

He walked along the river bank to the point where the water fell and saw that he was on the lip of an overhang, but rocks gleamed up at him from not too far below. Somewhat shamefacedly, he realised the "waterfall" fell only about 20 feet into another pool — his life was probably not quite at risk.

He moved the torch further out, and, at the far end of the pool below the water flowed out in another little waterfall into another pool further down, the three pools like great watery steps on the shelf of the mountain.

With a shock like a revelation, he realised where he was. He could have cried with relief. He slowly made his way back to the bank and tried to think. He prided himself on his sense of direction, and now realised he must be a little way above the pool where they had all gone swimming earlier in the week (*earlier in the week! It felt like years ago*).

In which case, the river he had fallen into wasn't the main river, but a tributary, which would explain why it wasn't as large or fierce.

So now he knew which way to go. Just find a way down to the second of the three pools and there was a path that led all the way to the resort.

He shut out all other thoughts of Maya and the mysterious men and just thought of home and began his journey.

He paused as a distant roaring sounded out behind him. What the hell was this new horror? He thought wildly of the black panther. A whole family of panthers? And then, he let out a yelp as the thought of flash floods came back to him.

Abandoning his caution, he somehow found the energy to start running again between the trees, away from that hateful river.

A bare minute after he had left, a wall of water came gushing down, engulfing the little pool and roaring over the edge in a torrent of foam.

How did people do it? Survive in the forest on berries and herbs or whatever? In reality, probably only about five minutes had passed since the ordeal of the river, but already, he was ready to give up, lie on the floor and give himself up to the elements.

Earlier that night, his fear of death had been overwhelming, but now he thought of death as a bringer of relief, as an end to the daily struggle of life.

The fading torch light showed a little man-made wall up ahead of him, stones piled up against a sand bank. He had no sensation left to feel any more relief. He just automatically registered that he was now at the campsite that Azhar had showed him some days ago. Towards one side of the wall was a set of steps and beyond that, the little hut where provisions were kept for campers.

Wearily climbing the steps, he remembered that the hut, while constructed with a thatch roof, was ingeniously built to keep out the rain. He stumbled to the entrance and pushed the door open. He would rest here. He quickly shone the torch around the room and nearly jumped out of his skin.

On the far corner was a little family of monkeys. One large one — presumably the mother — gibbered at him warily and wrapped two baby monkeys in her arms. The two cubs peeped out at him from behind her arms with wide eyes.

"Ok," Harsha said out loud. "You stay in your corner and I'll stay in mine, ok? No need to trouble each other."

The mother bared her sharp, pointy teeth at him, but he was too exhausted to care. He sank down against the wall, and, leaving the torch on, he looked wearily across at his odd companions. They didn't move.

Poor little buggers must be terrified of the storm, he thought, as a loud crash of thunder boomed through the room and the cubs cuddled up to their mother's chest. He wondered vaguely if monkeys felt fear. Of course they must, he thought, remembering how the stray dogs back home used to run terrified from the fireworks on Diwali.

With such irrelevant thoughts running through his mind, and with the eyes of the monkey family on him in the light of his torch, Harsha closed his eyes.

23. REVIVAL

He opened his eyes with a start and scrunched up his body defensively, blearily looking at the figure that stood in front of him. A surprisingly shapely figure.

Weariness turned to wonder, and his eyes widened as he recognised the contours of the face that had occupied his mind so much over the past week.

"M... Maya? Am I dreaming?"

Incredibly, it was Maya, smiling tremulously at him.

"So, you're not... you're..."

"I'm ok, Harry," she said, tearing up at the tenderness in his voice.

His eyes scanned her body for any other signs of wear and tear — she actually looked pretty fresh, until his eyes went back up to her face and saw that her forehead had been neatly bandaged up.

He reached his hand out as though to touch it, even though she was standing several feet away from him — for some reason — and he opened his mouth.

"It's fine," she said, quickly, still looking down at him from her vantage point at the door, an odd expression on her face.

He swallowed to remove the dryness from his throat and rasped out: "How did you find me?"

"By looking everywhere," she said, shaking her head slightly as though to come back to reality, and moved towards him. Harsha blinked when he saw a second person behind her. It took him a few seconds to recognise Murugayya. The resort manager was standing there quietly, looking concernedly at him with his sad eyes.

Maya hurried forward and bent over Harsha to check if he was ok, putting one hand on his forehead.

He closed his eyes at her touch and then rasped out: "Thank god you found me, Maya!"

"Thank Murugayya," she said, smiling through her tears. "It was his idea to check this place. He thought you would head here. I personally thought you had no idea where you were."

"I didn't," he said, trying to get up but falling to the floor again. She put one hand under his shoulder to try and lift him and he struggled to get up, his feet scrabbling on the dirt floor of the hut.

He leaned back exhausted, and then felt another, reassuringly strong grasp under his other arm as Murugayya came up to help. Between the two of them, they helped him up and he could feel Maya holding her breath as he gingerly tested his feet, and then sighing with relief when he was able to walk a few steps.

He felt the blood rushing back to his feet and kicked the floor, willing the tingling to stop.

"We thought you had died in the flood, sir!" Murugayya said, as though that was a consoling thought in some way.

"Right," Harsha said, limping towards the door, "I'm ok now. Hang on — where's my torch?"

Murugayya pulled out a torch of his own and shone it all around the room and finally located it — in the hand of one of the monkey cubs. The mother was nowhere to be seen.

"Goddamn monkey stole my torch! Maya, do something!" Harsha said childishly.

"Yes, Harry," she said, laughter in her voice. "I'll take you to the shop tomorrow and you can get a new one. I think this one is lost."

The monkey was now slapping its knobby palm against the torch, trying to make it turn on. Finally, when this method didn't work, it flung it at them and Murugayya calmly caught it and gave it to Harsha.

"Bloody monkeys," Harsha muttered, pocketing it and limping out.

Maya and Murugayya looked at each other over Harsha's shoulders. "I think he must be alright, if he can get this angry about monkeys," she said, smiling, getting a rare grin in response from the man.

They went out into the cold, sunny morning and flanked Harsha on either side, Murugayya guiding him through the scrub and rock that made up the floor of this particular patch of mountainside.

Harsha's teeth were chattering with cold now as he walked off his stiffness and looked around, marvelling at the tranquil landscape and contrasting it with the wildness of the night before. He flexed his fingers and tried not to think of the cold. He was sure to catch the flu or something, he thought gloomily to himself.

You are lucky to even be alive, a voice inside him said, and he felt a shiver of excitement go through his body as he remembered how oddly thrilling and terrifying the night before had been. His heart pounded again when he remembered the shadows of the men by the banks of the river as he was carried off by the raging waters, their *aruvals* gleaming in the light of their own torches.

"What happened to you, Maya," he asked, feeling ashamed at not having asked before, looking sideways at her bandaged head.

"Well, I waited by the bridge..."

"Why?" he cut in, angrily. "I told you to get away!"

"I couldn't just leave you Harry, and don't talk to me like that, I am a grown woman and make my own decisions!

"Anyway," she continued, when she was sure he wasn't going to argue any further, "They must have figured out what we were doing or something, because they split up and two or three of them came after me. They reached the bridge and saw me on the other side. And I... I panicked and left the path and went into the forest."

He clicked his tongue and shook his head.

She caught his eye. "I know," she said, quietly. "That particular decision wasn't the best." She shivered slightly, and Harsha could easily imagine what the journey through the forest must have been like.

"Don't worry, I'm not sure what I would have done if I hadn't fallen into the river. It saved my life."

"And nearly took it away," Maya said quietly, her grip on his arm tightening a little. "Anyway, I came out of the forest at some point, thank God, and found I was reasonably close to the village. I knew where Leela's house was, so I went and woke her up. She brought me to Murugayya, and he took care of me and organised a search party for you. I caught some sleep and then joined them for the second round of searches."

Harsha looked sideways at the man walking silently to his other side, his surprisingly strong grip propping up Harsha's arm, and felt a surge of affection towards him. He might be sycophantic at times, but clearly he also was able to take charge when needed. It meant a lot to have a dependable character like him to turn to whenever there was any trouble. No wonder Azhar spoke so highly of him.

"And how did you figure out where I was?" he asked Muragayya.

Murugayya kicked aside a rotting branch and said quietly: "Maya madam told me which path you took. I know where it ends, sir, and thought you would go downhill. And that leads to the campsite. In the rain, I thought you would look for shelter."

Simple, but still, remarkable that the man was able to pinpoint him exactly in the whole damn mountain.

"Clearly, Murugayya is crediting you with more intelligence than I would have done," Maya said, smiling and squeezing his arm.

Her touch oddly reminded him of what they had been planning the night before, and he looked away, confused.

"Murugayya," he said, "Any idea who those men were?"

The man shook his head.

They walked in silence, Harsha clenching his fists to try and stop from shivering, and the odd trio stopped for a second.

"Here," Maya said, pulling off her jacket and handing it to him.

He clutched at it gratefully but said: "I can't do that to you Maya, you..."

"Just shut up and take it and don't give me any of this chivalry bullshit. I've had a hot shower and I'm actually feeling a bit warm from the exertion of supporting your royal highness."

He was sure she was lying, but he pulled the jacket on. It was too tight for him to do up the front, but it felt like he was pulling on a delicious layer of warmth and he felt a small trickle of energy return to his aching body.

"Thank you!" he said, and they resumed their walking, Harsha holding his hands up to show them both he could manage on his own.

There was only the crunch of shoes on leaves for a minute, and then Maya asked: "Harry... Do you... do you think we overreacted?"

He looked at her, puzzled.

"I mean — do you think they were just ordinary men? Last night?" she persisted, panting a little now as the path took them uphill.

"Searching the mountain for something in the middle of the night, armed with those swords of theirs? And then chasing us? Splitting up so they could cover us both? No, Maya, we didn't imagine this.

Besides," he hesitated, wondering if he needed to scare her any more, but she had proved unbelievably tough, coming out to search for him after that ordeal. "I heard them say 'finish them off'. I think. In a mixture of Tamil and some other dialect."

Beside them, Murugayya jerked his face around and looked at him, a shocked look in his eyes.

Maya looked behind them furtively.

"And... where do you think they are now?"

"They must have gone away," Harsha said, trying to sound convincing, but he couldn't help glancing around nervously. There were no signs of humanity in the bright sunshine that suffused its way between the uneven spread of trees and onto the damp forest floor.

"Don't worry, madam. The whole resort is awake and looking for Harsha sir all over the mountain. They would have left long back," Murugayya said soothingly, and Harsha felt another surge of relief and affection for the man.

A few minutes later, they went over one side of the mountain and Harsha caught sight of the resort lying in front of them, the different rooms forming an oval shape on the side of the mountain, like a giant necklace glittering in the sunshine, and his heart lifted. For the rest of his life, he would never forget that moment.

"There you are!" Azhar said, banging into Harsha's room and taking stock of a fine domestic scene for a second. Harsha was sitting up in bed, the duvet covers pulled up to his waist, reading a book. Maya was sitting on a comfortable chair by one window with a magazine, the afternoon sunlight pouring in through the fronds of a sapling just outside. A cup of steaming tea was beside her, and the pair of them looked perfectly content, as though nothing had happened to disturb their equanimity in recent days.

Unimpressed by this, Azhar began: "Do you have any fucking idea..."

"Shhh..." Maya said, from her chair, without looking up from his magazine. "He's unwell."

"I'm not unwell, Maya, in fact I feel fine!" Harsha said, flinging his book down onto the bed and looking at Azhar with bright eyes.

Miraculously, he did feel fine. A few bruises aside, he felt as healthy as he had been since he first arrived at the resort. Murugayya had made him take a hot shower when he came back, gently insisting when Harsha had complained that all he wanted to do was sleep.

After a nap, Ammani had brought him a bowl of *rasam* and basmati rice for lunch, a dish he had sworn never to have again in his life once he left home. But on this occasion, the aroma of coriander and the tangy, spicy tomato flavours revived him like it was the elixir of life. Never again would he dispute *rasam*'s marvellous, healing qualities.

After a few hours' sleep, he felt fit and fine, except that everyone was insisting he stay in bed.

Azhar sat down by his feet, ignoring Maya and said: "What on Earth were you two..."

"Well, Maya was feeling unwell so I was bringing her back..."

"Yeah yeah, I wasn't born yesterday. Shane saw the two of you, and then we all watched you from the window," Azhar couldn't help grinning at this point. "Eating each other's faces, from the looks of it."

"Azhar!" Harsha said, sitting up further and going red in the face. But Maya was laughing.

"Seriously dude, I need to teach you a thing or two about kissing a... Anyway, never mind that! What the hell were you two thinking?"

Harsha sank back down in his bed. "Man, you make it sound like we wanted to play hide and seek with a bunch of murderous strangers in the forest at midnight — we were chased, you idiot. I have no idea why you are shouting at us."

"Oh I'm the idiot, is it? Why didn't you come straight back to Laurent's house?"

"They would have caught up with us well before that and we didn't want to lead them to the house, in case they were violent men. We got split up and..."

"How?"

"How what?"

"How did you get split up?"

Harsha shifted uncomfortably. "Well... I couldn't keep up with Maya and..."

"Hey!" Maya said, dropping her magazine in her lap. "Do you

think I would have just left you behind like that?" She turned to Azhar and said: "This chivalrous fool insisted on staying and distracting them."

"Oho, doing his Tintin act again, was he?" Azhar and Maya exchanged meaningful glances.

"Hello! Hang on! It made perfect sense — do you think we should have risked her getting raped?"

"What? When did I ever say anything like that?" Azhar said, understandably outraged by this.

Maya cut in once again: "It should have been me doing the distracting. I wasn't thinking straight, letting you do it. I can run much faster and longer than you."

"Ok, let's just shut up for a second!" Harsha thundered.

A silence fell, and the two of them looked expectantly, and a little warily, at him. Harsha took a deep breath and said: "Look, the truth is, we panicked. We had no idea what we were doing. But we got away with it and the important thing now is — what next? Who were these people? What were they doing? What the hell is still going on?"

Azhar shook his head to signify he didn't know. Maya looked thoughtful.

"Have you told the police?" Harsha asked Azhar.

Azhar nodded. "Police station is closed on Sunday, so I had to send someone to your buddy's house. He may come later today."

"The inspector? Good. I need to have a word with him."

Azhar looked at Harsha's grim expression and said: "Harry, don't piss the guy off, ok? He can make life very difficult for me."

Harsha threw off the bedsheets and said: "I need some breakfast. I mean, lunch or dinner, or whatever."

"Hey," Maya stood up, the book falling to the floor. "You're not supposed to get up today!"

"Maya, I will fall into depression if I have to sit in bed all day. Come on guys, let's go eat something."

24. REPORT

Harsha found that he hadn't quite recovered as much as he had thought. His knees and calves started to complain as soon as they made their way down the hill, and he tried not to wince with every step in case Azhar and Maya decided to bundle him back into bed. All the little scrapes and scratches from the river started to burn and he felt a horrible pain in his chest that he suspected was a bruised rib, if not a broken one.

Still, he tried to whistle as they walked down to try and allay suspicion. This seemed to have limited success, with Maya looking worriedly at him and asking after his wounds.

"These?" Harsha said cheerfully, holding his hands up to show all the plasters in various places across his knuckles and arms. "They just make me feel like a hero! How are you?"

Maya touched the bandage on her forehead and screwed her eyes shut for a second. "Fine," she said. "Just could do with some tea or coffee."

Azhar didn't say anything, but a strained look came over his face. Harsha knew that he was taking personal responsibility for all the things that had gone wrong in the last few days, and opened his mouth to say something to reassure him. But he closed it again, not knowing what to say.

"What a beautiful sunny day!" he said instead, trying to inject some cheer into the mood. "It feels like a different planet from last night."

They reached the dining hall and Azhar pushed his way in and held the door open for Harsha and Maya. Shane and Junaina were sitting in the sofa area of the hall, Shane looking as calm as ever while perusing a copy of *Southern Echo* and Junaina looking uncharacteristically serious.

"What kind of madhouse are you running here, Azhar?" she said by way of greeting when the three of them walked up to them. "Women getting murdered, people getting chased by some mad axe-wielding thugs in the middle of the night?"

Azhar ignored this remark and pulled the teapot on the table towards him, poured out a generous portion into a mug and passed it to Maya.

"Are you guys ok?" Shane asked, carefully folding up the newspaper and putting it away. "Murugayya told us the whole story."

"Yes, but God help me if I ever go into that forest again after dark," Harsha said, wincing as he sat down on one of the chairs.

Shane winked at him. "Once bitten, twice shy, eh?" he said, eliciting a reluctant laugh.

Azhar poured out some tea for himself as well and said to the group in general: "Look, guys, Harry is right. No more going out at night until someone finds out what the hell is happening here. Now, Harry — I think it is time you tell us what is going on."

Junaina said: "Eh! Leave the poor fellow alone, he just spent half the night swimming up a waterfall or some such thing, according to your Murugayya."

"No! He knows something and he's not sharing it with us. It's about time you told us, Harry. We are your friends and plus, this is my resort and if anyone here is in danger, I need to know. You are not doing anyone any favours by keeping it all to yourself!" Azhar said, glaring over his tea mug at Harsha.

Harsha looked at Azhar and felt a jolt of guilt at his friend's unusually disappointed expression. Azhar never got upset with him in that way. Angry, yes, but never disappointed. He looked around at the rest of his friends and saw that he was completely outnumbered. They were all looking at him keenly, and only Maya showed some sympathy.

"Ok look, it's not much that I do know, but I will share it all with you," he said, finally.

He started by giving a quick run through of the interviews he and Maya had done, for Junaina's benefit. He then gave them a more detailed account of the meeting with the inspector, ending with the inspector's theory that some important piece of jewellery or similar item had been taken from Lakshmi's hand — and that this item was the key to finding the killer.

"Well it explains the mystery of the men from last night, at least,"

Maya said.

Azhar turned to her: "How?"

"They were looking for this jewellery, stupid," she replied, feeling her bandaged head gingerly.

Junaina fell back on the sofa and looked at them all in turn, open mouthed. "Bloody hell, Harry! What a mess! I mean I don't even know what to say. You characters have got suspects and clues and shit! This is like being in an Agatha Christie novel!"

"Except that we have no clue what we are doing," Harsha said, heavily. He avoided looking at Azhar, who was still eyeing him somewhat reproachfully for not having shared all the details of the meeting with the inspector earlier .

Shane shifted in his chair, and everyone turned to look at him. He seemed mildly startled at the attention, but he cleared his throat and said: "It doesn't sound like you have no clue. You and Maya seem to have gathered some pretty good intel on the situation. I think it's safe to say this particular mystery hasn't been solved yet."

Azhar pulled the sugar pot towards him and frowned as he dropped a cube of sugar into his tea. "What do you mean, they haven't solved it yet? The police were very clear. They have arrested those quarry smugglers or whoever they are."

Maya sipped her tea, touched her bandage delicately again and said: "Azhar, after last night we have to assume there is more to it than that. Someone out there is still trying to find this missing object that the inspector is after, and I will bet my life that this person is Lakshmi's murderer — or at least the person behind Lakshmi's murder."

Harsha nodded at this.

"Bloody hell," Junaina said, shaking her head wonderingly. "*Bloody hell*. What a situation! And what do you think this missing object is?"

Her question was directed at Maya, but Maya turned to look at Harsha, who shook his head.

"Absolutely no clue."

They spent the next twenty minutes coming up with theories on what this object could be, and finally came to a consensus that it was either a ring or a pendant of some sort.

"Yeah that makes sense," Maya said slowly. "Imagine, you are being attacked," she said, making a grabbing motion. "You grab your attacker as you're trying to fight him away, and you grab his ring."

"It sounds a bit far-fetched to me," Shane said sceptically. "You are being attacked, and you take the time to pull a ring off someone's finger? A pendant makes more sense. You pull it off his neck."

"It could have happened by mistake."

They broke off the discussion as Ammani and Kuppi brought in an early dinner that Shane had had the foresight to order, Ammani grinning at Harsha as she left. They scrambled up and made their way towards the table, Azhar making a quick visit to the drinks cabinet to fetch some wine to go with the meal.

It was only around 6 pm, so the late evening light still streamed into the hall, giving the dinner a slightly forbidden feel. But Harsha felt his stomach rumble, and he remembered that he had only had *rasam* and rice for his lunch. He was definitely recovering and ready to have a proper dinner now.

"This is my kind of holiday," Shane said jovially, as he dusted biscuit crumbs off his khaki trousers and ambled up towards the table. "Moving from lunch to dinner seamlessly."

Harsha's mouth watered at the sight of the food that Kuppi had prepared, and a brief silence prevailed as they applied themselves to the *korma, sabzi* and *naan*. Azhar poured some wine for everyone after waffling on about it for a good ten minutes ("it has the right acidity levels to offset the spice of Indian food") before Junaina put a premature end to his lecture.

"Enough of this rubbish," she said, impatiently. "Let's talk about this pendant or ring, or whatever."

Harsha shook his head and winced slightly as one of the wounds on his hands scraped against the plate. "There's no point unless we find the damn thing. Azhar, I suggest we have another proper search of the whole resort for this object."

"What do you think I... fine, fine," Azhar said in a resigned voice. "I'll get Murugayya and co to comb through the whole bloody place, don't worry. First thing tomorrow."

"So there's nothing we can do till then?" Junaina asked, disappointed. "What about the suspects? Maybe we could approach it the other way round?"

Shane grinned at Harsha and cocked his head towards Junaina. "Looks like we have a new recruit to the team," he chortled.

"Just trying to help," Junaina muttered.

"Hang on, Shanny," Maya said, pushing her plate away and reaching for her mug of wine. "That's not a bad idea. Let's go through the three suspects we do have."

"The priest. Mahendra, or whatever his name is," Azhar said.

"Maheshwaran," Harsha said. "He seemed like a very decent guy. He even cried when he talked about Lakshmi. But then — wouldn't a killer also be a brilliant actor? We can't rule him out."

"Is he likely to wear any kind of jewellery though?"

"Possibly," Maya said, thoughtfully. "Many religious people wear a pendant with a holy symbol. I myself have a gold pendant with a carving of Saraswathi. It's back in my room."

"And Laurent?"

"Hang on," Harsha said, slowly. "Azhar, didn't you say he wears a wedding ring? Maya, do you remember seeing one on his fingers? I don't!"

Maya looked at him, startled. "Nor do I," she said in a hushed whisper. "I specifically remember because I watched him serve us all coffee. There was no ring on any of his fingers."

They all stared at each other around the table.

"Bloody hell," Azhar said, weakly. "Laurent. Loco! Always thought he was a bit weird but... this is insane."

Maya hesitated before saying: "Well, he definitely is intelligent enough to cover his tracks. And he is wealthy. He could easily hire people to look for a ring for him."

"He seems harmless, though," Shane said.

"That's the thing — we don't know what a killer behaves like. It might be sinister — or it might be harmless. We don't know enough to judge if any of these people are potential killers or not. We just have to find that ring. Or pendant."

Shane put down his glass of wine and nodded thoughtfully at this little speech from Maya. "Azhar, better ask Murugayya to look specifically for a wedding ring then, to narrow down the search a little."

"Hang on," Harsha said warningly. "Let's not jump to any

conclusions. What about Rajaratnam? Did he wear any jewellery? Do you remember, Maya?"

Maya thought deeply for a few seconds. What could she remember about Rajaratnam? He had worn his usual military brown shirt and khaki trousers when they met him. Was there a chain around his neck? She seemed to remember the man massaging his neck, scratching it. Would that be what you do if you were missing a pendant? She tentatively mentioned this to the group and they all mulled over this new bit of information. Azhar looked quite impressed but when Maya glanced at Harsha, she saw he was pursing his lips uncertainly. She couldn't blame him. It was pretty thin stuff.

Finally, Shane said: "Well, maybe he just lost his pendant or Laurent lost his ring. That could happen as well. Don't forget we don't know what this missing object is."

"Or maybe he had just been stung by a wasp or something," Junaina volunteered.

"Maybe..."

Harsha asked tersely: "Do you think we should tell the inspector any of this?"

"No! No way!" Azhar said.

"Ok, calm down Azhar."

"No, look, guys, I want this mystery to be solved as well, but we cannot accuse someone without proof, it is not right and I need to maintain relations with these people. Laurent is big cheese around here and Rajaratnam is *extremely* powerful, he could put me out of business like that," Azhar said, snapping his fingers. "As for a Muslim accusing a Hindu priest of murder — that could bring a lynch mob to my doorstep!"

"A lynch mob in this backwater," Junaina hooted. "No need to bring your Bollywood theatrics here."

"You have no idea, Juni. No idea," Azhar said, pouring himself another large glass of wine, and Maya thought his face had actually gone a bit white with fear.

Harsha hesitated, and then said: "Azhar — there's another reason why we have to help the police as much as we can."

There was something in his voice that made everyone sit up and look at him. Azhar looked most bitterly at Harsha and nodded his head. "Because I am a suspect," Azhar said, an uncharacteristic sneer appearing on his face. "I know. Is that why you didn't share the inspector's info with us earlier? Because you thought it could be me?"

Harsha leaned forward and clasped his friend's hand and looked at him earnestly. "Never," he said, firmly. The sneer disappeared from Azhar's face and he looked seriously back at Harsha and nodded.

Maya felt a little catch in her throat. She had just remembered how close Harsha and Azhar had been back in their university days. It had been a beautiful relationship, in its own way, and had always warmed her heart, even when she had broken up with Azhar. There was something so pure about friends and friendship that she had neglected for too long in her life. She looked at Junaina, who was fiddling with her nails, a look of concentration on her face, and then at Shane, who was sitting back with a sated expression, and vowed never to lose touch with these people again.

The group had fallen silent, and they all looked glumly down at their food. The light was fading quickly outside, and Maya was starting to feel the cut on her forehead throb again. She blinked and hoped it hadn't started bleeding. Kuppi came back into the room and asked them all, in her motherly way, if they would like dessert. Shane and Junaina gleefully accepted the offer of some *rava kesari* but Azhar and Harsha simply toyed with their sweet, not really eating it. Azhar kept his glass filled, though, and his eyes were starting to look bloodshot.

Maya looked out of the window at the darkening mountainside and shivered, remembering the terrifying events of the night before. Would she ever forget that night? The feeling of being so close to death — or worse? She glanced at Harsha and realised he had been right about one thing. Those men had been up to no good. She instinctively knew that they would have killed them both.

Oddly, it was Junaina who broke the silence. "Guys, you may think I'm being biased, but I just don't think a priest would do something like this. I just don't see how or why..."

"Come on, Juni!" Harry said. "You hear of priests getting up to all sorts of things in every religion!"

"Yes, but not murder. I just can't see how a priest could do it," Junaina said, and Maya was surprised to hear a pleading note in her voice. Harsha gave Maya a confused look, not knowing how to respond to this newfound religious zeal from Junaina.

Shane, as usual, came to the rescue. "Guys, who we think is likely or unlikely to do this is irrelevant," he said, putting a soothing hand on Junaina's shoulder. "We have neither the information nor the experience to judge who is the killer. Which is why we need to find that item of jewellery."

Harsha shot Shane a grateful look but he said: "We may not have the experience but one thing we can safely say is that each of these three men, in his own way, is extremely powerful. And we have to tread carefully."

"How is a simple temple priest powerful?" Junaina asked insistently.

"Being a religious figure does give you a sort of power over people, Juni," Maya said, gently.

"Power corrupts and absolute power corrupts absolutely," Shane added quickly, accompanied by his trademark chuckle.

Harsha grinned. "For once, one of your aphorisms actually makes a meaningful contribution to the discussion, Shanny."

"Even a broken clock tells time right twice a day," Shane countered, and everyone groaned.

"So what do we do, other than look for this piece of jewellery?" Maya asked.

A silence fell, during which Azhar got up to put on the ceiling lights. Indian nights always seemed to fall suddenly, Harsha thought idly to himself. They all watched as Azhar then busied himself by the wine cabinet in the corner, opening another bottle. They all seemed lost in thought, Azhar himself unusually preoccupied as he popped open the cork and filled their glasses, the garnet red of the liquid twinkling in the warm, golden-hued lights.

Harsha began tentatively: "If the inspector..."

"No."

"Azhar, listen, if we..."

"I said no, Harry. Not until we have proof."

They were interrupted by the door to the dining hall banging open, and Murugayya came rushing in, pausing only to close and shake the droplets off his umbrella. The entire group turned to see what the disturbance was all about, and Maya's heart pounded when she saw that Murugayya looked stressed and terrified. What fresh hell would they have to face now? Not another attack, surely? She suddenly felt extremely aware of how isolated they all were. When the hell was Azhar going to fix the cell phone signal?

"What the f... what is going on, Murugayya? Why are you looking like a dying duck?" Azhar asked sternly.

"The inspector... the inspector..." Murugayya puffed.

"What about the inspector?"

"He is here, sir! He is just outside!"

"Speak of the devil," Harry muttered under his breath.

In fact, Inspector Palanivel did have a slightly devilish air about him, as he strode darkly and silently into the cozy dining hall and looked critically about him.

He looked slightly odd in a checked shirt and jeans rather than his usual police outfit, the strange effect exacerbated by the fact that he was wearing hiking boots. His expression was forbidding.

"Good evening," he said formally, walking a few steps into the room and stopped to look at them all with his calculating eyes.

Kuppi came rushing in from the kitchen. "Inspector, would you like some dinner?" she smiled.

The man shook his head without looking at her.

"Some coffee? Tea?"

"No! I don't want anything, I am not here for a tea party!" he said harshly.

Kuppi withdrew, a shocked expression on her face, and everyone at the table sat up. Harsha and Azhar exchanged glances, and Harsha was pleased to see an annoyed expression come over his friend's face. More people needed to stand up to this inspector.

The man in question strode up to the table. Every eye was on him, and Harsha conceded to himself that Palanivel had a tremendous presence, a sort of charisma, about him.

"Thank you for bringing this latest episode to my attention," he said, an inflexion of irony apparent in his tone. "I would like to take statements from each and every one of you. Especially you two." He waved at Harsha and Maya.

"Please sit down, sir," said Azhar, who himself had stood up when the inspector walked in.

"In private, please. And then I would like to speak to you as well, Mr Azhar."

Azhar shrugged and said: "Maybe you can use my office. Murugayya! Show them to the office."

Murugayya stood to attention and scampered over to the door, opening up his umbrella and stepping out. The inspector clicked his tongue in annoyance at this delay and started to follow as Murugayya peeped back in inquiringly.

"Ok, let's go, Maya," Harsha said, standing up.

"Are you gonna be ok, Harry?" Shane asked. "Are you feeling well and everything?"

"Oh yes," Harsha said, pulling on his jacket, a determined expression on his face. "I am going to have a word with our dear inspector."

25. MOTIVES

"So," the inspector said, leaning back on Azhar's chair in the office and looking down at his notes. "Four or five men were on the mountainside. You ran from them. They ran after you. That's it."

"Well, what were they doing there at midnight?" Harsha asked, squirming uncomfortably in Murugayya's office chair, which was — typically for the man — utterly bare and clearly not designed with any regard given to comfort. It didn't help that Harsha's hip had started throbbing where he had banged it against a rock during the previous night's escapade.

The inspector leaned forward, resting his elbows on Azhar's oak table, looking slightly manic in the dimly lit office room. The conversation with Maya — who had given her statement before Harsha — hadn't seemed to have improved his mood.

"What were you doing there at midnight?" he asked, observing Harsha closely.

"We were watching football at Laurent's house. Maya was feeling unwell, so I was escorting her back to her room," Harsha said, speaking a little loudly so he could be heard over the drumming of the rain, which had increased in intensity in the last ten minutes.

The inspector wrote this down in his notebook, but with a sceptical smile on his face. *What was the man's problem?*

"And they were searching for something," Harsha added, trying to follow the inspector's squiggly handwriting without making it obvious he was doing so.

"Are you sure about that? Maybe they were just taking a late night walk?"

"They were spread out and shining their torches methodically across the ground."

"Yes, I made a note of that," the inspector said, looking down at his notebook.

"And they had *aruvals*," Harsha said, playing his trump card.

The inspector was not impressed. "Everyone in this place has *aruvals*, Mr Devnath. This is a farming village."

"And why would they take it with them for a late night walk?"

The inspector shrugged. "For protection? These villagers are a superstitious bunch, they think all kinds of ghosts and demons live in the forest. Plus, there are always stories about panthers and whatnot."

"But why were they there in the first place?"

"Did you think of just asking them?"

"They had *aruvals*, man!" Harsha said, in exasperation. His back was hurting from the effort of sitting on this ridiculous chair — he must be weaker than he thought — and a sharp pain in his chest made him wonder again if he had broken a rib.

"This is what I have from yours and Ms Pandey's statement," the inspector said. The emphasis on the 'Ms' made Harsha smile. Maya had clearly told the inspector off for calling her 'Mrs'. "You saw four men, apparently searching for something. They appeared to have hostile intent. You ran from them. You don't have any proper description of the men..."

"It was midnight, sir!"

"No proper description of them," the man continued. He sighed and leaned back, pushing his notebook away from him. "What do you expect me to do, Mr Devnath?"

"Inspector, I'm surprised you even have to ask. Didn't you say that there was something missing from Lakshmi's body? Surely you can put two and two together — these men were looking for..." Harsha stopped himself just as he was about to say 'the pendant'. "For the missing object?" he chose instead.

"That case is closed, Mr Devnath!" the inspector said sharply.

"So these sand burglars or whatever — they confessed to the crime?"

The inspector recoiled with anger, his nostrils flaring. "I don't have to answer that to *you*!"

"Did they?"

The inspector looked at him, breathing hard. "It is only a matter of time," he said, finally.

Harsha was about to reply caustically when Murugayya came banging in and said: "Does anyone want any tea or coffee?"

"What the hell is this place's obsession with tea!" the inspector thundered, causing Murugayya to recoil and take two steps back.

Harsha quickly interjected: "Just get us some tea, thank you Murugayya. And sugar separately please!"

As Murugayya withdrew, Harsha grinned at the fuming inspector and said: "Much quicker to just get something. And I could use a drink, couldn't you?"

The inspector closed his eyes and said: "Look Mr Devnath..."

"No, Mr Palanivel, I will not look. I want you to listen to me for a change." The man's eyes popped open in shock, and Harsha's stomach gave a nervous jolt. The policeman was still a scary man, and they were miles away from civilisation.

"How dare you..."

"Let me finish," Harsha said, lifting his hands in a placatory gesture. "You were the one who said that everything about that horrible crime did not add up. But now, you are saying the case is closed even though the questions you posed on that mountain have not been answered, and you have no confession?"

Harsha quailed for a second at the inspector's expression, but he was in now, and may as well go for broke. "Inspector, do you just care about closing the case or actually getting to the bottom of it?"

The inspector closed his notebook with a snap and stood up. "I don't have to justify myself to... to you."

Harsha stood up as well as the policeman strode towards the door and pulled it open. "Inspector, please forgive me, I didn't mean to insult you or your ability to do your job. Just hear me out!" he pleaded.

The inspector picked up his umbrella (which had a Manchester United Red Devils crest on it) and stepped out, wrestling with its clasp. "As far as I am concerned, this midnight encounter is not an incident and does not need further investigation," he declared, shaking the stubborn umbrella to try and get it open, spraying raindrops all over the threshold of the office.

"Inspector!" Harsha said desperately, walking to the centre of the office room. "I know all about you!"

The man stopped, umbrella forgotten and turned and looked at Harsha.

"I know you had an exemplary record in Chennai, you were awarded several medals for your outstanding work. And then you caught two young men who were driving drunk and ran over and killed a child on the street, the child of someone from the nearby slum. You arrested them and beat them in the police station. The newspaper reports say both of them had several fractures."

The man was looking at Harsha with a neutral expression, but his nostrils expanded a little as he breathed deeply in and out. Harsha pressed on.

"And it turned out one of them was a politician's son. So, you were rebuked for your actions and were transferred somewhere else. To Ramananpettai, in fact. Exiled, you could say. The boys walked free."

The man said, his voice trembling slightly with emotion: "And what is your point, Mr Devnath?"

"My point is," Harsha paused. He was in extremely dangerous territory and wanted to phrase this right. "The point is, I don't blame you for your actions at all. In fact, part of me even thinks you were right to do what you did. But... I wonder, would you do it again? Take on a priest or a powerful politician, for example?"

He quailed as the inspector dropped the umbrella with a clatter, strode up to him and looked him in the face. "Look," Harsha bleated, raising his hands again, "I just wanted to be sure, I don't mean any offence."

The inspector didn't say anything for a minute, just looked at him, his face three inches away from Harsha's. Then he said, softly: "Do you have any children, Mr Devnath?"

"No."

He nodded, and thankfully his expression changed a little. "Once you have children you will understand. We all want to save the world when we are young, Mr Devnath. But once you have children, your life changes."

He sighed and turned to leave once again. "Thank you for your help," he said and stooped to pick up the umbrella. As he got up, he nearly bumped into Murugayya, who was coming in with a tray with two steaming cups of tea and a bowl of sugar.

"Sir, your tea?"

"Sorry, I don't want it any more," the inspector said, and walked around Murugayya to the doorway.

"Mr Palanivel!" Harsha called out. The inspector looked back at him again.

"Isn't that why you beat those drunk drivers? Because you had a child of your own?"

The inspector's eyes widened, but he turned away from Harsha and walked out into the rain without a word and Harsha heard him curse — in his agitation, he had forgotten to open the umbrella.

"Phew," Harsha said, wiping the sweat from his forehead and collapsing onto the sofa that adorned one corner of Azhar's office. "Yes, don't worry, Murugayya, I will drink the tea. Ah, and here is Maya. You want some tea, Maddy?"

"Yes please," she said, pulling off her jacket and shaking the raindrops off it and hanging it up before collapsing on the sofa next to him. "Thank you, Murugayya."

"Madam," he said hesitantly, after placing the tray on a little coffee table in front of the sofa.

"Yes?"

"Sorry, madam, but my son..."

"Oh, yes! I am a little tired today, Murugayya, but I will teach him tomorrow."

"Of course, Madam, no problem at all!" the man bobbed his head and scuttled away.

Harsha looked enquiringly at her.

"Nothing much. The little devil is eager to learn all the time. Murugayya is very keen that he learns English, never lets me forget."

"So, I have some competition," Harsha said, catching hold of her hair and stroking it between his fingers.

She shifted slightly, so that he was forced to let go of her hair. He looked at her, a little puzzled. Perhaps something had changed for her since last night, and the physical intimacy they had enjoyed in the last couple of days had disappeared.

As though to underline this, she changed the subject and asked: "What did you say to the inspector? He looked pretty pissed off when he was leaving."

"Oh, that. I was just telling him how to do his job," he said, and laughed at the horrified expression on her face. "Well someone had to, Maya! The guy is shirking his responsibilities!"

She poured out tea for them both, shaking her head while she did it. "Well, at least I'm not the only person who has to put up with your bloody lectures."

Harsha grinned, watching the steam rise from the cups and said: "Yes, I am quite democratic with my lectures."

"Patronising asshole," she muttered.

"What's that?"

"Nothing, nothing. Here you go."

Harsha held the tea in his hands, feeling the warmth spread through his body, and looked a little wistfully at Maya, as she sipped delicately from her cup, looking beautiful even with half her head covered in bandages.

She curled up on the other end of the sofa and gave a sigh of contentment, holding the cup of tea with both hands. "God, it feels so good to be inside!" she said.

"Rather than running around in the dark?" he asked in amusement.

She shuddered. For her, it was clearly a traumatic memory. For him, it was something other-worldly. He looked back at it with fascination, and even a little excitement. For the first time in his somewhat predictable life, his life had been in danger on multiple fronts. And he had done well. Yes, he could say that he had done well. Harsha the adventurer was a new acquaintance of his, and he observed this new version of himself with interest.

"Was there anything important from the inspector?" Maya asked, cutting into his thoughts.

"Oh — yes! God, I almost forgot to tell you. These sand smugglers have not confessed to the crime. It's all a bloody set-up. I think the inspector well knows that they aren't the murderers. It's all just a convenient lie," Harsha said, smiling sarcastically.

Maya sat up and looked at Harsha in alarm. "Do you mean they are beating these random people to get a confession out of them that will never come?"

Harsha jumped guiltily. He hadn't given any thought to the treatment of these smugglers. "I don't know," he said, and squirmed at her disturbed expression. Was this investigation beating all the humanity out of him?

On the other hand, he had reacquainted himself with Maya quite well over the past week, and he felt a hot sensation inside him when he looked at her. She wasn't the same Maya from university; but the fire still burned within her. The desire to help people, the compassion for the downtrodden — all of that was in there, waiting to burst out. He wished he could be the one to help her express it, and be by her side and watch her as she did.

"Maya..." he said, hesitantly.

"Yes?" she asked, absentmindedly, staring at the carpet, probably worrying about the sand quarry thieves.

"I need to ask you something."

"Hmm?" Something about the urgency in his voice must have transmitted itself to her, because she shook her head and looked up at him seriously. Harsha took a deep breath before continuing. This was an almost impossible topic to bring up, the embarrassment burned almost as much as the cuts on his head and the pain in his chest, but he steeled himself.

"I guess... last night... that was a mistake?" he asked, his heart pounding a little. He wanted both answers — yes and no.

Maya sighed and turned away from him and took another sip of the tea.

"It was... a moment of madness, Harry," she said, finally, but not without a little undercurrent of wistfulness in her voice.

He looked back at her and smiled wryly. "I guess it doesn't matter right now. Compared to Lakshmi's death this feels..."

She turned and looked at him, her eyes suspiciously bright. "It feels?" she prompted.

"Trivial," he said.

He was right of course, but she still didn't enjoy hearing it. The maelstrom of emotion that was racking her body — how could it be trivial? She blinked tears away and tried to think about Lakshmi, and bringing her justice, instead of contemplating the miserable mess that was her life.

"Would you have gone through with it, if we hadn't been interrupted?" Harsha asked, and she heard the longing in his voice.

She brushed her eyes with the back of her hand, and said: "That interruption was sent to us, Harry. By God. Or the universe, if you prefer."

There was a brief silence, and then Harsha said: "I see."

She felt a terrible catch in her throat, and she stood up suddenly and said: "I'm sorry, Harry. I'm so sorry. Can we join the others? Or do you want to ask me anything else?"

He shook his head. He didn't need to ask her anything else. She had given him all the answers that he needed.

26. INTERLUDE

Sunday dawned warm and sunny, so they took a break from the case and went back to the pool, taking a picnic with them. Maya leaned back against the rocks and took a deep breath. This was so perfect. Strange, how she felt so comfortable in the company of these old university friends.

She was aware of Harsha's presence a few feet away. After the previous night's ordeal, it had been hard enough to convince him to return to anywhere near the river, but he point blank refused to do any swimming. So, he stayed on the edge of the beautiful little pool, leaning on the rocks.

She caught Harsha looking at the waterfall on the edge of this pool every now and then and shivering visibly. She knew he was picturing what it would have felt like to fall down. It would have been very unpleasant, at the very least, if not fatal.

Shane didn't get in the water either, but instead lay on a patch of grass nearby with a book. Harry Potter, to everyone's amusement, though he said he was only reading it to make it easier to read out to his kids. No one believed him.

Maya alone knew the extent of Shane's reading, his regrets at not pursuing English Literature further — the guy was naturally modest, letting the others do most of the talking, but there was a sharp brain behind the affable face, as she well knew.

Azhar and Junaina were bickering at the far end of the pool.

"Just get under here dude, it's bloody awesome," Azhar was saying, standing directly under a tiny portion of the waterfall, the water streaming off his head in a sort of liquid arc.

Harsha sighed beside her. "Why does beer taste so much better when you're out in the open?" he asked, taking a sip.

They sat in companionable silence, until Azhar and Junaina swam up to them and picked up the fluffy towels that had been placed on the edge of the pool. Junaina winked conspiratorially at Maya. "Still on for our girly catch-up later?"

"Can't wait!"

"What do you girls need to catch up on that we can't be part of?" Azhar demanded.

"Seriously, dude," Harsha said to him, shaking his head. "Just don't go there."

"I just don't want them gossiping about us behind our backs, fool," Azhar countered, vigorously towelling the top of his head.

"Yeah that's right, Azhar," Junaina said caustically, shaking her head to get rid of some water from her ears. "All women talk about when they are alone is about *boys*. Idiot," she added, for good measure.

Comfortable as she had been in the presence of the men, Maya was definitely grateful for some feminine company. Leela and Ammani had been wonderful to get to know, and she had become very close to them despite the difference in their backgrounds. But at the end of the day, they were working, and she was not. She couldn't make demands on their time.

The boys... well, they were boys. She had come here to clear her head and think a bit about what she wanted from life. And it had been useful in that respect, but what she really needed was a sounding board.

Of course, all of these men would give her their time willingly, they were good friends even after all these years, but... She had read somewhere that men were solution providers. And when there wasn't an obvious solution to a problem, they were either completely stumped or provided the most ridiculous, impractical solution. Sometimes you just needed someone to listen, not tell you how to do things.

Like Harsha telling her to "come back to India" and everything would be alright. How could leaving her husband and going to a different country be a constructive solution to a serious problem? And where would she stay in India? With a disapproving mother who would make her life miserable with condemnatory comments every minute of the day? And what would she do? It had been years since she last had a job in India, and she just did some editing of legal texts in Seattle to keep herself occupied. She found it hard to believe companies would all be lining up to hire her on the back of these qualifications.

Junaina, for all her tomboyish qualities, had always been great at listening. She looked at her friend, who was now out of the water and was towelling off, a slightly tired expression on her face. How much had she changed? The religious turn she had taken had definitely caught Maya by surprise, but she still seemed the same, good-natured soul, always there to take the boys down a peg or two when they were acting up. And Harsha definitely needed that balance.

She looked across at him, his arms spread out to take in the sunshine, eyes closed. Fortunately, he seemed to have accepted that there was going to be no repeat of the other night and was just treating her as a friend. That suited her fine.

She realised, with a rush, that she didn't want to leave this beautiful place.

Azhar rose out of the pool and reached for a towel, and Maya lazily eyed the gleaming muscles on his powerful arms. She may have been having a bit of a crush on Harsha, but that didn't mean she couldn't appreciate human beauty. She realised she was pursing her lips and straightened her face hurriedly.

Azhar prodded Harsha in the chest. "Oy, hand me a beer," he said, and Harsha opened his eyes and grunted.

"So, no luck with the search, huh?" Harsha asked as he took two bottles out of the nearby cooler, popped them open and handed them to Azhar and Junaina.

"Absolutely none. I made them search the whole damn place from top to bottom. Nothing," Azhar said, throwing the cap of his bottle at Shane, who waved it off as he would a fly, not taking his eyes from his book.

"Guys, this is getting ridiculous," Junaina said. "I only came here yesterday, and you still made me search for this damn pendant of yours. What do you think I would have done with the bloody thing?"

"We don't know if it's a pendant, it could also be a ring," Maya said.

"Yes, that makes searching for it so much easier! We don't know what we are looking for!" Junaina splashed a bit of water towards Harsha from a little puddle in exasperation.

"Junes, just drink your beer. It will calm you down a bit," Azhar said, grinning at Maya.

"Yeah, yeah," Junaina grumbled, but taking a pull of her beer nevertheless.

"How's the wine, Maddie?" Azhar asked. Maya felt a pang of guilt — she had said offhand she preferred wine to beer and Azhar had run back to the main complex to make sure someone brought some wine specially for her. She didn't even have the heart to tell him she preferred red wine.

"It's really good, Azhar, you've taken care of us beautifully," she said, putting a hand on his gleaming arm. Yes, pure muscle.

There was a general chorus of agreement at this point.

"Azhar, you've been amazing."

"Love you, man."

Even Shane looked up from his book and nodded.

"Dude, this is an amazing spot," Junaina said, giving her beer to Maya for safekeeping and turning around to take it all in. "It would be seriously amazing if we weren't doing this whole *Famous Five* thing."

Everyone chuckled. "Who's who?" Harsha asked.

"You can be George, bugger," Azhar said, handing him his beer bottle. "The woman pretending to be a man."

"You can be Dick," Harsha countered.

"And who gets to be Timmy the dog?"

Harsha grinned. "Well, Maya already has practice being Snowy, so maybe..."

"Careful, I bite," she said, baring her teeth.

Junaina stood up and walked to the edge of the pool and said: "Listen, you guys, we are only here until Wednesday now. Let's forget that damn case for a bit and do something fun. How about an elephant ride? Or a trek through the forest? Or do you have any more suggestions, Azhar?"

Azhar stood up as well and walked to the edge of the pool and said "We could do a road trip across these mountains — the roads are awesome, thanks to the panchayat dude, one good thing he has done anyway."

"Anything man, something more holiday-like, instead of searching for rings and shit," Junaina said.

"Yeah, I was thinking about that," Azhar said. "My original plan was to go camping when Juni got here, but given everything... Anyway, how about that road trip?"

Maya looked at Harsha, who was looking distinctly

uncomfortable.

"Are you going to be ok with that, Harry?" she asked, remembering his motion sickness.

"Yes," he said quickly. "It's totally fine. And we should have some fun. It's been too much of the *Famous Five* stuff, as Juni puts it. Azhar's car is a beauty and it will be really fun. I just need to buy some limes. And can I drive?"

They lazed by the pool until Maya's skin was starting to wrinkle, and then they stepped out for lunch by the pool, delivered by Murugayya ("you're supposed to be the *manager*, Murugayya!" Azhar complained, exasperatedly). It was incredibly peaceful to sit there, with nothing but birdsong around them and soft chatter by the pool. Harsha snoozed and Shane concentrated on his book, so Azhar and Maya taxed Junaina about her love life.

"You met him online, didn't you?"

"No dude, it was at a bar..."

"Yeah, we don't believe that," Azhar said. "Anyone who meets you in a bar is walking in the opposite direction straightaway."

Maya laughed gently, and lazily listened to them bicker, as she looked around, enjoying the surroundings. A few monkeys appeared on the trees, no doubt attracted by the smell of their food.

I should do this every now and then, Maya thought, feeling her breathing slowing — she felt — in time with the rhythm of the very earth. That's the sort of nutty, poetic thing that Harsha would say, she thought sleepily.

Just on cue, Harsha said: "How beautiful is this afternoon sunshine on the waterfall? 'The long light shakes across the lakes and the wild cataract leaps in glory.' Tennyson. Why are you laughing?"

"No reason," she murmured, her eyes fluttering.

Harsha didn't say anything, and Maya, in her half-asleep state, could just about follow Azhar and Junaina's conversation as they continued to chat quietly, their voices merging comfortably with the bird song around them. It reminded her of evenings lying on the couch and falling asleep while her dad watched cricket, and occasionally exclaimed at India's performance (or lack of it). She felt a pang of loss, all the more poignant in her current dream-like state.

"I miss this," Junaina was saying. "Just us old friends. I wonder why we lost touch."

Azhar shrugged. "I think Harsha was the glue that held us together. Once he went off..."

Maya knew they were thinking of the disastrous last meeting several years ago.

"Guys, I am sorry, I know I was different back then, but I am here now."

"Better late than never!" Shane chimed in from further away, raising soft laughter from the group.

"Well, anyway, let's not dig up old tragedies," Junaina said. "We are here now, and let's enjoy it. It may be the last time we are all together like this."

"Amen to that," Azhar said soberly.

That evening, as Maya stepped out of her shower and started drying herself, there was a knocking on the door.

"One minute!" she called out, and pulled on her clothes hurriedly.

She wondered who it was. Surely not Harsha? Surely, he had got the message... that she didn't want that anymore?

Her heart started beating slightly faster as she opened the door, smiling. And looked down.

"Oh... Jaggu," she said, looking down on Murugayya's son, trying to hide her confusion. "Er... yes, I said I would read some English stories to you, right?"

He just looked up at her with wide eyes, standing at attention in a little checked shirt and a pair of tiny khaki pants that brought a smile to Maya's face.

She sighed. "Ok, let's do it. Give me one minute."

The boy smiled broadly, displaying his little teeth.

"Where is your Appa?" she asked as she pulled on her shoes and reached for her jacket.

"Still working, miss," the boy managed, clasping his hands together bashfully.

They strode down towards the main dining hall, Jaggu skipping along happily to keep up with her. Evening was turning to night, and there was a slightly ethereal air to the mountainside. The lights had come on in the main dining room, making it look welcoming and warm. Maya took in the cold evening air and wondered if she would ever again experience anything as beautiful as this.

Of course you will, she scolded herself. She only had to make sure she made time for countryside getaways. And yet, the thought of driving out somewhere in the American countryside — as beautiful as it was — paled in comparison at that moment with the wild spookiness of Pipal Resorts and the surrounding mountain.

Eventually, they reached the dining hall and Maya ducked into the kitchen to ask when dinner was served, and to say a quick hello to her friends. Leela was perched on one of the counters, keeping Ammani company as she stirred some gigantic pot that was giving out the most delicious smell. Both women smiled broadly at Maya — the three of them were firmly part of the sisterhood now — and then went into transports of delight over Jaggu's little formal get up.

The boy patiently submitted to them pinching his cheeks, before turning to Maya inquiringly.

"Yes, let's go read now," she said, wondering why the boy hardly ever spoke, even though his Tamil was excellent and his English was improving all the time. "Where do you want to do this?"

"Under the tree, miss."

She waved goodbye to the other women and led Jaggu through the dining room, nodding to Shane and Junaina, who were playing a game of chess, beers by their elbows — before heading out to the cement dais beneath the pipal tree.

Someone had hung up lanterns on the branches of the trees, giving it an almost magical appearance, though clouds of little insects buzzed around each light.

As she sat down there with a sigh, Jaggu ran up to the central trunk and picked up his little knapsack and hurried back to her.

He unzipped it carefully, and she caught a glimpse of a variety of odds and ends that clearly made up his collection of toys. Jaggu took them out one by one as though they were precious gems and placed them on the floor, and then finally, out came the *piece de resistance* — a tattered children's book about ducks, probably given to him by one of the resort guests. Maya took this equally reverentially from him and carefully parted the pages.

"Mr Duck swims on the pond. Look at him go!" she read out absentmindedly, her mind wandering. Jaggu didn't seem to mind. He sat there, wide-eyed, drinking it all in.

When she finished the duck book, Jaggu leaning against her lap to get a better look at the pictures, she placed it to one side, much to the boy's disappointment.

She looked around at the hodge-podge of toys to try and find another way of entertaining him, as she was now heartily sick of the duck book. It was an odd collection, a mixture of cheap wooden toys, some genuinely beautiful hand-crafted pieces, one expensive-looking model of an Audi car — surely Azhar's contribution — and various other random items that the boy had picked up and stored in magpie-like fashion.

She picked up a plastic cell phone and said: "Hello, hello, calling Mr Jagannathan."

The boy giggled and giggled at this game.

"Hello, hello," he repeated. She had created a monster — whenever she tried to move on to some other toy, he just repeated "Hello, hello" until she picked up the cell phone again and pretended to call him.

She spotted Azhar in the distance, walking down the path from his office. "Hey, come and join us!" she yelled.

"Er... really busy, Maddie, lots of work to do..."

"Shut up and come!"

"Shut up!" the boy said delightedly, savouring this new English phrase.

"Good god, he's going to say that to his parents, isn't he?" she exclaimed.

"Probably," Azhar said, grumpily coming up and sitting down. "I'm supposed to be the owner of this resort, you know that Maya? Not some damn babysitter."

"Shut up!" the boy said, by way of greeting.

"You shut up!"

"Azhar! He's just a boy, you nut."

They played for a while, Azhar looking terribly pained by the boisterous treatment the Audi was receiving as Jaggu raced it around the floor of the dais.

"Oh god, I am so tired of this cell phone game!" Maya said, after what felt like the fiftieth time, dropping the plastic phone onto the floor. "What else does he have?"

Last Resort

She rummaged through Jaggu's things, surreptitiously pocketing a safety pin — surely, that was unsafe — and finally picking up a plastic tumbler. "Cheers, Jaggu!" she said, pretending to drink from the glass. She tossed her head back to empty her 'drink', and then yelped as something hard hit her lips.

"Ouch! What the hell..." Something fell from the plastic glass on to her face and then dropped with a clink on to her lap, and she picked it up.

The world went still, and the haze around them seemed to swell and the shadows lengthened as she picked up the shining object and watched it sparkle in a slightly sinister manner in the light of the lanterns above them.

"Azhar... Azhar!"

"Hang on Maya, I'm trying to explain something. Jaggu, look, this is a collector's item, you understand? Col-lec-tors i-tem! Very expensive!"

"Azhar shut up ('shut up!' the boy echoed) and look at this!"

Time seemed to stand still as two pairs of eyes focused on the shimmering object Maya was holding up with one thumb and forefinger. Azhar's jaw dropped.

From her fingers flowed a thick silver chain, winking in the light as it turned gently this way and that. At the bottom of the silver waterfall was a heavy golden pendant shaped like a sleek eagle, its merciless beak jutting out from the straight lines of its body, two bright red gems making up its cruel eyes, staring bleakly out at them.

"You don't think... I... Maya, that's not... No way..."

They both stared at the pendant in silence for a moment. Jaggu seemed to catch their sudden air of seriousness, as he stopped talking and looked at them fearfully.

Maya turned to him, staring at the boy as though she had never seen him before.

"Jaggu," she said urgently. "Where did you get this? Tell me, boy!"

Jaggu looked at the two adults one after the other and swallowed at their expectant, inquiring expressions. Complete silence descended on the courtyard for a minute, apart from the rasping of the crickets all around them.

"Come on, Jaggu, where did you get this?" Maya asked again,

urgently.

"Maya, the boy obviously has no idea."

"Lakshmi Akka gave it to me!" Jaggu suddenly declared.

"Lakshmi... Akka..." Azhar repeated, dazed.

They stared at the boy, speechless.

27. THE PENDANT

They sat around the table talking urgently, their sentences spilling over each other. The eagle pendant was placed at the centre of the table, fringed by beer bottles and wine glasses, and everyone's eyes were dragged towards it every now and then. Fortunately, there were no other guests in the dining hall, leaving them to talk freely.

Maya looked at the pendant with a slight sense of dread. She wasn't a particularly imaginative person, but she couldn't help picturing a dead hand wrapped around it. She picked up her glass of wine, took a deep gulp and looked distractedly at the windows of the main hall, wishing they were having this conversation during the day rather than in this eerie dusk light. She kept imagining that a stranger's face would suddenly appear in one of the window panes, the indistinct visage of one of her chasers from two nights ago...

"So, we finally got the truth out of that little devil," Azhar said, intruding into her thoughts. "Only after Murugayya clouted him a couple of times around the head," he added, an approving tone to his voice.

"So how did it happen? Why on earth did Jaggu decide to break her hand? It still makes no sense," Junaina said, cracking her knuckles speculatively. Shane was right — Junaina was really into this whole murder mystery thing in a sort of detached way. Her eyes were sparkling and she even looked a little amused. *If she had seen Lakshmi's body she may not have been so cheerful*, Maya thought darkly, and then felt ashamed of the thought. She wouldn't wish that sight on anyone, let alone a close friend.

"So, apparently Lakshmi used to bring the boy a little gift every now and then — a sweet or a toy or something like that," Azhar explained soberly. Unusually for him, he hadn't poured any wine for himself, and was just sipping a glass of cold water. "So, when he saw her lying there, he ran up to see what she had brought for him. When she refused to open her hand — probably because she was dead — the boy decided to pry it open to see what the gift was."

Maya shook off her sense of fear and said, as reasonably as she could: "I bet she used to play some sort of game with him, refusing to give to him the gift for a while, and then finally opening her hand with the promised present."

They looked at her, and she shrugged. "It's the kind of thing I do with my nieces and nephews," she said.

Shane, who was turning his beer bottle round and round on the table, as though playing spin-the-bottle, asked meditatively: "But how can a four-year-old boy break her hand? Would he have the strength?"

"The inspector said the fingers would be quite brittle after a few days of decomposing," Harsha said heavily.

"Besides, you would be surprised how strong he is. Jaggu, I mean," Maya added.

"But wouldn't he have been scared seeing her like that? I would have been terrified!"

"He's just a boy, Juni, he probably doesn't even understand what death is. He probably thought she was sleeping or something."

Shane added, his eyes still on the bottle: "And besides, I know for a fact that kids are fascinated by horrible things. Once, I cut my knee and it got infected. My boy spent hours staring at it and poking it and stuff. Kids are just strange, especially boys."

Harsha said: "Do we know for a fact that he took it from the dead body?"

"Oh yes," Azhar said. "He admitted he did it the day before you lovebirds found the body."

Maya let the 'lovebird' comment pass, and asked: "Yes, but the question is: what are we going to do now?"

A silence fell over the group.

Junaina looked around at all of them and then said: "Hello, what do you mean what are we going to do? Surely, we are going to tell the police? What on earth else *can* we do?"

Harsha folded his arms and said slowly: "Juni, I know you're not a fan of the *Famous Five* stuff, but the fact is, we are not sure the police will actually do anything unless we find out whose pendant this is. A couple of days ago, I would have gone straight to the inspector. But now I'm not sure he wants any more information — look at how they just completely ignored the murderous thugs who were wandering around at night!"

"How on earth are we going to find out whose pendant it is then?"

Maya glanced at Harsha, who shrugged his shoulders at her as though to say "as you wish", so she turned to Junaina and said: "We do have an idea of who it belongs to. Well — more than idea. We are pretty sure."

"And who is that?"

"Rajaratnam. He calls himself The Eagle and has the same eagle symbol on the gate of his house."

They all stared at her in astonishment and surprise. Azhar even made as though to stand up, but when she looked at him, he sat back down again, an expression of dawning realisation on his face. Shane was looking at her with uncharacteristic sharpness, his eyes seemingly trying to bore into her skull. Junaina was the only one who still looked puzzled.

"He has an eagle on his gate?" she finally asked, frowning. "What — like some sort of coat of arms or something?"

"Something like that," Harsha said, seriously. "Subhash, the shopkeeper, told us everyone calls him The Eagle. Something about it appeals to him — Rajaratnam himself banged on about it to us. Remember Maya? He sees himself as the man who got rid of a lot of unsavoury people in Arasur, like the eagle that eats snakes."

Junaina looked unconvinced, but Maya looked at Shane and Azhar, and knew that they instantly understood the significance of this piece of information. Azhar hesitated, before saying: "I have heard him referred to as The Eagle before. But even then I still don't see how you can prove that the pendant is his. It doesn't seem possible without putting ourselves at risk."

Harsha shook his head, and silence fell again.

They jumped as the door from the kitchen banged open and Ammani came in with her usual cheerful smile and said: "Dinner, sir?"

"Oh, yes please!" Azhar said, smiling gratefully at her. As she left, he turned conspiratorially to the group and said in a low tone: "Ok look guys, the first batch of Shane's corporate guests is arriving here next month. We need to get this place ready for them."

"Ready in what way?"

It was Shane who replied: "Some group activities — a treasure hunt maybe, and we'll have to set up a cricket pitch of some sort — I have a few ideas."

"So, the point is," Azhar cut in, "Shanny and I really need to get started on that stuff this week. Besides, you guys are leaving on Wednesday, unless you want me to change the tickets again?"

"And what about the road trip?" Junaina asked. They didn't say anything. "Oh fine, I can see that's not happening," she said, a little crestfallen.

Shane said: "Why don't you and I go for that elephant ride tomorrow, Juni, and leave the investigating to these people? I need to go anyway to discuss a group rate for the corporate retreat."

Harsha and Maya shot Shane a grateful look.

"Yeah ok," Junaina said reluctantly. "Though I thought the point was for all of us to be together."

"We can still hang out in the evening. We don't have to do everything together."

Junaina nodded. "Fair enough. A good chance to get away from this murder mystery rubbish, anyway."

"Right," Azhar said. "So, what are we going to do?"

They all looked expectantly at Harsha.

Harsha leaned over and picked up the pendant and rolled it across his fingers, clearly thinking. After a few minutes, he said: "There's sadly no magical way of tying this to Rajaratnam — they don't have DNA detection or anything like that here," he said, gazing down at the pendant as though he could penetrate its secrets by staring at it. "But I do have one or two ideas on how we can prove it is him. I need a bit of time to iron out the details."

"Let's hear your ideas," Azhar said, and a general buzz of agreement passed around the table.

Harsha paused for a minute and then said: "So I've read in this book..."

"Of course, you read it in a book," Maya said.

"Good old Harry, some things never change," Shane added, smiling affectionately at Harsha.

"Shut up guys and listen. There's this book where they need to prove this ring belongs to someone and..."

"What book is this?" Junaina asked, frowning slightly.

"Probably one of his Shakespeare things," Azhar said gloomily.

"No, it's not Shakespeare, it's..." Harsha hesitated for a second and then said: "Never mind what book it is. The point is, they need to prove this ring belongs to this man."

"*Arre*, why won't you tell us what book it is?" Junaina asked, impatiently.

"I think Harry's a bit embarrassed by it," Maya said shrewdly, smiling across at Harsha.

"Oh for God's sake! You people... fine! I'm not going to tell you my plan!"

"Stop being an idiot, we were just messing," Azhar said tersely. "You can tell us the plan."

"Come on, Harry! Tell us!"

But Harsha shook his head and said: "Seriously, I need to figure it out myself, and actually think it's better you don't know."

They tried wheedling it out of him for a good ten minutes, by which time the dinner was brought to the table, and they all served themselves and ate hungrily. But well after the *chapatis* and *kurma* had vanished, and dessert (Kuppi had excelled herself with homemade *gulab jamun*) was served, they still hadn't managed to get any details out of Harsha, except that he was looking a bit harassed.

"I need more time, guys, just give me some time!" he said for the umpteenth time.

Maya realised the conversation was running in pointless circles, and said: "Come on, guys, let's allow him to plot in peace. Meanwhile, what about telling us what you want us to do, Harry?"

Harsha threw her a grateful look and lapsed into silence. They all stared at him expectantly. He picked up his wine and looked at it meditatively, swilling it around in his glass.

Finally, he said: "I want you to invite Rajaratnam over. That's the most important thing."

"Invite him over? Bloody hell, Harry, how can I do that?" Azhar exploded. "The guy hates me and I hate him. What reason could I give?"

Shane piped up: "Tell him you've changed your mind about this resort — that you are now willing to discuss selling it."

Harsha pointed at Shane and said: "Genius! That's exactly it. Tell him that."

"But I'm not willing to sell, buggers! I can't just tell him..."

Harsha waved this away. "Just quote a ridiculous price, and you won't have to sell it," he said impatiently, as though this were a minor detail.

"But he never comes up here! We have done all our negotiations through his sidekick! That guy who is his secretary or whatever."

"Tell him you want to show him what you have done to this place. Show him where you want to put the football pitch or something. Come on, Azhar, show some imagination!"

Azhar looked around — everyone was staring at him. Finally, his shoulders slumped and he said: "Fine, I'll call him tomorrow. But what are you going to do once he is here?"

Harsha's hand closed around the pendant, and he stood up and threw it to Azhar, who fumbled before he caught it, staring at the elegantly crafted golden eagle.

"Only time will tell, my friends," Harsha said, and they could see that some of the sparkle had returned to his eyes. "I need to pay a visit to our friend the inspector tomorrow. And then, we shall see what we shall see."

28. RENDEZVOUS

She glided above the forest, only gently skimming the canopy every now and then to feel the leaves brushing against her underbelly.

The trees were sodden with rain water, and indeed, icy drops were striking her wings as she flew — it was uncomfortably cold, with a powerful easterly wind buffeting her from one side, but she revelled in it, enjoying the feel of the wind and that rain against her face, and the light fading in the west.

With a tremendous beating of her powerful wings she rose further and opened her beak to let out a cry that echoed across the lonely mountain.

Thunder broke out repeatedly, getting louder and louder. Time to fly home ...

Thunder again. But that wasn't thunder was it? It was too repetitive, the sound of something striking wood...

Maya's eyes opened and she lay in her bed in a daze, momentarily in that world between sleep and waking. She desperately tried to cling on to the dream. It had been so beautiful!

The thundering noise rang out again and she woke up with a start. The sun was streaming in from her window.

What was going on? Was someone knocking on her door? Surely it would be louder if they were?

She sprang up and ran lightly to her door and opened it.

"Come out of there you fool! Now!"

She shook her head to clear it and Azhar's slim frame came into focus. He was banging on Harsha's door, which was just adjacent to hers, his face red with agitation, as the mountainside stretched out peacefully behind him, smiling in the morning sunshine.

"Azhar! What the hell is going on? What's the matter?" she asked, rubbing her eyes blearily and trying to make sense of the scene.

Azhar turned from Harsha's door and looked urgently at her: "Maddie! Go get ready, I need you too!"

"But what..."

Harsha's door opened and its occupant stuck his head out. Maya had to suppress a giggle at the state of his hair, sticking up in odd directions.

"Wassgoingon man?" he slurred thickly. "Something on fire or something?"

Azhar caught hold of Harsha's shirt, pulled the door open and pulled him out bodily.

"Dammit Azhar," Harsha exclaimed, stumbling over the threshold and yelping as his bare feet hit the cold grass.

"Nice boxers," Maya chimed in.

"It was a gift," Harsha grinned, looking ruefully down at the clown's face plastered all over the front of his boxers, unmistakable below his plain white T-shirt.

"Why is the clown smoking a cigar?"

"Maya, stop staring at my..."

"Never mind his boxers, Maya! Harry, you idiot, you've messed everything up!"

Harsha blinked repeatedly in an attempt to wake himself up.

"Need a smoke," he said and turned unceremoniously and disappeared back into his bedroom.

"Man, there's no time to..." the rest of Azhar's words faded as he followed Harsha into the room and the door shut behind them.

Maya hesitated and then stepped into a pair of shoes, without bothering to pull them back over her heels, and followed the men into Harsha's room.

"... at 12 o' clock!" she heard Azhar say as pushed the door open and surveyed the chaos that was Harsha's room.

"And what time is it now?" Harsha was asking as he pulled on his jeans.

"Eight thirty!"

"Jesus, Azhar! There's ages left. Why are you getting so worked up?" Harsha demanded as he tugged at his belt and fixed the clasp, before grinning at Maya. "Glad you could join us," he added.

"How could I resist," she smiled. "Azhar, what is happening at 12 o' clock?"

"That Rajaratnam is coming here!" Azhar said, sitting down on a chair and putting his head in his hands.

"Azhar, couldn't you have told him to come later? Can't you still?" Maya asked, aghast.

"I tried! I told him to come this evening, but he just said if I want to seal the deal it must be now! I don't know how to deal with people like him, man! He scares the living shit out of me!" Azhar slammed his hands down on the arms of the chair and jumped up and paced the room. "What the hell will I say to him?"

"I don't care what you say. Just keep him talking. And give me your keys."

There was a second's silence as both of them stared at Harsha, who looked eerily calm, standing by his bed and running a hand over his T-shirt to smooth it out. In fact, he seemed completely in his element, Maya thought.

"What keys?" Azhar asked finally, sounding as baffled as Maya felt.

"The keys to the Audi, idiot. You have any mints?"

Still looking confused, Azhar fished in his pockets and found some chewing gum.

"No time to brush teeth," Harry explained. "Where's the car?"

"Just round the back of the building. Had to bring up some office supplies last night."

Maya sat on the bed, pushing aside a pile of Harsha's clothes, a little distastefully, and said: "Harry, is this really the time to go for a drive?"

"Why not? Looks like a beautiful day," he said flippantly, to her great annoyance, as he straightened his hair in front of the mirror on the door of the teak wardrobe.

"Are you going to explain, you... you... nimrod?"

He spun around and looked at her, amused. "Nimrod?" He asked.

"BLOODY HELL, HARRY!" Azhar yelled out so loudly that the others leaned back, Harsha stumbling against the great wardrobe. "Are you going to BLOODY EXPLAIN! Where are you going and what are you going to do?"

Harsha came up and put an arm on his shoulder.

"Azhar, there's no time. Besides, I myself am not too sure what I'm going to do. I'll think it through during the drive down to Ramananpettai. As for where I'm going, that I can tell you — I'm going to the police."

"And then?"

"I told you, I don't know — yet. But please, you *must* trust me, I will sort this out. All you have to do is keep Rajaratnam talking."

"Shall I come with you, Harry?"

Azhar froze in the act of handing over his car keys and turned to Maya as though she had gone mad. "Maddy, you are going nowhere!" he said, in a panicked voice. "You have to talk to Rajaratnam with me!"

She jumped at this sudden turn of events. "Get Shane to sit with you! I'll go with Harry."

Azhar hit his forehead. "Shane and Juni have buggered off to ride elephants!" he said, sounding disgusted. "Today of all days! Maddy I need you! I'll probably sell him this place and everything in it, including you lot, if I don't have some support!"

"Ok, calm down," she said, going up and putting one hand on Azhar's shoulder and kneading it slightly. His breathing eased a bit.

"Almost forgot," Harsha said, grabbing his jacket from the side table. "I need the pendant."

They stared at him again.

"Go and get the pendant!" Harsha snapped at Azhar, his calm assurance cracking for the first time, and Maya caught a glimpse of the tension beneath the façade, like a coiled spring.

Azhar almost saluted, before banging his way out of the room in a great hurry.

Harsha checked his pockets automatically for wallet and phone and then turned to Maya.

"What? Why are you looking at me like that?"

"Oh, nothing"

"Come on!"

She hesitated and then said: "I was just thinking that you seem to be enjoying this tremendously."

"I... I think I still love you," he blurted out, and then looked down at his feet.

A silence fell, and she said, as kindly as she could: "I'll let that pass, as it's all a bit tense right now and you probably are pumped up on adrenaline."

He looked up at her, and a bit of a smile returned to his face, and he nodded gratefully and then strode out of the room and they marched to the back of Azhar's office, where the car was parked. The sun was fully out now and streaming its way across Pipal Resorts. It was bidding to be the most beautiful day yet since they had arrived, and birdsong echoed its way across the slopes.

Azhar was standing by his Audi, a beautiful incongruity in the midst of the lush countryside. He held out the pendant between one finger and his thumb and hesitated before dropping it into Harsha's outstretched palm.

"I'll be careful with it, Azhar!" Harsha said impatiently.

"Careful Azhar, the two most precious possessions in this resort are now in Harry's hands. Bet you he is going to the nearest pawn shop," Maya said playfully, running one hand over the hood of the beautiful vehicle.

"What pawnshop and all in this god forsaken place," Azhar said dismissively.

Harsha pressed the button that released the car door and opened it reverentially, breathing deeply to take in the smell of leather. He then turned sharply to the two of them and said: "Just keep him talking!" He then slammed the door shut, creating a little divide between them.

"Until when?" Azhar yelled, banging on the car pane.

"Until I'm back!" Harsha said, lowering the window. "Or until something happens."

"Until what happens?"

Harsha turned on the ignition and the car purred into gear.

"You'll know when it happens. Maya, trusting you to take care of Azhar here!" he shouted above the sound of the engine.

She gave him a thumbs up, and he revved the car out (none too gently) and then eased his way into the little driveway that went from the office down to the resort, and suddenly accelerated down the slope with a roar, leaving a trail of dust behind.

"Right," Azhar said, staring gormlessly after the car. "How about some breakfast?" he added, a little helplessly.

"A great idea. Let me get changed first."

"Maybe he won't come!" Azhar said, hope dawning on his face.

"It's only 12.15, Azhar, Indian standard time. Just try and relax, ok?" Azhar's nervousness was starting to get on her nerves now.

Apart from being annoying, it was starting to transmit itself to her as well. She didn't quite have Shane's knack for calming things down.

She sighed and rearranged the notebook in front of her. She was going to try and take some notes, just in case they missed something. Perhaps a secretarial position might suit her — she had always looked down on it as a profession, but perhaps she hadn't thought it through. It would keep her from going out of her mind with boredom in the US anyway.

A knock on the door. Azhar sprang up from his position behind his desk. "Must be Murugayya," he muttered distractedly. "Murugayya! Murugayya! Is that you?"

The door opened and Maya recognised Rajaratnam's assistant, dressed in his weird dentist-like white uniform, before being followed by the man himself.

Rajaratnam was not as large as her imagination had made it. He was slightly rotund, of course, but his paunch was hidden by a loose, brown shirt with large breast pockets and his shoulders were broad and strong. His presence was undeniable, she acknowledged to herself, and reminded her a little bit of Inspector Palanivel for the effortless way in which he held the room.

She glanced at his bare neck and then looked away immediately. Very little seemed to escape those intelligent eyes, and she wanted to give him no hint of their suspicion. The assistant shrank into one corner and composed himself, standing. The contrast between his white shirt and Rajaratnam's light brown shirt made them look like some sort of military attache, Maya thought.

Rajaratnam advanced into the room, looking around the pleasant dining hall approvingly, and with a slightly proprietorial air.

"Oh... ah!" Azhar managed.

"Sorry to disappoint, you, I am not... did you say... Murugayya?" the man asked, smirking slightly at the name. Was it a dig at the hotel manager's caste, or just Rajaratnam's general air of menace that made his tone seem meaningful? Maya couldn't tell.

But certainly, the panchayat head was enjoying the discomfiture on Azhar's face, Maya thought, and felt a stab of resentment resurface in her. Once again, Rajaratnam was ignoring her. The irrelevant woman. Or was he?

This time he actually turned to look at her, as Azhar ushered him to a seat on the sofa. Maya followed and sat on a chair a little further back from the two adjacent sofas that made up the main living room space.

"And what is her role here?" Rajaratnam asked Azhar, politely enough, apart from his complete refusal to address her directly. Maya felt the blood rush to her head.

"Oh?" Azhar seemed thrown by this question. "I... er... I have hired her. As my se... my assistant," he said, unconsciously mirroring her own thoughts, as though she had telepathically sent him a message.

"I see. And you are going into business with your other friend — Shane Francis is it?"

"Eh? Oh, Shane, yes. How did you..." Azhar stopped himself. "Yes," he said, simply.

"And I hear you have been bringing in some other staff from the town as well?"

"Only to replace the ones who refused to come back after the... er... the accident. I mean, incident," Azhar babbled.

The man threw one arm casually over the back of the sofa, but his eyes narrowed as he looked at Azhar. "You seem to be on quite a recruitment drive for a man who wants to sell his business. New staff. New secretary."

A silence fell.

Finally, realising that Azhar had little to contribute, Maya spoke, using as much formal vocabulary as she could remember: "I am taking up a position as Mr Azhar's personal assistant, I am not an employee of the resort itself."

Rajaratnam had moved his head slightly in her direction to listen, though he still didn't look at her. But to her relief, he said nothing.

"So, Mr Azhar, assuming this isn't all a joke (Azhar shook his head vigorously) then we can proceed to business. Amarnath, go find me some coffee, please. Yes. Business," he said, as the assistant left in the direction of the kitchen.

Azhar just stared at the panchayat head blankly, to Maya's continued annoyance and growing panic. To her dismay, she realised that he was going to bottle it. She would have to step in or the plan would be sunk. But what could she say?

"Sir, shall I acquaint you with the details?" she cut in desperately. The man frowned without taking his eyes from Azhar, though Azhar himself turned and looked at her with obvious relief.

She ploughed on despite Rajaratnam's frosty attitude. She was in uncharted waters now — but what option did she have?

"Since I have been hired, I have been examining Mr Azhar's accounts, and I found that this business venture — this resort — has been increasing revenues at an exponential rate over the last two years," she said, trying to remember some jargon from financial documents she had typed up in her Seattle job. "It is on track to turn a strong profit at that rate over the course of the next summer vacation period."

She ended the final sentence with a squeak, and Rajaratnam frowned at the use of future tense for the profitability of the resort but didn't volunteer a comment.

"Unfortunately," she continued, her voice growing a little stronger now. "After the... incident... several guests wanted to leave with a full... er... refund, and given the difficult situation Mr Azhar was dealing with at the time, he agreed."

Still not looking at her, Rajaratnam gave a sardonic smile that clearly showed that he would have done things differently.

Azhar fidgeted. "Difficult situation... couldn't be bargaining with a bunch of... had things to organise..." he muttered.

"Anyway," Maya said sharply, cutting into Azhar's embarrassingly weak explanations while looking at Rajaratnam's profile. "The point is, I believe he and his family have decided that while potentially highly profitable, it was time to exit the business, having grown it so far. At the right price."

They were interrupted by the banging of the door as the assistant backed into it, carrying a tray with a pot of coffee and a cup. Just a single one, Maya noted. There was absolute silence as the man carefully approached the sofas and placed the tray on the coffee table. They all watched, entranced, as he poured out the coffee, so that there was no sound other than the trickling of the brown liquid as it steamed into the cup. Three cubes of sugar went in next and Amarnath stirred it carefully for a full ten seconds. Finally, he presented it with a flourish to his master.

As Amarnath retreated, Rajaratnam picked up his cup, delicately blew on its surface, took a sip and then said into his coffee: "And what might the right price be?"

Maya hesitated. Everything she had said so far had come straight from what little she remembered from her work. She had no idea what land prices were in these parts. She looked to Azhar for help, but he was just staring at her gormlessly. *What the hell, Azhar*, she thought to herself. What if she went for too low a number and the man accepted?

So, she went instead for the most ridiculous number she could think of.

"Considering the acreage, the proximity to the train station and the natural beauty of the surroundings — the number we are tentatively looking at is 20 crore rupees," she said.

"What?" the man literally jumped in his seat, the coffee slopping over the sides of his cup and onto the saucer. Finally, Rajaratnam turned to look at her.

"Did you say — twenty crores?" he asked, his eyes bulging. Even the assistant was staring at her.

Now was not the time to back down. "At the very least," she said firmly, ignoring Azhar's equally startled expression.

"Young lady... are you aware that the entire village... my whole farm... twenty crores is ridiculous!" Rajaratnam thundered, putting his coffee down on the table decisively.

"That's the price."

"This is a joke," the man said, wiping his hands with his handkerchief and then flinging it down on the table angrily. "I can't believe I wasted my time coming here to listen to some... some..."

"Some what?" Maya asked him, her back straightening and her eyes glinting dangerously as the assistant quickly scrambled towards the coffee table to pick up the handkerchief.

Rajaratnam caught the anger in her expression, and — perhaps realising she would not be as easily bullied as most of the people he encountered — calmed down a little. In fact, the sardonic little smile returned.

"Pardon me, Miss... Miss..."

"Maya," she said, too shaken to insist on 'Ms'.

"Miss Maya," he said, bowing his head exaggeratedly (as though he were in front of the queen or something, she thought to herself).

"Excuse my anger," he continued, suddenly all charm. "I was only a little surprised at the sum you quoted. Can I ask how you arrived at the figure?"

Why had she not foreseen this? Fighting down the rising panic, she said: "It is based on the revenues generated..."

"I thought you said he was making a loss?"

"Of course, but we are talking about revenues and the trajectory of the operating profits. A substantial investment was recently made in the resort to bring it up to modern standards. In terms of revenues the place is healthy, and from this point on the projections are for steady profits. I can run you through the numbers... er... at a slightly later point," she said, stumbling slightly.

"Also," she continued, mentally blessing the station master, who had insisted on gossiping to her at the train station while helping her with her luggage, "Consider that the Southern Express Mail is to change its route via the Ramananpettai station. So, you have a direct train from Bangalore in addition to Chennai from the start of next year. Ease of access, and potentially many more customers if you market it right."

She was on a roll, and she went for broke. "Finally, if you own this resort, you will own basically all the most valuable land on this side of the mountain."

"So?"

"So, the price for you is higher."

She had his entire attention now, she had him eating out of her hand. This was... exhilarating. The panic vanished.

"And what sort of logic is that?" he asked, breathing heavily.

She shrugged. "Simple supply and demand. This place means a lot more to you than it would to some random hotelier."

His smile returned. "You are... Mr Azhar's personal assistant, did you say?"

"More like a business consultant," she said, uncomfortably aware of how thin the story was. But fortunately, he seemed satisfied.

The man drummed his fingers on the arm of the sofa. She found herself staring at his neck again, trying to picture the eagle pendant there, and looked away again.

"To be frank, I came here prepared to pay a tenth of that sum. But I have to admit, your argument is good." He fell into silence again, staring at the wall opposite him and still drumming his fingers.

"I will have to see those numbers again..." he began but was interrupted by the opening of the door.

One of the cleaners came in from the kitchen and walked up to clear the coffee and wipe the coffee table. Rajaratnam glanced indifferently at her and then went back to contemplating the wall. His assistant continued to stand at attention by the door impassively.

But Maya and Azhar stared open-mouthed at this new entrant.

They had no idea who she was.

29. QUARRY

She was young and slim, and while she was wearing the red sari that all the cleaners in the resort wore, she was a complete stranger to them — though something about her slightly bored-looking expression did dislodge some memory at the back of Maya's mind.

They continued to stare at her as she picked up the tray with the coffee cup, balancing it with one hand while wiping the coffee table with the other. Finally, she stood up, and looking from Azhar to Maya, she said: "Good morning, sir, madam, can I get you any coffee or tea?"

Rajaratnam clicked his tongue at the interruption, but she ignored him and stood waiting for their response.

Why did she look so familiar? Suddenly, something clicked in Maya's mind and she shot a warning glance at Azhar.

"No, that's fine, thank you... er... Sanjana," she said, choosing a name at random.

"Some water, madam?"

"Er... alright, some water would be good."

The woman bowed her head slightly, the perfect model of submissiveness, and then was about to leave when she spotted an empty glass by the dresser in the corner. She hurried to pick it up.

"To continue, I would like to see the final numbers you mentioned, whenever convenient," Rajaratnam said. "How soon can you..."

"Oh!" the strange maid said, bending down to the floor. Rajaratnam broke off, looking doubly annoyed.

"What is it, Sanjana?" Maya asked.

"Oh! I'm so sorry, sir!" the maid said to Rajaratnam, sounding conscience stricken. "I didn't mean to interrupt your meeting. I just... found this on the floor in the corner... and... is this yours, sir?"

She walked into the full view of the room and held her hand out to Azhar.

Perched on her palm was a silver chain ending in a golden eagle, its ruby eyes glittering red.

The eyes of every single occupant in the room had only one focus

— the silver and gold chain that snaked its way around the maid's palm, twinkling in stark contrast with her delicate brown skin.

Maya was the first to break the gaze. She surreptitiously glanced around the room, first resting on Azhar — whose expression was one of blank astonishment, reflecting Maya's own state of mind — to Rajaratnam, who looked like he had seen a ghost — to the assistant, who looked puzzled, but with enlightenment appearing to dawn on his face. Maya turned back to the maid, who was looking at Azhar with an expression of barely-interested enquiry.

She was almost certain that she knew who this woman was. But even assuming she was right, there followed another urgent question.

What was she supposed to do next?

The silence in the room had been absolutely complete up to this point, but finally Azhar said: "What the f..."

But before he could complete the expletive, he was interrupted by another, most unexpected source.

Rajaratnam's assistant was the one who took a step forward and said in amazed tones: "Sir, isn't that your chain? Yes, yes!" The man strode forward purposefully, eager to be of help to his master.

"Madam, you can give that here, it belongs to Rajaratnam, sir," he said, confidently.

Maya glanced at Rajaratnam, who was just watching this scene open-mouthed, a ghastly expression on his face.

'Sanjana' turned towards the assistant, doubt clouding her brow, and she said: "This is yours? But I just found it in the corner here."

"It is Mr Rajaratnam's. You can ask anyone in the village. It is well known that it is his. The Eagle is his calling card, his lucky bird."

The woman turned uncertainly from him to Azhar, and then back again. It was plain that she didn't know what was the best thing to do — hand the chain over to the owner of the resort or to this strange person in front of her.

Her expression was almost too perfect. Maya was open-mouthed at how well this scene was orchestrated.

Harsha, you brilliant bastard, she thought to herself.

She glanced again at Azhar and Rajaratnam. They both hadn't a clue what was going on, but Maya was sure the panchayat head would cotton on quickly — the man was too sharp. She held her breath, waiting to see what would happen next.

"Please just hand it over, it belongs to Mr Rajaratnam, I have been working for him for 14 years and I know better than anyone," the assistant said, his moustache bristling with impatience as he stretched his hand out across the coffee table to receive the pendant.

"If you are sure," the woman began, moving towards the assistant and letting the chain trail down from her fingers as she reached over to him.

"AMARNATH!" Rajaratnam's hand came down heavily on the arm of the sofa. "Go wait outside for me!" he barked.

Everyone in the room jumped, no one more so than Amarnath himself, who hit his shin painfully on the coffee table and then scuttled towards his master, his back curving in a subservient bow.

"NOW!" Rajaratnam said, and Maya quailed to see his expression of fury. What Amarnath felt, she could only imagine.

The assistant turned hurriedly away from the sofa. "Yes sir! Sorry sir!" he said in trembling tones and scurried away towards the door.

The maid, who seemed to take this turn of events in her stride, took a step towards Rajaratnam as he sat bolt upright in the corner of the sofa.

"Is it yours, sir?" she asked pleasantly. "I just found it in that corner."

"Don't come near me!" he said sharply, and she froze where she was, a few feet away from him.

There was another brief silence and then Rajaratnam licked his lips and pulled his face into a sickly smile.

"Amarnath is just confused," he said in jovial tones that did not fool Maya one bit. "I have a similar chain — but I have sent it away for cleaning," he said, his left hand involuntarily going up to caress his throat.

"Sorry, sir," the maid said. She turned to Azhar and said, in submissive tones. "Shall I go now, sir? I'll put this in the lost property cupboard."

"Er... there is no lost pro... er... yes, you go do that," Azhar said, catching Maya's meaningful look.

The woman held the chain up with her finger and her thumb and slowly walked away, disappearing into the kitchen.

After she left, Rajaratnam stood up, stumbling slightly.

"I should be leaving," he said, distractedly, his face pale and aged all of a sudden.

"Oh... er... alright, best of luck," Azhar said, standing up and holding out his hand. Rajaratnam ignored this and stumbled towards the door.

Maya could not have stopped herself if she wanted to. "When should I send you the financial details?"

There was no reply, other than the slamming of the door behind the retreating Rajaratnam. "He doesn't want my numbers any more," Maya said, grinning at Azhar.

"Never mind the bloody numbers, what the hell just happened?" Azhar asked, looking at Maya with such a look of baffled confusion that she couldn't help laughing out loud.

"Stop giggling like an idiot, Maddy!" he said in exasperation. "Where did that damn pendant suddenly pop up from? Is it black magic or did that fool Harsha actually lose it somehow? I saw him drive off with it... And who the hell was that woman?"

Azhar flopped back on to the sofa in consternation, throwing his hands up.

They heard the tremendous revving of an engine from just outside — apparently, Amarnath had been instructed to step on the pedal.

"I think she is a policewoman. But we'd better ask Harsha about this," Maya said.

Azhar stood up hurriedly at this. "Are you telling me that ... that... *Bengali bastard* is behind this clown show we had to put up with? In my fucking resort?"

"I would bet my house on it."

Without another word, Azhar strode towards the entrance, muttering under his breath.

"Hey Azhar, come on, you have to admit it was effective!"

He turned around at this, bafflement and irritation etched on his face, so she had to suppress another gurgle of laughter.

"Effective how? I have no idea what's going on!"

He disappeared behind the front door, banging it behind him.

Maya hurried after him, laughing, out into warm sunshine to see him heading at a furious pace round the corner.

"What are you going to do?" she called out, running to keep up.

"Gonna find that fool and choke him to death! Ah there he is..."

Azhar broke into a run and Maya hurried to keep up, following him around a second corner.

She stopped short at a most incongruous sight: Harsha and the fake maid were smoking cigarettes and talking by the back entrance to the kitchen, Harsha leaning against a knobbly neem tree and grinning.

Azhar too paused in his run and approached the duo warily. It was possibly most fortunate for Harsha that the policewoman was there to prevent any attempts on his life.

She looked up coolly at the approaching pair, the cigarette dangling from the fingers of one hand, the elbow of which rested on the palm of the other. She looked decidedly odd, a sari-clad policewoman smoking a cigarette. Maya felt a fierce sense of affection for this woman, little as she knew her — she clearly did not care what anyone thought about her.

Harsha greeted them enthusiastically. "You guys were amazing! It actually worked! But what did you think of Gautami's ... sorry, Constable Gautami's performance?"

Astonished silence. And then Azhar cleared his throat. "Er... very good," he managed, nodding at the woman politely, and Maya had to stifle a laugh again. Azhar clearly still had no idea what was going on.

Gautami ignored Azhar and turned instead to Maya and gave a brief nod of acknowledgement for her role in the charade. The colour rose in Maya's face — for some reason she felt immensely flattered by the bored-looking woman's approval.

"What the... what was that all about, Harsha? Was this your great idea?" Azhar asked, his voice straining with the effort of keeping his anger in check.

Harsha shrugged his shoulders modestly, but the gleam in his eyes gave away his delight that the ruse had worked so well. "It was just a suggestion I made to the inspector — and he chose the constable here as the one person from the police force that Rajaratnam most certainly wouldn't know."

The constable's mouth twisted, and Maya thought she understood. Rajaratnam never seemed to acknowledge women.

Harsha added: "He also said she was the only person at the

station with half a brain."

Azhar gripped Harsha's shoulder and shook it slightly. "But what the hell does it all mean? What was it all about? Will someone explain?"

Harsha opened his mouth, but it was Maya who said: "If I understand correctly, Harsha, you wanted to prove to the police that this pendant belonged to Rajaratnam. And so you arranged for someone to 'find' it when he was nearby, and to try and get him to claim it as his — thus proving it belongs to him."

Harsha nodded. "Ideally, the man himself would have claimed it, but it sounds like his assistant did, which is just as good... I think," he said, glancing at Constable Gautami. Her silence took the wind out of his sails a little, but he did not say anything.

"But what now?" Azhar asked, frowning in concentration.

"Don't you see, Azhar? It was found on Lakshmi's body! The fact that Rajaratnam — well, his assistant anyway — acknowledged that the pendant is his ties him to the murder!"

Azhar looked at Maya blankly for a second and then understanding dawned on him, slowly. He looked from Maya to Harsha to Gautami and finally nodded. But he quickly rounded back to Harsha.

"Well, you might have warned us, you fool!" he said, indignantly. "I nearly blurted out that I didn't know who she was! Luckily, I got a look from Maya and I just kept quiet and let her handle the situation," Azhar turned to Maya and said: "You were bloody brilliant, by the way, Maya, absolutely *amazing*. How did you come up with all that accountancy stuff?"

She grinned and shrugged. "It just came to me. So, what happens now, Constable?"

"Now, I go make my report," she said, implacably, taking another drag of her cigarette and blowing smoke out in a thin stream.

"And does it mean Rajaratnam gets arrested?"

"It means I file my report," she said. "Then we will see."

And try as they might, they could get no more out of her — not even her opinion on Rajaratnam's guilt.

"I'll drive you down," Harsha said, a little crestfallen that she wasn't confirming the great victory of his plan.

"No, that you won't! I've seen the way you handle my car. Pass the keys over, you f... fool. This way... er... madam," Azhar said, giving a sort of half bow to the policewoman. The woman rolled her eyes and followed him, dropping her cigarette on the floor.

Harsha turned and grinned at Maya. "I knew you would wing it, Maya! I want to know *everything* — what you said, Rajaratnam's reaction — everything!"

She nodded towards the path and said: "It may have to wait."

Harsha turned to see Shane and Junaina making their way towards them.

"That was so weird!" Junaina said.

"What?"

"The elephant ride, numbnuts! So what have you guys been up to?"

Harsha took a deep drag of his cigarette and smiled at Maya as he blew the smoke out.

"Will you tell them or shall I?" he asked.

30. RITUAL

A keen wind picked up as they walked down the path that led into the village of Arasur. Junaina strode ahead, bickering softly with Azhar as usual, while Harsha, Maya and Shane brought up the rear. Harsha looked around him, trying to catch the eyes of the villagers. He had a distinct impression that many of them were also headed in the same direction.

"You ever been to a temple before, Shanny?" Maya asked.

"Several times," came the placid answer. "I have visited temples in Tanjore and Madurai — and of course, been to Mahabalipuram a few times."

Harsha's head snapped around in surprise towards his old friend. How many layers did this man have?

"How come?" Maya asked, though she didn't seem as surprised as he did.

Shane shrugged his shoulders. "I like architecture and history, and I like the kids to know a bit about the region they come from. Wouldn't you be interested in visiting the Armenian church in Chennai, even though you are Hindu?"

"There's an Armenian church in Chennai?"

Harsha tuned out the rest of this conversation and looked around at the village. They were close to its southern edge, beyond which the village ended at the edge of a shelf in the mountain, and the yawning slopes were visible beyond.

The sun beat down upon the mountainside, the long rays making Harsha feel like he was in one of Alfred, Lord Tennyson's poems. Perhaps aptly, his heart was heavy, as he stared out at the vast stretches of Indian landscape in front of him as he walked.

"You've done as much as you can, Harry – isn't that enough?" Maya asked quietly from beside him and he turned to see that she was looking concernedly at him, with Shane looking on with interest from her other side. Mild worry was etched on his face as well.

"It's ok guys, I'm over it," he said, trying to banish his

disappointment and forcing a smile on his face. "Let's just focus on Lakshmi now. That's why we are here."

They walked past the village square and, most unusually, Subhash's shop was closed, a rough wooden board placed against the cubbyhole where the genial shopkeeper usually stood leaning out and calling out to his would-be customers. Where had the man gone? The square itself was empty, the grand pipal tree – or *arasamaram* as the locals called it – casting its shade on an empty stone dais. Harsha presumed that with the shop closed, there was no reason for people to congregate there.

"We did our best, Harry," Maya said, insistently. "I don't think we could have expected this to end like a detective novel, with the criminal captured. This is India, after all."

"And what does that mean, this is India?" Harsha asked, bitterly. "Criminals walk free?"

"That's how it should be," Azhar cut in unexpectedly, and the three of them stopped and looked up at him. Harsha hadn't noticed that Azhar and Junaina had stopped at a fork in the road and were waiting for them, and had therefore heard the last part of their conversation. "It's the, what d'you call it, the democratic process. Innocent until proven guilty."

"You're telling me a rapist and murderer going free is democratic?" Harsha asked, nettled by this.

"I'm saying we need more proof than pendants and idiotic assistants to put someone in jail for life," Azhar said decisively as he chose the road on the right-hand side and starting striding along the small path, framed on either side by the colourful residences of Arasur. Harsha followed with the others, looking at Azhar's back in surprise. He hadn't expected his old friend to have such a strong view on judicial matters.

"So is this what they call a *shraddha*, Juni? I'm not fully familiar with Hindu death rituals," Shane asked Junaina as they proceeded down the dusty pathway and Harsha recognised a skillful and tactful change of topic.

But Junaina looked scandalised at the question. "This isn't a *shraadham*, fool. It's just a prayer for Lakshmi that the priest is giving, and inviting people to attend. Every Monday she used to pray at the temple, remember?" she asked. "A *shraadham* won't be done in the temple itself. Usually in the dead person's house. You see..."

Harsha tuned out the rest of Junaina's explanation and walked quietly behind the rest of his friends, alone with his own dark thoughts.

They didn't have much time to listen to Junaina's explanations in any case, because the road soon curved around a bend in the hill and led them out into the farmland, where the isolated little Murugan temple was situated at the far end of the village. As soon as they came out in front of the temple, they all stopped in their tracks and gaped at the scene in front of them.

Nearly a hundred people were thronging the front of the dilapidated and picturesque structure, and more and more were joining them every minute.

"Wow!" Azhar breathed. Junaina was smiling broadly at this sign of spiritual devotion and Maya, Shane and Harsha all looked at each other in astonishment. This was most unexpected.

They joined the general throng and saw that Maheshwaran Shastri was standing just outside the temple, directly under the statue of Lord Murugan, and addressing the crowd. Though the people were absolutely silent, they could barely hear his words over the sounds of the wind rushing through the fields and the call of the birds.

"... Now is the time for us to stand together as one..." Harsha heard him say, and looked at the noble lines of the priest's face, wondering how he had ever considered him a murder suspect. At this point, the man spotted them at the back of the crowd and nodded to Harsha.

There was a ripple in the crowd as everyone turned to look at them, and more than one villager nodded and smiled in their direction.

Harsha felt oddly gratified at this sign of acceptance. Perhaps some of them even knew the small role he had played in the investigation.

Maheshwaran Shastri went on with his speech, which was full of praise for Lakshmi and her place in the community. In one corner, Harsha spotted a tightly knit group that included Leela, Ammani, Kuppi and Selvam. Murugayya stood near them with a shy-looking, beautiful woman with olive skin who must have been his wife. They were all watching the priest intently.

"Is this a particular type of prayer? Anything special?" Shane asked Junaina quietly, and she shook her head, either in the negative or signalling that she didn't know — Harsha wasn't sure which.

Maya elbowed Harsha and nodded towards a few men in one corner of the gathering. They were talking quietly among themselves, and there was an expression of deep anger on their faces and a sort of steely determination. Harsha frowned.

"... In her death, Lakshmi has brought us together as a community. Now, in her honour, we must always stand up to injustice," the priest was saying. "Let the people of Arasur never allow injustice to rule us!"

Harsha's was reminded uncomfortably of Mark Anthony's speech in Shakespeare' Julius Caesar. Did Maheshwaran Shastri realise what an effect his words were having on these people?

"Now please come inside to get the Lord's blessings, and please be patient and wait your turn," the priest finished and turned to re-enter the temple.

A buzz of angry conversation broke out among the villagers, and there was a general movement towards the main temple building.

Harsha was about to join the queue when a hand plucked at his sleeve and he turned in surprise to see who was addressing him.

"Inspector!" he declared in astonishment, looking at Inspector Palanivel, who looked elegant and handsome in a white kurta and khaki trousers.

"Can I have a word with you, please, Mr Devnath?"

Harsha's friends all crowded up to see what he wanted, and he looked at them warily.

"Yes, you can all come too, if you like," he said magnanimously.

The friends all looked at one another in surprise and then silently accompanied the inspector to the side of the temple complex, leaving the people of Arasur behind them.

Even out here by the coffee plantations in the bright sunshine, Palanivel dominated the group effortlessly despite his slight, slim figure. The clean white kurta he was wearing accentuated the dark brown hues of his skin.

He looked over the nearby fields with his slightly cold eyes, his gaze resting on Harsha speculatively for a few seconds before he resumed his visual sweep of the area.

"Inspector!" Azhar said obsequiously. "You must come to Pipal Resorts for a meal sometime. Our cook makes an excellent chicken biriyani!"

The inspector's nose wrinkled as he looked at Azhar carefully. "Thank you for the invitation," he said neutrally. Harsha noticed that he didn't commit one way or another.

Junaina opened her mouth, no doubt to comment on Azhar's sycophantic tone, but Maya gripped her elbow urgently and she subsided.

Ignoring this exchange, the inspector leaned against the crumbling wall that surrounded the temple and looked around at the rest of the group. His eyes rested on Maya for a second with something like respect, and Harsha saw her blush slightly.

Then he turned to Harsha and said, this time in Tamil: "Well, Mr Devnath, it seems you will not be satisfied until you have cost me my job."

"What?" asked Harsha, genuinely baffled.

"Just my little joke," the inspector said.

Junaina muttered: "Hilarious," and Maya elbowed her.

Azhar scuffed his shoes in some weeds and looked eagerly at the inspector. The group had unconsciously formed a semi-circle around the policeman, boxing him into his position by the temple wall. Seemingly unconcerned by this, the inspector said: "What I mean is, I will have to formally open an investigation into Mr Rajaratnam and him being quite a powerful man, there is a real risk this could cost me a job."

Harsha felt a jolt of excitement shoot through his body. "So, you do believe it is him!" he said, loudly and excitedly. "I knew it! When are you going to arrest him?"

Inspector Palanivel looked around quickly to see if anyone was within earshot, but everyone had either gone into the hall next to the temple or were thronging its entrance. They were quite alone outside its walls. He turned back to Harsha, shaking his head.

"Arrest him? You must be joking," he said finally.

"Very strange sense of humour," Junaina whispered to Maya,

earning a pinch on the arm this time, as the elbow didn't seem to be quietening her down.

Harsha looked deflated. "You are not going to arrest him?"

"On the current evidence? Think about it, Mr Devnath. All we know is there was a pendant, possibly from the scene of the crime. When produced in front of the suspect, he denied it was his."

"But his assistant recognised it," Maya piped in.

"He did not say the actual words himself," the inspector said calmly. "Anyway, Rajaratnam was smart enough to stop him before it became too incriminating. It's all in Gautami's report.

The inspector sighed and fumbled in his kurta pocket for something. "Even if he had let it slip that the pendant had belonged to him, how could we possibly prove that it was in the victim's hand?" he continued. "Through the testimony of a four-year-old boy? And could there not be another explanation why she was holding it at the time? No, if we try to convict with this, the case will be laughed out of court. He won't even need a lawyer."

"So, it was all for nothing," Harsha said in a hollow voice, as the sound of chanting was heard from the hall, where Maheswaran was leading the prayer.

The inspector smiled at his disappointed face. "It wasn't for nothing," he said gently. At these words, they all looked expectantly at him.

The inspector paused (he has a keen sense of drama, Harsha thought) and said: "You have convinced me."

There was a moment's silence, and then Azhar voiced all of their sentiments when he said: "We have?"

"Yes."

"You believe Rajaratnam is the murderer?" Maya asked in an equally surprised tone.

"Yes. And so does Constable Gautami."

"And not the sand smugglers?" Harsha asked, unable to keep the accusation out of his voice.

"Oh, they are deeply involved as well. In fact they are Rajaratnam's men. Another little side hustle for our enterprising politician," Palanivel said, sneering.

The group gaped at him.

"So... they all committed the crime together?" Shane asked soberly.

"That is another thing we will try to establish. They won't give Rajaratnam away — they have clearly been paid well — but there are other ways to find out. By the way," Palanivel added hurriedly, looking at Harsha in particular, "This is all off the record. In fact, I will strenuously deny it if any of you brings it up again or tells anyone else."

They all nodded vigorously.

"Scouts' honour," Junaina said, holding up three fingers.

"But what's the use of convincing you, if you can't do anything about it?" Maya asked, ignoring Junaina's intervention this time.

The inspector's eyes glinted. "I said we can't convict him now. But what we can do — and by 'we', I mean me and my staff — is to formally investigate the case, establish a motive and find evidence, and so on. In short, do our jobs."

He paused and pulled out a sachet of *gutkha* and began the intricate process of trying to open it in one corner.

Harsha and Maya glanced at each other. "We do have some sort of idea about the motive, Inspector," Harsha said.

The inspector paused in his efforts with the tobacco and said: "Is this your theory about him wanting to buy Pipal Resorts and become the most powerful figure in Arasur?"

The neutral tone in his voice made Harsha frown, but he didn't say anything.

The policeman sighed and bent to resume his efforts with the plastic sachet. "That would take a very cold person indeed, to murder someone just as a power play. And maybe Rajaratnam *is* that cold. But we have some information that you don't, and couldn't have had, that gives him a clearer motive."

He finally managed to extricate some of the chewing tobacco from his little plastic packet and popped it in his mouth with every evidence of enjoyment. Harsha was a smoker, but he had to force himself not to shudder.

"So, what do you think is the real reason, Inspector," Maya asked, in as flattering a tone as she could manage.

The man hesitated, but he was not impervious to flattery, and that from an attractive woman.

"Still off the record?" he asked, after a minute. The group nodded. He turned to Harsha inquiringly.

"Yes," Harsha said curtly. He had gone very quiet. Maya looked at him sympathetically.

The inspector smiled briefly at him and then his face went serious, more serious than it had at any other point that evening.

"About a month ago, the victim ..."

"Lakshmi," Maya interjected.

"Yes, her, she came to the police station to report a case of sexual assault. She spoke to Gautami but before she could make a formal complaint, some other people from the village came and took her away from the station. I think it was her cousin or uncle or someone. Certainly, she didn't have any close relatives."

"Why did they take her away?" Even Junaina looked interested now.

"A good question. We have no idea, but in my experience, this is usually because the abuser is a relative, and they don't want any shame to be associated with the family. But, in some cases, also because the culprit is in a position of power."

"And which did you suspect?"

"I? I knew nothing of the case except what was in Gautami's report. And believe me, I read many, many reports. I looked at it again properly only after the death."

Maya noticed that the man had dropped his suave manner, and a trace of bitterness had replaced the slightly self-satisfied tone in his voice.

"Gautami, however, is relatively new to the job," he said. "All the other officers told her to let the villagers sort it out themselves, as they usually do, but she couldn't stop fretting about it. Finally, she went and confronted the vic... Lakshmi, in the village one day and pressed her to come back and register a formal case against whoever the abuser was. At this point — and I quote Gautami — Lakshmi looked at Rajaratnam's house and said: 'We are all scared of him.'

"Once again, this is not enough to convict anyone, but it is enough to raise some suspicions. Anyway, I don't know what magic Gautami weaved, but she finally convinced Lakshmi to make a statement. But before she could do it, well — you know what happened next."

There was a silence as they all stared at him. He, in turn, stared at his hands, turning some loose tobacco over and over in his palm.

"Do you know how he abused her?"

"No. It was too late," the inspector said into his hands.

Harsha said: "So... you think he killed her to keep her from making the statement?"

At this the man looked up straight at Harsha and said: "You tell me, Mr Devnath. You interviewed him. Why do you think he did it?"

Harsha thought for a second and said: "I think he did it to show that he is the boss. That no one in this village should dare to cross him."

The inspector didn't say anything, but his half-smile seemed to indicate agreement.

"But... but I don't get it," everyone turned to look at Junaina. "I mean, why do it himself? Why not just send his *chamchas* to do the dirty work by themselves? Why get involved at all? You guys keep saying he is intelligent but that was truly stupid."

Harsha said: "He just thought he was invincible. Hubris."

"Dude, this isn't a Shakespeare play," Azhar said in exasperation. "No need to bring Hamlet and all into it."

"Hubris is a real thing, idiot."

"Besides," Maya added, "He seemed like the sort of creepy bastard who would want to do it himself. Do you remember the way he looked at me, Harry, when he told that story about how women used to appear topless before the *zamindar* or whatever? Made my skin crawl."

The inspector stared at her open-mouthed. Possibly he wasn't used to women speaking so openly about such matters, let alone use profanity so casually.

"What are the chances of convicting him?" Harsha asked impatiently.

The inspector stopped staring at Maya and said: "I really don't know, Mr Devnath. We have an extremely powerful and intelligent opponent. I will try and build a case. We should get the DNA results in a few months' time, unless..." he broke off, frowning.

"Unless he bribes someone to doctor the results," Junaina finished for him. The inspector said nothing.

A silence fell over the group and they heard some bells sounding from inside the temple. Junaina stirred, and as though this were a cue, the rest of them straightened and got ready to go inside.

But Inspector Palanivel raised his hand and said: "Before we go in, Mr Devnath — let me say what I wanted to say. Firstly, I wanted to thank you all for your help. Secondly, I wanted to apologise."

Harsha and his friends looked puzzled. "To apologise?" Maya asked. "What for?"

"Well," the man said, still chewing at his tobacco. "I may have used you a little bit."

"How so?"

"Mr Devnath, remember when we met on the hillside and I told you about the missing item of jewellery?" Harsha nodded.

"Well, I am afraid that was part of my strategy."

"What? How?" Azhar asked.

Harsha stared at the inspector. "You were trying to spread a rumour... weren't you? I remember thinking at the time that it was strange you were telling me so much."

"Spread a rumour? But why?" Azhar demanded.

Harsha continued to look at the inspector. "Maybe to get the culprit to do something stupid? Or to get someone to come forward with some information? But, Mr Inspector, I didn't tell anyone about it until recently, and then only to this group."

The inspector spat discreetly into a nearby bush and then said: "You were not the only one I spoke to, Mr Devnath."

"I see. And what did you expect to happen, once the rumour spread?"

"Oh, something. My investigation was at a dead end and I needed to shake things up. You could call it — a last resort."

Maya interjected: "And of course, it worked — you did have a bunch of murderous men search the mountainside at night. Inspector, anything could have happened that night," she said, her tone betraying her anger.

The inspector nodded. "And that's why I wanted to apologise — that put you in a dangerous situation. I owe you both an apology."

"You don't sound apologetic at all, Inspector," Harsha pointed out. "In fact, I would say you sound pretty pleased with yourself."

"Do I?" the man said, grinning at him as he straightened and brushed off the front of his immaculate kurta. "Shall we go inside? We are missing the *puja*."

31. RESOLUTION

Harsha mechanically folded another shirt and put it in the open suitcase on his bed, humming along every now and then to the Oasis album playing from his phone. He hadn't listened to that band for years, but it somehow seemed appropriate — he was going back to London soon, and that was the music he most associated with England.

He wasn't sure how he felt. The last few days had been so invigorating. He felt like a fire was burning fiercely inside him, lit by all the passion and emotions he had felt over the period of the holiday. And some of his love for his country had returned forcefully.

As he carefully put away his headphones in the side sleeve of his suitcase, he thought of the afternoon light shining gently on the red roofs in London but felt cold and confused at the thought. He pictured himself getting off at Terminal 3 at Heathrow, buying a cappuccino to take away and getting into his underground train, and couldn't even believe that it was the same person who would be doing those things.

A knock on the door interrupted his thoughts. "Come in," he called out, and Maya walked in.

"Hallo, just thought I'd check if you were... wow, packing already! You have changed," she said, coming into his room. He looked up at her, smiling a little sadly. Her bandage had come off, and she had a deep scar on one side of her forehead, partly obscured by her tumbling hair. She was wearing that Pearl Jam T-shirt again, the one that ended slightly above her jeans, so that the buckle of her leather belt was visible. He thought she looked sophisticated and sexy, and felt a stab of sorrow that they would be in different countries, thousands of miles apart, within days.

"Oh, you know, it leaves me free to hang out with you guys this evening and tomorrow," he said heavily, trying to smile up at her.

She sat on one of the chairs, a ray of afternoon sunshine falling on her cheek from the open door, and watched him roll up his belt and place it on a neatly folded pair of cargo trousers.

"With the amount of lunch you ate, I thought you came back for a nap," she said, caustically.

He chuckled and said: "If you were buying sandwiches at Pret for lunch everyday, you wouldn't be surprised I'm tucking into as much Indian food as possible now."

There was a pause as he wrestled with the zip of one of his leather jackets before folding it as best he could to fit it in at the top of his suitcase.

"You can't wait to get back, huh?" Maya asked, finally, a slightly wistful tone in her voice.

"What?" he turned to face her from across the bed. "No! Not at all! In fact I was just thinking..." he broke off and turned back to his suitcase.

There was some awkward, but poignant, emotion in the air, and Maya didn't feel up to dealing with it. So, she resolutely returned to her original reason for coming there.

"I just thought I would check on you. You seemed really disappointed just now when you left the dining hall. But you should be proud, Harry, you did really help the investigation," she said, sitting down on the chair.

He pushed the suitcase to one side and sat on the bed, facing her. "You should be as well, Maya, you did more than me. You were *incredible*, and I think it's a travesty that..."

"That?"

"Nothing."

"Oh, come on," she said, getting up and walking up to him to give him a familiar poke on the side of his stomach. "You can't just start something and... Harry, no!" she said, pushing him away as he caught hold of her hands. He let go and watched her carefully.

After an awkward moment, he said: "It was strange."

"What was?" she asked, standing irresolute, halfway to the door. She really should leave right now. Part of her wanted her to respond to his move, but a larger and more vocal part knew it was not the right thing for her to do. But she had led him on, even asked him to sleep with her. How could she blame him for trying again?

But how could she explain why she had changed her mind? She felt close to tears at just how horrible the situation was, and with a stab of grief that came to her every now and again, she wished she could talk to her father.

To her immense relief, he changed the subject.

"Just the way in which the inspector used us."

"I know you have this weird admiration thing going for him, Harry, but that was horrible of him. I don't think I like him like you do," she said, sitting down on the chair again, and crossing her legs.

He laughed and sat cross legged on the bed. "I don't know. His hands are tied — he has no real means of investigating this crime except to be street-smart. I don't know what I would have done in his situation — probably just given up."

He took a deep breath and stared out of the window. She realised she would really miss the way he stared out into space and got lost in his own world, without warning, in the middle of a conversation.

"I guess," he said finally, thoughtfully, "I guess I had this weird idea. I felt like I was in a story, you know? A detective novel, if you like. We all were. And I guess I subconsciously thought I was the protagonist. But... in the end it was someone else's story and we all just played little cameos. It was Inspector Palanivel's story," he ended, on an ironic note.

"It was always Lakshmi's story, Harry," she said, gently chiding.

Still staring out the window, he winced slightly and said: "I guess I lost sight of that now and then. But... hearing her story from the inspector today kind of brought it home. That she was a real person, that it wasn't all a game — you know?"

"I know. Don't be too hard on yourself — we all got a bit carried away. For me the worst part is not being here to see the ending."

"Narrative anxiety," he said, nodding, reminding her pleasurably of university days, when he would teach the others about English literature. "Unfortunately, it could take months before anything happens. And even if they arrest him, knowing our legal system, several more months before conviction."

She sighed. "Makes you wonder what the point was at all."

He snapped out of his trance and smiled at her: "Our conversation is becoming quite morbid. Shall we go join the others?" He untangled his legs and jumped lightly on to the wooden floor.

She took a deep breath and said: "One second, Harry. I think I should explain something to you, first."

He smiled and sat back down on his bed and looked at her encouragingly. As though he knew exactly what she was going to say, and was gently encouraging her. The patronising idiot.

"I think... I led you on a bit, earlier."

"A bit?"

"Ok, I was ready to... to, well, sleep with you, to be frank. I don't know what came over me."

"And it was a big mistake, of course," he said, and she heard the bitterness in his voice, and found she couldn't continue.

"I'm sorry," Harsha added quickly, glancing at her stricken face. "It *was* a mistake. You are married, and I guess you could say I had my chance years ago. Though to be honest, my self-esteem was so low then I didn't even think I had a chance with you. But... I really," he hesitated, but what were the chances he was ever going to see her again? "I really loved you back then. And I think I still do now," he said.

She knew. Of course, how could anyone not know? And had he had a chance with her all those years ago, before she had gotten married? She had been angry with him for not even trying, thinking it impossible that a girl could hit on a guy. But given how shy he had been back then, maybe she should have...

She shook herself and said: "Harry there's no point in looking at what might have been. It's the past. As for the other night — I don't regret what we did, not at all. I don't think it was a mistake — it's what I wanted at that point. But God intervened and stopped me from making a mistake."

He cleared his throat in embarrassment, so she added quickly: "Not God then. The universe. Whatever you want to believe. And it was a real wake-up call. But, believe me, I did want it before we were... interrupted."

"And not any more?"

"No, I'm so sorry Harry, but I know what I need to do now."

"And what is that?"

"I need to give my husband a chance. I never really did," she said.

"Societal pressures..." he began.

"Not this time, Harry," she said, shaking her head decisively. "I got married to him because of societal pressures, yes. But now I am making my own choice. I am prepared to leave him and live my own life, but first, I have to give him a chance. And sleeping with another man is not a good start," she said.

He looked at her and nodded. Though he looked sad, he forced himself to smile. "You have grown, Maya, just in these last few days. I feel like you are beyond my understanding now — but you look peaceful, and I am happy for you. Really."

He took a deep breath and added: "I just want you to remember this — you are so intelligent and compassionate and so filled with fire — you should be doing great things with your life."

"And I am going to," she said.

He looked at her, sitting there composedly, a new confidence in her, and thought she had never looked more beautiful.

He stood up and said, with difficulty: "Let's go join the others now, Maya."

"You seem to be in a hurry to get rid of me," she said, smiling.

"It's not that. You are in my room, and I only have so much self-control," he said, cheekily.

She laughed and jumped up and stood in front of him, looking up into his eyes. Those long lashes again, she thought to herself, so incongruous with the straight lines of his face, and yet so alluring.

"You never know, Harry. Maybe one day," she said, gently touching his cheek.

"Maybe one day, Maya," he said, and he managed to smile again.

They stood like that for a few minutes, staring into each other's eyes. Harsha asked himself — what exactly constitutes cheating on your spouse? Kissing the way they had done the other night? Actually sleeping with each other? Or simply standing here and feeling what they felt, looking at one another? This felt far more powerful than any other sordid form of cheating, and he found himself exasperated at the choices he had made that had led him to this point.

The door banged open and they both jumped and turned towards it in alarm.

Harsha was the first to recover. "Murugayya! I feel like it's been at least a few hours before you interrupted some crucial moment... are you ok?" he ended sharply, stepping forward.

Murugayya stood at the threshold, doubled up, and wheezing from the effort of having run up to the room, and finally said between great breaths: "Azhar sir... calling you... now... main hall!"

Maya and Harsha glanced at each other apprehensively and made their way towards the doorway.

"What fresh hell does this damned resort have in store for us now?" Harsha asked, though the spring was back in his step as they stepped out on to the beautiful mountain path, which was bathed in afternoon sunshine, all traces of that morning's mist vanished.

"Better go find out," Maya responded, and they hurried down the hill.

32. LAST RESORT

Harsha hurried down the path, his heart thumping again. He had no idea what to expect, but something told him that the incredible events of the past week hadn't quite run to a close.

As they rounded the avenue of trees and got a clear view of the dining hall below them, they stopped short. Harsha squinted to make sure he was seeing right.

Normally, the area surrounding the dining hall was tranquil, with a few of the staff perhaps visible in their red saris, or Selvam sauntering by, grinning at staff and guests alike.

On this occasion, the area ahead of the dining room entrance was teeming with people.

"Who the..." Harsha turned to Maya, and saw that she had turned white with apprehension.

Without looking at him, she said in a panicked voice: "Azhar!" And then she took off without warning, running down the path.

"Maddie!" he yelled after her. "What are you doing, you fool! Go down the back! The back of the hall! Don't go near them!"

He started running himself, hoping against hope that Maya wouldn't do anything crazy like charge into the crowd and try to explain matters. Who were these people anyway? He couldn't make out individual faces from this distance but judging by the sunburnt darkness of their skins and the faded white of their clothes, they were the villagers of Arasur.

As he drew closer, he could hear an angry buzz, as though a wasp's nest had been disturbed, and could sense a palpable anger in the air.

He ducked behind a clump of trees and approached the great dining hall from the kitchen entrance. The door was shut, but he saw Maya knock softly and a very frightened Leela open the door and look out. Seeing Maya, she quickly swung the door wide open to let her in when Harsha finally caught up and said: "Hang on!"

Leela broke into a brief smile at his appearance and ushered him in as well and then locked the door securely.

"What's going on, Leela," Harsha asked, trying to sound as calm as possible while also taking in raking breaths after the brief sprint down the hill.

She just shook her head and pointed them towards the main hall.

Maya and Harsha walked past the pots of food, eased past the stacks of steel and aluminium vessels, and reached the main hall. And stopped short.

Rajaratnam was back, seated on the sofa, leaning forward, his elbows resting on his thighs. An extremely harassed looking Azhar was standing opposite him, in an almost comical attitude of confusion.

Shane and Junaina were standing by the doorway, looking out through one of the French windows at the angry group of villagers outside.

"But how the hell will we... Harry! Maddy!" Azhar spun around, and Shane and Junaina turned to contemplate the pair who had just walked into the room.

"What's going on?" Harsha asked Azhar quietly.

Azhar pointed querulously at Rajaratnam and said: "This... this... man, wants me to keep him safe here!"

Harsha looked at Rajaratnam and felt a slight sense of shock. Gone was the bombast, the confidence, the air of menace. Now he just looked tired, his face crumpled, his skin rugged and flaky. He looked a pathetic figure, and Harsha barely recognised him any more.

"Protect him from whom?"

Azhar gesticulated distractedly at the villagers outside.

"From the whole bloody village! They are after him! And he has come *here*!" he said, ending in a squeak.

"Where is Amarnath?" Maya asked, stepping forward.

Azhar sighed and said: "Maddie, who cares where that idi..."

"He has left me," Rajaratnam cut in, desperately, looking up. "They have all left me. I have no one left."

Harsha looked at the pair of them for a second, Rajaratnam a pathetic figure, looking up beseechingly at Maya, who stood tall and firm, and wondered at how the roles had reversed completely from that first meeting.

"This fool wants me to protect him," Azhar said despairingly to

Harsha. "How am I supposed to? What if they burn down this place and we all die? Why us?" This last remark was to Rajaratnam.

Rajaratnam waved exhaustedly across his face. "There is no one else," he said.

A silence fell, into which Shane said: "I don't think they will burn the place down, or do anything like that. They are not even trying to get in. They are just waiting out there."

"Waiting for what?"

Shane nodded significantly towards Rajaratnam. "For him to come out."

"And what do they want with him," Harsha asked, looking at Rajaratnam carefully. The man flinched at the question.

Junaina stirred at this: "They want to take him out clubbing," she said, sardonically. "Come on, Harry, of course you know what they want. They want to finish him off! What a bloody holiday. Lynch mobs, murderous jungle men, you with your Tintin act, megalomaniac inspectors — why the hell does anyone come here at all? Why does this place even exist?"

Maya turned at the word "inspector" and asked: "Has anyone called the police?"

"Oh! The police!" Junaina said in mock astonishment. She flicked Shane's arm and said: "Why didn't we think of that! What complete morons we are."

"This isn't helping, Juni," Shane said quietly, and to Harsha's surprise, Junaina subsided.

Harsha glanced at Rajaratnam and then spoke quietly, so that his voice didn't carry over, and said: "How many people are out there?"

"I think around 50 people."

"Shit. And they want to... kill him? Are you sure?"

"Kill him, beat him up, we don't know," Azhar said, not bothering to keep his voice down. "But what the hell are we supposed to do? Why has he come *here*?"

Rajaratnam stirred at this and looked up bleakly at Harsha, who felt an involuntary stab of pity for him. He tried to remind himself that this man was a murderer. A rapist and murderer. But was he? Was it up to him, Harsha, to decide? No. But the people who were supposed to make the decisions had failed. The system had failed.

What was left for the villagers?

With a rush of insight, he understood why vigilante justice was so pervasive in India. What else could people do when there was no other way of giving Rajaratnam what he deserved?

And yet — it was wrong. Whatever happened, it was very clear in his mind that they couldn't let this mob take Rajaratnam, if they could help it.

"Leela," he said finally.

"What?" Azhar asked, peering concernedly at him.

"Call Leela here. She must know these people, understand what they want."

Azhar nodded, marched over to the kitchen door, flung it open, and started. Leela and Ammani were both right there, their ears pressed against the door.

With a flicker of his old spirit, Azhar held the door open with a flourish for them to enter the dining room.

Leela looked fearfully at Harsha and said: "I don't know why they are doing this, sir. My father begged his friends not to. But they are determined. I don't know how to change it."

But Harsha had noticed that while Leela was wringing her hands, Ammani was smiling, a cruel smile of triumph that was directed towards Rajaratnam. The man looked up at her and his face crumpled even further.

"Ammani — what are you doing?" Maya asked, sharply. She had noticed as well, Harsha thought.

"Just looking at that man," Ammani said between her teeth, and everyone in the room turned to look at her. She raised her arm and pointed at Rajaratnam, looking for all the world like an avenging spirit, and said: "Just looking at that devil."

Harsha's mouth dropped. Was this the same Ammani that cheerfully brought *dosais* for them and greeted them every morning with coffee and a warm smile?

He collected himself and said: "Ammani. Whatever it is, surely we can't just leave them to take him? Shouldn't we get him out somehow?"

She turned to Harsha, her eyes burning, and then said: "Why should we? I'm sorry, Harsha, you are a good man, but maybe now you should stop interfering in the situation and let the village take care of it on its own."

She said this with such authority and confidence that Harsha felt utterly sure, for a second, that there was nothing they could do to prevent a killing. He glanced over at Rajaratnam, and, whatever he was, the idea of turning him over to the mob turned Harsha's stomach. He looked over at Maya and their eyes met and he knew she felt the same way.

But apparently not everyone did. Azhar sidled up to him and whispered: "Is it such a bad idea? What the fuck can we do anyway? Let's leave these mad villagers to sort out their own problems."

"You don't mean that, Azhar," Harsha said, with as much conviction as he could muster. To his relief, Azhar looked sheepish, though he said defiantly: "My priority is to keep you all safe, especially Maya here."

Ammani lifted her chin at that and said: "They will not hurt any of you. Never, never, never. They are not criminals. They just want justice." She turned to Rajaratnam again, her eyes burning ferociously.

Harsha looked around at Shane and Junaina, both of whom shook their heads, and then back to Maya. His mind was racing with ideas, each more unrealistic than the next. Could they smuggle Rajaratnam out through the back? Could they race off in Azhar's car? And could they do it in any way that wouldn't bring the wrath of the local villagers down on them?

He was about to make another plea to Ammani and Leela to help them out — which he knew was hopeless, especially in the case of Ammani — when they heard the sounds of sirens in the distance.

All of them froze and then turned towards the doorway as the sounds grew louder and louder, finally obscuring the angry buzz of the crowd outside, followed by a screeching of tires. For the first time since he had entered that room, hope returned to Rajaratnam's face, and even some of his swagger, to Harsha's disgust.

Time crawled for the next few seconds, while the entire group listened for sounds of activity outside. A slamming of car doors, a heavy scraping, indistinct shapes flitting in front of their vision, the distinctive brown of police uniforms and then, finally — a heavy knocking on the door.

They all watched mutely as Shane pulled the door open a crack, looked out, and then swung it open wide.

For what felt like the hundredth time over the past week, Inspector Palanivel swaggered in, this time in full uniform, the buckles on his belt and the badge on his chest sparkling clean, the outfit clinging to his slim and strong frame.

He was followed by five other police officers, among them Constables Gautami and Ezhumalai. Two of them held massive rifles, which explained how they had easily got through the villagers. These two stationed themselves on either side of the door and the rest proceeded into the room. Harsha felt Maya step back a few yards. *Almost as though she were more nervous about the police than the lynch mob,* he thought cynically to himself.

Palanivel looked around at all of them, glanced at Rajaratnam, and then turned to Harsha and said: "What's going on here?"

Harsha looked briefly at Shane, who looked so alarmed at the idea of admitting to having made the phone call, that Harsha wearily took charge, and said: "We called you to help us in a difficult situation. It looks like these villagers are chasing this man," he pointed limply at Rajaratnam. "Who seems to want us to protect him. As you can see, we have no means to protect anyone here."

Rajaratnam tottered to his feet and, recovering his poise, said to the inspector: "Inspector, you have done a great job in coming here today. It seems some villagers are taking matters into their own hands, and taking out their dissatisfactions on me, as the closest authority figure. It is misguided but understandable," he said indulgently, before becoming serious again. "I ask you to give me your protection until I have made preparations to... er... visit my relatives until this blows over."

All of them gaped at Rajaratnam. He had been a broken shell of a man minutes ago, and here he was, talking with assurance and authority, as though his own life did not depend on the inspector's response. Harsha could not help admiring the man's brazen courage. Or was it hubris again?

And more importantly, would he get away with it?

One glance at the Inspector shattered that possibility. He shot the panchayat head a look of such contempt that even Maya was taken aback. Palanivel sauntered in Rajaratnam's direction, hands behind his back, and the two men looked at each other. Each powerful in their own right, alpha males staring each other down — the air was thick with tension. Then the inspector smiled, his neat moustache curving above his thin lips.

"Protect you, sir? What from?"

Rajaratnam looked taken aback. "From... the mob outside, you fo... from the people out there! They are ready to tear me to pieces!"

The inspector turned away from the man and sauntered over towards the table, apparently inspecting its contents, and said: "Really? Why?"

The question threw Rajaratnam. He stared in disbelief at the man's back and then said, stumbling over his words: "Some dissatisfaction on how the area is being run — you know how it is — lack of respect for authority, mob rule. It is an affront to the great democracy that we have built here in India!" he said, ending on a strong note and standing erect by his sofa. "They are taking the law into their own hands, and it is your duty to uphold the law!"

The inspector turned and considered Rajaratnam carefully, staying silent for a minute, and then said: "I have spoken to some of these people and they said all they wanted to do was to talk to their leader. The head of their panchayat, in an open forum. I think this is democracy in action!"

Harsha glanced at the other police officers, and every single face was watching Palanivel in fascination.

"Democracy? They want to kill me, man!" Rajaratnam said, his voice breaking slightly and his arms stretched out as though in entreaty.

Palanivel's lips curled again and he shook his head. "You must be crazy, Mr Rajaratnam. I see no evidence of any violent intent among these simple village folk. In fact, I might caution Mr Devnath here for wasting police time."

Though Harsha did not understand what was happening, he recognised his role in this little charade, and did not object to this. Palanivel nodded to the other officers and started to make his way towards the door.

Rajaratnam stumbled forward. "You are not going to take me with you?" he asked, pitifully.

Palanivel turned with another look of surprise. "Why would we?

There is no danger here, we have established that. The only reason to take you with us is if we were arresting you."

A frisson went through the room and Harsha and Maya glanced at each other. So that was his game! The inspector was actually using the threat of the mob to force a confession out of Rajaratnam! Behind Maya, Harsha could see Ammani smiling triumphantly. The smile sent a shiver down Harsha's spine.

"A... arrest me?" Rajaratnam asked.

"Yes. Do we have any cause to arrest you?"

Rajaratnam licked his lips. He wasn't a fool, he knew what was happening, and clearly he was trying to think of a way out. "I may have taken some campaign money for myself. In my wife's bank account," he said. "And... and... these roads, I used government infrastructure money to build them but kept some of it for..."

Harsha watched in fascination as Rajaratnam babbled out a list of crimes, the type most people in India would suspect most politicians of. It was small-time stuff in a country where creaming a little off the top was mostly tolerated.

As Rajaratnam's little confessions petered out, the inspector shook his head. "All very interesting Mr Rajaratnam. I will ask the constable here to open those cases. I will be in touch shortly."

He spun on his heel and Rajaratnam started forward again: "Wait! Wait! Are you not going to arrest me?"

Azhar muttered something under his breath, clearly astonished at this sight of a man desperate to be arrested.

The inspector turned again and said: "Those are all new cases or old cases, sir. Right now, we only have one major case open. The murder of Lakshmi Nathan."

He stepped right up to the panchayat head and said: "I don't suppose you know anything about that?"

The pause was electric this time, as Rajaratnam's mouth opened and closed, the angry buzzing of the crowd the only accompaniment to the silence inside the hall.

The inspector's eyes opened wide as he looked into the terrified slits of Rajaratnam's eyes. "Did you kill her?" he asked.

Rajaratnam's mouth quivered and then he finally, finally whispered: "Yes!"

"Did you have any help?"

Rajaratnam said nothing, his lower lip quivering as he looked at the inspector, beaten.

"I asked, did you have any…"

"Yes!"

"Is it the same men who have been arrested for quarrying sand illegally?"

"I… yes. I think so."

"You think so?"

"I can provide you with a full list of names," Palanivel said, without any visible sign of remorse.

"And a full statement?"

"Yes."

"Now?"

A hesitation, and then finally, in a whisper, Rajaratnam said: "Yes!"

Inspector Palanivel's shoulders slumped slightly in relief and then he said: "Mani! Gautami! Arrest this man."

Rajaratnam closed his eyes, his face crumpling again, as the two police officers strode up to him, put his hands behind his back and handcuffed him.

As they marched him towards the door, Leela started silently crying, and Ammani put her arm around her. The rest of them looked at each other in horror. Much as they knew Rajaratnam probably deserved it, that scene had been difficult to watch for all of them.

As the police officers left the room with their quarry, Gautami turned to give Maya and Harsha a brief, but warm smile. At that, Inspector Palanivel also turned and nodded his acknowledgement to Harsha, before they silently left the room.

The buzzing of the crowd increased, but a few sharp orders from Palanivel seemed to quieten everyone down.

No one in the room said a word until they heard the roaring of the two police jeeps. Then Shane peered out and said: "The villagers are leaving."

Azhar turned with a sigh to Leela and Ammani and said: "You both take the rest of the day off. I will take care of dinner. Don't worry about it. Please… take care of yourselves." Harsha was touched by the concern in his old friend's voice for the two women.

Azhar then turned to Harsha and then said: "Well, Tintin, you got your happy ending. Happy?"

Harsha shook his head. "To be honest, I don't know. But I could do with a drink. You?"

"Smartest thing you said all day," Azhar returned, grinning, as he walked towards the drinks cabinet.

33. GOODBYES

"Now Juni! Get your ass in here!" Azhar yelled as Junaina paused and bent over her sandals on her way to the resort's car park.

"Just need to get this buckle straight, you fool, will only take a second!"

Harsha turned for one last glance at the beautiful stretch of mountainside that had been his place of abode for the last ten days. Leaving it felt oddly like leaving home. He thought, with a pang, of the beautiful pool where they had gone bathing and the multiple waterfalls that threaded their way to the green valley below.

"Harry! Enough sightseeing, bugger! We'll be late for the train!"

He sighed and turned and came up to Azhar's Audi. "Selvam going to be ok?"

"Oh yes — he will be back next week from his break," Azhar said. "Thank God. Had enough of buying provisions for this place — seems to hoover up food even when there are no guests, god knows how. Maya! What *now!*"

Harsha turned to see that Maya had stopped dead in her tracks, a look of angst on her face. She suddenly spun around and ran away from them.

"Oy! Where are you off to? We'll miss the train, for God's sake!"

"Have to say goodbye!" she yelled back. And at that moment, Harsha saw Ammani and Leela stepping out of the kitchen and walking up towards Maya. She charged up to the pair of them and hugged them close, one by one and then turned and ran back towards them.,

"About ti..." Harsha pinched Azhar's elbow to stop him remonstrating. He could see the tears on Maya's face. Instead, he waved up at Ammani and Leela himself and they waved frantically back. He was touched to see the tears on Leela's face.

"Say hi to your father from me, Leela!" he bellowed up the hill towards them and saw Leela bob her head vigorously.

He turned towards Azhar's Audi and saw Shane standing by one of the doors, hands in his pocket, resolutely trying to control his emotions.

"Shanny," he said and went up to his friend. "You not coming with us to the station?"

"Can't fit this fat bugger into the car on top of all of you," Azhar said briskly, opening the boot and checking all the suitcases were there, counting them with his fingers.

Shane held out a hand and Harsha brushed it away and pulled the man into a bear hug, clapping his back loudly before letting go.

"Thank you for being such a rock, Shane. You lifted us all when things were looking dark," he said, quietly.

Shane grinned. "The night is always darkest just before dawn," he said, and Harsha clapped his hand to his forehead, and, smiling, jumped into the passenger seat. Junaina gave Shane a quick pat on the shoulder — she had never been the touchy-feely type, and turned to Harry and said: "Oy, how come you get to sit in front?"

"Car sickness, dude."

"Convenient!"

Maya pushed Junaina aside and wrapped her arms around Shane and squeezed as tightly as she could, trying to put all her emotions into her hug. Her tears leaked out onto his shoulder.

"Harry is right. You are a rock, Shane. Never change, my friend," she said, stepping back and wiping her eyes with the back of her hand.

She half-expected another cliché or aphorism, but he simply said: "I never will. Be in touch — tell me how it all goes."

She nodded and then slipped into the back of the car wordlessly, still wiping away tears. The others had already taken their seats, so the car slid smoothly into gear and she turned to wave goodbye to Shane and Ammani and Leela, and behind them, to Pipal Resorts.

They drove in silence for a while and then Azhar cleared his throat and said: "Guys, hope you all had a good holiday."

Junaina snorted. "Yes, amazing, thanks. I especially enjoyed hiding from the mob yesterday, that was my personal highlight. You, Harry? Was it running from a bunch of *goondas* or drowning in the waterfall?"

"Hush," Maya said, seeing Azhar's crestfallen expression in the rear-view mirror. "Azhar, what you did was amazing. The way you held it together. And we did some really important work this week. We found a killer."

"But how?" Harsha asked tersely, looking unseeingly out at the countryside that was flying past them.

"What do you mean, how?" Azhar asked, querulously. "I thought we all agreed this panchayat dude was the killer? So what's the problem?"

They drove into a little patch of forest, plunging into the darkness of the canopy, and Maya gave a little shiver. "Harry," she said, trying to sound reassuring. "We have to trust the process. It will go to court now. We did what we had to do."

"I'm just..." Harsha sighed. "I'm just having doubts about whether we did it the right way. If the end justifies the means, as Shane would say."

Azhar shook his head. "You are saying that because you don't know that panchayat guy. This murder or whatever is only the tip of the iceberg. If all the shit comes out about him, he'll be in jail forever. Don't second-guess yourself, bugger. You have done this region a big favour."

Maya cleared her throat and said: "I think Harry, you are worrying because of the nature of the arrest. That policeman..."

"Bloody hell. He was cold as ice, wasn't he?" Junaina said, shivering slightly, and the two women exchanged glances at the back of the car.

"Harry, remember what you told me," Maya said insistently. "That he has limited options and has to work with what he has? The mob was the only leverage he had over Rajaratnam and he used it. Fair play to him — what else could he have done? Rajaratnam is wealthy and will have good lawyers. Trust the process! We did good."

Harsha turned around in the seat and looked gratefully back at Maya. "You are right. As usual. Thanks Maddie."

She smiled at his use of her old nickname and leaned back. They came out of the forest at this point and she looked out of Junaina's window at the green slopes and the valley below them, the town of Ramananpettai snoozing by the gleaming river.

"Guys, investigation or not, I am so grateful you all came," Azhar said. "Even Juni, believe it or not."

"Azhar, I can't tell you how great it was to see you all," Harsha said. "Let's never lose touch again."

"Amen to that," Junaina added.

The sadness of parting was weighing heavily on Maya's heart, so she tried to lighten the mood: "We must tie ourselves together with hoops of steel. Is that the quote, Harry? From Merchant of Venice? Come on, don't pretend you don't remember it!"

There was a pause and then Harsha said: "Those friends thou hast, grapple them to thy soul with hoops of steel," he said, turning briefly to smile at her.

"Oh god, not this 'thee thou' shit again! I thought I would never have to listen to it again in my life!" Azhar declared and they all laughed, and the rest of the journey passed in laughter and sweet remembrance of their university days.

As they sped through the dusty roads of Ramananpettai and pulled into the little toy station, they could already see the train approaching from the distance. Azhar screeched to a halt as the carriages emerged from a break in the trees, a copper-coloured line contrasting with the dark green of the forest, and they quickly pulled the suitcases out and hurriedly rushed towards the platform, waking up the portly station master who was enjoying a little snooze in the sunshine. Seeing the train approaching, the man stood up and followed them sedately and importantly as they arrived on the platform in a flurry of tumbling suitcases and rasping breaths.

As the train pulled into the platform, Junaina and Maya gave Azhar quick hugs before Harsha strode up to him and pulled him into an even bigger bear hug than the one he had given Shane. Azhar disengaged first and said: "Right, so don't forget me — us — when you're back with your English friends."

"Azhar — you will always be my best friend, dude."

"Yeah, yeah," Azhar said, turning away and surreptitiously wiping one eye.

With a hiss and a crash, the train came to a halt and a handful of people jumped out, as luck would have it, exactly where they were trying to gain entry.

"It only stays for two minutes!" Azhar called out warningly and Harsha threw courtesy to one side, shoved past one of the exiting passengers and flung his suitcase in and turned to receive Junaina's.

As whistles rang out in the air, Maya ran to the next door and picked up her suitcase and jumped in with irritating ease, but even so, the train was already moving as Junaina moved in and Harsha clambered into the open door behind her.

"Best of luck! Text me when you reach Chennai!" Azhar roared above the din of the departing train.

"Will do!" Junaina yelled after him and then grinned at Harsha and said: "I'll go find us a seat."

But Harsha wasn't prepared to leave just yet. Instead, he leaned dangerously out of the train door and waved violently to Azhar — nearly losing his hand to a passing telegraph post in the process — and yelled out: "Thanks for everything, legend!"

"Goodbye!"

"Goodbye, Azhar!" Harsha yelled, his voice breaking slightly. He looked up at the mountain above Ramananpettai and said softly: "And goodbye, Arasur. Goodbye, Pipal Resorts. I wonder if I will ever see you again."

"And why would you not?" asked a beloved voice right next to him, and he turned to smile at Maya. She squeezed beside him onto the threshold of the open train door and leaned out and waved at Azhar, who was now a tiny figure in the distance, still waving to the train.

Once past, they both looked up at the mountain in silence.

"I want to come back to India. To live," he said, finally. "I forgot how much I love this country."

"Me too," she said, simply.

She leaned against him and sighed, and for once, he switched off his mind and just enjoyed feeling the warmth of her body against his, without asking if it meant something or if it would lead to anything. In fact, he knew it wouldn't.

He breathed the moment in, trying to etch it in his memory — the wind, Maya's skin, the forest flying by and the smell of metal and leaves.

"Oy, lovebirds. Want some coffee? Vendor just came by. Proper south Indian brew, too," Junaina yelled out from behind them.

They both turned and smiled at Junaina, their faces framed by the lush Indian countryside flying by behind them as the train picked up speed.

"Coffee sounds perfect, Juni."

Junaina hesitated, and then said: "Well — I'm sure he'll be back again a bit later. Why don't you two take some more time. I'll call you again later when he is back from his rounds."

Harsha and Maya looked at each other and then Harsha said: "Just give us five minutes, and then we will join you."

As Junaina left, Maya's hand reached out and held Harsha's and he gripped it tightly and they looked out at the mountain of Arasur one last time as it retreated into the distance.

YOUR FREE BOOK IS WAITING

A gang of misfit English literature students. A despotic and racist professor. A strict Catholic university. Harsha and his friends master their growing pangs, love lives and struggles with Shakespeare to fight for change – with explosive results.

Get a free copy of *Joint Study*, the prequel to Last Resort, here:

Download Joint Study at www.abhinavramnarayan.com

I wrote the first draft of *Last Resort* in a mad frenzy in November 2014, after my flatmate at the time introduced me to National Novel Writing Month (NaNoWriMo). I had been sitting in front of one of those American crime TV series and idly wondering how a murder mystery would play out in a remote part of India and then decided to have a go at putting my thoughts down on paper. *Last Resort* ensued.

But that proved only the very beginning. I abandoned the manuscript as a pile of rubbish for several years and focused on writing other, more "literary", novels before my partner Anne McHale convinced me to stop trying to win over agents and publishers and actually get a book out there instead, especially given how much easier it is to self-publish online.

I returned to *Last Resort* and found, to my pleasant surprise, that the book wasn't as bad as I had thought for so long. With a bit of work, I might even be convinced to show it to other people!

The first of these other people was erstwhile colleague and fellow novelist Mike Turner (remember the name) who actually took the trouble to read it from beginning to end. His positive response was a huge encouragement but he did not mince his words on some of *Last Resort*'s flaws — and I owe him a huge debt of gratitude for that.

It took me another couple of years, plenty of early mornings, excitement and more heartache than I can measure, to get *Last Resort* to its current form. My editor Parimala Rao and book cover designer Cherie Fox were instrumental in bringing it to its current state, and the support from my parents and my sister Akhila was valuable beyond measure.

That said, I may still have bottled it if it hadn't been for one other factor — my early readers. Before pressing the button on *Last Resort*, I released a prequel novella *Joint Study* on my personal website to try and drum up some interest in my writing.

The buzz it generated went way beyond what I had expected. I don't know if I would have had the courage to go ahead with *Last Resort* if it hadn't been for the enthusiasm and kindness of my earliest readers. I won't name names here because I will inevitably forget someone — but you know who you are, though perhaps you will never know how much your support and patronage meant to me. Thank you from the bottom of my heart.

Readers are everything for a writer. Whatever you thought of *Last Resort* (and I encourage you to let me know via a review or by getting in touch directly) I am so very grateful that you have given my work your time and attention. I do hope you will stay in touch.

Happy reading!

Abhinav

Printed in Great Britain
by Amazon